things
that
happened
before
the
earthquake

things

that

happened

before

the

earthquake

CHIARA BARZINI

 Doubleday New York London Toronto Sydney Auckland

All rights reserved. Published in the United States by Doubleday, a division of Penguin Random House LLC, New York, and distributed in Canada by Random House of Canada, a division of Penguin Random House Canada Limited, Toronto.

www.doubleday.com

DOUBLEDAY and the portrayal of an anchor with a dolphin are registered trademarks of Penguin Random House LLC.

A portion of this novel first appeared in *East* magazine (Summer 2017)

Book design by Maria Carella
Jacket photograph by Dennis Stock/Magnum Photos
Jacket design by Emily Mahon

Library of Congress Control Number: 2017941177
ISBN: 978-0-385-54227-2 (hardcover)
ISBN: 978-0-385-54228-9 (ebook)

MANUFACTURED IN THE UNITED STATES OF AMERICA

First Edition

10 9 8 7 6 5 4 3 2 1

To Luca who makes everything possible

And to Stefania, Andrea, and Matteo for always being up for an adventure

One gets the impression that people come to Los Angeles in order to divorce themselves from the past, here to live or try to live in the rootless pleasure world of an adult child. One knows that if the cities of the world were destroyed by a new war, the architecture of the rebuilding would create a landscape which looked, subject to specification of climate, exactly and entirely like the San Fernando Valley.

Norman Mailer
"Superman Comes to the Supermarket"

part one

departure

1

I was looking at my grandmother, sitting cross-legged and top-less on El Matador Beach in Malibu, and remembered that we used to make out. She would stick her tongue out and I had to lick it. She called it the "tongue-to-tongue game." A soggy dumpling asking to be joined by mine. I couldn't say no. The smell of her saliva repelled me. I didn't like this activity, but I was told I should do it because she was old and I was a little girl. We played the game until I was eight. That day on the beach the vision of her pendulous naked breasts seemed as out of context as her tongue in my mouth did when I was little. I wondered what it was about my family. Why we could never make it right.

I sat on a rock in front of the waves—tall, ferocious waves. Even though it was summer, it was freezing. The beach was empty. I hated my parents for bringing me there. They were both sprawled on the sand, leaning their heads against a pole that held a SHARK ALERT sign. Their bathing suits were in a heap on top of a Positano-style sarong. They lounged nude as if they were in a beach town off the Mediterranean Sea. The wind thrust sand and towels in my face. It was so strong, I couldn't even hear my brother's voice close to me, but our parents were content, like that was just exactly what they had in mind when they moved to California. It wasn't what I had in mind.

My mother took four soggy cream-cheese sandwiches out of her bag and a gallon of warm water she'd bought at the gas station a few days earlier and left in the car. The water tasted like plastic.

"Lunch!"

She invited my brother and me over and kept smiling even though we were visibly angry. This made us angrier.

"No thanks."

We'd rather sit here and hate you, was what we thought.

They moved into the shade, nibbling on their soggy sandwiches, chunks of cream cheese getting stuck in their pubic hair. Grandma graced us by putting her shirt back on for the duration of the picnic. I didn't want to be there. I wanted to be where the young people were, at the skate park we had passed on the highway coming in. If I was to live in that labyrinth of a city, that vast region, I should have the right to be with people my own age. But no, we were supposed to have lunch together, like a real Italian family.

It was August of 1992. Three months before standing on that windy beach, our father had announced we would be moving to Hollywood to become rich and famous. What he didn't tell us was that we'd be moving to the vast and scorching basin that sprawled seamlessly for miles north of Los Angeles, the San Fernando Valley.

"Don't you want to go where it's always summer?" he asked my brother and me during a shoot for a commercial for canned meat in Rome.

Our entire family had been cast to be the national face of Italian Spam. This was encouraging, according to our father. A rich destiny awaited on the other side of the ocean. None of us had ever acted except as extras in our father's films, but the commercial's producers insisted.

"You are perfect for our product! You *look* like you're related!" they screamed during our audition.

We were promised extra money for this reason.

"It'll be practice for Hollywood," our father said when we got the parts.

In the commercial we had to act like a traditional Italian family: a sporty fifteen-year-old daughter, a kooky younger brother, and two unconditionally loving parents. We had lunch together on a terrace overlooking Saint Peter's Basilica—no waves, no sharks. The stylist put Band-Aids on my nipples because they got hard in the breeze. Girls were not supposed to have erect nipples. Our mother, Serena, dressed like a southern Italian housewife, a *casalinga* from the fifties, prepared a big salad topped with cadaverous red meat that had been duly molded, painted, and sprayed by the "food stylist" to deliver what the director called "a glorious, meaty glow."

It smelled like dog food.

"Who's hungry for thinly sliced vegetables on a bed of chopped meat?" she asked on camera.

"Me! Me! Me!" my brother and I cried, raising our arms to the sky.

"Time for a healthy lunch!" our father exclaimed, skipping over to the lavishly decked-out table after putting away the pot of azaleas he had just finished trimming.

We chewed the meat and spat it in a bin by our chairs after each take. I liked acting as a perfect family. I liked seeing my father play a patriarchal role, watering plants on the aristocratic Roman terrace the production company had rented for the shoot. In real life he rejected authorities and institutions. He wore pink and aquamarine shirts, called himself an anarchist, and practiced yoga and Transcendental Meditation. Now he was forced to wear ordinary dad clothes and say ordinary dad things. In my mind that really was our practice for Hollywood. We needed to learn how to become a normal family.

———

When I told my Roman schoolmates we were moving to America they all gasped. I should refuse to move to an imperialist country. America was evil. That was the bottom line. Ours was a politically active institution. Every year students conducted a sit-in on the school grounds to protest government decisions about public education. The real activists printed pamphlets and screamed communist slogans into megaphones. The rest of us liked the excuse of sleeping away from home. We camped in sleeping bags inside the freezing gym, smoked hash, and talked about "the system." Nobody washed for days. Halls were littered with cigarette butts, posters, and empty cartons of pizza—our only sustenance. Most of the boys had anxious Italian mothers who snuck home-cooked meals through the gates. They didn't want to look like mama's boys so they ate their food alone in the restrooms.

One night Alessandro, the school's most popular political leader, woke us up in the gym and ordered everyone to follow him to the principal's office.

"Get the girl who's moving to LA!" he screamed.

He identified as Rastafarian even though he was white and came from Trastevere. He had not rinsed his dreadlocks in so long that one of them had hardened to the point of breaking off. It was said that he'd found so many lice eggs inside that it looked like a cannoli pastry.

The old black-and-white television in the back of the principal's office showed images of a city under siege. It was Los Angeles. Alessandro looked at me and nodded his head. "This is where you're off to."

News had arrived that the four police officers who were on trial for brutally beating the African American construction worker Rodney King had been acquitted. We had all seen images of the assault on television. It took place on a dark Los Angeles street and was videotaped by chance by a red-haired Argentinian who witnessed it from the balcony of his apartment. It was the first time that police brutality had been caught on tape and the video had gone viral even without the benefit of the Internet. The world expected justice. But justice didn't come, so half an hour after the acquittal, more than three hundred people started protesting in front of police headquarters. By that evening the protesters outnumbered the police officers. Riots, burning, and looting began.

Sitting around the black-and-white TV in Rome, we felt like we were watching footage from a war.

When I went home the following day I screamed at my parents that we could not move to a country where the police were allowed to beat people with impunity. Serena and Ettore had been politically active radicals in their youth. My father had been part of Autonomia Operaia, the autonomist leftist movement, in the seventies. If I had any sense of political justice ingrained in me, it was because of the stories he told us about workers' autonomy growing up. I thought I could count on their leftist ethos to change their minds. I was wrong.

The riots went on for six consecutive days. I looked at the flaming streets from our television in Rome and tried to imagine our new home somewhere among those fires. While Los Angeles was facing the largest insurrection in the United States since the sixties, my family was packing boxes for our move. Our grandmother Celeste would come along to help us settle in California. She walked around the house shaking her head at everything we were leaving behind.

"Poveri ragazzi," she kept saying about my brother and me. "Poor kids."

Serena turned off the TV and handed me a copy of American *Vogue*. There was a photo of happy girls on a beach wearing heart-shaped sunglasses and bikinis.

"This could be you. Try to look at the bright side."

The Los Angeles airport was just a few miles from the epicenter of the riots. It was dusk when our airplane drew closer to the landing strip. I could see, amid the streets lined with identical one-story houses, a lack of something. An absence. Fifty-one men and seven women died in the riots—shot, burned, beaten to death, stabbed. That same airport where we were landing had been shut down by violence and then for cleanup. There had been fires, hundreds of buildings and homes burned down. Large parts of the city, famed for its lights, were still obscured. The power cut during the rioting left the south corner of the city in a dark hole. But the gloom I saw from the plane the day we arrived was not caused by lack of power. Order had been restored, but stores and businesses had shut down never to be rebuilt, leaving a sense of permanent dimness, like the bulb of a flashlight whose batteries were beginning to die.

It felt like the city was still burning when we stepped off the airplane. Or maybe I was yet to get used to the incendiary quality of the warm Santa Ana, the "devil winds" that blew in from the desert. The sun set behind the freeway. As we drove toward our house, we saw police choppers in the sky, metallic dragonflies emitting shafts of white beams moving probingly over the concrete below. Our cat, Mao, who had traveled from Rome with us, miaowed inconsolably. Nothing felt welcoming, and my father knew it.

It took us a long time to get to the house. My grandmother clutched her purse through the whole cab ride.

"It's not like you're going to get mugged in a taxi!" my mother reproached her, but she would not let go.

"Señora is right. We're in Van Nuys, barrio Nuys as the local gangs say," the cabdriver said with a smirk. "Better safe than sorry."

"*Visto*, Serena?" my grandmother sniffed. "Marida was right. Whenever you told her you wanted to move out here, she always said it was the worst place to raise a family."

Marida was my father's mother who had died earlier that year at the age of ninety. She had grown up drinking champagne and twirling pearls in her fingers, but a few years before her death, she'd been conned by a Vatican priest who took advantage of her Alzheimer's and asked her daily to withdraw large sums of money from her bank account to give to the church. She was convinced she could pay her way into heaven. By the time she died, there was very little left of the great inheritance my family was counting on. This, according to my father, was the reason why instead of living in Beverly Hills, like all decent filmmaking families, we had to live in barrio Nuys.

We had smuggled her ashes with us. They'd been divided among her four sons and even though my father was angry at her for leaving him with no patrimony, he was also superstitious and felt that something bad might happen if he left his share of his dead mother in Rome. On the flight over she had come to him in a dream, explicitly telling him to go back to Rome and forget about Los Angeles and filmmaking altogether. In her lifetime she had refused to see most of my father's films. He invited her to premieres and even asked her to be his date the one time he had been accepted at the Cannes Film Festival, with a Pasolini-inspired story about a homosexual couple, but she bluntly declined. "I don't like stories about pederasts."

Ettore was disturbed by his dream and said his mother had ruined his life while she was alive and now she was trying to ruin it in death. He would make films. He didn't care what she had to say.

The first thing he did when we entered our home on Sunny Slope Drive—an all-American haven in the middle of what felt and looked like the ghetto—was to move her ashes into the backyard. He placed the urn under a lemon tree in hopes she would not come back to taunt him in his sleep again.

My brother, Timoteo, and I explored the new grounds. It was a spacious house with a front yard dominated by a colossal oak and a backyard with lemon and orange trees—a residual taste of the many years in which the entire Valley was nothing but orange groves and farms. It featured hardwood floors, large windows, a sun-filled studio for my father's work, and a kitchen that fascinated us from the start. Not only did we have a vintage soda fountain but our sink came equipped with something we had never seen in Italy, something we did not know could exist—a garbage disposal. It allowed us to dump and grind leftovers in the sink without having to empty our plates in the trash can first. Where the food went and who was responsible for it ultimately, we had no idea and did not care. Timoteo and I imagined a food cemetery for liquefied burgers and fries that created a foul, toxic hummus people were warned to stay away from. If pet cemeteries existed—we heard there was a famous one just a few miles from our house—why wouldn't Americans think about having cholesterol graves too?

My father's first important entry point into American life involved the purchase of a huge, white 1962 Cadillac convertible he bought at the Pasadena antique car mall—a suburban warehouse filled with classic American cars from the fifties and sixties. He loaded us into the car and drove triumphantly along Van Nuys Boulevard with the top down. In the early 1900s Van Nuys and the southeastern part of the San Fernando Valley, with their "preserved Western landscapes," had been the perfect neighborhoods for movie shoots, he explained.

"Stars lived here, *right here*! They strolled down Van Nuys Boulevard like it was Rodeo Drive. Our neighborhood was hipper than Hollywood. Did you know even Marilyn Monroe went to Van Nuys High in 1941?"

"Exactly. In 1941. Now it's just homeless people, prostitutes, and 99 Cent stores!" I complained to him while he parked in front of a head shop where he wanted to buy a tie-dyed Grateful Dead T-shirt he'd seen a few days earlier.

I took the presence of all those head shops and *tiendas baratas* by our house as a bad omen. How could my father become rich and famous if he surrounded himself with cheapness? It wasn't just our neighborhood; the whole Valley was disconsolate—a pale, discount imitation of the grandeur that existed on the other side of the hills. The actors who lived here were B-rated stars or grown child actors who got in trouble with the law. Corey Feldman, my favorite Goonie, got caught with heroin and Todd Bridges, the elder brother from *Diff'rent Strokes,* whom every Italian child from the eighties adored, had been arrested for trying to kill his drug dealer when he was high. Down the street from our house lived Desmond. He was on TV and had a comedy show called *Desmond.* His wife was a former Miss Virginia. His mother had been a department-store cashier but now lived with him and took care of the house. His sister worked as his personal assistant. We were told he was not as friendly in person as he was on TV and that he carried loaded guns. From the street you could see parts of his house: a cement garden, a pool surrounded by mildewed deck chairs, a collapsed faux-antique lamppost. Two guard dogs rushed forward barking when you approached the iron fence. One had a transparent eye. Those were the kinds of celebrities who lived in the Valley. Even their dogs were defective.

I started adding these facts to my list of bad omens. The signs that we were in the wrong city at the wrong time were unignorable. We were surrounded by them. My father's dream on the airplane, the echoes of the riots, the smell of ash and

dirt and anger in the air, the failed celebrities. Within the first
two weeks of living in Van Nuys we received an array of bad
news: our trunks from Italy had gotten lost and our cat, Mao,
died under a car in front of the driveway. Timoteo had fallen off
his bicycle on a winding road during a day trip to the Mojave
Desert and split open his knee. We had to give the hospital
fake names and Social Security numbers because we didn't have
insurance. One day we received a phone call from a company in
Palm Springs. The guy on the phone knew my father's name and
kept congratulating him on having won a brand-new car. We
got dizzy with excitement. What a country. People just got on
the phone with you and gave you things. We drove out to Palm
Springs convinced we'd be heading home with a brand-new car
but ended up spending the day in a lecture hall with a bunch
of gullible families like ours, eating stale muffins, and listening
to real estate agents on microphones who tried to sell us vacation condos. If we did our part, they promised they'd do theirs
and we'd be eligible to win a car. "Eligible!" my grandmother
screamed at my father. "That's the key word you failed to understand! You didn't *win* a car, you were eligible to win one. You and
the four hundred idiots in this room." We all drove home and
never talked about it again. The oracles were speaking clearly
to us: Go back to your country now. Do not try to figure out
how to conquer the golden sun of California, for it is ungraspable. But my father would not budge, blinded as he was by the
promise of something better. "And cheaper!" he screamed. "LA
is much, much cheaper than Rome. There are department stores
where clothes, *real clothes,* important, brand-name clothes cost a
quarter of what they do in Italy."

Suddenly we belonged to those canyons with mountain
lions yowling in the night; we belonged to Pick 'n Save, the discount store where all our new plates and cutlery came from; we
belonged to the 405 freeway that roared incessantly in our ears
like a huge hair dryer. We belonged. It was decided.

———

Back on the shark-infested Malibu beach, my naked parents and topless grandmother now read out loud from the *LA Weekly* classified ads.

"Canoga Park!"

"No, not the Valley section. Go to the other side," my father instructed Serena.

"West Hollywood?" my grandmother proposed.

"Mmm, what about Bel Air?" Serena replied.

The neighborhoods were not, as I hoped, options for new places where we could live but addresses of yard sales that might be in good-enough areas to guarantee high-quality secondhand household appliances. My parents' friend Max, a Cuban producer who was friends with Phil Collins and lived next door to him in Beverly Hills, had instructed them on the art of accumulating goods without spending much. All they needed was a full tank of gas, a map of the city, and an *LA Weekly* with yard-sale addresses. He was our go-to man for any questions regarding heat, pain, and glory.

When he took us garage sale-ing, he drove us around Bel Air and pointed out which celebrity each mansion belonged to. We never saw the actual houses from the car. They were protected by brick walls and gates, but I could tell things smelled different in those neighborhoods. The grass was greener—something zesty and hygienic in the air. I imagined kitchen counters filled with fresh limes and oranges. Chlorine-free sprinkler water. "The magic of this city," Max explained, "is not in the mansions but in the smell of the cedar trees that are planted in front of them. It's not in the beautifully tiled pools but in the way the sunlight reflects on the water in them. It's what keeps people here," he added with an air of mystery. "The *luminous unseen*." I stared intently at tree trunks and tried to peek at the swimming pools through the fences, hoping to catch a glimpse of that invisible California life-form Max spoke of, but I couldn't. The city appeared to me always in the same way, a fatuous leaden expanse.

"Remember, Eugenia," Max warned me when he saw me squint, "if you look too hard it disappears."

So I stopped looking for the magic and focused on the stuff instead: blenders, canoes, rocking chairs, broken phones, and microwaves. We were furnishing our house with other people's rejects.

My brother ran up to my parents and sat beside them to oversee their yard-sale research—a lean, pale body among my family's overflowing dark, tanned flesh. He hunted for water-bed mattresses, icons of adolescent freedom. For an Italian kid a water bed had the same mystical effect a bottle of Chianti had on an underage American. America was to "cool" what Italy was to "grown-up."

From a solitary rock, I looked at the Malibu waves cream-ing on the sand. I swung my legs into the air and hopped off. On the other side of the beach there were no nudists. A family of Mexicans with four coolers—one for each family member—sculpted mermaids on the sand. An Armenian father sat on a fold-up chair drinking beer out of a brown bag while his girls frolicked in the water. I climbed over the cliff and walked along the freeway back to the skate park we had passed earlier. I leaned against a wall of arid earth, looking at the skaters rolling up and down the ramps in hypnotic loops. There were girls on bleachers in skintight T-shirts. They had pigtails and sucked on lollipops. I felt the cold wind against my skin. Nature in Califor-nia was hostile and unforgiving, but the skaters—so vigorous, their hair so blond it was almost white—didn't seem fazed by it. The girls' legs were strong, legs that surfed and pushed boards against thrusting water. Legs that could keep a violent nature at bay. I looked at my own skinny, pale limbs, bruised and covered with goose bumps, and I closed my eyes.

Dear Mary, I need your help. Speak to this ocean, these waves, the wind, and the sun. Tell this city to smooth its edges, to show me some kindness, to give me something to hang on to. Dear Mary, appear to me in all your beauty. Make it good or at least better. Amen.

Since we'd moved, the Virgin Mary had become my role model. Being away from the motherland called for motherly reassurance. I wasn't getting it from my creator, so who could be better than the mother of all mothers? I asked her daily to perform miracles for me as auspicious signs that would cancel out the bad omens. Sometimes I felt like she listened.

The wind blew hard. I put my hoodie on and suddenly the heavens opened with a roaring sound. Mary had heard me, I knew it. The sound became stronger. The skaters stopped skating and looked up to the sky.

She was coming for me.

She was going to take me away.

It was the sound of a helicopter, floating above the beach where my parents were reading out yard-sale listings. From the loudspeakers came the voice of God. It said, "Put your bathing suits back on. I repeat, put your bathing suits back on! You are committing a felony. Ma'am, put your top back on."

"Dear Mary," I closed my eyes and kept praying. "Tell me this isn't happening. Tell me a policeman is not telling my grandmother to put her top back on."

The skaters started laughing. One of them rolled his pants down, extracted his big cock, and waved it around toward the helicopter.

"Want me to put my bathing suit back on too, officer?"

His friends rode their boards down along the coast to see

the nudist outlaws from the top of the cliff. I didn't want to go.
I couldn't. So I stayed there staring as the helicopter picked up
dust and sand and landed on an opening by the beach.

I imagined my parents getting handcuffed and deported,
and me condemned to stay alone on that beach forever. Maybe I
would fall in love with a skater and we could hitch a ride to San
Francisco. I heard that it was more of a European city. But did I
want that? To betray my family so soon after our arrival?

I ran back to the beach. From the street above, the skaters
laughed and screamed at my grandmother.

"Sexy granny, take it off! Take it off!"

A police officer was writing out a ticket as my family stood
half dressed and bewildered before him.

"What happened?" I asked when I finally reached them.

"The officer was explaining to us that we cannot be naked
here," my mother whispered in a sultry voice, trying to give herself a distinguished British accent. She thought that by prov-
ing her—in her mind superior—European heritage, the cops
would be more lenient, but the policeman stared her down and
nodded his head.

"Italians, huh?"

The British affectation had failed her.

"You guys like your topless tans. Well, you're in Los Angeles now, and if you are going to lay naked on a beach, you have
to take responsibility for things that might happen."

"But what's the worst thing that can happen, sir? Nudity is
only natural," my father replied with a Gandhian smile.

It was so like him to try and get a muscle-bound authority
figure to level with him in his down-to-earth way. The cop slid
his sunglasses down his nose.

"The worst thing that might happen, sir, is that a maniac
could be standing right on top of that cliff looking at you naked
people, masturbating, and traumatizing children and civilians."

I tried to imagine a pervert jacking off to my grandmother's formless bosom.

"I've seen it happen," he confirmed, noticing my doubtful expression.

My brother looked at me and rolled his eyes.

"This is a warning. Now don't let me find you without bathing suits on here again . . . And ma'am?" he said, turning to my grandmother who, speaking not a word of English, sat on a rock with furrowed brows. "Don't you know sun is carcinogenic? At your age you should be guarding certain . . . *delicate* . . . private parts."

"I don't understand you and I think you are an ugly asshole," my grandmother replied in Italian.

He tilted his head and climbed back up the cliff to the helicopter landing. The pilot revamped the engine. The blades spun and the heavens roared. The officers flew above my now fully clothed parents toward the ocean.

"If this isn't another bad omen I don't know what is!" I screamed at my parents.

"Ma'am . . . Put your top back on, ma'am," my father replied doing a nasal policeman impersonation.

"It's not funny, Dad!"

"Oh come on, get a sense of humor—"

"I hate you. I hate this beach and I hate this city. I want to go back to Rome!"

"I want to go back to Rome as well," my brother interjected.

My father put his arms around us and started walking. "Let's get out of here, kids. These people are fascists."

We pulled away from the windy coast into a cool, shaded canyon and climbed inside curve by curve, entering a great protective womb—the car like an old steady boat. The ocean wind ceased and the goose bumps on my thighs disappeared. I leaned back on the leather seat, calm. We all stopped speaking. My grandmother took my hand and looked at me with pity. *Where the hell are we?* her eyes asked. Minutes earlier on the coast I would have been comforted by that droopy, empathic look, but now it was me who had to reassure her. With each curve the forest precipices softened, and what seemed wild and dramatic from one position, transformed into something intimate and natural as we moved farther in. We were inside Topanga Canyon. In the twenties the place had been a weekend getaway for Hollywood stars. The rolling hills and vegetation created hidden alcoves everywhere. The indigenous Tongva people gave that land its name. The word meant "the place above" and I could see why. We were suspended in the air. I leaned back and closed my eyes. We were up high, where nobody could see us.

2

Dear Mary, this is the most important day of my life and you have to be part of it. I dipped my rosary into my grandma's ashes for blessings. I hope that's okay. I hate milk in the mornings. It makes me sick, but tea is too diuretic and I don't want to have to look for a bathroom. I'm scared to ask for a bathroom. I'm scared I won't find one and will look stupid trying to find one. My English is bad. I don't want to have to ask anyone for anything. Please, make it so I don't have to go pee. Or worse. Amen.

On my first day of public high school in America my mother dropped me off in front of the entrance gate and handed me a campus map the principal had given her when they went to enroll me. She kissed me goodbye in the car.

"Don't worry. If you worry just pump your shoes." She winked.

I wore Reebok Pumps that day. We bought them at Ross Dress for Less, my parents' new favorite department store. The internal inflation mechanism of the shoes fascinated me, and when I pumped them I felt I had power feet. I could run faster, jump higher, and have quicker reflexes.

I stepped out of the car and reached the other backpacks swarming through the main gate. When I crossed the entrance I turned on my heels and walked back to the car. I climbed inside.

"I'm not going in. There's a fucking metal detector!"

"I know," my mother said smiling reassuringly, opening the car door again to let me back out. "That way you'll be safer, no? No shootings!"

We picked the high school I would go to based on three elements: The first was the school having no record of firearms being brought in by students—as part of my parents' "make love not war disposition," they were conscious of the problem of guns in America. The second was the fact that the principal, Donald Peters, had a name that resembled our own family name, Petri. This was encouraging according to them. And the third was that it was in one of the San Fernando Valley's rich residential neighborhoods, Woodland Hills.

"Oh, this place is awesome," said Mr. Douglas, the man in charge of security who gave us a tour of the campus during orientation. We'd gone in through the side doors at the time, no signs of metal detectors. "Ice Cube came here," Douglas continued. "He wrote the lyrics to 'Boyz-n-the-Hood' during his English class right over there. Smart motherfucker he was." Douglas had been a stunt man for Bruce Willis in *Die Hard* and worked closely with the LAPD on gang control. He explained it was imperative that I not wear the colors red or blue in school.

"No C-walking. No gang clothes. No gang moves. Unless you want to get shot." He winked. "Kidding, just kidding . . ."

I tried to smile and looked at my parents who kept walking down the hall, unperturbed. The Bloods and the Crips were the two biggest gangs in Los Angeles. Their gang colors were red for the Bloods and blue for the Crips. The two basic colors were banned from most public schools in the city. This complicated fashion policy made for very original color-scheme solutions. There were a lot of fluorescent pinks and greens around.

"C-walking" meant any kind of jittery stutter-step combination of foot pivots and shuffles. The dance move originated with the Crips, which meant that nobody in school was allowed any kind of funky or playful walking style. We were to walk in straight lines and wear bland clothes.

My brother's middle school in Van Nuys was worse. It had barbed-wire fences everywhere. The most stimulating class they offered was Hydraulics, which taught the basics of plumbing.

I stood in the hallway looking at the crowds pouring in, not knowing what to do next. My school in Rome had two hundred students. This one had four thousand. My Reebok Pumps were the wrong choice. Most girls wore heels.

Somehow I managed to get to my English class. Since I was Italian I had been assigned to a class for people who spoke English as a second language, but when I got there I realized it was more for people who didn't speak English at all. I tried to put on the most American-sounding accent I could. I felt like a show-off when I approached the teacher and told her I desperately wanted to get out of there. It was true my English was not perfect, but I could read and write it, and put sentences together. The teacher was not interested. ESL was a standard class for anyone who came from another country. I'd just have to sit down and follow her lesson.

Bells kept ringing. I did not understand what they referred to. I walked to my locker and observed other students flipping their little knobs clockwise and counterclockwise with rapid hand movements. I tried to do the same but failed, and since I didn't want anybody to notice, I decided to carry the books in my backpack instead. The slip of paper with my schedule was confusing, the campus map far too complex. I couldn't decipher how to get to the phantom building D where my math class was, and according to the schedule, it was time for something called "Nutrition" soon. Perhaps I should go and feed myself somewhere, but where? The cafeteria was crowded with rowdy kids throwing grapes and scraps of pancakes at each other. I looked at them wondering if I should get in line, but another bell rang and everyone scuttled away.

Mr. Douglas and an overweight police officer in Bermuda shorts circled the campus on a golf cart with a megaphone, screaming at everyone to get out of the way and hurry to class. "Let's go, let's go! Tardy sweep-up!"

I didn't know what that meant, but since I was lost and meandering, I was mistaken for someone who wanted to ditch class. I was loaded, alongside other roaming teenagers, onto Douglas's golf cart. On board, two Persian kids improvised a rap song, pretending like they were riding a Bentley in a hip-hop video. I looked at them and did not say a word. I preferred my schoolmates to think of me as a thug rather than an idiot who could not figure out how to get to class.

We got dropped off in front of the "tardy hall," a storage room for students who were late for class. A twenty-year-old New Age teacher in tie-dye sweatpants watched over students and gave them speeches about how to avoid gang confrontations. There were about fifteen of us—mostly African American, Persian, and Hispanic students. The tardy hall was also known as the "gang prevention room," but the correlation between being late to class and wanting to shoot people eluded me.

"You start off tardy and you end up dead on a sidewalk," the teacher explained right away. The new post-riot theory was that teenagers who resisted getting to class on time were more likely to drop out of high school and fall into violent patterns. If you were "swept" more than three times in a year, you were profiled and eventually suspended or expelled.

The teacher gave us a handout of gang signs we should know and never imitate.

Another laugh. Nobody needed an instruction manual about these gestures. The Persian guys from the golf cart gathered in the back of the room. They hugged each other and laughed, looking at photos of their summers, commenting on the girls they'd been with.

One of them with a baseball cap and deep brown eyes sat next to me.

"Where you from?"

"West side," I replied, referencing the gang handout.

"You smoke weed?"

"Yes."

"Where's your accent from? You Mexican?"

The Hispanic girls in class huffed at me and shook their heads.

"She ain't no freaking Latina. Look at what she's wearing."

"You Persian?" he asked.

"I'm Italian."

"I'm Arash." He shook my hand, looking confused. "Italian? For real?"

"No, that bitch is *Sicilian*!" a girl named Ajane screamed from the back of the class.

"Duh," said the first Latina girl. "Why you think she's wearing Reebok Pumps? They are way behind with fashion there. They got that dictator there, what's his name? The bald guy who got rid of all the Jews along with the German hater?"

"Mussolini?" I asked.

"Yeah. If I had that fool for president I wouldn't be thinking about what shoes to wear, I'd just be thinking of getting the fuck out of that country . . ."

Everyone started laughing.

I stayed in my seat listening to Tupac Shakur airing from an eighties boom box on the teacher's desk. The deal was that she'd play music as long as we let her lecture us about its lyrical contents.

"When Tupac says *'I bail and spray with my AK,'* what he really is trying to say is: The fact that you are racist really hurts my feelings and now I want to hurt your feelings back."

She had a degree in teen psychology with a focus on decoding gang semiotics, but it didn't seem to help much.

"Tupac speaks out of fear," she explained expertly. "Does anybody have any examples of when we act out of fear?"

"I know I ain't afraid of that Sicilian bitch!" Ajane snickered, pointing at me. Everybody laughed.

Arash raised his hand to interrupt the laughter.

"Yeah, miss, sometimes people think we're haters 'cause we're Persian and have Persian pride. They think it's a gang, while actually we just love our people—"

"Hairy wannabe rappers with big egos and small dicks!" Ajane sneered, causing another stir.

"Shut the fuck up," one of Arash's friends intervened.

"Gold-chain-wearing cheap asses driving old-ass beamers, trying to distract everybody from your nasty monobrows," Ajane's neighbor pitched in, laughing.

A chorus of "ooohs" and giggles rose from the desks.

"What did you say, bitch?" Arash and his friends got up from their seats and moved to the other side of the room where the girls were. "You wish we drove old-ass BMWs. Our shit is brand-new. And it's ours. You just ride a bus!"

A rumble of desks and chairs. Ajane and her friends met the Persians halfway. Ajane elbowed me and swiped my books from the desk to the floor.

"Hey!" I complained.

She turned to me. "What, you want to get your ass kicked too?"

The New Age teacher in sweatpants tried to intervene, but Ajane resisted her. She leaned over and stared at me, bobbing her head.

"You wanna fight? I got my sneakers in my bag, you wanna fight?"

"Not really." I looked down at my own shoes. How ugly they seemed to me now.

"Fight! Fight! Fight!" Arash's Iranian friends began to cheer.

Arash glanced at me. If I got into a fight, I kept thinking, I would have to update my list of bad omens. The teacher tried again to keep everyone on their own side of the room, but the groups spilled over, waiting to combust, and I was stuck in the middle. That's when I saw Arash suddenly retreat. He lifted his hands as a sign of truce.

"Leave it alone, y'all."

His friends started teasing him. They screamed, *"Kuni! Kuni!"*—the Farsi word for "faggot"—at him for backing off.

I shrank in my desk and kept looking ahead, avoiding eye contact with anyone. Alone in the front row of the room a beautiful girl with auburn hair was putting lipstick on in front of a compact mirror, deliberately not participating in anything. She was full of freckles that made a striking contrast with her bright green eyes. She was the only thing I could look at—a haven to rest my eyes on as my breathing went back to normal. She giggled to herself listening to everyone's bragging and when the teacher wasn't looking, she packed her backpack in haste, got up from her seat, and snuck out of the classroom. The door swung shut behind her. From the small glass window I saw her ponytail bounce down the hallway, then she disappeared.

The bell rang. I was headed to Health Class, my paper said, but I didn't know what that meant and I wondered if I'd learn about prescription medications. I was bound to get lost again in the crowded hallways so I turned instinctively to the one person who seemed less threatening: Arash.

"Do you know how I can get to building H?" I asked in a rush, terrified of getting swept up again.

His friends clustered around him throwing up signs. They created *P*s with their hands facing each other. "Persian pride!"

Arash looked at me with sweet eyes and pointed in the direction of a military-looking barrack at the edge of a barren baseball field. I thanked him and started walking.

"Hey Sicily!" he called after me.

I turned. He was smiling.

"I was fucking with you. H building is in the other direction."

I turned and started walking in the opposite direction, passing in front of his friends who all laughed. As soon as they were gone, he caught up with me.

"I'll walk you to class, man."

"Thanks. You don't have to."

But I was too desperate to refuse his help.

"So is Sicily close to Greece? I was there one year with my family . . . We visited the Pantheon."

"The Parthenon?"

"Yeah, whatever. The big old white building with all the columns."

"Great. Look. Just for future reference, Sicily is not a country. It's a region that is *part* of Italy. Kind of like a state here."

"That's tight." He winked at me and dropped me off in front of a yellow door. "I always get those two confused. See you around, Greek goddess." He spat on the floor and walked away.

"Rome, Georgia?" Mrs. Anders, my health teacher with fake breasts asked in front of my new class members.

"No. Rome, Italy."

"Wow, that's neat."

We sang the American national anthem with hands on our hearts. I did not know the words but opened my mouth in wide oval shapes. Mrs. Anders passed a picture of an overweight Hispanic teenager looking down at a newborn child.

"Does anyone know what the best prevention for pregnancy and sexually transmitted diseases is?" Mrs. Anders asked.

The word *condom* was muttered by students, but of course

it was a trick question. Mrs. Anders looked at us with a grave expression. Below the photo was a handwritten paragraph:

> *Hello, I'm Marcia Espandola. I'm 16 years old. One year ago I thought it would be a good idea to use a fake ID to buy a bottle of Jack Daniel's with my boyfriend. We got drunk, partied, and had unprotected sex. A month later I discovered I was pregnant with Julia. My boyfriend left me and now I'm a single teen mother. I had dreams of attending my Junior Prom. That's not going to happen. I can't afford to pay for a babysitter.*

"The number-one prevention against pregnancy and sexually transmitted diseases is *abstinence.* Write this down in your notebooks. It's going to be on your quiz next week."

I looked around. It was obvious none of the girls in my class were virgins.

Mrs. Anders handed us a "self-esteem contract." We were to write a goal we wanted to pursue in the course of the following ten weeks. Each day we would fill in an empty column with the steps we were taking toward our goal. The goal had to reflect something that would boost our self-esteem and steer us away from drinking, sex, and drugs. Alcohol was conducive to unforeseen acts of libidinous lasciviousness that had catastrophic consequences. We needed to steer away from turning into Marcia Espandola.

I wrote down my goal: "In ten weeks I want to be back in Rome."

When class was done I felt a surge of loneliness. I glanced at Mrs. Anders with her full melon breasts. I needed empathy. I put on a deep guttural voice like the ones from the soap operas my grandmother watched at home. America was five hundred episodes ahead on *The Bold and the Beautiful.* Key characters had already died and been resurrected here, twin sisters had popped up out of nowhere, new actors had taken over main roles. I watched and translated every episode for my grandmother so that on Sundays she could ring her friends in Rome and report back. My favorite character was Brooke Logan, the troubled wife of Ridge Forrester, the alien-faced foppish son of the fashion tycoon Eric Forrester. I liked her pink lip gloss and stern, dramatic tone, always on the verge of a desperate revelation.

"Mrs. Anders." I looked at her, channeling my inner Brooke. "Where I come from, students are forced to take over their high schools and do sit-ins because teachers are fascists. My family moved to America to escape constant political oppression and I thought I should be honest with you and tell you these things about me. I understand American teachers to be more democratic than Italian ones."

Her eyes lit up. "Oh, dear. I'm so sorry. Families from all parts of the world flee persecution and find safety and opportunity in America. Our school welcomes all refugees. We are happy to help you rebuild your life here."

She thought I was a refugee from war. I did not tell her World War II had ended. Did not explain that we used "fascist" to describe any teacher who disagreed with us on anything, particularly on granting students the right to have sit-ins at their high schools in order to smoke hash and have sleep-ins in the gym.

I shook her hand. "Thank you, Mrs. Anders. It feels good to know I can count on someone here."

I walked out of the classroom and made a mental note to change my self-esteem contract. Returning to a war-infested country in ten weeks was an unlikely objective. Under "self-esteem goal" I would write: "Rebuilding my life in the United States."

3

From the shade of the lemon tree my brother and I spied on my father in his studio. He had signed with a minor agency and was working with Robert, his new writing partner—a CalArts film student with two pierced eyebrows who wore black lipstick and talked to himself like he was in on a plan nobody else knew about. Robert bit his nails while my father twisted his curls with his index finger and looked at the computer screen. They never spoke when they worked.

"Do you think he'll give you the Terminator face today?" my brother asked as he coughed up smoke from the cigarette I was teaching him to inhale.

"I hope not." I sighed.

Like the Terminator, Robert was expressionless and never removed his black boxy sunglasses. This made us all self-conscious when we saw him around the house. It was hard to say if he had emotions. It was hard to say if he saw anything.

Ettore met the kid through Max, who thought they were a perfect match. Robert had a fascination with World War II and was uninterested in most things except for Hitler's biography and horror films, but this, according to Max, was his virtue. "He's hyper-focused and completely ignorant. Like a street kid from a Pasolini film, but living in Los Angeles thirty years later."

Our father devotedly listened to anything Max had to say. He was a big reason why we had moved to LA. We were in awe of his friendship with Phil Collins. He had written the lyrics to the semi-recent hit "Another Day in Paradise." We felt proud to say we'd known him before he was famous. In the eighties he had produced horror films, including an American cult movie about android chameleons that was shot in the studios of Cinecittà in Rome. He and Ettore met on set in Rome and became close friends, carousing around town in search of remnants of *La Dolce Vita*. Every year since Max left Rome, he sent us Christmas cards and tried to lure my parents to Hollywood. He told us about working with the studios, writing for Phil Collins, and life in Beverly Hills. When we left for Los Angeles nobody knew whether Ettore and Max would be compatible. His last film, *Devourandia,* was a cannibalism tale about old Texas farmers in a small border town who discovered that the blood of drug addicts had the power to prolong lives. My father usually fainted at the sight of blood, but he was willing to take a chance because Max knew musicians, actors, and producers. He was the only person who seemed to know about the underground jazz club in the back of a Long Beach soul food restaurant. And one of the few who was allowed in. I always had a hard time finding a connection between producing horror movies about cannibals and writing humanitarian hit songs about homelessness like "Another Day in Paradise," but we were all fascinated by his eclecticism.

"We don't even have a pool. Everyone in LA has a pool." My brother sighed, looking at our mother at the other end of the yard as she bathed in a pink inflatable pool from Pick 'n Save. It was half tilted on its side and water leaked out. We were allowed to refill it only once every three days. Our father said Los Angeles was a desert, and water in deserts cost more than gold. Right now the water was lukewarm and filled with insects and rancid lemons, but Serena did not care. She glistened top-less in a layer of Johnson's Baby Oil, squirting it on her eyes and breasts, ignoring the side effects the unfiltered California sun would have on her skin. Her new cat-eye sunglasses from the 99 Cent store slipped down her shiny nose. She pushed them up each time she turned the page of her book—her fourth Sitting Bull biography. The grass around the pool area was cluttered with newspaper clippings, cutouts, and books about Native Americans. If you asked her what she was doing, she glared at you and said she was working.

Her passions emerged in serial fashion. Each one entailed reclining on a bed or in a pool or tub, surrounded by piles of clippings and books. In Rome she went through a Gypsy phase. She read about Eastern Europe's nomadic culture for months, forced my brother and me to watch documentaries about the Chernobyl nuclear disaster, and organized playdates with a group of children living in a Romany camp on the city outskirts. She had been lured by a Gypsy woman she met at a traffic light, whom she recognized as a sister from a past life. They hung out and became friends, then the woman hypnotized our mother. Ettore found her wandering the Piazza del Popolo in the center of Rome with no purse, no jewelry, and no car. We got picked up from the nomad camp and never saw our Gypsy friends again.

My brother put out his half-smoked cigarette and went rollerblading with Creedence, one of eight Mormon brothers who lived with their parents in the long shotgun house down the street. Creedence was his first and only friend. Not having a friend was worse than not having a pool, I thought. Three months had passed and I felt invisible. In school I was alone. At home I was alone. Robert was a breath of fresh air—or dead air since he looked like a corpse. But it didn't matter. It was something. I pulled out my copy of Simone de Beauvoir's *The Second Sex*, hoping he might notice me through the window and be attracted by my intellectually committed reading. It didn't work. Like my mother, I took off all my clothes except for a bathing-suit bottom and sat on a towel reading in the burning sun, eyeing him from under the lemon tree. It was hard to tell whether he could see me through the Terminator glasses, but he faced my general direction a few times. My eyebrows thickened and my cheeks swelled with the heat as I tried to delve into existentialist feminism. I fell asleep in the sun.

When I woke up an hour later, I was dripping with sweat. Serena was no longer in the pool. My grandmother ironed clothes on the fold-out board on the patio while humming Claudio Villa songs to herself. She also owned cat-eye sunglasses now. After helping us move, and disdaining Van Nuys and everything about America she could think of, she had decided to stick around a little longer. The California heat was good for her arthritis, she said, and Rome was already rainy and cold. She called Alitalia and befriended an airline representative from Torrance who changed her return ticket without charge in exchange for health tips.

I stumbled to the plastic pool and collapsed in the warm, oily water Serena had left behind. Inside, the house was empty. A television was turned on. I could hear it from the yard. I splashed around, did some lazy sit-ups, and came out. In the living room I found Robert sitting in darkness, sunglasses still on, staring at the screen.

"Your parents went to buy groceries. They invited me to lunch," he said without looking at me.

I was wrapped in a white towel. The bottom of the bathing suit dripped dirty pool water on the hardwood floors.

"I don't usually eat anything so I think it'll be weird, but whatever. Your mom doesn't take no for an answer."

"Do you want a snack?" I asked him.

"A snack?" he asked with a vampire smirk.

"Yes, a snack."

"No thanks. I said I don't eat. Food is weird."

I turned around, embarrassed, and headed for my bedroom.

"Hey!" he called after me. "I'm watching *Nekromantik*. You want to watch it with me?"

"Sure. Is it a comedy?"

"It's a story of a couple that gets off on fucking corpses."

"Oh, okay."

"It's the sexiest thing in the world."

We sat side by side in the dark, never touching. I could smell him. My first American male smell. It wasn't a great smell, a bit sickly, but I welcomed it. We could be friends, I thought. We had things in common. I didn't know what they were, but I was sure they existed.

On screen the male protagonist unearthed a dead body from a cemetery and started to fuck it. Robert said that was so hot. I glanced at him from the corner of my eyes.

"Yeah, that *is* hot," I said.

He drummed his fingers on his knees and picked his nose once, but I told myself I wouldn't mind.

Later on we all gathered at the table. Serena had cooked lunch. When I sat down, Ettore said that sunbathing topless by the blow-up pool made me look like a poor man's Lolita. "It's very cheap and you're distracting my co-worker," he complained in Italian. Never mind that he and Serena walked around the yard completely naked every day. I was to follow different rules. Especially when Robert was present.

Robert was uncomfortable with his name being tossed around in another language. He was also uncomfortable with the quantity of food on the table and the number of family members gathered around it. Serena served spaghetti with fried zucchini flowers, humming over the awkward silence.

Robert stared down at his pasta and tried to roll it in his fork.

My grandmother sneered at him and pointed to his plate.

"Americans don't know how to roll spaghetti."

Robert looked at me for guidance. "What's everyone saying about me?"

"She said you're no good at rolling your noodles," Timoteo explained.

I kicked him under the table.

Exasperated by his bowl of recalcitrant food, Robert finally asked my mother for a knife, but they all stared him down and shook their heads disapprovingly.

"*Macché,* knife! If you go to Italy and cut spaghetti, what will people think of you?" my father scoffed.

"That you're an idiot! A dumb American idiot!" my grandmother lashed out.

Robert put his fork down.

"Was it too al dente?" Serena asked, desperate for approval. "You don't like it? But you are like a skeleton! Do you eat at home?"

"We eat, just not all eat at the same time or around a table. Normal people don't always eat together, you know," Robert mumbled.

Timoteo translated for my grandmother.

"*Normal people?*" she said, gasping at his black lipstick and piercings. "He looks like the Antichrist!"

"What did she say again?" Robert asked.

"She thinks it's not true American families don't always eat at the table together," I said, lying.

"That's terrible!" Serena sighed. "Your mom doesn't cook for you?"

"My mom is dead."

Everyone finally shut up.

That night I had a high fever from extreme sun exposure. I closed my eyes in bed, hallucinating and meditating on the effects Robert and the necrophiliac couple had on me. I was a corpse dressed in rags, washed up on a riverbank. Robert carried my limp body in the moonlight. My consumed, translucent flesh—soft and covered in mud—was his. His bony fingers crept up my legs, pulling rags up my thighs. My impotence got him hard. He made love to me, respectfully at first and becoming progressively rougher, pulling clumps of dead hair out of my skull until, when my head was almost shiny, he shoved me firmly against a tree and fucked me. I came and then fell asleep. I dreamed I was Sue Lyon, the actress from *Lolita,* aged and overweight, sipping on milk shakes and chewing on pizza. A poor man's Lolita.

4

After the first month of school I'd earned my right to attend a
regular English class, but I soon realized it was just a few steps
above the ESL class. Most of my classmates could not read or
write. Spelling tests included words like "tomorrow" and "teenager." Arash sat in my row and left the page blank. He did not
speak to me in class, but when his friends weren't looking, he
rolled his eyes and asked me to speak Greek to him because he
thought it was hot. I didn't know what to say so I listed Italian
food items.

"Prosciutto, mortadella, carciofi alla giudìa, melanzane alla
parmigiana."

"*Man o bokon*—have sex with me," he answered, thinking I
was trying to seduce him.

He spat out the window and whistled at the girls who passed
by below our classroom. The teacher could not keep him or anyone else under control. The rest of the students only stopped
screaming when she sniveled.

My most challenging course was Physical Education. A
gigantic coach with shiny red hair who looked like a walrus
commanded us to run for what felt like miles around a football
field. My legs were long, but I was stooped and slow. There was
only one person worse than me on the track—a tiny Persian

doll with a seventies wedge hairstyle and a big mole on her chin. Her head was disproportionately large and looked like it would unhinge from her neck with a small push. Neither the coach nor any of our classmates seemed to have any interest in her. She could not run. She could not jump. She could not catch balls. Under a slight mustache her swollen lips exuded a patina of saliva. Nobody got close to her. She stared vacantly into space until she caught up with me on the racetrack. I was dragging my feet to finish my first mile—hand lodged over my aching spleen. We'd been lapped by our classmates and still managed to be the last ones running. She gave me her bony hand to shake. Her name was Azar and her wrist was the size of two fingers squeezed together. She looked ill and desperate and begged me to be her friend. "Or just pretend like you are my friend in this class," she said. "Be my PE buddy, please."

I agreed to be Azar's friend in gym class, but when I saw Arash again during lunch break he said that was a terrible choice for a new girl in school. He tapped my shoulder in front of the football field, cigarette dangling from his lips, waiting for me. His theory was that as long as you kept moving nobody noticed.

"Azar is a weirdo. Like she's actually half mentally retarded and has a growth disorder. If you hang out with her, people will think you're a loser like her."

"It's okay. She's not a loser."

"I'm just saying. She's totally uncool. She's like a half cousin so I feel bad saying it, but it's true. I'm just trying to help you out."

We crossed a picnic bench area and Arash flipped his cigarette butt into the dirt, quietly agreeing to guide me through the school grounds so I'd get my bearings. He didn't say it, but I knew that's what he was doing and I was grateful for it.

"Hey, is it true women in Greece don't shave their armpits?"

"Look, I'm Italian, not Greek. And anyway it's a political choice," I said, trying to defend myself.

"You go topless at the beach, right?"

"Yes, of course. We are topless and proud and we don't get stupid tickets for being naked," I insisted.

"You know what? You're kind of hot the way you talk all strict and serious and shit. Makes me pop a boner."

"Makes you what?"

He took my hand and put it on his jeans. "New girl in town gotta learn what's what." He giggled.

We arrived in front of the cafeteria area. Arash stole a small carton of chocolate milk from a tray on a table and opened it. He said I looked like a sorry ass walking around not knowing what to do. There was no Greek-Sicilian section in school, but I might get along with Jewish Israelis. They were peaceful and hung out under the only trees in the school yard. "They listen to Dylan and dye their hair green," he said. I could also become friends with Chris. He pointed him out. He was a kind of stoner-looking dude with a beanie, bloodshot almond-shaped eyes, and beautiful long brown hair partly tied back with hemp string and beads. He was playing hacky sack alone. He was *always* alone, Arash said. He'd grown up in some kind of hippie situation in Topanga Canyon and had no social skills. But the good thing about that was that he had access to incredible weed. He was a superb pot dealer and if I wanted to purchase anything I should always go to him. His stuff came from a commune up in the canyon. It was the best in the Valley.

Arash led the way out of the cafeteria toward an abandoned baseball field where he dropped me off. A group of Mexican punk rockers with bags under their eyes were smoking cigarettes.

"For now hang out with these guys. They are anarchists. They don't give a fuck who you are or where you come from."

"Thanks."

"Hey! Don't you fucking say 'hi' to me when you see me with my friends, though. I only like you 'cause I went to Greece that one time."

He came close to me and gave me a hug.

"And don't look so scared all the time. It's a sign of weakness."

I forced a confident smirk and wiped a chocolate-milk stain from his lips. "So is milk on your lips."

He had long lashes and dark eyes that were more profound than he thought. He also had a boxy, fat chin. It was manly and square with a deep dimple in the center that made me think he was courageous, like Kirk Douglas. A chin that was ready for fatherhood or gladiatorhood. A chin that made me trust him. I now had a PE buddy and a protector in school. I was moving up.

The Mexicans on the field all looked younger than me. Many didn't speak English. They barely said hello, but it was true, they did not mind having me there. I sat on the ground, smoked cigarettes, and read my feminist tract. At the edge of the field I noticed the girl who had snuck out of the tardy hall on the first day of school. She was a roamer, never remaining in one place. Every time I saw her, a door was opening before or closing behind her. She walked swiftly alongside the school fence. She threw her backpack over it, climbed up, and jumped off, disappearing down a residential street—long copper hair bouncing off her shoulders. In just a few seconds she was free.

When school was out I emulated her. Wandering and meandering across the grids that formed the San Fernando Valley became part of my daily ritual. I picked Sepulveda. It was the longest road in Los Angeles and the closest big boulevard to my house. Nobody walked there, but I did. It happened naturally. At first I thought it was the ugliest street I'd ever seen. Every parking lot was fenced with barbed wire and there were often rags and bibs stuck in the metal spikes. There was a series of dismal strip malls featuring obscure Mexican fast-food chains,

cycles of used-car lots, and Jenny Craigs. But day after day, the
street began to transform in my eyes. The more I walked, the
more the ugliness became part of my everyday life and those
barbed-wire fences and strip malls became what I began to
recognize as my neighborhood. A local reality. It didn't smell
like freshly baked pizza from Campo de' Fiori in Rome, but it
was familiar. A new form of familiar. I knew, for example, that
when I saw the neon sombrero of the Mexican fast-food restaurant or the golden crown from the Crown Car Wash sign, it
meant I was approaching my house. I started to look forward
to those little landmarks and creating my own mythological
stories about the place I inhabited. I stumbled on Sound City
Studios, a crumbling recording studio just a few blocks from
my house. It was a former Vox music-equipment factory nes-
tled in front of a Budweiser Brewery that spouted nauseating
fumes from its chimneys. From the parking lot it looked like
another desolate Van Nuys store, but one day I saw Zack de la
Rocha from Rage Against the Machine leaning on a car outside,
smoking a cigarette. I came closer and since the studio door was
open, I peeked inside. It smelled like cat urine. It was dark and
dirty, but the walls were lined with rows of gold and platinum
records: Neil Young, Fleetwood Mac, the Grateful Dead had all
recorded their most iconic albums there. The place had almost
gone bankrupt in the eighties until Nirvana decided it would be
where they would record *Nevermind*. That had happened just a
year earlier. On the walls I saw intimate snapshots pinned to a
corkboard of Kurt Cobain and Dave Grohl playfully grappling
each other. As for many people my age, Nirvana was the fuel
to deal with pain and anxiety. Kurt's deep blue eyes seemed to
reassure me. If he had turned Van Nuys in his favor, I could too.

Walking in LA meant crossing paths with people you
wouldn't normally mix with. If you were a girl it also meant getting honked at. On Sepulveda a car passenger rolled down the

window and screamed at me once. I didn't understand anything
except for "Baby," but a tall Hispanic girl wearing a sequined
minidress and slouched against a streetlight in front of a Food
4 Less stared me down, thinking I was trying to steal her job.
She was as big as a man, with broad shoulders and a faint beard
stubble. "It's my block, girl," she hissed and I kept going. I'd
cross paths with her again and always made sure she understood
I was just a pedestrian, one of the few.

During one of my treks down Sepulveda I ended up on
Ventura Boulevard—the only Valley street that did not have
a cookie-cutter suburban feel. A sign in front of a shop called
Archstone Vintage and Rentals read: "Welcome to the world's
longest avenue of contiguous businesses. We apologize for not
living up to your expectations." The place seemed closed. The
storefront was a dusty display of antique dolls in Western costumes, some with no eyes or hair. A scarecrow sat in a wheelchair holding on its lap a pile of lunch boxes from the eighties.
I pushed the door open. A guy with long hair and a Metallica
T-shirt sat on a swivel chair with his feet up on a counter.

"What's up?" he greeted me.

"Can I come in?"

He shrugged his shoulders and laughed. "You sure this is
what you were looking for? Nobody comes in here."

"The storefront seemed interesting."

"Oh, the broken dolls? Phoebe says they're antique."

I made my way into the dusty alcove.

"Which they are if you consider that this one"—he got up
and pulled a doll with a half-shut glass eye from a shelf—"was
the initial tester for Chucky."

"Who's Chucky?"

"You're not from around here?"

"No, I have no idea what you're talking about. Is it something from a film?"

"Almost everything you see in this shop was, once. Even the scarecrow on the wheelchair. It was in *Devourandia*. Ever seen that weird film?"

I couldn't believe a prop from Max's movie had made it to the store.

"I know the person who produced it. He's a family friend."

The guy didn't seem impressed. "Max Velasquez? He's the one who sold me the pieces. I think he was a bit low on cash."

"I doubt it. He's friends with Phil Collins, you know. He wrote the lyrics to 'Another Day in Paradise.' "

"It's a shitty song," he said with a sneer. "He should be punished for that."

I was surprised to think that Max, with his grandiose attitude, would be selling props to a store like this one.

"Simone de Beauvoir, huh?" he said, noticing the book peeking out of my bag. "Why are you reading that? Didn't she, like, promote castration or something?"

"What? No! She was an existentialist. She thought women were condemned in a world built for men."

"A ballbuster."

"She laid the foundations for the second wave of feminism. She's incredible. I take this book with me wherever I go. As a statement," I said, proudly.

"Well, you shouldn't. In fact you should hide it. Nobody reads in LA." When he spoke, his lips curled forward in a heart shape that gave him a gay affectation. He had an aquiline nose and wild, squinty, light blue eyes.

"I'm Eugenia. I'm Italian."

"Hey, I'm Henry and I'm poor."

We shook hands. His was pudgy and dirty.

"You hate it here, I can tell."

I nodded.

"How's school? Have you been recruited by cheerleaders?"

"I can't even jump on one leg."

"Sad. Want to smoke pot?" he proposed, bouncing off his chair. He locked the front door and huffed. "Nobody is going to come in anyway."

We walked to a small bathroom in the back. He loaded a bong and passed it to me. I'd never seen such an instrument. I took one hit and soon the store felt like a cozy gigantic piece of velvety fabric. I walked around the dusty wonderland in awe: Elvira's original makeup set was on display in the Thriller section next to a hat that belonged to Bela Lugosi. Capes from *Dracula* went for under $100. Wonder Woman belts sold for $90. There were three of them on the hips of disfigured mannequins.

A photo album from the fifties traced the history of the training of Lassie, the collie dog from the TV series. Vinyl records, old photos stuck together, ice skates—everything was bundled in moldy piles.

"Phoebe is a fat-ass hoarder," Henry explained. "She has a hard time letting go of things. I hate working here. It's all going to shit."

"Phoebe is the owner?"

"Yes. She's my mother. She used to be a costume designer in the seventies, but then got addicted to crack, got out of crack, started shooting heroin, then got clean. Now she just drinks diet soda and eats junk food."

I liked his matter-of-fact way of speaking. He handed me a picture of an airline attendant from the sixties that was hanging next to a mirror.

"That's her when she was young. She was actually beautiful before she started using. So, like, she was beautiful until she was twelve."

I arched my brow at him.

"I'm kidding, but not really." He chuckled.

He took out a big cardboard box from the back of the room and stabbed it with a knife. It was full of vintage clothes. I passed my fingers over a flimsy Dracula cape. It seemed too cheap to

have been in a movie, but Henry explained that everything that
was made for films was that way. It wasn't meant to last.

"Can't you just sell fake things and pretend they're original?" I asked.

"You wish. Every film costume comes with a certificate of
authenticity from the studio. Falsifying one of those is worse
than murder in this city."

"Wow."

"Last week a store down the street bought the DeLorean
from *Back to the Future*. It was sitting on the back lot at Univer-
sal rotting away. You should go check it out if you're into these
things. This area is full of film-memorabilia stores."

Henry moved his long hair away from his eyes and I noticed
there was something wrong with his ear. It was almost nonex-
istent, eaten away. I tried to look elsewhere, pretending not to
notice, but he sighed immediately.

"Yep . . . I don't have an ear."

"I'm sorry, I didn't mean to—"

"No problem. That's why I keep my hair over it. I hate getting those fake heartfelt looks. It's just an ear."

"Yes, well . . ."

"Did you drive here?" he asked.

"No, I walked."

"You live close?"

"Not really."

"A Valley walker. I used to do that. Met a lot of weirdos
that way."

"Well I'm sure they must have said the same about you."

"Right."

We both laughed.

Henry walked me home. He said the sameness of Sepulveda
soothed him also.

"Every time I walk in front of this place I think about my
mom. I imagine dropping her off here and never picking her up

again," he said, pointing to an overweight lady in a Jenny Craig parking lot.

"So where is she?" I asked. "Your mom."

Henry tilted his head toward me to hear me better from his functioning ear. He shifted his weight from one side to the other, leaning in just enough to not look like a deaf old man.

"At home. She can't really move. She's obese."

"Oh, come on."

"Not kidding. She's huge. Like seriously morbidly obese. She's horrible. I hate her."

"But you work in her shop."

"It's a job."

"Wouldn't you rather have a different employer?"

"Well, it's actually kind of awesome having a boss who is never around. I do whatever I want, like walk sad Italians home in the middle of the afternoon."

I laughed. I was drawn to his missing ear. It wasn't entirely missing. The lower lobe was there, just curled inward, like the tail end of a fat snail. I tried to scrutinize it from up close each time the wind stirred his long mane, but Henry was quick to pat the hair back down.

We walked past the Crown Car Wash and Henry turned in to a strip mall. He asked me if I had ever been to the twenty-four-hour Taiwanese party store. I had to meet those guys, he said. They sold everything from balloons to drugs to desserts and iced teas.

"They'll sell you cigarettes even if you're underage. Two bucks for a pack of Camel Lights."

Inside the store Henry high-fived a group of quiet Taiwanese kids in oversize starched baseball caps. He introduced me and ordered us a bubble tea, an ice-blended drink filled with floating fruit jellies. It was overly sweet and toxic and delicious. That taste was the first magical thing that had happened in my neighborhood.

When we reached Sunny Slope Drive, Henry took a look at my house from the front yard. The lights were on inside. We could see Serena in the kitchen with her apron on.

"Seems like a nice place to be."

"Sometimes." I smiled.

He leaned into me and kissed both my cheeks.

"Isn't that how you Italians do it?"

5

"**We cannot be** happy in this land if we don't pay tribute to the people who originally inhabited it," my mother proclaimed. She had concluded her repertoire of books and biographies on the Sioux tribe and felt that in order to *love* America, we had to see it as it was originally imagined. Shortly after our family-lunch fiasco, Robert the Goth went off his medications and had a psychotic breakdown. He ran away from his art-school campus and tried to electrocute himself on a high-voltage security fence. He needed a couple of weeks off from work while he got back on his feet and started his new pills, so my father had time to kill.

We made a Thanksgiving trip of it and visited the battlefield of the Wounded Knee Massacre of the Lakota at the Pine Ridge Indian Reservation in South Dakota. My grandmother would not come in the Cadillac convertible. She hated it and said it was ridiculous and uncomfortable, so we bought a used Pontiac station wagon with tinted windows for $500. It took us three days and a few mechanical problems to get to South Dakota.

When we arrived we drove straight to the reservation. We parked in an empty lot by the mass grave. When the engine was turned off, the valley around us hummed. My mother got out and scurried to the trunk. She had been preparing for this moment.

We would pay tribute to the deceased souls of the Lakota and honor the fact that they were there before anybody else. She decided we would plant cyclamen bulbs by the graves and say a prayer. She had packed a suitcase full of loose flower seeds as well as a pile of white rags we should wear for the ceremony.

"A hundred years ago, three hundred Indian men, women, and children were massacred by American troops," Serena said solemnly as she passed around the faded garments. She did not find anything that fit my grandmother, so she gave her an old white bedsheet, insisting she take her clothes off and wrap herself in it "as a sign of respect."

"I'm not going to do that," my grandmother replied. She got back in the car and shut the door. "I am not getting arrested for being naked again, and I am not walking around in a bedsheet."

"Stop acting like a baby!" Serena complained.

My grandmother stomped her feet and remained glued to the backseat of the Pontiac.

"You can't make me do this."

"Fine! When the spirit of Spotted Elk comes to you in the form of a fierce antelope and tries to stab you with his horns, don't tell me I didn't warn you!"

Timoteo and I rolled our eyes. This was a typical phenomenon that followed our mother's intensive research phases: clippings, books, excessive enthusiasm, then playing the victim if others dissented from her opinions.

"I'm not going to that stupid grave site. I'm not afraid of Spotted Elk and I am not wearing *this*!" My grandmother took the bedsheet, threw it out the window, and locked the car.

"These people were here first!" Serena pounded her fist on the glass.

"They can stay here for all I care! I'm going back to Italy in one month and you know what?" She rolled down the window so we could all hear her. "I think you should do the same! You can't just carry your kids with you everywhere you go."

"I do whatever I want with my children!" my mother screamed at her. "They love me and are happy to follow us whatever we choose to do, right, kids?"

We did not answer.

"See!" my grandmother squealed.

Serena's lip started to quiver. I knew what was coming.

"There you go. I can never do anything right, can I?" She broke down crying in the barren South Dakota field. "All you do is complain! I'm just trying my best!" she wailed in a fit of self-pity.

Making a scene inside the quiet cemetery seemed wrong. I hated seeing my mother sob. Her melodramatic tantrums always caught me off guard. I didn't like it when our roles reversed, when she cried like a baby and I had to be the grown-up. I would do everything I could to stop her from going down that route.

"We'd follow you anywhere. We are all happy to be here." I tried to console her with a hug.

My father wrapped his arms around her also. He knew the drill. He told her how much we all adored Native Americans. There was no other place we'd rather be than the barren battlefield of Wounded Knee.

"Then is it so much to ask of you to put some white clothes on?" Serena whimpered.

My grandmother scoffed from her seat in the car, crossed her arms, and mumbled, "Manipulative bitch."

"What did you say, *Mom*?" my mother snapped, peering through the window.

"Nothing," I interjected. "She just doesn't want to wear the white robe."

"Sheet!" my grandmother screamed from the car. "Bedsheet, not robe!"

I found a sleeveless baby doll nightgown in my suitcase and gave it to my grandmother to wear over her clothes, but Serena kept frowning, unconvinced. She handed my brother his out-

fit: extra-large white boxers and a T-shirt that belonged to my
father.

"I don't want to go around in Dad's underwear," he complained, but our mother's lip trembled again and he put on the
boxers without further discussion.

My father wore yoga pants and a long-sleeved Indian shirt.
My mother slipped into a white tunic-style nightgown and I put
on yellowing thermal pajamas from the Salvation Army.

Together, finally, we walked toward the site.

The aluminum fence that guarded the Wounded Knee
burial grounds was shut. Inside were dusty graves and a chapel
that was missing part of its roof. White bunnies scavenged for
food, unafraid to get close. We hopped over and pried the gate
open so grandma could get in. The great battlefield was silent. It
was freezing. A brutal, dry wind scratched our skins. We stood
next to one another in front of the mass grave where hundreds
of Sioux had been buried. A wooden plaque told us we were
officially on a U.S. National Historic Landmark, but it didn't
feel like it. We were the only visitors. The graves were falling
apart, some were so dirty it was impossible to read them. Others
were made from mud, decorated with skimpy wooden crosses
impaled in the soil before them.

My mother's eyes swelled with tears. She had been reading
about this battle for months. She thought we would be visiting some kind of Holocaust museum, but we were all discover-
ing America wasn't interested in conserving certain chapters of
its history. She read out loud from a cement slab that vaguely
resembled an obelisk: "In memory of the Chief Big Foot massacre December 29, 1890. Many innocent women and children
who knew no wrong died here."

"Is this *it*?" My grandmother sighed as tears rolled down
her cheeks. "I didn't want to come to this stupid site anyway."

Serena ignored her and let her grumble away. She held my
hand and my brother's, then closed her eyes in prayer.

"Dear Sioux, I bring you my family and ask you to welcome them to your land. We know this country belonged to you first and we want you to know we come in peace. *Namaste.*"

My brother elbowed me.

"That's not the Native American way of saying 'peace.' It's Indians from India who say that," I corrected her timidly.

Serena shot me a look.

"It doesn't matter. It's the energy the word carries that counts. You should know that."

"Amen," concluded my father.

The high sun emanated a metallic light that cast a wild luminescence on the tall grass around us. The wind blew through the holes in my Salvation Army thermal underwear. We were all too vulnerable under the huge South Dakota sky. It felt like it would swallow us whole, inter us into its sacred land with the lost tribes.

We planted Serena's cyclamen bulbs close to the mass grave. We all knew they would never turn into flowers. A graceful hawk circled in the sky. On our way out we noticed a large FOR SALE sign on the back side of the cemetery's fence. The eighty acres of the Wounded Knee Historic Landmark were being offered for more than a million dollars by the owner of the land. What was left of the Sioux tribe could not afford the price.

From the parking lot, the Prairie Wind Casino and Hotel looked more like a warehouse than a hotel. A long, horizontal cement structure extended from both sides of a faux-tepee sculpture that served as an iconic entrance gate. On each side of the building, rusty billboards depicted multicolored horses galloping into the wind.

"Feel the Wind and Feel the Win!" an advertisement said.

My mother was drawn to the idea that the place was owned and run by the Sioux. Choosing to stay there was a way to pay them back. While my parents checked in, through the revolving doors I caught a glimpse of a lonely Native American Elvis impersonator getting hammered at the bar, preparing for his evening performance. We were all aware we had ended up in a desperate place in the middle of nowhere, but we also knew that saying anything would precipitate Serena's final breakdown and ruin the rest of our vacation. We made a silent pact not to mention drunk Elvis or the senile gamblers who sat like zombies in front of the slot machines next door.

Thanksgiving lunch was served at the casino buffet. We could eat all we wanted for $13.99. My mother's quasi-religious views about Indians and their tribes, about the purity we had to give back to the once-virgin land, disappeared into a plate of turkey nuggets and canned cranberry sauce. Over our heads TV screens looped diamond-studded gambling catchphrases: "Cold Days, Hot Cash!"

A giant turkey with dollar bills coming out of its tail fan winked: "Free Thanksgiving bingo. We'll give you something to be thankful for!"

I forced myself to eat and smile and prayed that my mother's furrowed brows would smooth out over her eyes, that her lip would stop trembling and time would go by fast.

The five of us stayed in the casino's Black Elk Imperial Suite so we could all fit. The kitchenette was decorated with a framed portrait of the very white Charles Fey of San Francisco, the man who invented the first slot machine. "A big THANK YOU Mr. Fey!" read a golden plaque beneath him. We visited a hot tub in a glass house in the casino's internal courtyard. The water was lukewarm and brownish, but hot tubs were exciting for my family. Any kind of pool or water container that fit people was. If it had the ability to produce bubbles, generate heat, and massage body parts with jets, it made an entire journey worthwhile.

We bathed in silence. Nobody else was in the glass house.

My grandmother, in a golden one-piece bathing suit, exhaled through the vapors. Her hair turned turquoise under the neon lights. She was trying to get the sore parts of her lower back directly in front of the tub's jet. I imitated her and sat in front of the gushing water, pretending I also suffered from incurable ailments.

"Watch out for hemorrhoids! They can creep up on you if you let the jets in your anus" she warned me.

I didn't know what hemorrhoids were but I knew I didn't want anything in my anus that was problematic for my grandmother's. I floated under the neon lights. The windows got fogged up. We were bathing in a hospital room and I knew then, with complete lucidity, I did not want to be there.

6

Dear Mary, please forgive me and please make sure my parents forgive me. It is time for me to leave. I cannot stay in this country with them. I must find a solution. I know you were a teenager when you had Jesus so you must know what it feels like to be handed a situation that is unmanageable. You might think giving birth to the son of God is more traumatic than living in Van Nuys, but I think that's because when you were alive you never visited the San Fernando Valley. It's easier to be a virgin who gives birth than to be an Italian who lives on Victory and Sepulveda. Amen.

Ettore and Serena came back that night elated from playing blackjack—the free drinks in the game room yielded the desired effect. When they fell asleep I packed a bag with peanuts, tonic water, two small bottles of vodka, a banana from the minibar, and ran away from the Prairie Wind Casino and Hotel. A bunch of local kids were partying at the hot-tub glass house, skinny-dipping and drinking whiskey from bottles. A good sign from Mother Mary. I walked straight into the glass house and picked out the man I thought might save me: Alo. He vaguely resembled Ethan Hawke. If I worked with my imagination, I could pretend he was a celebrity. I didn't know how to approach him because he was naked and pale, so I went back outside, opened my bag, and downed my minibar vodkas for courage. I waited a few minutes until I was sure my good judgment was impaired. In my mind it was imperative that I make a wrong choice that night. *Any* wrong choice. It was the only way to break free.

I observed the vaporous glass house from outside and admired the flashing breasts and butts simmering in the tub. As soon as Alo left the group to get cigarettes, I took a breath and made my move. I asked him for a smoke and drunkenly introduced myself to him, trying not to look below his waistline. I told him I was Italian and traveling around the United States alone, looking to have fun.

"Do you have any weed or hash or Jack Daniel's?" I asked plainly.

Alo exhaled his Marlboro Red and looked at me with focused, excited eyes.

"Are you for real? Where have you been all my life?"

I laughed lasciviously.

He said smoking pot was a sacred thing and it was important to do it in the solitude of nature. He saluted his drunk naked friends and loaded me into a pickup truck. We drove toward the hills.

Alo was half white and half Native American. His name meant "he who looks up," he said. Normally he lived in Ventura, a small surfing town north of Los Angeles, but on holidays he came to South Dakota to visit his mother—a cocktail waitress from Nevada who worked at the Prairie Wind Casino. She had married and divorced a Sioux man with a drinking problem who lived on the reservation and got in trouble. Alo didn't say how, but I gathered he was in jail.

"Oh my God, we, like, share so much!" I exclaimed, forcing a Valley girl accent. "I *totally* live in Los Angeles also. I mean that's where my stuff is while I travel around." It was the first time the Greater Los Angeles area had given me something in common with somebody else.

"That's cool. I escaped South Dakota when I was your age, but it was too far away to get anywhere. I had to wait a few years before things got fun."

"Oh, I'm not a runaway. My parents know I travel. They're bohemians."

I didn't know where my proclamations came from but I felt they were sending me in the right direction.

We were the only car on the interstate. The full moon was rising in the sky. I had never seen such a gleaming ball of light. Everything in America—even the moon—was bigger. We pulled off the highway onto a winding dirt road that led into the woods.

"Where are we going?" I asked after another swig of Jack Daniel's.

Alo leaned toward me and wrapped his hand around my neck, half petting, half caressing my hair in a way that was supposed to be reassuring but had the opposite effect.

"I think Moira is very happy. She has never seen someone from France."

"Italy," I corrected him with a low tone of voice. "Who's Moira?"

"My car." He smiled and patted the dashboard of the pickup with the palm of his hand like a proud father. My eyes fell on the vagrant bottles of whiskey on the floor and the ashtray brimming with cigarette butts.

"Where are we going?" I asked again, sniffing the stale carpets.

The moon crept up higher into the sky, obscured by a row of thick pine trees that curved in toward one another, forming a natural tunnel for our crossing. When we reached a plateau in the forest, Alo turned off the engine and the headlights and let the truck roll down the other side into the darkness.

I tensed up, but he said not to worry. He did this all the time. He knew the road so well he could drive with his eyes closed. And that's what he did. He shut his eyes and let the truck go. I grabbed the steering wheel but could not see. The truck coasted downhill, picking up speed through the black sea of trees. There were no sounds except for the thumping tires on the loose gravel, repeating their cycle at a faster and faster pace.

"Stop!" I screamed. "Turn the lights on."

We zoomed down until the pine trees became sparser and the moonlight began to trickle back in. Moira shot us at full speed out of the dark tunnel into an iridescent wide-open prairie below.

We had landed.

Alo stopped the truck and let out a long laugh, releasing adrenaline. I got out of the truck and started walking as far away from it as I could, into the light of the field.

"Oh, don't be mad. I told you I had it under control," he called after me.

The grass glowed under the moon. It was then I realized we were back at the Wounded Knee burial ground. Alo caught up with me and handed me a blanket and his bottle of whiskey. We treaded through the field. A drumming sound came from the hills.

"Lakota." Alo signaled for me to hush up. "It's their purification ritual to bless the land. They come here on horses every winter from different parts of America as a spiritual journey to heal their ancestors' souls."

I felt a pang in my heart. My poor mother, with her ragged white lingerie and cyclamen bulbs, was right then. She was in tune with the Lakota people who flocked in from all over the country, migrating on horses in arctic weather.

We walked toward the drumming sound, hiding in the long-stemmed grass.

"They asked me to join them the first year, 'cause my dad

is Lakota, but you're supposed to spend months preparing with sweat lodges, meditations, and vision quests. I couldn't swing it. You basically starve yourself, then walk aimlessly in the wilderness for days until some kind of spirit guide or animal appears to you and shows you what the purpose of your life is. Not something you can do in Los Angeles, unless you want to go into the ocean and get eaten by sharks. Plus I like whiskey too much."

We walked further and found a large group of men, women, and horses gathered around a cottonwood tree, close to the burial site. We tried to stay hidden in the shadier parts of the field. Alo unfolded the blanket and sat down. It was freezing.

The tribal drumming intensified and a stout man with face paint started speaking Sioux to the other members.

"Enjoy the show," Alo said while he loaded a pipe. He took a long hit, then passed it to me.

"I feel like we shouldn't be spying on them."

"It's okay." He cuddled me, trying to be romantic or reassuring, succeeding in neither attempt. "They know we're here. They'll let us hang out as long as we don't bother them."

He passed me the incandescent pipe again.

I inhaled deeply, the way Henry taught me back at the vintage store. I kept the smoke in my lungs as long as I could, then spat out with a cough. Alo offered a sip of whiskey to warm up. I downed a quarter of the bottle and almost choked. The alcohol flushed through my throat. An unfamiliar burning began in my stomach. I was suddenly aware of the exact consistency of the liquid. I felt the thick malt condense inside me, and all the way down. I began to see the precise molecule formations that made up whiskey drift into the air. They slid into my esophagus, burning my insides.

I got up in a panic screaming about fire. Everything was burning.

Alo took my hand and sat me back down.

"Chill out or they'll send us away. It's okay, breathe. I just sprinkled a bit of peyote with the weed. Relax. You won't even feel it, I promise," he said as an insidious red dragon made its way out of his throat. I opened my mouth hoping to extinguish the fire burning inside me with the cold air outside, but it got worse.

I was high.

A woman's voice inside my head—the Virgin Mary's—told me to keep breathing and not move.

"Still fires eventually extinguish themselves," she said.

"As long as the wind doesn't blow them elsewhere," replied another voice inside.

I stayed paralyzed.

The Lakota in the circle began to throw things in the fire as part of their ritual. I kept my gaze on their flames. The closer I looked, the more appalled I was: the objects tossed in the pit were, I was sure of it now, turkey nuggets from the casino's Thanksgiving lunch. The Indians were throwing streams of them into the fire: fat, crispy nuggets. It was, of course, their way of rejecting the hypocritical American festivity with its false display of brotherly love between Pilgrims and Native Americans. They were punishing my family for celebrating Thanksgiving and eating McDonald's-style fast food on their reservation. In my mind we had wronged them terribly and there was no turning back. This was it.

I felt a sharp pain in my lower back as if a dog snout made of steel was sniffing me out, pushing away my panties. I pulled Alo's arm to get his attention and only then noticed the dog snout was actually his hand. He had unbuttoned my pants and gotten past my underwear. His fingers were inside my ass.

"What are you doing?" I asked. "Don't you see they are burning the turkey nuggets?"

He laughed. "I know . . . damn turkey nuggets."

I tried to thrust him away, but he stumbled on his side and pushed me further down on the ground.

"Just relax."

"My family is so fucked up! I can't believe we *ate* those nuggets!"

"We *all* ate the nuggets. We're *all* fucked up," Alo said, trying to reason with me.

He was on top of me now. I began to cry, not so much because of his fingers in my ass but because I suddenly remembered reading that McDonald's Chicken McNuggets were a puree of chopped chicken beaks and bones mixed with a pinkish coloring substance, deep-fried in grease. We had sinned against the tribe with our imperialist appetite for fried turkey. What would my Roman schoolmates think?

"It was so wrong to eat those nuggets. On Thanksgiving! On an *Indian* reservation!" I finally cried. The panic was getting worse. Alo pushed farther inside me and told me to stop thinking about the nuggets and to think about the moon instead. It was so beautiful, just like me. He started kissing my neck.

"Surrender," the voice inside my head said. "Surrender or it will be worse."

"You're so hot," Alo whispered sloppily.

I closed my eyes and let myself go on the grass. The sound of drums reverberated in my ears and the fire inside me started to die down. Alo unzipped his pants, keeping his fingers in my ass, and took out his penis. Even though it was freezing cold, his penis stood boldly in the prairie wind. He pulled down my jeans and pushed his way inside me. Surrender or it will be worse, I kept thinking. And we started to fuck.

"Are you a virgin?" he asked, frustrated by my dryness and the friction between our cold bodies. I was. He said I was a lot of work and then pushed harder. I felt the lower part of my body spring from the ground. It undulated over the Lakota fire in the field and hinged there, warming up over the flames. The drumming created a soothing spongelike protection that guarded my insides. Everything turned into a rubbery, senseless composite of two people making love. I was full of him. His flesh expanded inside my crevices, but it was okay because I didn't feel anything. My body wasn't with him. It danced in the field under the full moon. I could see my bare feet touch the ground and bounce on the dirt. My legs moved to the right rhythm, my hips swayed into the fire. The flames made everything numb.

A fastidious tremor pulsed somewhere beneath me as the drugs started to fade. It was my ass. It had been rammed. I heard my grandmother's voice repeating her words of wisdom, "Watch out for hemorrhoids. They can creep up on you if you let the jets in your anus."

And then I passed out.

In a dream I saw escalators descending toward an underground train. They were long and steep and covered in packaged turkey. Yellow turkey breasts, red beaks, and fluffy body parts scattered about. It was a turkey-filled descent into the underworld. The passengers were being asked to be courageous.

"Be strong!" the engineer screamed from his perch in the locomotive. "Be strong in the face of packaged turkey!"

The challenge, I realized, was to not interact with turkeys. No matter how many pieces of meat I found along the way, I knew my mission was to get on the train. I stayed focused. Didn't even look at the dead birds until I reached the cars. I leaped through the closing doors and squeezed in just in time. I did it. I had been strong in the face of packaged turkey and when I looked back at the red beaks and fluffy parts amassed on the moving escalators, I knew I was safe.

I woke up in a damp bed in a house with plastic walls and linoleum floors to the smell of fried bacon. I had no clothes on. I slid into a T-shirt and pretended not to notice. I told myself it was normal. I always slept naked. When I went downstairs a woman in Daisy Dukes was frying sausages and pancakes on a stove. On a stool next to her was a greasy plate piled with layers of bacon. She looked up at me and smiled.

"Ah, the French girl!"

"I'm Italian."

"Oh, I love Italy. I've never been but I *love* the food."

I wanted to make small talk, but words would not come out. Never mind, I thought. I had other priorities.

"Where am I?"

Alo came into the kitchen wearing a pair of dirty over-alls. He'd been out chopping wood. I smiled at him because he looked familiar. The woman in the Daisy Dukes wiggled her butt at him, teasingly. He walked behind her and gave her a hug. They kissed on the lips.

I shuddered thinking about my underground train. Where did it take me? I tried to remember the woman's face. Was she with us on the field? Did I lose my virginity to two people at once? I forced my mind to stop asking questions.

"Good morning, Ma, smells good," Alo said.

He smacked the woman's behind jokingly as she pulled away from him with an excited shrill.

"Watch it, I'm frying!"

I glared at them.

"You're . . . Alo's . . ."

The woman turned toward me, rolling her eyes to the sky.

"Yeah, I had him when I was fifteen," she replied, not real-izing it wasn't the narrow age difference I found perplexing but the fact they'd just kissed on the lips for a long enough amount of time to be awkward. A pot of coffee rested on the kitchen table next to the fried bacon.

"Have a seat! You guys probably need some coffee . . . you were up late." She giggled, eyeing us.

She grabbed the bacon and made plates for us. She poured

herself a cup of coffee and sat on her son's lap. Her tank top
rode up, revealing her butt crack and two dimples on her lower
back. She had a Tasmanian devil tattooed over her right hip. I
sat on the other side of the table, looking at them, not knowing
what to say, where to start. Alo did not glance at me. I could not
eat, but I needed a way out, so I stared out the window: pine
trees and great boulders. We were in a parking lot in the middle
of some kind of rock formation. Outside, children with dirty
mouths played with broken tractors in front of prefabricated
trailer homes. How could I get out of there?

The mother sipped on, staring at me inquisitively with
blinking eyes.

Silence.

She turned to Alo with a worried pout and pushed his hair
back to examine his face, the bags under his eyes, the cracks
that grooved his dehydrated skin. She scratched his stubble
and stretched out his cheeks with her fingers. The way she
was sitting on top of him made it so that when she turned to
him, her breasts came right up to his face. They were solid,
rubbery balloons. Her nipples poked through the white tank
top. Alo nuzzled his head between them and shook it in mock
despair.

"I'm soooo tired, Mom! Put me to bed! Please!" He laughed,
then lit a Marlboro Red.

She took the cigarette from his mouth and put it in hers.

"Alo has throat cancer," she declared with nonchalance.
"He shouldn't smoke."

I understood now why his voice was so raspy.

"Shouldn't you not smoke at all?" I asked, but Alo said he'd
rather die than not smoke.

His mother rolled her broken watery eyes at me.

"It's a lost cause," she said, then got up and waddled to the
pantry where the washer and dryer were, suddenly uninterested
in our company.

"Do you remember last night at the sacred grounds?" Alo finally lifted his eyes. He got up from his chair and came close to me, warm and intimate. "You were so tight. I didn't want to break you."

"Break me?"

I had wanted him to break me. Because now nobody else could. Trying to remember how it happened or what had happened would only make things harder. I did not want to have that conversation. For me what mattered was that I was okay. I had no scars or bruises. I survived the loss of my virginity. I made good my escape. But now I was cold and I wanted to go back.

I imagined my parents going crazy looking for me, blaming each other, incited by my grandmother. I saw police cars piling into the casino's parking lot, detectives taking notes, a Native American psychic conjuring visions of my alcohol-stashed backpack through her third eye. All of them devastated by my absence, rethinking all their choices.

"Can you take me back now?" I asked.

Alo came closer and kissed my lips.

I wanted to steer away from the chance of having him inside me again so I told him I was sorry he had cancer and hoped he wouldn't have to put a creepy voice box in his throat.

"I'm not putting any box in my fucking throat," he said with a glare. And I knew my vagina was safe.

We drove back and on the way Alo gave me a romantic tour of the Badlands, the great rocky expanse of battered buttes that stretches over the southwestern part of South Dakota. He stopped his pickup on a dirt road overlooking miles of dry pinnacles eroded by wind and water. Every cone composition formed clusters of breast-like sculptures emerging out of the earth. They went as far as I could see.

"Infinite tits, man," said Alo. I smiled and shivered. He removed his leather jacket and placed it over my shoulders, a chivalrous gesture I didn't know how to take in. He said I could keep it, that he wanted me to have it. It came from Germany. The Suicidal Tendencies patch on the back was very rare. We should exchange numbers. We could see each other in California. He'd like that, he said, and scribbled his phone number on a piece of paper with a violet pen he found floating between the cigarette butts. I told him I didn't have a phone yet and wrote down my address. I knew I never wanted to see him again.

I rolled Alo's leather jacket under my arm and stumbled toward the Black Elk Imperial Suite, sure I would find a team of detectives huddled around my sobbing family. I told myself I would hug my mother and tell her I was sorry for making fun of her, that packing white clothes and insisting, even crying, so that we would wear them was the right thing to do. I would reassure her that the Lakota had their ways of taking care of themselves. They had horses and rode across barren, frigid fields to commemorate their ancestors. They fasted and went on vision quests and knew how to do things the correct way. She was right. We were wrong.

When I opened the door my father was leaning against the wall in a sirsasana headstand pose while my mother read to him out loud from a yoga exercise book.

"There you are." She turned with a radiant, vacant smile. "We were looking for you."

No detectives. I was not happy about it.

I waited for Serena to scream, for my father to get back on his feet and slap my face savagely.

"I went on a hike. There's a trail behind the casino," I said.

"What a great idea."

My mother got up, came close to me, and stroked my hair.

"Good news. Max got Dad an appointment with a co-producer who is really interested in financing a new project.

Robert is out of the psychiatric ward and ready to finish the script. We're going back to LA today."

In the bedroom my grandmother sat on my bed while my brother played *Tetris* on his Game Boy. He didn't lift his head.

"They didn't even realize you were gone the whole night." She shook her head as she folded my clothes into neat piles.

"I didn't leave," I said firmly.

Then I sat on the bed, curled up on her lap, and fell asleep.

I stayed asleep through most of the ride back. We drove without stopping because my father didn't want to waste money on food or lodging since the casino charged us for leaving early. Outside the car window I saw smoke signals and trails infused by the colors of mutating nature: the Black Hills of Wyoming, the iridescent crystals of Utah's salt flats, waves of neon lights in Las Vegas. We rode through the Strip. Night was not night, but a darker, permanent day, and I felt how small we were compared to all that. In the dawn effulgence we passed the low desert shrubs of Barstow and drove across the suburban Inland Empire of San Bernardino. Then traffic thickened. Freeways began climbing over each other, intersecting, shifting alignments and directions, telling us we were at the end of our trip.

I opened my eyes to the smoggy capsule that towered above downtown Los Angeles. The sunlight diluted into a thick polluted haze and I knew home was somewhere behind those freeways, off a green exit sign that looked like the one before and after it. Home was in this place. We were almost there.

7

*Dear Mary, penetration doesn't hurt! I can make love whenever
I want now. I have a pain-repellent internal rubber suit and no
longer want to pass through school like a ghost. I want to be seen
and I want to be held. Amen.*

My rubber suit was the perfect accessory for anyone facing
fear, change, disorientation. It had a hood that functioned like
a helmet. You could bang your head on a wall and feel no pain.
It had been consigned to me by Alo on a cold night, and one of
its perks was to insulate you from climate conditions. Also you
never saw what you were doing because rubber got in the way,
protecting and isolating you at the same time. I started going
through my day as if it were one of those dreams where you can't
see clearly even though your eyes are open. My peripheral vision
was blocked by the suit's substance, and I filled that unknown
space with the presence of sex, as much as I could, as hard as I
could. Whatever it took to get noticed.

I started with Arash because even though he was cocky and
spat from classroom windows, he was my secret protector, was
occasionally nice to me, and smelled of dryer sheets and flannel. There were traces of talcum powder in his skin that made
me think he was sheltered and loved like an overgrown baby.

The scent of his clothes spoke of mothers who did laundry and prepared lunch bags—dutiful, reliable mothers who owned machines that washed and dried clothes. We, of course, did not own a dryer. In our lives there was no space for "real thrills," as my grandmother called them. The dryer—that was the true frontier, and the fact that my father refused to purchase one confirmed what she always thought of him: He was all talk. We were the only ones in our neighborhood with a clothesline in our garden, a reimagined Neapolitan alleyway. My grandmother's oversize faux-silk underwear from Ross Dress for Less hung over the blow-up pool, firm and heavy like chastity belts. But my father didn't care. If grandma didn't like our house she was most welcome to return to Rome. It wasn't like he was dying to live with her.

My English teacher realized I didn't enjoy spitting out the window or making her cry like the other students did. I could read and write and even liked doing it. She gave me a library pass to go and read on my own during class. It was our secret. I'd be one less person to have to worry about and nobody except for Arash was going to notice my absence. During those stretches of time to myself I often spied on the girl with freckles who hopped fences. I examined the natural flow she had in closing and opening portals, climbing walls, disappearing behind staircases. She was agile and fearless and I wanted to be like her. She waited for the tardy bell to ring so the hallways would be empty and, just before the security guards started their rounds, she opened the doors and escaped. That's how I discovered that the side doors in school did not lock after you shut them.

I never knew where she disappeared to until the day I followed her. We exchanged glances as she stood on the threshold of the side doors. She smiled warmly when she saw me, then put a finger to her lips to suggest we were to operate quietly.

"Wanna come with me?" she said in a husky voice. She had a look that said goodbye at the exact moment it was saying hello. I could not turn away from her darting eyes and freckled cheeks. She was hypnotic, like one of those precious stones from a treasure chest in a Walt Disney movie. A big gem that sparkled under any light, so beautiful it hurt.

She slipped away from me. Before the doors could shut behind her, I stepped out using a foot to prop one of them open. I stood midway between the school hall and the outside world, staring at her, in awe of her moves. The outer school fence had two small holes, just big enough to fit a climbing foot. The girl slid her toes into the first one, then inserted the other foot into the second hole and pushed herself up. When she reached the top of the fence, she looked back at me with dazed green eyes, the wind blowing in her swaying ponytail. She squeezed her thumb and index together and pointed them toward the sun, pinching out a drop of light. She pointed her fingers toward my eyelids.

"There you are, some light in your eyes. That's all you need to hop over. Just look at the sun. Think of the other side. Don't ever think of what's behind you."

Just like that she was free.

"Don't tell anyone about the holes, okay? I made them myself." Then she smiled. In a few moments she was speeding down the sidewalk.

I stayed there, looking at her like a dumb thing, stuck between two worlds, my foot still propping the door open. When she reached the end of the sidewalk she looked back at me and pointed to the sun again.

"Just look up and keep moving!"

I waved at her awkwardly, but she was already gone. I looked at the fence and knew I wouldn't do it. I cowered back inside the school building and heard the door shut behind me. I didn't have the courage to take those risks alone. I kept roaming the hall and made my way outside to a hidden cement spot by a fire hydrant where the sun shone. I preferred reading there rather than in the library. Nobody ever came. On the path I passed by Ajane and her friends. I knew when to look away now, how to distance myself from them so words and provocations would not be uttered. In the quad, cheerleaders arranged themselves in diamond-shaped choreographies to the rhythm of a Snap! song. I kept moving until I reached my safe corner. A small hibiscus shrub grew there. I lay on the concrete. The school's marching band practiced nearby. Proud trumpets echoed in my ear. I felt my legs open on the hot ground. A whiff of ocean made its way across the canyons. If I closed my eyes I could smell salt in the air. I thought about what the ponytail girl said about heading for the sun and not looking back. I saw her fingers pinching light and placing it in my eyes. I pretended I was on a Mediterranean beach and let the rays fill the dark circles around my sockets.

"Hey Greece," a voice called to me. "What's up with not coming to class?"

There was Arash, alone, in a white T-shirt against the blue sky. And that's when I chose him.

Two days later it was the two of us swinging open the school's side doors. We went to the fence and I showed him where to put his feet to climb up. We threw our backpacks to the other side so they wouldn't get in the way, and when I reached the top I looked at the sun and told myself everything was easy and safe. I didn't look back, just like the girl said. We jumped down to the other side and started running. On a residential street we laughed and panted and took each other's hands. We were alone and the Valley was quiet, almost beautiful. The few green bumps that gave Woodland Hills its name looked like imperial knolls to me now.

Arash pulled me closer to him.

"You're a ballsy chick. How did you know about that fence?"

"Just don't tell your friends."

After a few turns, we stumbled on an abandoned junior high tucked between two small mountains. A team of Hispanic gardeners in bright orange vests was at work in the hills—the guardian angels of the San Fernando Valley's natural world. They looked after its ecosystem, contained biological rebelliousness, removed leaves, bark, and moles. We used a faded RESERVED WHEELCHAIR ACCESS sign that was screwed into the parking-lot fence as a foothold and hopped over.

Tall grass sprouted from the courtyard and through the cracked cement of the basketball courts. The gardeners up in the hills weren't paid to keep this nature at bay. Nobody noticed or cared about the weeds that grew outside the boarded-up classrooms or the ivy that crept along the rusted fences. A sign in one of the abandoned buildings read PROHIBIDO ENTRAR. Perhaps the people of Woodland Hills thought the only ones interested in trespassing at an abandoned junior high were Latinos. We walked around the ghost school's echoing hallways. Arash pushed his shoulder against the wooden door of a sealed classroom, but it wouldn't open. We found a discarded shopping cart and rammed it against the door a few times until it busted open. Shafts of light illuminated dust particles that shimmered over piled-up desks. A blackboard still hung on the wall. Someone had tagged "NWA" on it.

We sat on a bed of dry leaves on the classroom floor. Arash leaned back against the wall and lit a cigarette. He spat on the ground beside me, then looked me in the eyes.

"It's kind of cozy here," he said, smiling.

"Why do you spit so much?" I asked.

"I dunno. Habit, I guess. Plus I don't want to have my mouth all full when I kiss you."

"When you what?"

He leaned over and kissed me, bumping my head on the wall. I kissed him back. I didn't expect it to be good, but it was. His lips were soft and I liked how big and sweet his tongue felt.

I kept my eyes closed and undid his jeans, sniffing the aroma of the softener his mother used for his flannel underwear. It smelled better than his lips.

He had a dark, compact cock—an adult penis, more mature than the person behind it. I wrapped my lips around it and tasted the bittersweet drops at the tip. Arash's head fell back and hit the wall. His fingers began to tremble on the side of my ears, attempting to caress my temples. I opened my mouth wider and sucked mechanically—rubber suit intact. He rolled his eyes in disbelief.

"You mean just like that? I don't even have to work on it or nothin'?"

I looked up and smiled. "Just like that."

I pulled him closer to me from his hips. He was breathing hard, more from stupefaction than from pleasure. I felt liquid moving up and so I pushed him farther down my throat. I let him come inside my mouth and swallowed because I was embarrassed to spit and didn't want to add to his pile on the floor.

Afterward we sat hugging each other on the dusty floor, listening to the hypnotic hum of chain saws in the hills, a distant bark, birds twittering. The gardeners did their job, vacuuming gravel and chopping trees, doing what they did in their orange vests. They were the only ones who knew how fast the grass grew, how far elm branches reached. They were paid—very little—to bind and limit the explosiveness of the city's macrocosm, to get rid of the beautiful trees with loose, flimsy leaves that lined the hillcrests. They had to intervene when white people planted weeping willows where they weren't supposed to—their deep roots digging for moisture, breaking pipes and clogging water systems. As I lay there I imagined the men in orange vests shaking their heads, speaking to trees and plants, apologizing for all the times they had to cut them down for stupid reasons.

I rested my head on Arash's shoulders.

"Want me to go down on you?" he asked politely.

"No, I'm fine. Thanks for coming here with me."

He shifted in his seat and held me closer.

"All you Persian guys in class call each other *kuni* all the time, but then you're always grinding each other and grabbing each other's dicks . . . Don't you think there's something homoerotic between all of you or something?"

"Uh, I don't know. Probably. What do you mean *homoerotic*?"

"Gay."

"Fuck that. I'm not fucking gay. Did I seem gay to you when I busted a nut in your mouth just now?" he snapped defensively.

"No. I don't know. Never mind."

"Hey, Greece, you think too much. Give me a kiss."

He leaned over and kissed me again.

"I'm fucking Italian, you idiot."

I was happy to be with him.

"You taste like jizz," he said.

I had my library pass and Arash made it a habit to skip English class so we could go to the abandoned junior high. It was always the same thing when we went. I made him come, but never came myself. I never took my own clothes off. I let him kiss me and touch my breasts while I stayed focused on our actions so I wouldn't start to feel things. In school he pretended not to know me. He didn't want his friends to know. I wasn't allowed to say hello when he was with them, but I didn't care. I took my outcast status out on Simon, the school's reigning nerd: tall, bookish, and already hunchbacked at sixteen, with wide teeth and thick gums. I had observed him during my library hours. He spent time there, reading and practicing for Speech and Debate. He was the captain of the team and of any other school team that didn't involve having to move your body. He was a year ahead of me and always carried around a huge book that looked like a brown brick. I asked him if I could look at it one day. It had thin pages. There was a painting of a beautiful woman in colorful clothes on the cover. It was an anthology of American literature. Simon spoke to me about his Advanced English class. That was the place to be if you wanted to go to a good college. He had done so well on his tests that he had applied to college early and had already been accepted to Harvard. I leafed through the pages of his book and fell in love with it. Edgar Allan Poe, Harriet Beecher Stowe. I loved Thoreau and the way he wrote about nature. I cried reading Harriet Jacobs, became obsessed with Emily Dickinson's poetry, and wrote down every Gertrude Stein title I could find so I could get all her books. Simon talked about what life at a university would be like and made it sound nothing like the Valley. He used a language I had never heard anyone my age use. His nose was thin and long, his eyes focused. Soon I started noticing other kids in school walking around with that same anthology. They were like a nerd cult, but I felt I had something in common with them. They were calmer, almost invisible, a kind of substrata. I wanted that book. I wanted to be where that book was, but I was not willing to take my suit off yet. So I kept it on and followed my usual procedure. I invited myself over to Simon's house, asking him to tutor me. I told him I wanted to move up from my regular window-spitting English class and join the league of Advanced English students like himself. He had no friends and neither did I. Plus he wore Birkenstock sandals with white socks. Nobody in socks and sandals could reject me.

I showed up at his house with a short, glittering dress and no underwear. His parents were at work. Their cocker spaniel, Leonard, minded his own business. Simon tried to explain to me how to answer the analogy questions on SAT tests, but I just looked him straight in the eyes until he blushed and turned away. His big toes wriggled inside the spongy white socks. I slid his hand under my dress and opened my legs, staring at his feet. Why would anyone wear socks with sandals? I kept thinking. It looked so bad that I promised myself I would never tell anyone about us. I'd just close my eyes and pretend like it never happened. A hard-on poked through his matted sweatpants. I got up, lifted my dress, and sat on his lap, letting the ugly polyester rub against my naked skin. Simon turned red. Leonard barked. Simon kicked him under the table while I pulled down his pants. He turned me around and kissed me with an uncertain jolt. We groped each other toward his bed and fell over. Then we were both naked and soon even he wasn't a virgin anymore.

We had tutoring and sex sessions twice a week after school. We did everything together. I was unashamed and felt fine bossing him around. I warned him not to tell anyone about us, just like Arash warned me. On his birthday I put his penis on my ass and slid it inside. It felt too deep and I got scared because for a moment my rubber suit had come off and I felt my legs trembling. I breathed my way back into numbness and then went to the bathroom to shower off. The suit functioned within certain boundaries. It was important not to overstep them. My writing improved and so did my English. Finally Simon introduced me to Mrs. Perks, the Advanced English teacher. She asked me to give her some writing samples and said she'd consider me for the future.

During school I hooked up with Arash, after school I hooked up with Simon, and at home I started making out with Robert the Goth screenwriter. I finally got to him. He slipped notes inside my backpack and doodled in my schoolbooks. I lured him into the bathroom one day, kissed him hard against the shower curtain, and asked him to tell me about the crazy things he did and the drugs he had to take for his mental problems. I hoped showing interest in his dark side would make me intriguing in his eyes.

When I went out with him I told my parents I was going

bowling in the Valley with friends from school. They were too happy to hear the word *friends* to not let me go.

Robert and I drove an hour to get to an animation festival in Pomona. On our way I asked him if I could smoke a cigarette and he said he hated smokers.

"You guys always open a crack in the window like it's going to make the car less smoky. That's bullshit. Cracks don't help. Just smoke, okay? But leave the window closed."

The theater was filled with drunk college students.

Robert offered me the Valium his doctors prescribed for his mood swings. I washed the pill down with vodka from his flask. When the lights went down I began to feel heavy. It was one of those festivals where audience participation was required and everybody screamed at the screen. A bird molested a cat on top of a tree. Robert, elated, launched his flask at him and yelled, "Fuck you."

The rest of the audience joined him and started throwing random objects at the screen. Tomatoes were involved. When it was over, Robert burped and said he didn't really know any other date-y type places. I was on my first American date, it occurred to me—the kind where you wore cardigans and drove to lookout spots. A date where I was supposed to wear a bra he could clumsily undo, but I knew it was too late to have romantic expectations about this city. My weeks with Arash and Simon said things would not happen that way for me.

I asked Robert to take me to his favorite place and he drove me to an old sewer tunnel beneath the Pomona freeway where a small gathering of homeless people slept on blankets on the ground. I stumbled over one of them, but he was too drunk to notice. There were murals and graffiti on the walls, remnants of the LA riots: "Riots Not Diets!" "Crips, Bloods, Mexicans Together. Fuck LAPD." The sound of water trickling through the tunnel made it hard to tell if there was anything to be scared of. Robert and I walked into darkness and sat in a dry area at the end of the path. He finally kissed me and rolled down my tights and underwear. I was so cold I barely recognized his small tongue coming at me, insidious and ineffective. All I could feel was the freezing air scratching my naked thighs. I turned over and tried to give him a blow job. He was so cold that his penis had shriveled into a stub, and though I breathed my inner vapors onto it, it stayed flaccid. Robert mumbled something about how cold it was and how the Valium did something. We decided to just make out. He gave me a hickey and laughed.

"I fucked up your neck," he said.

I remembered an episode of *Happy Days* when everybody gathered around Ralph Malph at Arnold's so he could show off his new hickey to his friends. Wasn't it supposed to be romantic and exciting to receive hickeys?

Our date was not working out, so Robert proposed we go to his house. He lived in a place called Soledad Canyon. The landscape was so barren and lunar that many *Star Trek* episodes had been shot there. His house was in a cul-de-sac in the middle of nowhere. The place was pristine and cold, the furniture preserved in shiny protective plastic covers. His father, a downtown LAPD detective, snored in front of the TV next to a pair of crutches that leaned by him on the couch. He woke up when he heard us and gurgled something about Robert having to warn him when he left home.

Robert ignored him and headed straight for his bedroom. I nodded hello, but the man growled at me and closed his eyes again, curling up in a fetal position, squeaking against the cushions of the plastic-covered sofa.

"Can you work as a cop when you have crutches?" I asked Robert when we stepped in his room.

"He's on leave. He was on duty during the riots and got fucked up by the assholes who were looting."

"Wow, I can't believe he was there. He was *part* of it."

Over the bed was a framed *Nekromantik* poster showing a skeleton clutching a woman's breast. Robert opened a drawer and pulled out a switchblade.

"Yeah, I wish they'd killed him."

"Why?"

"I'm just kidding," he mumbled. "You don't get my sense of humor, huh?"

I tried to laugh. I didn't want him to think I wasn't tough enough.

"Anyway, he hit a couple of bastards with the butt of his gun They hit him back. It was crazy."

"Why the hell did he hit them? Don't you think the police have done enough hitting?"

"There's never enough hitting." Robert smirked and passed me the knife. It was the original one from *Nekromantik*. Worth money, he said, and gave it to me as a gift.

"You want to see what I've been working on?" he asked, as I rolled the knife over the palm of my hand. "It's a short film I shot in school. It might make you vomit."

He plugged a camera in to the TV. He was on the screen, walking in a parking lot toward a high-voltage barbed-wire fence. He electrocuted his arm on the fence, then fell to the ground.

I realized it was the film that had gotten him locked into the psychiatric ward.

"Isn't that awesome?" he asked.

"Totally," I answered.

Robert lifted his sleeve and showed me four parallel lines of raw, red flesh. "You like my electrocution scars? I think they changed my life."

"Didn't you go to an asylum after this film?"

"Yeah man. It was nuts. They thought I was crazy and suicidal."

"I wonder why."

"They also didn't like it when I told them Hitler was my role model."

"Hitler?"

"Yeah man. I fucking love Hitler."

I couldn't smile at any of the things he told me, so I accepted one more Valium instead. We turned the TV on and I placed my head on his thin torso, letting the rest of my body twist on the hard cold floor. I thought about my friends in Rome, the ones I'd had sit-ins with at my high school, the ones who taught me to be interested in politics and suspicious of America, the *imperialist devil*. What would they think of me if they saw me bundled on that floor, clinging to a Hitler fanatic? But again, the rubber-suit rules were clear. If I wanted it to work, I should not think too much. I should not feel too much.

We undressed and embraced. Robert threw my underwear on the floor. I noticed it had discharge on it and turned it upside down. Then I felt a tremor, an imperceptible quiver, and his minuscule penis rose. He put a condom on and pushed me on top of him. I spilled over his bony hips trying to keep myself light, afraid I might suffocate him with my curves. I moved up and down, back and forth, feeling nothing inside me, hoping his facial expressions would betray a sensation of pleasure or presence, but they didn't. I thought of the bowls of pasta my mother tried to shove down his throat, our little Italian world with our sit-down lunches in the middle of Van Nuys, and the screenplay he was writing with my father—all those things standing between us.

It lasted two minutes—the apathetic humping disguised as sex. I looked down at him, a strange, small creature with vacant eyes. He was gazing at a commercial on TV. Then it was over. He rolled off the condom. I couldn't tell if there was anything in it.

In the car ride back home we didn't speak. This time I smoked my cigarette without asking if it was okay. He coughed and rolled the window down a crack.

8

Ugly men who do not read. I'm attracted to them. If one is to have meaningless sex, one should at least pick people with admirable physical qualities. Sex with pretty, stupid men is never as fun as sex with ugly, stupid men. Ugly men who do not read might not become prominent people, but they sure have prominent chins. Like, maybe they have boxy chins or chins with dimples—chins that trick you into thinking they are brave. They enjoy spitting and groping girls in abandoned buildings. They want to do simple things that feel right, like electrocuting themselves on high-voltage barbed-wire fences. Sometimes they look stupid in public situations, like when they crawl in sewer canals or scream inside movie theaters. They might like visual things like art or film. They watch movies about people having sex with dead people. They call them romantic comedies.

In moments of solitude, an ugly man who doesn't read will be exactly where you want him to be. He will give you moral support or a leather jacket from Berlin with a rare patch on the back. They can only have certain pieces of a girl's flesh in their mouths at a time, but you are still willing to give them what they want because nothing better is coming along.

This was the excerpt of the essay I wrote for health class that Mrs. Anders read over the phone to my parents when she called and asked them to come in. The topic of our final exam was abstinence and STDs. I got suspended. I could not understand why. I thought I'd written a great paper. I was so excited about it I even sent it to a literary journal I found out about at the library. They were looking for submissions for their next issue. The theme would be "Bad Sex." I thought I'd fit right in. But it wasn't just the essay that got me in trouble. Leafing through my health textbook, Mrs. Anders discovered horrific Nazi phrases and swastika scribbles. Someone had transformed the face of a Boy Scout into that of a young Hitler by giving him a mustache and parting his hair on the side. I realized it must have been Robert. All those times he slid into my room and infiltrated my backpack, he wasn't just leaving me notes, he was defacing my books.

The principal called me in to his office and asked to see the rest of my schoolbooks. We found plenty more drawings and offensive writings.

"I wasn't expecting this from you," Mrs. Anders said while I waited for my parents to pick me up. "After everything your country is going through." I tried to convince her I had not done the drawings. I was a communist's daughter. I couldn't draw that well and it wasn't my handwriting. It did not matter. If someone I knew had done that to the books, it said something about me, about my own immorality.

I stayed on the office chair waiting. Azar, my macrocephalic PE buddy, peeked her big head inside. I lied and told her I was going home because I was feeling sick. She became frantic and asked me if I thought I'd be better by the following day. She crept inside the room.

"It's my birthday tomorrow. You must bring me a balloon."

I was confused.

"That's what friends do here when it's someone's birthday. The more balloons a girl has on her birthday, the more popular she is. My mom said she'd get me two, but I don't want it to look like I'm buying my own balloons." She looked at me with serious, pleading eyes. "You have to bring me one and give it to me in front of everyone in class. They need to see."

"Of course, Azar."

I was moved by her big head. I wanted to tell her she should grow her hair out so it wouldn't look like a ball.

"The balloon should be pink. It should say 'Happy Birthday.' Better if you find something with hearts or kittens."

I promised her I would bring her the balloon.

"I have no words." My mother looked like a martyr as we walked to the school parking lot with a handful of papers that determined the amount of days of suspension—three plus a week of community service cleaning up school grounds after hours.

"Slut!" my father screamed at me as we got inside the car. "My daughter is a total slut!"

Suddenly Ettore had transformed into an Italian patriarch I had never met before.

"You were the one working with a psychopath. It's not my fault if Robert's hero is Adolf Hitler!" I tried to defend myself.

"Well it's your fault for having intercourse with him and it's your fault for writing this delirious essay!" my father yelled.

"How irresponsible of you! Who are these men you've been sleeping with? And Robert? Robert! Of all people! Do you know he could have killed you?" my mother burst out.

"It's great that you guys had a murderer at our dinner table then!"

"We didn't know at the time. That was before the episode!"

"The episode" as Max and, consequently, my parents called it, was the reason Robert eventually stopped showing up at our place. Without anyone knowing, he'd obtained an appointment with two powerful Jewish Hollywood producers and pitched them his new solo film idea: *Holocaust 2: The Party's Just Getting*

Started—a horror movie about Jewish zombies who organized raves in Dachau. The producers, who, thanks to Max, were faintly interested in the project Robert was working on with my father, were horrified and vowed Robert would never set foot in their offices again. Robert showed up a few days later and threatened them with a blunt razor saying they were making a big mistake. He was arrested, but his father—the downtown LAPD officer on crutches—got him out with the paperwork from the insane asylum where he had been locked up weeks earlier. The producers were so disgusted by Robert and the whole event that they stopped responding to my father's calls. He was back to square one, without prospects.

From my bedroom that night I heard Max at the dinner table.

"She's turning into a nymphomaniac! Keep her home," he commanded, explaining to my parents what people did to their kids in America when they got suspended from school.

I sneered at him from under my blankets. "Nymphomaniac" was a bit strong, I thought, but it served a purpose. For the first time since we arrived, my parents were worried. I finally heard them consider the possibility of having made the wrong choices. They feared their daughter was turning into a sex maniac. Their son got beat up regularly in school for not having a group to hang out with. He was known by the nickname "the Italian Tomato." It was one thing to be part of a racial minority. It was difficult and you were discriminated against, but at least you knew you were backed up by those who shared your origins. But Italians had no reference points and were hard to classify.

"You can't just let these kids float. They need rules. Eugenia has to be grounded," Max explained. "This sex rampage is a cry for help. Take away her private phone," he ordered them.

"She doesn't have one," my father replied.

"Then take away her TV!"

"It's broken," my mother admitted.

"Take away her monthly allowance."

"Umm . . . she doesn't have one."

"Well, just keep her inside the house, then," Max groaned impatiently.

"*Keep?*" my mother said. "She's *always* home. I don't know when she even had time to *meet* all these boys."

I liked hearing their concerned voices. I liked that people were gathered around a table to talk about me—even if it was about the best form of punishment for my wild spree.

On my fourth night of being grounded, I lay in bed struck by the sudden awareness that I'd missed Azar's birthday. She had been alone on her special day—no balloons, no friends. The thought of her by the track, waiting for me to show up with the kitten balloon, was devastating. I would tell her I was sick. I would tell her a tragedy occurred. Better a late balloon than no balloon. I'd make it up to her.

I slipped into a dirty pair of sweatpants and tennis shoes, snuck out through my bedroom window, and walked to the twenty-four-hour party shop on Sepulveda that Henry had introduced me to. The Taiwanese kids at the register were sucking nitrous from balloons, laughing. A different kind of partying went on in the back of the store compared to what was showcased in the front. I bought my usual bubble tea, a pack of cigarettes, and a pink-and-silver balloon with puppies for Azar. They didn't have kittens.

With the string wrapped around my wrist, I was headed home feeling festive when I heard an insistent honk on the road.

"Is it your birthday or somethin'?" a voice shouted at me.

A metallic blue BMW pulled up to the curb. I peered in.

It was Arash. Without thinking I opened the door, stuffed the balloon inside, and jumped in.

"I missed your cousin's birthday and I promised her a balloon. I'll bring it to school on Monday."

"When are you going to stop hanging out with that weirdo?"

"Never. Don't be mean."

We were happy to see each other, but we didn't want to say it.

"So is it true you got suspended?"

"Yes, and now I'm grounded."

"So what are you doing walking around?"

"My parents think I'm in my room. They won't check. They don't really notice when I run away. It's very convenient."

Arash's car moved past my house. I didn't tell him where I lived and didn't ask him to stop. I just wanted to stay with him without having to think about anything.

"You seem happy to see me," I teased him.

"It's Saturday night. You're lucky I had no plans," he said with his usual cocky tone, but his eyes had a little warm light burning in them and I told him I was happy to see him too.

Arash was dressed up. Beneath his Yankees cap, the gel on his hair had turned strands of it into rigid, oily spikes and he had layers of gold on his chest.

"Why are you so dressed up if you have no plans?"

"My stupid homeys flaked on me 'cause they scored some pussy."

"Oh." I looked down and leaned back against the seat.

We drove by the Sound City Studios hoping to catch a rock star on a cigarette break, but the parking lot was empty. The smoke from the Budweiser factory next door was sickly and Arash kept driving. We reached the far eastern edge of the San Fernando Valley at Chatsworth, an old agricultural community flanked by the Santa Susana Mountains. We stopped the car in front of Stoney Point, a huge set of boulders on a hilltop, a classic Valley hangout spot for kids. The rocks were etched with marijuana-leaf drawings.

We climbed to the top and Arash spread his hooded sweatshirt on the ground. We sat overlooking the flat lights of Chatsworth and the black mountain range to the east. Arash exhaled into the sky and took my hand.

"This is a good place for weirdos like you." He smiled.

"I'm not a weirdo," I said leaning against him, too tired to fight back.

"What the fuck you wearing?" he said, noticing my sweatpants.

I looked down, embarrassed. "I wasn't planning on going out."

"So that's your home-alone outfit?"

"Oh no, that one's much worse!"

Arash giggled.

A warm night wind blew on our faces, thick with smog fumes from the end of the day. I inhaled everything and kissed him hard. I kneeled over on automatic pilot and pushed him back on the rock, ready to go down on him, but Arash put his hand on my forehead and lifted it.

"Stop," he said and pulled a strand of hair away from my eyes.

I looked up at the drowned-out stars trying to shine through the polluted purple Valley sky and felt relieved.

"They still look pretty even when they're fuzzy," I said, but what I really wanted to say was "thank you."

"You're getting romantic," Arash teased. He pulled me toward him and smiled. "We're just lying under a hood of smog, actually."

He kissed me, pushing my hands into his, and we just kissed and kissed until our lips went blue. We were trying to find out who we were when we weren't people who hid in abandoned buildings. Who we were at night, as equals.

"You know what? Fuck it. We should just go out and do something," he said quietly.

"Like where there's other people?" I laughed.

"You want to go see a movie? *Reservoir Dogs* is playing at the Woodland Hills Mall," he asked with a tentative tone.

"Together?" I asked, worried about how quickly we were changing the parameters of our unspoken understanding.

"Why not?" he said to reassure me.

The mall was filled with the excited shrieks of adolescents set free. They were everywhere, the people our age. They swarmed out of minivans in packs. That's where they all went, I realized. That's why the streets were silent. They hid inside shopping malls, scattering popcorn and teasing each other, chewing gum, burping, exploding with soda.

We gave Azar's balloon to a ticket-booth salesperson to watch over and crossed the large entrance hall. In the mirrors that lined the hallways I saw the reflection of an ill-matched couple walking in slow motion: the awkward Italian girl in sweatpants and the macho Persian guy with the perfectly starched Yankees cap and clean shirt. Arash reverted to a nighttime version of his school self. He walked in wide oblique strides with a laid-back but vigilant bounce. I didn't match that stride. My steps were rigid, contained. My body had no messages to share.

The posters for *Reservoir Dogs* were beautiful and everyone stood around looking at the men in black suits, splattered in blood. Arash bought us butter-infused popcorn and Cokes. The way he sipped his drink—sucking the straw with a tough smirk from the side of his mouth—was a performance, but I told myself I didn't care because I felt that I was part of a performance also. The one in which we were adults, sharing things. Man and woman, popcorn and soda, ascending escalators side by side.

When we reached the theater entrance Arash went pale.

Hovering in front of the entrance, his friends from school with another group of bearded guys, maybe their older brothers, were fighting with an usher to let them sit close to one another. They pushed him around playfully. They all wore sagging khakis, gold chains, and buttoned-up flannel shirts just like Arash's. They looked like a squadron. We were still at a safe distance, but I caught a glimpse of us again in the mirror as we started to break apart—a little tear. Arash turned to me, tense.

"Your friends?" I said, without expecting an answer or an explanation.

One of the younger ones, Faraj, recognized Arash and walked over. His eyes turned into a question mark the closer he got to us.

"Yo, fool! What are you doing out here? We paged you all night."

Arash's body shrunk, his gestures were not grand now.

"Yeah, I know. I couldn't get to a pay phone to call you back on time."

He glanced over at me. So it wasn't true they'd flaked on him, I realized. He wanted to be alone with me. For an instant this made me smile, but when I saw myself in the mirror I looked smaller now. Folded arms protecting my chest, ugly sweatpants. Why did I get in that car?

"What's up with her?" Faraj asked with a smirk.

Arash looked away and said he'd bumped into me. I was just a girl from his English class. Someone who wrote his essays for him.

His eyes wavered for a moment.

Faraj peered at me again, vaguely interested.

"How much you charge? I gotta get my college application essay done by someone. Been looking into that."

I told him I was too busy.

In the mirror an older boy questioned a younger boy about

the presence of a young Italian girl. The younger boy replied with a nod and a wave of a hand, signaling he had this under control. He'd get rid of her in a second.

And so it went.

Faraj nodded at me and edged away.

I crumpled the ticket stub in my hand and stashed it inside my pocket.

Arash's eyes had time to recover. They were stronger and tougher when they turned to me again.

In the mirror the older boy joined his friends waiting in line. The younger one took his wallet out of his back pocket, withdrew a twenty-dollar bill, and handed it to the Italian girl.

"There's pay phones downstairs. You can call a cab to take you home."

His friends at the tail end of the line were almost inside the theater, looking back at him.

"Hurry up, *kuni*!"

He shrugged his shoulders at me. "I'm sorry. We should have gone somewhere else."

He picked up his bouncy stride and caught up with his friends, pants sagging below his waistline.

Look at those flannel boxers popping out, I thought. I bet they smell good.

9

Monday morning Arash didn't show up to English class. This
was a relief because I didn't know how to look at him without
rage and embarrassment. On my way to PE I went to retrieve
Azar's balloon from my locker. It had shriveled, but I decided I
would give it to her anyway. I found a note inside the locker. It
was from Mrs. Perks, the Advanced English teacher Simon had
introduced me to. I had given her some literary essays before
getting suspended, but I didn't think I'd hear back from her
because of what happened. Her note didn't mention my bad
conduct. She said she'd read my essays and was willing to let me
try her class the following semester. She gave me a list of books
to read over Christmas break. If I came back with satisfactory
reports and committed to more writing and reading tasks than
my peers, she'd take me on. "English is not your first language,
but I can get it to become your first language's bright younger
sister," she wrote. I read those exotic book titles and her note,
smiling as I walked to my PE class. I felt like I had a foot out of
the ditch.

When I got to class Azar was sitting on the track staring at
her feet. She looked more depressed than usual. She glanced at
me and my shrunken balloon and sighed.

"Thanks," she said without looking up. Her eyes had dark

circles around them. I sat next to her, waiting for the coach to take roll. Then the school speakers began to crackle. The principal's voice came on.

"Good morning, students. It is with great sadness that we make the following announcement: On Saturday evening, Winnetka High School tenth-grader Arash Yekta was shot and killed at the Woodland Hills Mall. Eleventh-grader Nadir Javan was also shot and remains in stable condition at the Encino Medical Center. Arash will be remembered fondly by family, friends, and the Winnetka High community. He was vivacious and good-natured, and will remain in our hearts. We send our best wishes for recovery to Nadir and his family. There will be a gathering this afternoon at the Woodland Hills Mall, at four o'clock, for those who wish to mourn Arash together. We will now have a moment of silence."

On the speakers, the *S* sounds broke, screeching into our ears, and this reassured me. I thought if we couldn't properly hear what was being said maybe it wasn't really true. A gust of wind blew across the football field. The seagulls scavenged for leftovers from the weekend's football game. They shrieked and sunk their claws into the ground, bickering over soggy fries. Azar's birthday balloon was a lump of sparkly plastic hanging from her wrist. I batted my lashes a few times. All I could think was that I should have gotten her a new one that morning. I should have woken up early and gone to the twenty-four-hour Taiwanese party store. I should have gotten her five balloons with kittens and I should have thrown a teddy bear in there also—but why was everyone getting quiet all of a sudden? Why were they all looking down at the ground? Didn't they also know this was just a misunderstanding? I would see Arash. We'd go to the abandoned middle school, like always. I know I told myself I wouldn't speak to him again, that I would not know how to look at him without rage, but I changed my mind—I took it back, I swore. We were going to bust through the side doors and break free on the sidewalks like we always did. We'd go to the building with the cracked pavement and the tall grass and the shafts of light that made dust sparkle—that school, tucked between the hills with the lonely gardeners in orange vests. We would talk about nothing and spit on the ground and listen to the chain saws. That school. We went there every day. That's what we did, so he wasn't dead.

Some students started to cry. Azar looked for someone to comfort her. She was Arash's cousin, but nobody knew that except for me. I hugged her tight and my hug communicated something like we were going to get to the bottom of that misunderstanding together. She hugged me back, pretending to believe me. She was wrapped around my waist and I felt like a mother. Her feeble body was like a cracked branch inside my arms. Her big black hair tickled my neck. Black hair on her arms embracing me. Black hair over her lips pressed against my chest. Black eyebrow shutters, opening and closing onto my clavicles while she cried. She unwrapped the balloon's silver string from her tiny wrist, hoping for a cathartic moment, a liberating flight, but the balloon had lost helium and gravitated in front of us. Even the wind couldn't carry it away. It wouldn't fly up and it wouldn't lie down. It just lingered like a piece of bad news we did not know what to do with.

The last time Arash and I had escaped to the abandoned school in the hills I tried to take a photo of him with a camera I bought at a garage sale for three dollars, but he pushed my hand away. He said I might blackmail him and tell his friends about us. Then he hugged me and pushed the hair from my eyes. When I developed the photo it looked like Arash was saying goodbye with the hand he was using to distance me.

"I know we're just fooling around. But you know, this is the best part of my days," he had said.

"It's the best part of my days too," I told him. And it was true.

"I could never come to such a shitty place with my friends."

No, he couldn't. I smiled and lifted my face from his chest. I looked at him, half naked—his pants still unbuttoned and his soft white T-shirt rolled up against his chest. The cars cruising the residential streets were in another world and we lay in our made-up living room on the cold classroom floor. I looked at him and he seemed like just a boy. A boy with a penis. A man. One of those beings stripped to their essence. No Persian pride, no gold necklaces, no oversize pants. It was him—naked with his deep dark eyes, long lashes, and dimpled chin. But on that Saturday night when he was shot, I knew what he wanted to be. I felt it just looking at his undulating stride the second we crossed the mall's sliding doors.

After he got rid of me, he performed the essence of his public self: loud, crude, offensive. Inside the theater Arash and his friends had screamed at the screen and gotten kicked out for being too rowdy. Who knew why Arash had screamed at the screen, why Robert did—why they all did. Maybe screaming at screens was the only way young people had to be part of the city's culture, to subvert it. Movie theaters were places where we were expected to be silent and still, but they were also the few places where underage people were free to go on Saturday nights. That freedom was too small an allowance.

The newspapers said the drive-by shooting revealed the allure of gangster culture among Valley teens. I read the articles over and over because it was the only way to know what had happened. Nobody knew about my relationship with Arash. I had no access to direct information. So I read and imagined and placed details where none were given. I filled in the blanks.

The night I rode the bus home from the Woodland Hills mall, eating stale buttered popcorn, saving the twenty-dollar bill Arash had given me for a taxi, while Arash and his friends screamed in Farsi and threw candy at each other, in another part of the city, not far away, three bored private-school Valley girls with no criminal records were figuring out what to do with their weekend.

I read their descriptions. They could have been any number of girls from our school. Natalie was blond and had perfect bangs. She had a job at the Sherman Oaks Galleria Gap. Audrey was identical to her, but with longer eyelashes and greener eyes. They looked like sisters, everybody said, except one had bangs and the other didn't. Erica, the third, was overweight and nobody bothered to describe her beyond that. The girls were hanging out in a hot tub in the backyard of Erica's luxury home in Encino. As I read, I could feel the Santa Ana wind blowing on their skin, the temperature of the lukewarm water—how it made everybody look and feel the same. I imagined Erica floating with her big arms spread open, a wet T-shirt over her bathing suit to cover her rolls, staring at the sky. She knew she'd spend her Saturday night watching a movie. It was probably what she did every Saturday night while her prettier friends called boys and snuck out of her bedroom window. I imagined the giddy girls murmuring about parties into Erica's pink phone. All rich Valley girls had private lines. Erica never went with them. She stayed behind because boys called her "Big Bertha" and said she took up too much space. I thought she probably didn't mind, though. Maybe it was enough to see her friends getting ready— living the excitement and anticipation of a night out without running any of the risks.

The night of the shooting Natalie, the girl with the perfect bangs, called two guys she'd met at the DMV. They were older and belonged to a San Fernando Valley gang. I read their gang names and thought they were out of a movie: No Good Capone and Baby Huey. Natalie had picked them because they were "different." They knew Ice Cube and Eazy-E from when they went to school in the Valley. They'd lured the girls with fun nights at Dr. Dre's mansion in Woodland Hills. They had guns, which was hot. Their gang was called Every Woman's Fantasy. It was a promising name. They had the best parties in the Valley and both Natalie and Audrey were fed up with Saturday nights doing drugs in McDonald's parking lots.

It made sense.

I imagined Natalie and Audrey climbing out of the window, leaving Erica behind, warning her not to pick up the phone in case their parents called. I pictured Erica, disappointed, pushing *The Bodyguard* tape into the VCR deck, telling herself to pretend she was Whitney Houston, lighting a candle, closing her eyes. Kevin Costner would lift her up. He didn't think she was too fat.

Audrey and Natalie cruised the Valley with the boys. No Good Capone knew someone who knew someone who hung out at Suge Knight's Death Row recording studio in Tarzana, but that night he was nowhere to be found. The four of them kept driving, waiting for a plan to come up. Every Woman's Fantasy members were famous for their wild parties, but where was the party now? Where were Dr. Dre and Suge Knight? Where was Ice Cube's mansion? The girls became restless. Suburban somnolence, more warm wind, a succession of strip malls. No guns, no fun, no music, no party. Just a crack pipe in a Carl's Jr. parking lot. Another Saturday night taking drugs in a fast-food parking lot after all.

"What are we going to do?" "What is there to *do*?" "Where should we *go*?" The girls asked the same questions over and over. They were high. They forgot what they just said. They said it again. The articles made it clear that there was some kind of role-playing. Everyone had a part. Natalie and Audrey did what was expected of them: raspberry body spray, apple shampoo, Victoria's Secret lingerie stolen from the Sherman Oaks Galleria. But No Good Capone and Baby Huey weren't living up to their end of the deal. The boys kept their eyes on their pagers. Why weren't they blowing up like they said they would?

In an interview Audrey said she became a little bit worried when one of the guys decided to call a friend from West Adams. He boasted about how the guy had done drive-by shootings, kidnapped babies, and killed people. That was the moment when she realized maybe things could have taken a wrong turn. But her friend Natalie, she said, wasn't afraid. She thought it was a game and going to West Adams was perfect because it was a chance to get out of the Valley.

Once they decided to go over the hill, they stopped by a pay phone in the parking lot of the Woodland Hills Mall so No Good Capone could page his friend and tell him they were on their way. The pay phone was crowded with a rowdy squadron of Persian kids. After getting kicked out of the theater Arash and his friends were making calls, looking for something to do—same as No Good Capone and Baby Huey. They wore baggy khakis, gold, buttoned-up flannel shirts. Baby Huey and No Good Capone wore the same clothes but were part of a different kind of squadron.

Arash's friends who spoke to the journalists explained that No Good Capone didn't want to wait his turn to use the phone. He did not want it to seem like he was the type of man who waited in silence for other men to do things.

No Good went up to Arash with a confident stride, the same one Arash always had, but less undulant, less bouncy, more like warfare.

"Where are you from?" he asked him.

Arash turned from the receiver and rolled his eyes at him without answering. From the car the girls were now paying attention.

"Where are you from?" he repeated.

Arash told him to back off. He was trying to talk on the

phone and was annoyed, his friends told the reporters. He didn't think the guy was for real. He looked like a kid, a little older than them, but still just a kid.

No Good insisted.

"Do you gangbang?" He asked the question forcefully. But Arash wasn't intimidated. He lifted his face from the receiver, annoyed.

"Do we fucking *look* like gangbangers?" he replied, then turned his back to No Good.

Too mercurial. I could just see him. And then that question hovered. Arash's simple reply had left No Good Capone speechless and he didn't like being speechless. He did not want to use the phone after that.

He returned to the parked car. Natalie laughed. "I know that fool. I thought you were badass. I thought you're Every Woman's Fantasy. You gonna let him get away with that?"

Natalie said she recognized Arash from summer camp a few years back. He'd peed his bed. The papers said she tried to speak with a gangster inflection, but I was sure she still sounded like a rich, white Valley girl.

No Good Capone asked her to get on the wheel and got Audrey to sit in the front next to her. He and Baby Huey climbed into the back. It felt innocent, like a game of musical chairs, Natalie told a journalist. No Good asked her to circle the parking lot a few times while he got ready. Then they drove back to the dimly lit rear of the mall where the pay phones were. No Good asked Natalie to douse the headlights and drive slowly toward the Persian group.

I imagined Natalie turning to her friend, proud. It wasn't going to be another boring Saturday night. The car slowed down and started to creep forward. Arash and his friends didn't see it approaching. They were busy laughing at someone's joke—laughing so hard that Nadir had tears in his eyes.

Natalie pressed her foot on the accelerator. The car caught up with the group, then slowed down almost to a halt.

"Duck now!" Baby Huey screamed to the girls. Everyone heard that scream, even the Persian kids, but before they could realize what was going on, No Good Capone was already leaning out the window shooting in their direction. He shot ten times, hitting Arash in the stomach six times. Nadir was wounded in the left leg.

"You don't gangbang?" No Good Capone screamed at Arash as he fell to the ground. "Well you do now!"

He leaned back in the car and they sped out of the parking lot. The girls said the sound of gunfire was louder than they thought, the consequences so much more real. Audrey turned around and saw bodies on the ground. Sirens started blaring almost at once.

Arash was bleeding, squeezing Nadir's hand.

"My stomach hurts" were his last words.

He died a few hours later in a hospital in Encino, five blocks from Erica's mansion.

After the shootout, the group scattered. The girls went back to their friend. They told her that no matter who came and asked, she was to say they'd been together that night. Erica agreed, but a few hours later, at dawn, she woke up her parents and told them to call the police. Audrey and Natalie were promised immunity for their testimonies. No Good Capone and Baby Huey would get life sentences.

After school I walked by myself to the Woodland Hills Mall. Everyone was there, behind the Cineplex where Arash had been shot. Students, teachers, and relatives lit candles and placed flowers. There were tears. The sidewalk was covered in spray-painted *Goodbye* graffiti.

"Keep smiling," "R.I.P. from your homeys," "We love you."

TV and print journalists circled the pay-phone area, reconstructing the events from Saturday night.

"They think we're a gang," one of Arash's friends explained to a journalist. "But Persian pride just means we take pride in our native culture. We flip signs and wear baggy pants, but it's fashion. All kids wear baggy pants. They sell them at the Gap."

The parking lot got crowded. Arash's presence was in the air. He had just been there, alive, himself, doing the normal things we all did, except—I now realized—we lived in a place where normal things could get you killed. I stood on the periphery of the mourning human cluster, alone. I could not share my grief with his sisters like the other girls did. I could not say what I thought, that if his friends hadn't noticed him at the end of that theater's entrance hall, standing next to that awkward Italian girl—if he'd been alone with me that night, walking with no particular stride, away from that mall—he would have still been here today.

I grabbed a lonely red candle from the asphalt and left the parking lot. I walked to our ghost middle school and hopped the fence. In our classroom I lit the candle for Arash. It was almost Christmas and I was wearing a T-shirt. I thought about that—and only that: That things were not what they seemed. That winter was summer, Christmas was Easter, and death was another incongruous detail that made up the landscape of the city. I did not cry. I thought about the freckled girl from school and pulled my hair up in a ponytail. I hopped on top of the fence and looked up at the sun as it set behind the hills. "Think of the other side. Don't think of what's behind you," she had said. It always worked when I climbed over with Arash. I hoped it would now too.

I left our spot and walked by rich mansions, shitty condos, and family homes. When the last rays of the sun disappeared, the street I was on suddenly lit up. A plastic Santa Claus hovered over my head with a big sign: "*Ho ho ho* and welcome to Candy Cane Lane. Our holiday display can be enjoyed from the comfort of your own vehicle, but please don't feed the penguins!"

I'd heard people in school talk about this extravaganza but didn't believe it actually existed. A manic celebration of Christmas unfolded before my eyes. The entire street was one huge kitsch holiday decoration asserting the city's right to enjoy a jolly Christmas in spite of the tropical temperatures. A blanket of fake snow had been distributed over each home's freshly cut front lawn. Insane sums of money and thousands of kilowatts of energy were spent on lights, plastic snowmen, and animatronic Santas. Disney-themed installations—Robin Hoods, Aladdins, Little Mermaids everywhere. Hollywood was a hill away. A life-size inflatable Santa Claus on a motorcycle chased a helicopter with candy-cane blades. Bejeweled, tired palm trees swayed in the hot wind. There were no firs in sight. The street ended under the Ventura Freeway. In front of the last house three Hispanic gardeners carried heavy generators across a yard. They looked up at me and rolled their eyes.

"Crazy, right?" One of them laughed as the other settled a glowing baby Jesus into the earth. He dug holes for Mary and Joseph to rest in, stabbing the lawn with a shovel, chuckling to himself.

At the beginning of the street, cars got in line for a tour of the lane. They couldn't park and walk to see the show. Shooting people and celebrating Christmas: Everything in LA could be done from the comfort of one's vehicle.

The gardeners plugged a plastivity scene in to the generator.

Mary's electric dress sparkled like a holy disco ball. She looked so beautiful shining on that lawn, under the freeway overpass. I got on my knees, crossed myself, clasped my hands, and closed my eyes in front of the sacred family.

*Dear Mary, please be nice to Arash's soul. Help him fly
away, out of the Valley, over the Woodland Hills Mall, across
the canyons. Move him on a string through the western surf,
into the setting sun. Plunge him into the ocean and push him
through the depths of the earth, far from the coast of California.
Bring him back to Persia. May he be greeted by a potent red
sun and a noble lion. May the melodies of lute players from all
time resonate when he enters his skies. Undress him. He is so
beautiful when he is naked. Cover him in jewels. Throw his
baggy pants away. Let him know I plan to join an advanced
literature class next semester, a class where people read. We
would have had to stop going to the abandoned school anyway.
Amen.*

I decided that would be my last prayer, the last chance I'd
give Mary to make things right. When I reached Sepulveda
Boulevard, instead of going home I kept walking. I headed to
Henry's store. I didn't know why I felt like being with him in
that moment. Maybe it was the missing ear. I too felt like an
amputee, missing limbs here and there. Missing parts of my
heart.

part two

return

———————————

10

Alma stood on a rock in the middle of the Mediterranean Sea, shampooing. She had long curly black hair on her legs.

"Come and take your showers," she invited my brother and me.

She poured expired body wash on our heads, massaging our skulls. We dove from the rock into the clear water. Soapy foam rolled down our spines, caressing the back of our necks and slipping off our naked shoulders.

"That's it. Clean now!" she screamed, and dove after us into the dirty wake. It was our daily ritual, Neptune's private bubble bath. There was no running water at home.

A tourist boat passed. There were several of them each day from neighboring islands. They circled ours without stopping to let passengers off. On the loudspeakers the captain entertained passengers with folkloristic tales of our island's main attractions: the tiny population, the predominance of donkeys, the absence of cars, roads, and food—total wilderness. The captain honked at us as we finished our sea showers. Alma climbed out of the water and flipped him off. She hated tourists. A British woman on the boat deck screamed at her that we were polluting the sea.

Alma yelled back, *"Verpiss dich!"* "Fuck you" in German.

"We have no running water here! How would *you* wash your hair?"

From the sea our island looked like a truncated cone rising vertically from the water. Like all the Aeolian Islands of Sicily it used to be a volcano, but it had been inactive for thousands of years. It was hard to believe the green pastures on the top of the crater were once fumaroles emitting vaporous liquids and lava. Everything on the island was built upward on blocks of coarse basaltic stones. The winding *mulattiera,* a donkey path climbing from the sea to the top of the mountain, was the only road. At the port an Alfa Romeo convertible had been parked between rusting barrels for twenty years. A fisherman won it in a lottery. It came on a boat and hadn't moved from that spot since. There were no roads to drive it on.

It was June 1993 and we were on the most isolated island of the Aeolian archipelago. Our parents had decided we would spend our summer there while recovering from our difficult first year in Los Angeles. Timoteo and I knew the place. We'd spent childhood summers there in the care of our uncle.

"Don't send them to those horrible beaches filled with deck chairs and umbrellas. Kids need to learn about wilderness or they'll never survive in the world, let alone LA," my uncle Antonio told my parents. It had not taken much to convince them. In Los Angeles Max was on the brink of getting money for a new film he wanted my father to direct and co-produce. They all stayed behind, supposedly to work, but I often wondered if it was just that they couldn't afford the airfare.

At the southern end of the island was the meager port with the *alimentari,* bar, and newspaper stand. Hydrofoils docked at the tiny pier. The port was flanked by lavic boulders that functioned as beaches. We stayed with my uncle and his German wife, Alma, on a central plateau halfway up the mountain, about two thousand steps. It was a small village area stippled with limestone houses supported by dazzlingly white masonry col-

umns and decorated with built-in *bisuoli*—benches. At the tip of
the volcano was the ghost village, inhabited by a small colony
of German hippies who squatted in the abandoned houses of
fishermen who had immigrated to Australia at the turn of the
nineteenth century. They lived off potatoes and solar energy.
Alma had been one of them before meeting my uncle and mar-
rying into "civilization," as she said. Her face was rough from
years in the sun.

They lived year-round in a sophisticated ruin perched on
a cliff overlooking the archipelago. No electricity, no running
water, but plenty of organized harmony. Cisterns collected rain-
water. When they traveled off the island, the islanders built pipe-
lines to steal water from their cisterns, leaving just enough for
a few summer showers and occasional dishwashing. My uncle
didn't complain about it. It was the price they had to pay to live
on the island, he said.

"We're in Sicily. Do you know anybody who doesn't pay
protection money here?"

I liked the feeling of being cloistered on the island. Wind-
less heat, cicadas, no air conditioning. After overabundance
came restriction. After supermarket aisles stashed with nineteen
varieties of milk, came the relaxing Sicilian communist regime:
milk, cheese, bread, eggs. You had to take things at face value or
starve. The "all or nothing" approach was easier than anything
in between. Timoteo and I had passed through Rome for a few
days on our way to the island. We stayed with our grandmother
and slept on her couch. I read stories from the American literature anthology all night long because the jet lag wouldn't let me
fall asleep. The city was empty and quiet. None of my old friends
were around and it was impossible for me to get my bearings.
I did bump into Alessandro, the school's Rastafarian political
leader. He'd cut off his dreadlocks and was working the door at
a summer disco-bar on the Tiber. He had graduated from high
school, refused to go to university, and didn't have any plans.

"Rome is depressing, man. There's nothing to look forward to
here." I tried to console him. I told him about the evil imperialist America. He'd been right. It was a place from hell. Every
other store was part of a big chain. But he shrugged his shoulders and said I was lucky I didn't have to wear ugly, itchy wool
sweaters from Peru in the winters like all the other lefties from
school. "Get a tan and stay away from here. You won't regret it."
Then he stamped my wrist and let me in for free.

With almost no people on the island I focused on the animals instead. Mice were everywhere. Timoteo feared their
insidious tails. He imagined them creeping into his bathing suit.
From the cots in the kitchen where we slept, we heard them
crawl in search of crumbs and leftovers. As a solution my uncle
adopted, for the time of our stay, ten of the hundreds of wild
cats that lived on the central plateau. Most lacked bits of paws,
eyes, or tails.

"They are perfect. They eat everything, even ants!" Alma
proclaimed.

"Better than your California sinkerator," Antonio chimed in.

We threw dinner leftovers from the terrace at night. The
cats ate the food but didn't touch the mice. It was the kind of
place where animals agreed not to recognize each other's differ-
ences. They came in different shapes but faced the same chal-
lenges. The deal was no eating each other.

The animals I loved most lived on a makeshift farm that
belonged to Santino, the island handyman. He had two donkeys,
Angelina and Maradona (because he was a hard kicker, just like
Napoli's football idol), two ostriches, a cow, a watchdog, cats,
and chickens. They were badly matched yet they fit together
like a dysfunctional family. I liked them because they made me
think of home. Santino could move fridges and furniture up the
mountain—alone or with the help of the donkeys. He loaded
mules with groceries and water for tourists and hauled them up
the hill in exchange for cash. He lived with his wife, Rosalia,

and two daughters next to a metal trash container by the sea—a miniature Sicilian trashopolis like Dharavi in Mumbai. The animals rummaged close to the trash piles, inhaling the stench of garbage and melting plastic. It yielded a thick, sickly-sweet smell under the sun.

Everyone on the island recognized my brother and me from the Spam commercial we'd shot in Italy the previous year. When we disembarked from the hydrofoil it was a walk of shame. Kids chased us with cameras and papers so we could sign autographs.

"The Americans are here!" they screamed.

We stopped for refreshments at the bar and were welcomed like movie stars with free mulberry granita and iced tea.

"Who's hungry for thinly sliced vegetables on a bed of chopped meat?" the barman winked at us, quoting our mother's line in the commercial.

The islanders cackled.

"Canned meat anyone?" another intervened.

"Can we come out to your beautiful house?" a little girl asked, prompted by her aunt.

"*Macché!* They live in America. That wasn't their *real* house," one of the local boys interjected.

"They're rich! They have a house in Rome *and* one in Los Angeles. Don't you know?" the little girl's aunt answered in dialect.

They spoke their ideas out loud, talking about us as if we weren't there. The teenage girls hissed when they looked at me. I wanted to tell them they had nothing to be envious of. Nearly a year had passed since we moved to the United States and little had changed. Part of the canned-meat company's payment to us was a long-lasting supply of Spam. My parents had shipped the cans over to the island so Alma could feed the stray cats. Not a glamorous story so far. When they asked me if I'd seen any celebrities in LA, I told them about the day on the freeway when I passed the actor who played Eric Forrester, the powerful father figure in *The Bold and the Beautiful*. His custom license plate read PATRIARCH. I had also seen David Hasselhoff at a mall in Encino. I lied and told them he'd pulled in to the parking lot in a black sports car with tinted windows and a roving red sensor on the hood.

The boat my uncle bought from a fisherman a few years earlier had a name painted in blue on the bow: *Samantha Fox IV.* It was flimsy and filled with stagnant seawater, but dignity was bestowed upon her by the Roman numerals that followed her name. We took off from the small port, trudging slowly across the calm sea. Alma bailed out the yellowing seawater inside with a sawed-off two-liter water bottle. She wore crooked, imitation Ray-Ban aviator sunglasses and liked repeating that the last time she bought something for herself was 1979. She clipped her toenails on board, then threw them in the sea—the usual open-air toiletry method. Her feet were permanently dirty from walking barefoot on the island rocks. My uncle didn't speak with us much. He didn't approve of Ettore's move. He and Alma lived off sun and water and the vegetables they grew on the plains on top of the mountain.

"Why would anyone need more than that? Why move somewhere far away when all you'll ever need in life is right *here*?" he asked my brother and me, tapping his heart demonstratively with one hand and clasping the tiller with the other, a cigarette dangling from his lips.

We shrugged our shoulders.

"To make movies?" I ventured.

Alma shook her head disapprovingly.

"America!" she groaned. "Full of *shit* films!"

"Ettore and Serena should bring culture where it's appreciated. Not stupid Hollywood!"

"It's not exactly Hollywood where we live, so don't worry," I said.

I curled onto a wet cushion and closed my eyes in the sun, lulled by the hum of the slow motor. It seemed to repeat the same monotonous words over and over, *Lay low, even out. Lay low, even out.* I followed its orders and compressed my body against the spongy cushion. *Lay low and make yourself small,* a voice inside me said. *Lay low and even out.*

We anchored the *Samantha Fox* by the Scoglio Galera, the prison rock, a conglomeration of isolated rust-colored cliffs in the middle of the sea. My uncle opened the canopy for shade.

"You don't need to watch movies when you can live inside them. Welcome to Jurassic Park," he announced, smiling and looking up at the uncontaminated sky.

I hadn't been to that side of the island in years. I'd forgotten how wild it was—a prehistoric enclave with no humans, just wild goats and large birds flying over the black lava shores. Alma removed her bathing suit top and dove into the green-and-purple algae that floated beneath the surface of the water. Timoteo, smeared in fluorescent white sunblock from America—our mother's only recommendation was that he protect his pale skin—jumped off and paddled away with a blunted trident in search of octopus dens. Birds circled the lava accumulations that spilled from the tip of the mountain, squeaking fiercely at each other like pterodactyls, ancient wails that belonged to no other birds on earth. They picked on the wild goats hinging off the slippery rocks, and the wild goats bleated back defensively. Their interactions were like emergency calls, the bird cries strident requests to be rewound to the era they actually belonged to.

———

I swam to shore and dried on the black rocks. My uncle appeared, water dripping from his chest, holding a swim mask filled with sea urchins. He opened them against a stone and removed eggs from inside with his finger, offering me part of the beheaded creature. I let the urchin spikes prickle my palm and nudged the eggs with my fingertips. Antonio looked back up at the wild goats battling the birds, and pointed to a row of chewed-off prickly pear cacti that looked like apocalyptic wishbones.

"Everyone's either hungry or dying here. No more fish. The fishermen from the other islands use underwater explosives in the winter. By summer there's nothing left."

He threw out the empty urchin shells and pointed to a small recess in the mountain.

"Alma and I lived there for six months. We filtered our water and ate fish and prickly pear fruit. I think I didn't go to the bathroom for months." He laughed.

He sprawled out and rolled a bundle of lavic stones on his body, arranging them like a black cross over his torso. I saw traces of my father's pioneering spirit in him, but wilder. His lean, tapered fingers placed stones up his chest all the way to the center of his forehead.

"The cross is for Tindara. In case she's watching," he explained, glancing up at the mountain. "She lives up there. She was our neighbor at the time."

I had heard stories about Tindara since I was a kid. She was the island's evil-eye remover. I knew she lived alone off the eastern flank of the island in a cliff dwelling inside a canyon, and hardly ever came down to the shores. She grew her own vegetables and performed rituals in a round cement court she built with her own hands. She didn't need men. She didn't like them and didn't like the sun. A nocturnal creature, with frozen blue eyes. The fishermen anchored their boats below her cave at night for good luck. Some said she had the power to filter moonlight and change sea tides, some had seen her reflection beam under the stars. They believed she magnetized fish to nets with only a gesture of her hands.

"One day we had a squabble with her and a rock tumbled down the mountain close to where Alma was swimming. We knew it was time to leave."

My uncle cackled and made another cross with his hands to ward off Tindara's evil eye.

"She's a powerful one," he explained, and grabbed his testicles three times—a superstitious Italian ritual I had forgotten about.

I walked to the dump next to Santino's farm with a dripping trash bag over my shoulders. The dumpster was so tall I couldn't manage to swing the bag over the top. Donkeys and ostriches stared blankly at my maneuvers. Angelina, the older donkey, was pregnant. I left the bag on the ground and crept into the farm to take a closer look at her belly. She was swollen. It was impossible to make out where nipples began and breasts ended. I put my hands over her belly to feel if anything was moving inside her. She blinked, swatting flies out of her doey eyes. I fell in love with that look right away. I kissed her forehead and petted her crimped mane and snout.

"You're getting there."

The ostrich sisters stood next to each other, perfectly still on their two-toed feet in a corner of the muddy farm. They'd lost most of their feathers in the sun and seemed confused— but that was the thing about the animals of the island. They all looked confused and I felt pity for them—the ones in the sky, on the rocks, and inside the sea—sparse and ugly as they were, with their missing paws, their dirty dens, and the patchy body hair that burned under the sun. I was drawn to their cries. It's too hot, it's too hard, it's too rocky, we're too hungry, they all seemed to say. Even the mice, squeaking through our kitchen drawers at night, sounded desperate.

I heard a thud from the dumpster. When I turned around I noticed my trash bag was gone. Santino stood next to the big metal container, barefoot on the dirty ground. He didn't say hello, didn't even look at my face.

"Too heavy for you," he muttered. "I threw it out."

He approached me, locking eyes with mine.

"You've grown, Eugenia. You were a kid the last time I saw you. You like my farm?" He chuckled. "All Americans like animals, right?"

"I like animals. I'm not American." I smiled.

"Yes, sure."

I glanced over to his house behind him. Rosalia was leaning over the small balcony—suspicious eyes staring at me below wild graying curls. As far back as I could remember I had never seen her communicate anything warm toward a living being. Even with her daughters she was distant. The most affectionate gesture I'd seen from her was tying their shoelaces or feeding them a sausage sandwich. When they were too loud she hit them over the head and told them to shut up.

"You like staying up at Antonio and Alma's house?" Santino asked with smiley eyes.

"It's nice . . ."

"Does Alma still walk around naked?"

I blushed.

"All those Germans do. They think we can't see them." He cackled. "You do that too?"

"Do what?"

"Go around naked?"

I glanced up toward his wife and blushed again. She was still on the balcony, staring.

"No. I don't . . ."

He was a wild, beautiful thing. Now that I saw him up close,

I remembered his green eyes from childhood. His whole story suddenly came back to me: Santino the crossbreed, Santino the orphan, Santino the Egyptian. He was the son of a pale fisherman, but his mother had an affair with a migrant worker from Egypt one summer, and he was born nine months later with dark skin, green eyes, and curly black hair. His father rejected him and after his mother died, when the boy was five, he stopped taking care of him. Santino grew up without parents like a savage creature climbing barefoot on the island rocks. He never went to school, couldn't even sign his name. Islanders took him in when they could. They fed him until he was old enough and strong enough to tough it out on his own. I remembered as a little girl noticing his solitary tours. He hiked to the top of the crater, screaming at bulls and mules. Animals were his life. Owning beasts on the island was more convenient than owning a house.

"Why do you keep ostriches? Don't they need to run? They have nowhere to run to here. There are just stairs," I asked.

"They need to run? I decide what they need," he told me with a smug look.

It was the end of July and there was no more air. The sea was still like a lake at dusk. The first fishermen were beginning to go out for squid. When the sun disappeared, their boat lights turned on. They looked like suspended Florence Nightingale lamps, caring for the wounded waters, looking after exploded aquatic animals with missing body parts. No donkey screams, no mice squeaks. It was so still I could hear the Mediterranean lapping gently and the fishermen's voices chatting in dialect as if we were all inside the same blue room. I was on the island's second plateau, taking a break from carrying groceries up the stairs. The thin plastic handles had sawed through my fingers, but I insisted on bringing up the bags on my own because I didn't want to overload the donkeys. I sat down on a cement bench and noticed a shadow move across the heather bushes. I recognized her from the shape of her hair—a frizzy mass pinned down by three aquamarine plastic clasps. Rosalia.

She hovered toward me awkwardly, like a troll.

"Is it true you're prominent overseas?" she asked without looking up.

It was the first time I'd heard her speak.

"No," I replied, confused by her use of the word *prominent*.

She looked disappointed and sat down next to me on the bench.

"You're not famous?" She sighed. "But everyone says you're famous. You do commercials."

"I did one commercial, a year ago."

"But it was for canned meat! You were on RAI 3. We saw you. I'm sorry, but you're famous."

I let her win.

"Look," she said obstinately, "there's a weight on my chest. No matter what I do, I can't get rid of it. It comes down on me the minute I close the blinds to put the girls to sleep and stays there until early morning. I can't breathe. I can't sleep. Tindara says you can make it go away. 'The woman who will help you is a prominent person who comes from a country overseas.' That's what she said. Exact words. She read the olive oil in my water and the coffee in my cup."

She was rushing and fueled with adrenaline, eating up her words in strict Sicilian dialect. I barely understood anything, but I gathered she was convinced I was the one person who could help her. She stared at me with focused, transfixed eyes.

"I'm not leaving," she said.

She looked wrinkled, tired, and ugly and that was all I could think—how ugly she was, with her small mouth and hairy chin, her rough skin covered in scars and freckles, wild hair graying prematurely, not caring about any of it. I searched for glimpses

of the person she might have been before isolation and rough-
ness, before the husband and the kids and the dumpster smell
outside the window—and I saw a way out.

"I can make you beautiful," I offered tentatively.

It was the first time America had come to my rescue. I was
thinking about the Niki Taylor Cover Girl commercials I'd been
watching in LA. "Beautiful is fresh, beautiful is alive" was the
tagline and I repeated it with flair. I don't know why I said it. I
didn't mean it like that, but when I uttered the words, she parted
her lips with an imperceptible, feline smile. Everything in her
body said yes.

"Do you think that will take the evil eye away?" she asked.

"I'm sure of it."

Lay low, even out. Lay low, even out, my uncle's motorboat had
warned me, but there I was proclaiming cures for evil eyes,
promising remedies, announcing makeovers.

Rosalia and Santino's house was excavated out of the mountain. The rock walls sheltered the family from the dumpster's
stench. I walked up the creaking wooden stairs and stepped
inside: a kitchen and living-room area with two mattresses on
the floor for the girls, a small bedroom with a queen bed, and
a bathroom. No doors, just strings of plastic beads hanging
across doorframes. A faded *pescheria* calendar from the previous year hung over the fridge next to a crucifix with a dried-out
olive branch from the past Palm Sunday. Rosalia grunted hello.
She gave me water and showed me to the bathroom.

I'd filled my backpack with used beauty products I found
in Alma's bathroom: rusty tweezers, blunt scissors, an old electronic hair-pulling machine that made a mean sound, melted
waxing strips, expired highlighting shampoo and conditioner.
I bought a hair straightener from the "beauty" section of the
alimentari. It was next to the nail files, between the hairpins and

glittery jelly sandals—the whole of the beauty accessories available to islanders.

Rosalia sat on a stool inside her broken shower. Her crisp curls sizzled under the straightener, and when I pulled it away, they came off her head in clumps and I panicked. I did not know what I was doing. What if Tindara had misread the coffee cup and olive oil? I pictured her directing many evil eyes my way. I imagined altars of Italian Spam covered in pine needles as she howled at the winds and the gods from her cement terrace, agitating goats and pterodactyls, proclaiming revenge against the American impostor.

Santino's bare feet dragged up the wood stairs. Rosalia shifted in her seat and covered her cleavage with a towel, defensively.

He peeked his head into the bathroom and snickered at his wife.

"You look like a crazy person. What's for lunch?"

Rosalia got up from her stool and walked to the kitchen area—her fried hair flopping to one side. She threw an old bread bun on a plastic plate, opened the fridge, took out a shriveled sausage, and slapped it on the bread. She handed the plate to her husband. Santino glared at me and walked out.

The next morning Rosalia was waiting for me, leaning on the back porch door with burned hair—exhilarated.

"Something is happening. Last night before going to bed the pounding rocks on my chest only lasted a few minutes. We're on our way."

I thought about Niki Taylor's hair blowing over the rooftops of the small Greek island village in the Cover Girl commercial. "Cover Girl: Redefining Beautiful." I would turn our crumbling Sicilian island into a clean Greek Cyclades. I'd introduce Rosalia to the concept they told us about in health and PE classes: Looking good is feeling good.

We started over.

I sat her on the stool in the shower and patted her hair with conditioner. Now that it was moisturized it didn't break under the hair straightener. Her frizzy curls began to unfurl on her shoulders in delicate waves. When the hair was straight we moved to the porch and she dried off in a sliver of sunlight that filtered through a crack in the mountain. Her usual mouse hue faded. The colors of the mountain began to blend into her hair and eyes. It was the first time she was letting the island into her body.

I shaved her and waxed her, focused like a scientist in a lab—the lab of infinite dark follicles. I pressed olive oil over her legs and thighs and tweezed her eyebrows in perfect arches. Her face transformed. I watched the angles of her eyes soften as she looked at her reflection in the mirror.

"Nobody has ever touched me with the intention of making me beautiful," she said.

Her daughters came home, fishing rods dangling with hooked worms at their sides. They ran over to touch their mother's face.

"*Mamma, sembri una principessa!*" they screamed. "You look like a princess!"

A small revolution broke out around town. Rosalia wore new clothes and walked with her chin up. The older women sat on stoops, dressed in black, hissing at her when she passed with her hips swaying. She used to walk straight like a piece of wood, but now there was this waving thing she did and everyone was suspicious of it.

"*Era beddu u putrusinu. Arrivò u iattu e ci pisciò,*" they whispered in strict Sicilian dialect, meaning she was ugly from the start and the makeover only made it worse. "And with those legs! Who does she think she is, showing so much skin?"

It wasn't just physically that Rosalia changed, her whole attitude had new potency, and Santino could not stand it. He started criticizing her lightly at first, telling her she could not sleep in his bed because he didn't recognize her. Then he got heavy-handed, at times even physical, and Rosalia began detouring him. The island women dressed in black crossed their hearts when they saw her pass by. They thought she was possessed by "*u spiritu du Donna Nzula,*" the spirit of Lady Nunzia, the island's only professional prostitute who had taunted married women until her death. They thought Tindara had invoked Nunzia and placed her inside Rosalia's body. Santino was right if he chose to disown her. Rosalia was offending his honor. It didn't matter that nobody on the island had cared enough about him to send him to school or give him decent clothes. Now he was suddenly one of them—a fellow islander ranged against his immoral, dissolute wife.

"The whole island is talking about it," Alma announced with a tinge of excited local gossip at dinner.

"About what?" I asked.

"What you did to Rosalia." My uncle spoke with a grave expression. "Why did you do it?"

He got up and cleared the table, annoyed.

"You've become so American," he groaned. "All this stuff about self-improvement and looking pretty and making the best out of what you have. It's silly. Like those stupid American commercials. We never had that kind of business on this island. People here don't even know how to read and write. Why should they care about straightening their hair when they barely have food to eat?"

Suddenly I felt stupid, as if I'd toyed with a pillar of society, a fixed ancient law that had been there before I landed on the island and would be there when I left. A law not worth questioning.

Lay low, even out. Lay low, even out. I thought about the motorboat warning. Why did I ignore it? Why couldn't I stay put? Where did that restlessness come from? I knew the answer, but kept tiptoeing around it. I tiptoed around the memory of Arash's doey eyes, so similar to the ones of the island donkeys. I looked away when the porous lava rocks reminded me of the little dimple on his chin. I avoided men in white T-shirts and despised the darker Sicilians who looked Middle Eastern because they reminded me of him. My grief for Arash was a brick I'd safely packed in a box, something tangible I had to carry with me. The box was heavy but sealed, the contents perfectly isolated. As long as I didn't open the packaging I'd be fine. I shifted the load from one side of my head to the other, never finding the courage to throw it off. I knew I couldn't change Rosalia's life, but I could help a new person emerge from her armature because it was the same thing I was trying to do with myself.

"She's not your experiment, you know," Alma asserted dryly.

"But she's happy. She's happier. She smiles now. What's wrong with that?" I asked.

Nobody answered.

Rosalia started spending more time in nature to avoid her husband. After twenty-three years living life indoors she was curious and alive. The pangs in her chest had diminished. Sometimes they were barely noticeable, she told me. Tindara said it was because she was on the right track. There were moments when I looked at her on the rocks by the sea, and she seemed beautiful, like a new being.

Her daughters were inspired by their mother's new freedom. They all hiked to the top of the island to look at wild goats and chase the rabbits that lived in the crater's shrubs. During winter, islanders hunted them with rifles. The girls were used to eating them off the grill, but now all they wanted was to hold them in their arms.

"Are we allowed to *pet* them?" the younger one asked as she ran after a bunny.

"Are we allowed to *love* them?"

"Yes, yes, yes!" Rosalia replied in the grip of newfound mirth. What she felt in her chest for the first time in years was the feeling of love, an expanse of possibilities, a lighthearted-ness. It made her jump out of bed at dawn and go to sleep with a smile on her face. No pangs. She was in love, she said. Not with her husband or *with* anyone. Just in love: a fluttering heart and air in her legs. The island beasts sang to her. She sat on the stairs and spoke to lizards. She started to take care of Angelina and Maradona and the ostriches, cleaning them, curing their sores. Everything on the island seemed interconnected in her eyes, unified and divine—people and prickly pears and prehistoric canyons, the wild and tame animals, the disappearing fish in the sea—all bound together under the same wide moon, the same relentless sun.

The former schedule of the house—lunch at noon, dinner at eight—ceased.

"Eat when you're hungry," Rosalia told the girls. "Sleep when you're tired."

The sisters descended the mountain with bunnies in their arms. They brought them home and kept them as pets. Rabbits chewed through electrical cords. The refrigerator broke, the TV short-circuited. Santino went wild with rage. Out of all the beings his wife seemed to have chosen to share her love with, he was not one of them.

He took out his revenge on me because I'd started it. At first he stopped saying hello. He avoided me at all costs and if we ever crossed paths he wheezed, spat on the ground, and moved on.

I bumped into him as he climbed the mountain one day. He was whipping Maradona's flanks with a switch, urging him up the shaky path, loaded with water and beer for the Germans who lived on top. I was coming down with his girls, bunnies in our arms. He elbowed his way past them and kept walking up.

"No more rabbits," he commanded.

The girls looked down and giggled.

"Go back home! You look like feral children," he screamed at them. He huffed and kept making his way up the mountain without acknowledging me.

"Accà!" he brayed at Maradona, whipping him harder. The word meant "right here," but it had the same sound as *casa,* meaning "home." *Here. At home. With me. Stay. Do as you're told.* Those small ideas were the only things he had to latch onto—the reassurance that everything had a place that could not be altered. *Stick to me!* his eyes cried, but he cringed inside. He clung to little convictions—home, wife, food, quiet—with all his strength, but nobody listened anymore: not his wife, not his animals, not his daughters. A silent rebellion had insinuated itself under their skin and there was no going back.

At night Timoteo and I talked for hours while on our cots in the kitchen with mice and geckos to keep us company. Hearing his voice on the other side of the room made me feel safe and I knew it was the same for him. We couldn't call our parents because there was only one pay phone on the island and it was expensive, but we had each other. In the darkness we spoke in English and it was like we became two different people, different siblings with different personalities. Language became an escape route. We could switch from one personality to another without being afraid of anyone's judgment.

Sometimes if my heart beat too fast I crawled into his cot

and hugged him. He knew how to make me laugh. We were both learning how to bridge two worlds.

"Max or Robert?" he asked.

"Robert."

"Zio Antonio or grandma?"

"Antonio, *ovviamente*!"

We played our game of "Sophie's choice." Who would we be more willing to throw off a cliff into burning flames below? Our potential victims were always well calibrated and tough on the conscience.

To know that humans were inevitably bound to make choices, even the hardest ones, gave us peace of mind. Someone always had to go off the cliff and if we could choose between two unbearable options, we'd be able to face any no-win situation. If we could toss grandmothers, pets, parents, and friends into the flames, then we could live anywhere in the world, pick any persona we wanted, accept our own parents' poor judgment. We played into the morning hours, commenting on each other's choices, mostly agreeing on them. Except that between our father's film in LA working out and being given the chance to move back to Rome, I picked our father's film. Timoteo said he'd move back to Italy no matter what was on the other side of the cliff.

11

Naked on the rocks by the sea the Germans looked like dying bulls with sagging sacs and flat asses. They brought homemade picnics with them, complaining the panini at the *alimentari* cost a fortune. The yolk from their soft-boiled eggs dripped from their mouths onto their naked bellies. They drank warm beer and laughed. My uncle and Alma conversed with them, sometimes partly undressed, sometimes completely nude—depending on whether my brother and I were around. They told stories from the long winters and gossiped about which islanders had stolen water from whose wells.

I had chased Arash out of my dreams that morning. I learned to control his incursions during my sleep. I knew how to blur the edges of his face into the periphery. My rubber suit kept him mostly at bay, but sometimes not enough. It wasn't just him. It was the feeling of him that wouldn't go away. The packaged brick was with me and I kept waiting for the right moment to get rid of it. I reassured myself that Iran and California were far away, that I was safe on my small island. No riots or guns, just the purifying waters of the quiet Mediterranean Sea. I thought being there would cure me. I'd find a rocky alcove where I could dispose of my grief. I looked for that nook every day.

I left my uncle and the German nudists. I swam out to

the open water farther down the coast. On the isolated shore
I started walking past the natural arch that divided civilization
from the wilder side of the island. I walked for hours, teetering
on the edge of the boulders, until I reached the ancient lava
flow beneath Tindara's house on the other side of the island.
From the shore I could see the emerging red cliffs of the Scoglio
Galera in the middle of the sea. They seemed taller now that
the tide was low. I swam out to them and climbed up, squinting
my eyes to catch a glimpse of Tindara's cliff dwelling, hoping
to see her fluttering a symbolic white flag in the middle of the
canyon, proclaiming a truce. "Your duty is terminated. You and
Rosalia may consider yourselves healed. Enjoy the rest of your
vacation." But Tindara wasn't there and the only things flying in
the wind were hungry birds.

I took my bathing suit off, closed my eyes, and jumped from
the tallest cliff into the water. It felt good to jump into space, so I
got back up and jumped again. I did it over and over as the birds
quarreled with the goats in the ancient sunlight. I closed my
eyes and sprawled my body on the high rock, drying in the sun.

When I opened them again, the tide had come in and
the sun was disappearing behind the mountain. The stones I
treaded upon on my way in were now submerged and the only
way back was by water. It was a long stretch, a quarter of the
island's circumference. I was tired from diving, but I had no
choice but to swim.

Back in the water the black shadows underneath the sea
looked like gigantic whales. I kicked harder, afraid they might
emerge and eat me up. I didn't have the strength to swim the
crawl, so I turned over and tried backstrokes. I could see the
dividing line of the natural arch in the distance turned upside
down, still too far away. A captain's megaphone from a tourist
boat reverberated somewhere, but I could not see it. A sailboat
swept by peacefully on the horizon. No other boats were in
sight. I was getting cold and I was now too far from the Sco-

glio Galera to come out of the water. I tried to hold to a wall of shadowy rocks that hung over the sea, but the tide had risen and there was nothing to latch onto. I thrust my hips against the cliff walls and fell back in. I ran out of breath and closed my eyes, floating, too tired to do anything else.

I drifted over the coal-black lava flows that tainted the submerged world and remembered being four, on a beach in Rome. I had told my father I was ready to swim on my own without water wings, but it wasn't true. I wanted to test him. He had been away working for a long time and I didn't like how little he knew about us when he returned. He didn't know my brother had started walking and I had started swim classes. Some part of me wanted to punish him for this. He let me go in the sea alone. I swam out feeling tall and brave, but when a wave pushed me down, I didn't make my way back to the surface and I fainted. A tall man in a red Speedo saved me. When I regained consciousness I was in his arms. I hugged him tight pretending he was my father, pretending my father had saved my life. Back on the beach the man scolded my real father and told him he'd report him to the police.

Ettore lifted his arms defensively in the air. "Stop attacking me, *man*. She *told* me she could swim."

I remembered the disbelief on the face of the red Speedo man. He had gray hair and thick, buttery skin. I looked for him now instinctively, as my backstrokes got weaker. I was shivering and my fingers were waterlogged and wrinkled. The tide rose, making the cliffs darker. I heard the sound of a motor underwater. I looked up. In the distance was Santino on his small fiberglass boat. I waved at him with the little strength I had left. He looked straight past me, but started to veer slowly in my direction.

I got picked up and slid on board, letting my limp body collapse on the floor over a pile of squirming fish. I wrapped my hand around Santino's ankle to make sure things were solid.

Fish wriggled up against my nose, under my legs. What were they doing there? Santino was a terrible fisherman. Everybody on the island knew it. He broke motorboats and cussed at the water. I pressed harder on his legs, smelling juniper and sweat— the acrid scent of sun, dirt, and seclusion. His body was not welcoming. It was hard and his leg hair was rough like a steel-wool pad. But I let myself go. I was shivering and the fish kept gasping and flopping over my thighs. Santino was the only warm thing, the only dry thing. I hung on to him, my savior, and pressed my lips hard against his ankle. I didn't want to open my eyes.

I stayed there, rescued and in shock. As the boat proceeded toward the port, the sun peeked out of the mountain again and my body began to warm up.

I opened my eyes a few moments later. Santino smiled a forced smile I had never seen. I gathered enough strength to sit.

"Thank you for saving my life."

"Thank you for saving my *wife*," he replied sarcastically, keeping his gaze on the horizon. "What were you doing out there? You're a good swimmer, why were you drowning?"

"I didn't realize the tide would come in so fast. I thought I could walk back."

"Watch out. The next time I might not see you."

It sounded like a threat.

One more curve and the port would be in our reach, but Santino slowed down the boat and turned the engine off in the middle of the sea.

"You were naked at the Scoglio Galera. I saw you. Why don't you take your wet bathing suit off now?" he said. "Take it off. The Germans are naked. Alma is always naked and so is your uncle. It's natural, right? If it's so natural then why keep your bathing suit on with me? 'Cause I'm an islander? You think I can't understand? I understand. Take it off."

I looked around. We were far from shore and I could not swim anywhere. I didn't have the strength to fight back.

I pulled down my top and looked him in the eyes, establishing that we were not to go further than that.

"You're pretty good at being a slut, right?"

He got on his knees. The flopping fish slid across his legs. His face was in front of my crotch and he looked up at me.

"Take these off or I'll bite you."

I removed my wet bathing suit bottom and scrunched it in a fist.

I looked up at the mainland. Maybe I could still swim. It wasn't that far. Maybe I'd make it.

"Yes," he said, examining my naked body. "You're pretty good at being a slut. But that doesn't mean you have to turn everyone else into a slut. You understand?"

I nodded yes, that I understood. He pressed his front teeth hard into my hip bone, then backed off, squishing the fish with his feet.

"Especially not my wife or daughters," he concluded.

I put my bathing suit back on, keeping my eyes down. I wasn't afraid.

We stayed quiet until he started the motor again. The boat began to move toward the mainland.

"Won't you put the fish back in the water? You can't eat them. They're too small," I said as we got closer to the port.

"They keep me company," he said and smirked.

"They're just piled up in here. They're useless."

We passed by the dump and the animal farm. Angelina looked pregnant even from far away.

"She's getting there," I mumbled.

Santino didn't answer.

He raised the motor when we reached the shore so the propeller wouldn't scrape the rocks on the bottom of the sea.

I hopped off and looked back at him, thankful he had not hurt me.

"You'll throw the fish back in the water?"

He nodded yes. *"Tutti a mare!"* he winked reassuringly. "All back at sea!"

That night the island shuddered with the sound of donkeys braying—a continuous, repetitive wail that went on in twenty-minute increments. It stopped and started over. Angelina was giving birth. I got up from bed, sweating in the sticky night heat, and dashed down the stairs to Santino and Rosalia's barn. Angelina was sprawled on a patch of hay, her eyes open wide. She was dilated. Two small legs wrapped in a liquid sac were making their way out of her body. It seemed impossible that something so big could emerge from a living being. Rosalia and the girls stood by. The vigilant ostriches had developed protective sisterly instincts. Angelina stretched out more as the foal's legs pushed out, but the baby was stuck halfway and she was too exhausted to keep pushing. She stayed on the hay, her head drooped on one side. Rosalia turned to us and signaled to help. She squatted over the donkey, grabbed the small emerging legs, and began to pull. She put a hand on Angelina's head and kissed her forehead. The girls looked at her in awe.

"Mom!"

She turned back to us.

"Don't just stand there. Help me!"

We awoke to a primal call of duty and grabbed parts of the baby, whatever we could get our hands on. The amniotic sac was slimy and hot. It drooped over our fingers, covering our wrists, but we didn't care. We pulled gently and firmly until the little one slipped out in a blob. He squirmed to the ground, not knowing how to get up, engulfed in slime. Angelina pierced the sac with her teeth, then licked him to clean him off. It was her first baby yet she knew exactly what to do. The ostrich sisters grunted, impressed with everyone's performance. The girls hugged their mother. Maradona brayed so loud he woke up half the island. We all had tears in our eyes.

Santino didn't come out for the birth.

We called the baby Nerino because he was darker than the other donkeys. He emitted a sound like a loud frog croak. Angelina licked his face until his eyes opened and in no time he could walk.

On my way home I passed by the quiet port. Santino's boat was anchored at the end of the dock, shimmering in the dim village lights, water slapping against it.

I walked over. I could not see much, but I caught glimpses of a dark mass at the bottom. I knew what was there. I could smell it. I pulled the boat closer with the rope and stopped it under a sliver of light. It was the fish. They were all still there, piled on top of one another, covered in flies.

Toward the end of summer, the skies turned against the sea. Thunderstorms shook the island and hailstones strafed the rocks. We thought the mountain would explode or sink under the sea. A feeling of doom and catastrophe cloaked the island. No commercial boats could get to our shores. No fishing, no food, no supplies. The storms banged against the sky for days, until finally the sun came back, ripping into the heavens, and everything turned metallic and wild. The island's long stairway became tufted in moss—a green carpet leading to the heavens. Alma and my uncle decided it would be a good time to camp out on the crater. We had no tents, but we brought blankets, eggs, and the cans of Italian Spam we'd been feeding the cats with.

As we made our way up, the port became smaller, the island got quieter, filled with the ghosts of the immigrants' empty houses. At the top, a few German Vikings with shaved testicles did sun salutations on their terraces. We said hello but they didn't respond, too immersed in their spiritual practice. The mountain was different from the seaside. Nobody smiled there. People didn't look at each other if they crossed paths. It was the place for everyone's personal mission.

When we reached the crater, we felt as if we'd landed in space. The sun was setting over the sea while the full moon rose behind our backs. One side of the crater was infused in a pale, glowing light, the other blazed in warm red. Looming fig trees, heavy with fruit, sprawled on the basin's edges. Wild rabbits scurried from one end to the other, electrified by the day's end. We camped next to a stone cabin overlooking the sea. In the sunset the other Aeolian Islands looked like submerged boots left behind by a giant who had walked off barefoot into space.

We lit a bonfire. My uncle took out a banged-up guitar and prompted Alma to sing in German in front of the flames. My brother opened his first can of Italian Spam and burped.

In the crater's basin, glowing in the moonlight, I noticed Rosalia. She was floating toward the stairs wrapped in a silvery gown I had never seen her wear. Alone with a basket of vegetables in her hand, she looked like a new being, an island spirit. Sometimes, like the village women, I too wondered whether it was still Rosalia inside that new body, if Nunzia hadn't taken over after all. I hadn't spoken to her since my incident on Santino's boat and Angelina's birth-giving night. In truth there was nothing left for me to do or say and Santino's warning to keep away had been enough to make me falter every time I entertained the possibility of knocking on their door. But now she was alone. I walked toward her golden, bare back. Her flowing gown scurried down the staircase.

It was only when I took a few steps down that I realized why I had followed her. It was the presence of a sound. It chiseled its way into my ears now: Angelina's bray. She was right below us, coming up the ramp of stairs, loaded with groceries. It was her first trip to the top since Nerino. Santino trudged next to her, flailing his switch on her buttocks. She was soaked in sweat, a shiny seal. She was too loaded and it was early to bring her all the way up. Nerino was probably suffering without her, with no milk for so many hours. From the face he made I could tell Santino hadn't expected to meet Rosalia on the path. She was too beautiful with her loose hair falling over her shoulders. The words between husband and wife flew into the wind. I couldn't hear anything from where I stood, but I could see they were tense. Rosalia waved her vegetables in the air defensively, as if she were smacking truth in his face.

I walked down a few steps to hear better, making sure they would not see me.

"She's not ready for runs yet," Rosalia said, pointing to the donkey's stretched belly.

"Mind your own business!" Santino replied.

His arms moved in grand circles, then turned to smaller, contrite movements. His right hand sealed into a crooked fist like a capricious child's. He stomped his foot, demanding attention. His rage mounted. There was no way out of it. A fury was taking over his body as he screamed nonsense against rabbits and donkeys and chewed-up electrical cords.

The mosquitoes were starting to come out. I could feel them on my bare legs. I wanted to swat them against my thighs and ankles, to splatter myself in blood marks, but I let them eat me. My eyes were fixed on Rosalia and Santino's lips.

"Accà!" he screamed to the donkey. "Let's go."

He pushed Rosalia out of his way and hit Angelina on her side.

Angelina trotted up a few more stairs and stopped in front of Rosalia, asking for help with her eyes. Even though it was almost dark, I could see her expression and what I couldn't see, I could imagine. She wanted to go back to her baby.

Santino flogged her again to keep her moving up, but Angelina stood stubbornly next to Rosalia, her heavy eyes as big as a cow's, begging for help.

"Stop it! Can't you see she's tired? She just had a baby," Rosalia protested.

"*Accà!*" Santino screamed, ignoring her.

I walked down the steps, trying to catch every bit of their wind-distorted words.

Rosalia now faced her husband, appearing stronger than him, like a bigger and better person.

"Let me take her back down with me. You're almost there. You can unload her here and bring the rest of the stuff by hand," she said as she patted Angelina's soft snout.

"You think I'm going to do ten trips back and forth for a donkey?" Santino's chest grew wider as he spoke—the man of the stairs.

"*Accà!*" He hit Angelina harder, staring into Rosalia's eyes.

He grabbed a thick branch from a dry olive tree next to the stairs and doubled his whipping. He beat Angelina again, this time on the belly.

"She just had a baby!" Rosalia screamed.

I felt my legs tremble. I was outside my body, right there next to Angelina.

"I'm taking her up, you understand? And you're going home!"

Santino hit Angelina harder, a second time, and a third. He stared down at his wife and raised his arm toward her, threateningly now. Either she got out of the way or she'd be the next one to get hurt.

"*Basta,* Santino," Rosalia screamed. "That's enough!"

She pushed him away from the donkey. Santino pulled a loose rock from the staircase, sending part of it crumbling down. He hit Angelina with it. She pulled back and started braying, hopping in place, trotting from front to back legs, trying to kick up, but was blocked by Santino's reins. I noticed her belly bleeding and stepped down farther, emitting a small cry to get their attention. They didn't look up at me.

"What are you doing? She's bleeding!"

"Shut up!" Santino replied. He searched for another rock and lifted it toward Rosalia to scare her off. "I said go home! And don't tell me we're having scrambled eggs for dinner tonight. I'm not eating them!" he screamed after her.

Rosalia started running down the stairs, looking for help. She peered through the sparse windows of the empty houses, crying. Nobody heard her. Nobody was around except for me, but I was paralyzed with fear at the top of the stairs. I wanted to rush back to the crater and get my uncle, but I couldn't stop staring, afraid something terrible would happen if I moved away, convinced my mere presence might be enough to protect Angelina.

The donkey pulled on Santino's reins and kicked backward. For an instant she freed herself and I felt my body open up. My foot stomped the ground with the same urgency that was in her trot. *Go, run! Fast!* The words wouldn't leave my mouth. Angelina ran down the stairs with wild, uncoordinated movements. I saw her eyes flash sideways like those of a crazy horse—all tenderness gone. Santino leapt down four steps at a time and caught the tail end of the reins. He pulled her back and fell forward, scraping his knee, the reins never leaving his grip.

"Look, stupid donkey! *Scemunita!* Look! I'm bleeding now!"

He held Angelina's reins under his foot to keep her still. With both free hands now, he hauled out another boulder from a different part of the staircase and threw it on her back.

"*Accà!*" Santino hit Angelina with it.

He beat her again on the flanks, on the belly, on her legs. Every time the rock fell off his hands, he picked it up and bashed it against her. She knew she couldn't win and stood, impassive—no trotting, no kicking. She took it all until she fell to the ground. The groceries for the Germans spilled off her saddle. Tomatoes and bottles of water rolled down the stairs.

Finally my voice came back. I let out a shriek—a loud, desperate cry like that of a gutted chicken. Santino glanced up, squinting. He waved at me, his hands soaked in blood.

"There you are! The animal-rights and wife-rights girl. You think my wife is done showing herself around to the entire island?"

He turned toward the bottom of the staircase, addressing Rosalia, who didn't answer. She just stood there panting and staring.

"Yes. I'm done," I said. "Now leave Angelina alone, though, okay?"

Santino grabbed the reins, trying to get Angelina back on her feet again, but she was bleeding too much and could not move.

He picked up the loose groceries that had fallen off the saddle and tried to load them on her back.

"Leave her alone, Santino. I'll deliver the groceries myself. Just leave her alone," I screamed.

I began to walk down the stairs as nonthreateningly as I could. Angelina did not move from the ground. Blood gushed out her legs and back. Her eyes stared into space. She panted so heavily I could hear her breath from where I stood.

"*Lasciala!* Leave her," Rosalia yelled from the bottom of the stairs, encouraged by my presence.

Santino glanced up at me, then back down at his wife. "Stop! Stop talking to each other, you two!"

He sprawled himself over the donkey, claiming her body like a child claims a toy when he feels the presence of another wanting to take it away.

I made my way down more steps with caution.

"Don't fence me in!" he screamed.

He pranced up a few steps, and extracted another stone from the now disheveled staircase.

Angelina wasn't moving.

Santino raised the rock to the sky and crashed it on her head. He lifted it up and came down on the center of her forehead—the space I used to kiss her on. He did it again and again until blood streamed out. It flowed down the stairs, onto the caper plants and dry olive tree roots.

Before dying, Angelina made a sound that was different from her usual bray. It was a kind of "Oooh" or maybe a "Noo." It was the sound of disappointment.

Santino untied the remaining groceries from her saddle and stacked water bottles on both his shoulders. He started walking up the stairs toward me, swaying from side to side to keep his balance.

"Are you happy now? I'm delivering the water on my own."

I turned away and ran back up the steps, afraid I might be next.

When I reached my uncle and Alma at the crater, we heard the sound of the islanders rushing up the mountain followed by Rosalia's wails. Alma and Antonio went to take a look. My brother came close to me and squeezed my hand. We spent the night under the moon. Antonio and Alma didn't return until hours later. They spoke in whispers and went to sleep on the other side of the stone cabin.

At dawn when I got up, their clothes were in a bundle on the ground, covered in blood. I woke Timoteo and we went back to the staircase. The blood was still there, mixed with donkey mane and a few tomatoes from the lost groceries, but Angelina's body was gone.

"Maybe she survived," my brother suggested.

I shook my head.

———

Over dinner I asked Alma who was going to be in charge of reporting Santino to the police.

"There are worse things happening on this island than a donkey dying," my uncle replied dryly.

"Islanders settle these matters by themselves," Alma answered simply. "There are different rules here."

My brother and I looked at each other like everyone was crazy, like they were going to stop talking like that soon, and we would finally have the conversation about what happened the night before, but the conversation never came.

"Nobody can afford to have Santino in trouble. He's the only handyman we have, the only one who knows how to get furniture up all the stairs." My uncle picked up his fish leftovers and scattered them off the terrace to the cats.

I went to the public pay phone at the travel agency and called the carabinieri on the mainland, convinced I could take matters into my own hands. The police laughed at me.

"You want us to get all the way there on an *aliscafo,* because on your island, in the middle of nowhere, a donkey died? I'm sorry. Call back in December when we have nothing to do."

They hung up.

On my cot in the kitchen, I thought about the islanders' quiet pact and the silence that followed Santino's actions over the next days. I thought about how Alma and my uncle had gotten rid of Angelina's body with the islanders in the night, how they came back with their clothes covered in blood and just went to sleep. People on that island developed a forced affinity to nature, but something arid also grew in their chests. The volcano's barrenness was present in every living thing. They were all like rocks. Rock people. My mind wandered back to the parking lot of the Woodland Hills Mall and I thought about Audrey and Natalie and how they were rock people too, and how wrong my uncle was. Rules in America were not so different after all. They'd gotten away with murder while two black kids would spend their lives in jail. A matter of convenience. White girls were needed more than black boys, and Santino was more necessary on the island than in jail because he lifted heavy objects and hauled furniture. I thought about the weight on Rosalia's chest and how she was a rock person who had tried not to be a rock person anymore. Toward the end of August Tindara had announced her take on what happened. She said domestic animals were our filters, our shields against people's envies like the island's stray cats with their missing paws and the half decapitated fish in the sea. Maybe Angelina had been a screen, placed at the right place at the right time. A body taken in place of Rosalia's. The weight Rosalia had felt all winter long, the one she begged me to get rid of, were the rocks pressed against Angelina's heart now.

Santino abandoned his farm and moved to the top of the mountain. He came down infrequently. I never saw him again. The night ship that would take us back to the mainland was delayed because of more storms. Each day my brother and I waited on the dock, dressed in our American clothes, waiting to go back. Each day the sea told us it wasn't time yet. But when the boat finally came, I ran back to Nerino before embarking.

I opened the farm gate and threw my arms around his neck as he walked in circles around the big metal container, looking for his mother.

"You are lucky she never came back," I whispered in his ear. "Sometimes coming home only makes it worse."

He brayed. It sounded different now. It was a sad, lonely cry, like the sounds of all the animals on that island. He'd become one of them.

part three

arrival

12

In the customs area at LAX, the immigration officer asked my brother and me where we'd spent our summer and whether we had a right to be back in Los Angeles. I knew the drill. Ettore had told us, "Whatever they ask, say you are entitled to everything and are dependent on your father who is a journalist."

Our passports said we depended on his visa, but my father had gotten us in the States on the pretense of his being a journalist, so there were always difficult questions to answer. We looked at the long line behind us in the huge hall. It was such a big room, so promising. Anything could happen in a country that had a room like that. American citizens zipped right through the lines. They were greeted with smiles and questions about their holidays, but everyone else had to answer a different set of questions.

"Where are your parents now?" the officer asked.

"In the arrivals hall, I think."

"Yes, but why are you traveling alone?"

"Because we spent our summer in Italy and our parents didn't come."

"Why not?"

"Because . . . they were working?" I ventured.

"Here?"

"Yes . . . here, but for an Italian company."

The extent of their work permit was never clear. The gist of it was that the government was willing to look the other way for people working in the media as long as they paid taxes and stayed in that realm.

"Say you're dependent on your father who is working as a journalist. Tell them I work here, but don't ever tell them I work here." Those were the kind of paradoxical instructions our father gave us regarding immigration officers.

"What do you mean, Dad?"

"That we work here, but we don't *work* here. You know what I mean."

I pretended I did, but I didn't and I always thought he'd do all the talking if it ever came down to it. But now it was on me. I tried to bring back memories of our conversations.

"Don't fall for those Nazi immigration officers' intimidations. They'll interrogate you like SS sergeants, but they have nothing on you. Everyone is innocent until proven guilty. So fuck them and their deportation tactics. If they press, tell them you are visiting your father, but don't tell them your father *lives* here. Just tell them he is *temporarily* working here. The purpose of your trip is *not* business related. You are here to go to school. Actually forget it, never mind. Don't tell them you go to school here. I'm not sure you're actually allowed to go to public school. Whatever you do, do not mention the fact that I'm a director. Oh, yes, and if it looks like they're really getting pissed off, just take back everything and say you're on vacation."

"I'm going to ask you this again, miss: Why did your parents *not* come to Italy with you? Let me remind you that lying to the government will jeopardize your entrance to the United States."

"Because they're making a movie!" I broke down, feeling at once guilty and relieved.

"They're making a movie?"

"Yes?"

"Do they have a permit to work in the United States?"

"I'm sure they do," Timoteo intervened.

"You're not allowed to make movies with an Italian media visa. You're only allowed to work for your Italian employer. So are they making an *Italian* movie?"

I remembered my father's advice and took it all back.

"No, I'm sorry, I got confused. I meant to say they're on vacation . . . we're on vacation . . . we're . . . all on an extended family vacation."

"Please step aside. Take your passports and follow us."

"Where are we going?"

"I'll tell you where you're not going, and that's inside this country."

We were escorted to the baggage claim area where our bags were sniffed at by a German shepherd.

"Must be the island cats," I joked to the officer. He arched his eyebrow at me.

"Our dogs are not trained to smell *cats*. You spent your whole summer in Italy and you are trying to tell me you have nothing to declare?"

I looked away. How did he know?

Our bags were opened and displayed for public shaming: prosciutto, mortadella, pecorino, parmigiano reggiano, pizza bianca—my favorite—from the oven in Campo de' Fiori in Rome, salami, and a huge wheel of caciocavallo cheese. Officers came by and shook their heads at us.

The other Italian passengers from the flight walked by our cured-meat and cheese exposition.

"Oh my God," a perky Louis Vuitton–covered woman I had spotted in business class exclaimed, covering her nose. "What are you, Sicilian immigrants from the 1800s? We're in LA and it's the twentieth century. International food markets exist, you know."

We were removed from the baggage claim area into a private security room surrounded with one-way mirrors. We sat there on the other side of the mirror, the side where they kept the bad people.

A Pakistani guy next to us cried, saying his family was in the arrivals hall and they wouldn't let him see them. He had to go back to Pakistan. The last time he'd seen his daughter was three years ago. When I tried to console him he looked at me hopefully and asked if I had kids. For some reason I replied yes, that I did.

My brother furrowed his brow. "What the fuck are you talking about?" he asked in Italian.

"Shut up," I replied and turned back to the Pakistani guy. "My daughter is here . . . with my husband."

The guy shook his head. It made him feel better.

A British man came in arguing with an officer. He was a writer and performance artist who wasn't being allowed to tour the United States on account of his "moral turpitude."

"I've been questioned for eight hours in the other room. I'm not going to tell you anything I haven't said before. It's all in the book. My whole life. You can read about it. It's a best seller in England . . . that's why I'm on tour here, you know."

He was tall and handsome with glazed brown eyes and full lips. He looked more like a rock star than a writer. I had heard about the book. It was a hit in Europe.

"Travelers who have been convicted of crimes such as controlled-substance violations are not admissible to our country."

"So why don't you kick out all your crack fiends? Just dump them in the ocean! I hear we're close to South Central. There's a lot of them there."

The writer turned to me. "I can't believe I even removed my bloody nail polish for them."

I shook my head to show support, but I was too tired to feel properly sorry for him.

The writer was escorted out the door to be put on a plane back to England.

The Pakistani guy looked at us and tapped his left temple with his index finger to suggest everyone in the room was crazy.

After hours in the interrogation room, surrounded by waves of strangers, screaming with papers in hand, I realized it wasn't the officers I was afraid of, nor their SS interrogation tactics, as my father called them. What I was really afraid of was being sent back. A year earlier I would have made any false statements in order to have a free pass back to Italy, but after that summer, I wasn't sure.

"Why the hell did you tell them you were on vacation?" my parents both screamed at us before saying hello, when we finally stepped into the arrivals hall.

"I don't know! You told me if all else failed to play the vacation card."

"Yes, but not when you mention my *work* here first!"

"I told you it was a bad idea," my brother interjected.

They grabbed our luggage and rushed us out. Neither of them hugged us. It was late afternoon. We'd been gone for two months.

My mother looked younger after a summer without us. She wore a fringed leather jacket and cowboy boots. Her tan was deep brown and golden, her hair short and spiky and platinum blond. She looked somehow Australian and also a bit like a python.

"Do you like it?" she asked, combing her fingers across her new chunky locks. "It's a Meg Ryan haircut. Very trendy right now."

I nodded absently, noticing her ivory-colored French manicured fingernails and that she was clasping a Starbucks iced tea.

She shook the ice in the cup impatiently as if she didn't have time to listen to my answer.

"What happened?" I asked. "How did you get us out of there?"

"Let's go, quickly, before they change their minds."

We sped down the hall, out the sliding doors toward the parking lot.

Los Angeles. We were back to the leaden sun. The familiar distant haze engulfed us. A feeling similar to the mirrored room we left behind, another no-man's-land.

Max was waiting for us inside our old Cadillac.

"Ooh la la, here's our little girl with the big mouth!" He hugged me, shaking his head in mock disapproval.

My parents rolled their eyes and got in. Over the summer they had installed a car phone, but it didn't work. Ettore now owned a lot of leather binders from Office Depot. They rested on the dashboard with credit card receipts sticking out.

On the ride home, the lapping sounds of the Mediterranean were zapped out of our ears, absorbed into a funnel that pulled out silence and poured in airplanes and choppers flying over Compton.

This was one of those times when the ambiguous nature of Italy's post-communist government-owned regimes came in handy. RAI, Italy's public-broadcasting company, had originally sponsored my father's visa. In typically Italian style, RAI was an *everything* medium: a national radio network, a television network, a cable channel, and a film production company. If you worked under its broad wings—I understood then why Italians called it Mamma RAI—you could be anything from a big-time film producer to a news anchor to a talk-show host. Max figured this ambiguity would be our way out, or rather our way back in. He showed up at the airport disguised as my father's lawyer—he had passed the bar exam and had been a practicing lawyer before venturing into film—and argued with the officer that the film my father was preparing was in fact a documentary for RAI, and therefore perfectly within the boundaries of his visa permit.

"So you're not working illegally?" I asked, relaxing into the rubbery backseat.

"Of course we are," my father answered.

Ettore's film production had taken over the house. Two fax machines beeped incessantly. Piles of papers and Post-its were stacked next to one another. The kitchen was littered with fast-food bags, leftovers, wrapped straws, and binders full of documents and photos. Max prepared a pitcher of sangria, blasting Phil Collins's "One More Night" from a new multidisc CD player, ignoring the chaos. He whistled to the rhythm of the cheesy song. Over the summer he had befriended Johnny Depp's agent, who invited my parents to the Viper Room regularly. They had gone to parties with Brad Pitt and met a group of actors from the movie *Dazed and Confused,* which was about to be released. Things were happening, they said.

"So Johnny Depp is going to be in your film?" I asked, excited.

Max poured me a glass of wine and fruit. "We're working on it, *chica.*"

My father put his hand on my shoulder. "Do you know that we are growing vegetables in the yard now?" He opened the fridge, pointing to bowls filled with fresh vegetables and fruits. "We have amazing tomatoes and zucchini. And you know *why* they grow so well?" He picked out an overgrown zucchini and held it between us like a powerful scepter.

"The sun?" I asked.

My father shook his head and threw the huge green thing back in the fridge.

"Compost," he said with a knowing grin. "Compost is

everything from lemon peel, to garlic cloves, to rotten cheese."
He pulled my brother and me closer to him. "You need to create a fertile terrain for things to come to fruition, kids. Johnny
Depp's agent is my lemon peel. The Viper Room is my garlic
clove, and the film Max and I are going to make is delicious rotten cheese. We are officially in the right milieu."

"So Johnny Depp is *not* going to be in your film, then?" my
brother concluded.

I kept walking around the house, amazed at how different
it looked. My father's office extended into the backyard, where
a workstation had been set up on the patio with a desk, a computer, and another phone.

"What's all this stuff?" I turned to my parents again.

"We didn't want to tell you over the phone because we
didn't want you to be worried and think it was worse than it is,"
my mother said.

"Worse than what?"

"We've started preproduction on the film and we're using
the house as a—"

"Production office," my father concluded with a professional tone.

"We have a crew of people working for us already and we
didn't know where to put them. We couldn't, you know . . ." Serena faltered.

"Afford an office," my father finished. "Yet. It's all going to
change when the money comes in. We might even move out of
the Valley."

"Move out of the Valley?" I gasped with a shiver of exhila-
ration. Now I was glad they'd stayed behind.

The hallways were lined with black-and-white portfolio pictures of important-looking yet obscure Hollywood actors. Next
to them were Post-its of their possible roles in Ettore's film.
Tamara Landkin: Grace? Ellen Studelli: Stephanie? *If These*

Walls Could Talk was the title of Ettore's movie, and it would be a psychological horror film, a *Poltergeist*-style ghost story inspired by the haunted Hotel Alexandria in downtown LA—one of the most prestigious venues in the city during the heyday of the motion-picture business, which had since turned into a low-income housing cluster of rooms and apartments. Shooting at the Alexandria was cheap, especially on the eleventh floor because the hotel owners believed it to be infested by ghosts and wanted nothing to do with it. That was where most of the paranormal activities took place, they said.

"It's actually completely haunted, which is great for the actors. Less work to get in character," my mother explained.

I entered the dining room. It was sealed off by a makeshift sliding door. On the other side were a bunch of suitcases and some furniture I recognized from Max's old house.

"This is where Max is storing his things," Serena announced timidly.

Max gave me a sly, melodramatic look. "*Lo siento, chica.* Just for now."

He slid through the door, whistling. My father pretended he just remembered something urgent and followed him out. My brother and I stayed, question marks in our eyes.

"He didn't have anywhere else to go!" Serena finally broke down. "He was evicted. His landlord was a real bastard, you know."

"What about Phil Collins? Isn't he his friend and neighbor? He has a mansion. Can't he stay with him?"

"It would look bad," Serena said with pride.

"When were you going to tell us this?"

"Aren't you happy?" she asked, her quivering lip ready to go off. "Max is fun to have around and Dad is finally going to make his American film. You should be happy. I don't understand why you can never just *be happy*."

Max, in a bathrobe, crossed the kitchen with a Dorito chip popping out of his mouth.

"We're deducting rent from his production fees," my mother explained.

"You're paying him to produce the film?"

"It's a co-production," my mother sighed. She seemed annoyed, like we were stupid for not understanding this thing that happened in Hollywood where people converted their homes into offices and gave out free rooms to producers.

"Dad gets the money from Italy and Max is going to get money here. Then they put the money together and we make the film. Once Max gets his money, he'll pay off production expenses and contribute with rent for his room here."

"So where does he sleep?" I asked.

Silence.

I dashed out of the dining room. My mother caught up to me, trying to delay the inevitable. I reached my bedroom. Serena leaned on the door to block me.

"It's temporary," she pleaded.

I pushed her aside and opened the door. My clothes had been stacked at the far end of my closet. My posters had been removed and folded onto my desk. An ashtray filled with Cuban cigars and joint butts sat on the windowsill. The yellowing walls were staled by smoke and the bed was covered in bundles of sweatpants and dirty emerald green silk boxers.

I let out a scream.

"Just until he finds a new place. It's easier if we're all in the same house."

"Where do I sleep?"

In my brother's room Serena had created a Eugenia corner with a desk, garage-sale lava lamp, and Nirvana poster.

"Cool lamp, right? When I saw it I thought of you right away."

I poked my brother's water bed with the tip of my shoe. It gurgled and moved in tiny waves.

"If you don't like it we'll put a real mattress on the floor for you. How does that sound?"

My brother shrugged his shoulders, looking at the wall. "I hate Nirvana."

13

I didn't wear Reebok Pumps to school that fall. I wore sandals and shorts and let my tanned legs be part of the scenery. I was equipped. I had my big anthology. I knew where the buildings were. I knew how to open my locker. I knew where to go for naps, where the holes in the fences were, and thanks to the freckled girl with the bouncing ponytail, I knew how to hop them. Arash's death left me unexpectedly confident, as if I were the heir to a very important secret. He left a space nobody was willing to fill and maybe because of this, everyone was a bit more tolerant. There was a truce—temporary but effective. I walked by the Persian tables on the upper quad. They had allowed Azar in. She waved rapidly but full of pride when I passed by—head still fuzzy and disproportionate but smiling. I felt the weight of Arash's absence still there on my shoulders, but I aligned with the others and pretended I too had turned a page because the more I pretended the more I felt like turning pages was easy.

I'd spent my summer reading from the American literature anthology and even though my English wasn't perfect, Mrs. Perks kept me in her class. I wasn't an excellent student. She was hard on me and was never sentimental, but I could tell she cared. She wore suits. She knew where Rome was. She'd been to Italy. Her breasts were real. She was perfect. Twice a week we met privately during lunch to go over the Italianisms in my essays. I started collecting books at yard sales and writing stories. When Simon came looking for me—wearing sandals with no socks now—I got rid of him fast because nothing about sex with him was appealing any longer. I was on my feet. It wasn't going to be that kind of year. I would try to get to college without his tutoring. Early in the summer the literary journal with the "Bad Love" theme to which I had submitted my essay about ugly men who didn't read—the one that got me suspended—published it. The editor said my piece had "reflected the contemporary attitude over the no-strings-attached lifestyle." They used the essay as a kind of decoration piece for the last page. It was printed in a tiny font and I was sure nobody had read it, but I didn't care. I felt encouraged for the first time. Henry was wrong: I didn't have to hide books to be accepted.

It wasn't just Arash's death that made the difference but also that enough time had passed since the riots. In the fall of 1993 the city had started to function again, the wound was beginning to heal. Anger against injustice had transformed into silent sorrow, a suffering acceptance that we were all in the same boat—no use fighting. Or maybe, as with any army, one had to know when it was time to withdraw the troops and care for the wounded in order to prepare for the next battle. After all the violence the city seemed to open up to its more benevolent nature—especially the flora and fauna. Elm trees with bulging roots cracked through the pavement of residential streets. Mountain lions climbed down from the canyons and walked stealthily toward the sea. Hawks circled the hills saluting mourners, reminding them of a life up high, away from bus stops brimming with homeless people, away from the LAPD and patrol helicopters. The city had been shocked by the Rodney King riots. Every corner had buzzed with the electric field of war zones and injustice. Everyone had been on the edge over spilled blood and burned buildings, but we'd entered a different stage of mourning now. After adrenaline came anger. After anger, pain. Then peace or the vanishing of something. Nature was the biological aftermath to the riots' mourning cycle, and it took precedence over everything else. Ivy grew quicker over the industrial buildings downtown. Polluted waterways cleansed themselves spontaneously. The Santa Monica pier became populated by more seagulls than humans. Seals and otters occupied the wood foundations below. You could feel the city's parameters changing. Its new essence was friendlier, part of an organic order of things. It was right, or at least it felt right. And I wanted to be part of it.

"Hey, I heard you give good head," a voice called to me as I lay in the shade of the magnolia tree in my new hiding place at school.

I propped myself up, the sun in my eyes. A blazing silhouette came into focus. A guy with a beanie and long hair stood in front of me. He kicked a hacky sack that landed on my legs. Chunks of his hair were twisted inside beaded hemp strings.

"What?" I asked defensively, throwing the hacky sack back at him.

"Wanna suck mine?"

"No."

I looked at him up close and realized I'd seen him before. Arash had pointed him out to me the day he briefed me on every group in school. He was Chris, Arash's pot dealer. I remembered Arash mentioning the fact that he'd grown up in some kind of hippie situation and had no social skills, hence the crack about my oral-sex abilities. Arash must have told him about us. He probably thought the guy was too much of an outcast for the news to get out.

"Well, do you at least want to come over to my house after school and listen to music, then?" he asked.

I felt a rush of longing for Arash, as if he were back in a

new form but with the same audacity and cockiness. I wanted to draw out the line that could connect me to him a little further, and so I said yes. The tacit agreement with my parents was that I was granted more freedom because Max had taken over my bedroom. I needed to get out of the house to obtain privacy, I explained. So far that had translated into uneventful strolls up and down the grids of the San Fernando Valley, but that day I was invited to experience the thrill of a different area code.

Chris lived in a funky collective of wooden cottages on a slope at the top of Topanga Canyon. The main house on the property had a panopticon-like presence and floor-to-ceiling windows overlooking a valley of oak trees. The smaller cottages below—creaking wood satellites to the master house—served as bedrooms for him and his twin sister. Between the main house and the cabins there was a kind of small amphitheater; the bricks on the edge had crumbled apart a bit, but the semicircular shape was intact. Chris hopped in the center of the miniature arena and let out a small scream. There was a specific point that generated an echo.

"You have to stand right here or it won't work."

Chris showed me to a little dent in the ground.

I screamed an "Oh" sound that bounced back to us. Chris said that when he and his sister were kids their father told them "echo" was a man who lived in the air and he only stayed alive if you screamed at him.

"We had to scream for so long every day because we were worried he'd die. It was his way of keeping us busy without having to play with us."

We both laughed. We heard the thump of a glass bottle falling to the floor in the balcony of the main house. Chris shoved me inside his cabin furtively and peeked out the window.

"Oh . . . It's just a bottle of beer that fell with the wind."

He kept an eye out toward the balcony.

"Are we not supposed to be here?" I asked.

"My dad doesn't allow us to have guests. He's at his studio now. He's a musician. Classic rock. Terrible shit."

The cottage was small and damp. Chris plugged in an electric heater with frayed wires. It smelled like a burned animal. He pulled out a box hidden beneath one of the floorboards, took out a bong, and loaded it with weed. There were spiderwebs on the ceiling and a branch of wild laurel had squeezed its way into the room through a cracked floorboard. There was a mattress in the corner, a guitar, a beanbag, and a pile of CDs and tapes stashed neatly under the window. Next to them was a framed picture of Neil Young. He was standing next to a younger man with long brown hair similar to Chris's. They wore slightly torn T-shirts and had big smiles on their faces. Both held beers. I noticed they were standing in the same echo spot where Chris and I just were. The amphitheater was brand-new, though, no chipped bricks. There were musical instruments in the background.

"This is here?" I asked.

Chris smiled. "A long time ago . . . That's my dad. He was a studio player for a couple of Neil Young's albums. They used to jam a bit out here. My twin sister and I would put on plays for them." He chuckled. "We asked for lots of money after we performed because Dad told us Neil was famous. To us he was just Neil." Chris turned the frame over and looked me in the eyes nervously. After his initial bold approach in school, he was now timid and didn't know what to do with himself. He kissed me abruptly. His lips didn't know when to part and when I didn't kiss him back, he pulled away and glanced nervously at his wrist to check the time. He offered me a bowl of his famed pot.

"Yes, let's get some air," I suggested. I took his sweaty palm and guided him out the door. We climbed up the slope, past the main house toward the top edge of the garden, and curled into a hammock that hung between two trees. We smoked in silence. Eucalyptus trees shot up behind the fence in the neighbor's yard.

Their silvery leaves hovered over us, releasing a minty scent that crawled into our nostrils. I loved that smell. I had begun to associate it with certain good parts of the city, the parts where the natural order of things wasn't just restored but was a constant, a steady state. A spongy green moss carpeted the bottom edge of a wooden fence. Stoned, I stared at its microcosm, noticing the minuscule strands that composed the whole. Each green crevice looked like a portal that could open into a magic world, funneling beings from the valley into the canyon, out to the sea on the other side.

This was Topanga, still and solemn and unscathed by the city. We had driven through that canyon coming back from the beach when our grandmother went topless and my parents were fined for nude sunbathing. I had felt peaceful inside the canyon's womb. She was there and had been for a long time. I felt welcomed in a place of rest. I smelled the new air and looked up. No Valley fog, but solid blue colors, rapacious birds soaring in the sky.

"I like being up here," I said. "The natives were right to call it 'the place above.'"

We swung lazily in the hammock. Chris crawled toward me and put his arm around my sun-warmed shoulders.

"That's what everyone here likes about it. Feels like you're on top of the world."

I nodded. I sensed time slipping off the edges of my body and it felt good.

"It makes sense that you'd like it," he continued. "Europeans settled here first. It reminded them of home. My sister and I used to sneak into the old celebrity holiday cottages in the mountains. Some have been rebuilt, but you can always tell when something belonged to a star. There's a different smell."

He shifted his position, keeping a vigilant eye out for what was happening in the main house below. I hooked onto the sparse roots crawling out of the earth and pulled the hammock

back toward the fence. A warm breeze began to blow behind
my neck and down my legs, pouring in from many directions
at the same time. It breathed on the corners of my eyes, electri-
fying my hair. I listened to the sounds of the canyon and felt,
for the first time, I had been granted access to that magic LA
feeling Max had tried to explain to us when we first arrived,
that ungraspable, comforting light: the luminous unseen. It was
what in Hollywood translated to a sudden stroke of luck, something divine and invisible that could heal you instantly from
pain, smog, and rejection. I was so hungry for it that I opened my
eyes wider, hoping I could extract its essence and store it inside
me, somewhere between the layers of my rubber suit. I pushed
the hammock against the fence. With every swing I inspected
parts of that luminosity and tried to bask in it. I smelled new air
and looked up at the blue sky. But the moment I tried to capture
that feeling, the light faded. Objects returned inside their contours and the luminous unseen was gone. "If you look too hard
it disappears," Max had said. And he was right.

I retracted into the earth and considered our positions. The
top of the hill pointed west, into the canyon and toward the
ocean, while the lower part and front of the main house faced
east over the Valley, creating an imaginary line with Woodland
Hills and the mall where nine months earlier Arash had been
shot. We were swinging between two worlds and Chris's house
was in the middle. The back façade was slanted upward inside
the canyon, high above the city, severed from the Valley, levitat-
ing toward "the place above," while the front aimed at the flat
roads of the San Fernando basin and the dim parking lot of
the Woodland Hills Mall. Echoes of gunshots reverberated in
the living room. The smell of butter-infused popcorn stunk
up the kitchen. The floor-to-ceiling windows were eyes, the
front door a gaping mouth, aghast in front of the spectacle of
blood. Inside Chris's house I heard silence followed by gun-

shots. Through the windows I saw Arash scramble on the floor, screaming for help.

"You don't gangbang? Well you do now," I said out loud, swinging us back out on the hammock.

Chris nuzzled into my neck. "What did you say?"

"You do now," I repeated.

It hit me then, with my fingers still clasped on the earthy roots, that I had not yet given myself the time to let those words sink in.

"It's what that guy told Arash before he shot him. I read it in the newspapers," I said. "You knew him, right? He told you about us?"

Chris shrugged his shoulders. "Don't think about that shit now," he said.

But I couldn't help myself. I turned my head away from the mall and the parking lot back toward the damp earth of Topanga Canyon. No guns, no cars would ever drive across these eucalyptus trees and I knew I wanted to stay here.

I turned my back to Chris and closed my eyes, lulled, unafraid to slip into unconsciousness. When I opened them again it was because someone was screaming in the house below. Chris wasn't in the hammock anymore. Through the back windows I could see into the living room. A long, warm copper ponytail passed by, swinging back and forth. I recognized the motion immediately. I knew who it was: the pale ghost I'd seen move through school doors and hallways, hopping over fences, the girl who taught me to look at the sun and never look back. Seeing her inside a house with nothing to jump over seemed odd. Even now when she stood leaning on the kitchen counter, I felt like some part of her still swayed.

The male voice kept yelling at Chris.

I saw him cower. A slightly hunchbacked man with a long graying beard, a red cap—scrawny ponytail escaping behind it like a rat's tail—entered the picture, hands in the air waving in discontent.

The girl, I now realized, was the twin sister Chris had been talking about. I scanned his face back in my mind to find similarities. He had no freckles, no striking green eyes. They didn't have the same life pulse inside them. She leaned in and touched the man's arm while he screamed. She wore elegant black pants and a tuxedo shirt. She looked different from how she did in school. The man interrupted his screaming to look at her. He pulled her toward him by her white shirt and kissed her cheek, giving her some sort of last-minute instruction I could not hear. She nodded at him and walked out.

I slid off the hammock and snuck back down the hill, following the girl at a safe distance. She darted ahead of me, floating down the driveway and over bushes. She crossed the main canyon road and ventured down a trail that led toward a creek, stooping over a few times to remove the wild thorns that kept clinging to her elegant trousers. When she did this, her swinging ponytail came undone and flopped against her back like a golden bridal veil. She reached the creek, sat on a rock in the middle of the water by a lavender bush, and lit a cigarette. I stayed behind on the trail, careful not to make the leaves crackle under my feet. Ribbons of smoke circled in and out of her auburn locks as the sun hit her face. Her freckles sparkled, part of the canyon's landscape. Her hair changed hue with every glimmer of light, reflecting the tones of the earth. I stayed there for the duration of her cigarette, so close I could hear every inhalation. I remained silent, immersed in the miraculous feeling of having found a treasure. If I picked a single ruby out of the chest, a pirate would come and snatch it all away. A car passed on the road above us and the girl turned her face up and saw me.

"Hey . . ." Her eyes softened. "What are you doing up here?"

I removed the last thorns from my shirt and reached her.

"I guess I was visiting your brother."

She rolled her eyes like she'd heard that line before.

I sat on the bank of the stream and lit a cigarette. I could not keep my eyes off her face.

"So did you figure it out?" she asked.

"What?"

"How to skip the broken fence?"

"I did. I practiced what you showed me."

"Good," she smiled. "I've seen you do it a few times, actually. With that guy."

"Thanks for teaching me the art of skipping," I said quickly, not wanting to imagine Arash's climbing feet.

"That's what I do." She exhaled in my face. "I skip out."

She leaned her head against her shoulder and examined me. Her freckled cheeks caught a ray of sun and turned red. She closed her eyes and rubbed her lips with a bay leaf she'd ripped from a wild strand growing by the water.

"If you're ever in trouble for drinking or smoking, these take the smell away. They are my remedy. What's yours?" she asked, propping herself up.

"I'm from Italy . . . Everyone drinks and smokes there."

"Everybody drinks and smokes here in Topanga also. I guess that's what my father is worried about."

"I saw him with your brother earlier, I think."

"Yes." She turned quiet. "That's what happens when we don't mop the house. Can you believe it? Who mops? Nobody mops. Do you mop?"

"No, I don't mop."

We both laughed.

"It's my dad's thing." She sighed. "He's a single parent so he treats us like housekeepers sometimes. He grew up in Montana. They really teach you to pull your own weight there. Sometimes I hate my mother for leaving just because of all the chores she left us with. Fucking raking leaves."

"Where is your mother?"

"She moved to Utah with a creep."

"Sorry."

"They funded a Christian café in their town. It's called the Holy Grail."

I laughed.

"Coffee beans from heaven," she added sarcastically, blowing out smoke. "She really lost it. I never want to visit her because she forces us to go to church. I hate church. I even got de-baptized last year. My mom doesn't know. She'd take it super personally."

"De-baptized?"

"Yes, I even have a certificate. You would have done the same thing if you were me. You probably don't get it if you're from Italy."

"I do come from the cradle of Christianity."

The girl put her cigarette out on the rock and stood up, blocking the sun, glazing over me with a bright but absent smile. She put a hand in the pocket of her pants and took a roll of cash out.

"I can't buy smokes in Topanga. My father checks in on me and knows the store's owner, so could you get me a pack before school?"

"That's too much for a pack of cigarettes," I replied.

"I make lots of money as a waitress. Half of it I give to my dad, the other half I never have time to spend. My brother and I are basically not allowed out of the house except for school and work. I'm going to the restaurant now. Hence the ridiculous clothes."

She pointed to her tuxedo shirt and patted her black pants. I put the shriveled money back in her palm.

"Save it for when you do get out. I'll be happy to buy you cigarettes."

We walked up the river as the afternoon sunlight filtered

through the trees. She hopped from rock to rock and I followed in her footsteps until we reached the foundations of a brightly lit restaurant overlooking the creek. She took out a small mirror and put lipstick on.

"Good for tips." She winked and straightened out her elegant trousers. We climbed up to the side of the restaurant. The humid terrain slipped under our feet, but she was agile and fast. Those minutes with her in that stream felt like shapes fitting into slots, like a giant game of *Tetris* placing us perfectly in each other's company.

New Age harp music played from loudspeakers on the restaurant's terrace, strings of round lightbulbs hung from tree branches creating a warm glow—a quiet, health-food atmosphere. The restaurant was being made ready for the evening.

The girl turned to me and extended her hand. Her name was Deva.

"Do you party?" she asked with a liquid sparkle in her eyes.

"What do you mean?"

She took a flyer for a rave from her pocket and handed it to me: a neon-yellow sun setting over a desert landscape. Fluorescent lettering announced what must have been the party of the century—or so it seemed from the looks of the crowds in the flyer's background.

"It's the moon tribe party in January. I really want to go."

"Well . . . we have time then." I winked at her.

"You can dance for three days in the middle of the desert. Nobody knows where you are and you don't either. It's so much fun." She sighed longingly.

It sounded like an agoraphobic nightmare to me.

"I can't wait," I said.

It was impossible to tell what it was that ailed her, but it was all right there in the way she looked through me, engaging only my contours, avoiding my eyes and trying to get close at the same time. I wanted to talk more, but she pulled her hair back up into a ponytail and trailed off through the restaurant's back door. She ran into the kitchen and jumped on a sous-chef who was assembling sprouts and tofu inside a bowl.

"What's up, José! Let's have a shot of tequila before we get to work!"

The door swung shut and I was left alone on the quiet terrace. Frogs croaked in the brook below. Shadows were setting in the canyon and the wooden cottages lit up.

The main house at Deva and Chris's place looked dark. Everything was silent now. I took a few steps on the birch in the yard. Chris's cabin door was cracked open, but when I tried to creep in, a hand tapped my shoulder. His father was behind me. A red, plump nose erupted out of his puffy beard. His cap was off now, revealing his thinning ponytail and receding hairline. He told me his children were not allowed to have friends over during the week. He had Deva's eyes, except hers were hypnotic and otherworldly, his beady and exact. They peered inside you and made their mind up fast.

Chris was inside the room on his mattress, drawing. He looked up at his father and straightened his back.

"I just came to get my backpack," I said.

His father waited in the doorway for me to get my bag and leave. While I gathered my things, he disappeared into Deva's cottage. She had locked the door, but he unscrewed the handle with a tool and pried it open, screaming about how she would get in trouble for locking her room and how rules were rules and he was sick of this shit.

I glanced down at Chris.

"I thought you were gone," he said in a whisper.

"I saw you fighting with him. I didn't want to interrupt."

He looked away, worried. "He wasn't supposed to be back

so early. We'll do it some other time, okay?" His eyes were gloomy with defeat.

"Yeah, for sure," I answered, but I didn't really believe that we would.

We heard the shuffling sound of plastic from Deva's cabin, things getting slammed to the floor. Chris's father rushed out with two full trash bags on his shoulders and marched to the bins at the end of the driveway.

"I told her I'd throw her shit out if she keeps this mess up! And I am. I'm throwing it all out," he proclaimed.

"Dad, come on," Chris tried to call after him, but the man didn't listen. He threw the bags in the bins and headed back up without looking at him.

"You gonna go or what?" he asked, realizing I was still in his way.

I grabbed my backpack and ran down the driveway without saying goodbye. I waited around the corner a few minutes, then returned to the bins. I picked up the trash bags with Deva's stuff and headed down the canyon toward the Valley.

The air was light and warm. The rocks on the side of the road turned gold in the afterglow of the day's end. Wind chimes tinkled. In a distant pasture I could hear the bells of a flock of sheep heading home for the night. What was this place where sheep grazed and time stopped, this canyon brimming with luminous corners and oak trees that looked like they'd been air-lifted from Tuscan hilltops? How was it possible that all this could exist above the Valley's sirens and boulevards and strip malls? My fingers buzzed with the same electricity that moved leaves in the wind. I was welcomed to the place above. I knew it would be my haven from the place below.

At home I dumped Deva's trash bags on my bed and examined my loot: fairy-princess dresses, silk tops, velvet bell-bottoms, and turquoise shirts woven with golden threads. I slept in them and what I couldn't wear I spread out on the bed to keep close to me. They smelled of incense and patchouli and essential oils I'd never encountered before. I wanted those new smells inside me so much that I tried not to let them end after each inhale. I trapped them in my nostrils and then inhaled some more. Every sniff was a trip to another place that didn't look like lava lamps and didn't smell like Max's cigars.

14

"**What the fuck** are you wearing?" Henry sneered at me, turning on his swivel chair, plastic wheels screeching against the floor.

"It's a fairy-princess dress," I replied, defensively.

"A fairy what?"

"Fairy-princess dress."

"More like a grandma's baby doll."

"It's Deva's."

"Who is that?"

He rolled the chair over to *Street Fighter*. He had carved out a pathway between the cash register and the video game so he would never have to get up from the chair.

I knocked him off his seat.

"Put double player on."

T. Hawk, the exiled Indian warrior, versus E. Honda, the sumo wrestler.

"So, who's this girl?" he asked again.

"Oh my God, Henry. She's amazing. You would love her. She's, like, the most beautiful girl I've ever seen."

"Oh yeah? Does she like handicapped men?"

"Shut up."

"What? Some women are kinky like that."

"You are not handicapped!"

"Dude, I'm missing an ear."

"Could be worse. You could be missing a leg."

"Not like I use these much. I'm always in this shitty store. Oh, you fucking cunt!" he screamed at the screen while my wrestler unleashed his hundred violent sumo hands move.

"I kicked your ass. And I haven't even played in two days! It's not like I practice constantly like you."

Since I'd been back from Italy I'd started to spend my afternoons at Henry's store playing *Street Fighter* on an arcade video game he had stolen from a doughnut store, smoking pot, and redecorating the shop. I was obsessed with Bargain Barn, a warehouse in Anaheim where furniture and clothes were sold by the pound. Bel Air sold rich people's leftovers while Anaheim collected the dreams of society's dropouts: desks from offices of failed businesses, corporate couches, synthetic orange armchairs from the seventies, and, since Disneyland was in the neighborhood, plenty of dated cartoon memorabilia. Once in a while a gem popped up: a Louis Vuitton handbag, a Chanel purse, or a velvet Valentino jacket.

I fixed up a set of glass cases for Henry's store. I baptized them with the switchblade knife from *Nekromantik* that Robert had given me on our first and last date. I also got a set of matching rust-colored velvet chairs and an antique two-tier paper cutter. I spent close to nothing to refurbish the store. It happened naturally. I started off bringing him pieces I thought might look good, then I began to stick around in the afternoons, unpacking boxes of vintage clothes, dividing garments into different categories and labeling them by color and style. "We have customers," Henry cheered one day after I sold a stack of moldy DeFranco Family records. And since that day they kept coming back. I reorganized stashes of old portfolio pictures that

Henry had never even leafed through and pulled out the ones of actresses who had made it. The real prizes were the portfolio images of stars before they were famous. We called them PFCs—pre-fame celebrities—and sold them for twenty dollars apiece. Familiar faces: Julia Roberts at seventeen, Meg Ryan at twenty, an awkward post-teen image of Diane Keaton—my favorite. She presided over the store, hanging above the counter like an Italian patron saint. I put a constellation of anonymous angels from the seventies and eighties around her: Nina Sanchez, Elodie Verve, Tania Beloved—the incredible names of those who never made it. I wanted them to have a shot too, if not in a film, at least in a store.

Henry paused the game and looked at me with pinched brows.

"So how did you meet this Deva girl? Weird fucking name anyway. Are her parents hippies or something?"

"Maybe. The house looks kind of hippie. Her dad is a rock musician with a biker beard, but he's super strict. Her mom lives in Utah and has a Christian coffee shop."

Henry moaned, "Gross."

"Have you ever been to Topanga?" I asked him. It was difficult to imagine Henry anywhere outside that store. "It's another world from the Valley. I want to live there."

"I don't know. It reminds me of *Twin Peaks*."

Henry lit himself another cigarette. I emptied the overflowing ashtray that was sitting on the dashboard and went back to play.

T. Hawk had floored me with his kicks.

"You asshole! I was dumping your disgusting ashtray!"

Henry butted me off the chair so he could go back to playing alone.

"Anyway, Topanga is, like, so not like *Twin Peaks*," I squealed.

Henry gave me a complacent smirk. "Did you just say two *likes* in the same sentence? You're starting to sound like a Valley girl, you know that?"

I blushed. I knew he was right.

"You're worse, an *Italian* Valley girl. You've invented a new LA subculture."

"Want some weed? It might make you feel better."

Cinderella looked at us with a glimmer of hope. Her tiara was off and her hair was down.

"I'd love to get stoned, man."

She scratched her scalp, relieved. The Disney goo on her face was coming apart.

We were in the smoking section at Disneyland and Cinderella had been crying and screaming at her boyfriend over the pay phone, telling him he was a motherfucker and she wished that he would die slowly.

Henry had agreed to take me to the Anaheim market with the promise that we could get stoned at Disneyland. I never imagined I'd end up getting high with Cinderella as well.

We took hits from Henry's metal pipe.

Cinderella held the smoke in, then exhaled with a cough.

"I'm so pissed." She sighed, drying tears from her eyes. "He fucked my best friend."

"I'm sorry," I said.

Some children walked by our designated area and got excited about seeing Cinderella. She got up with a grunt and walked toward them to pose for a photo.

She tried to smile benevolently—in character. The little girls looked up at her in awe, but the older ones could tell something was off. As soon as they moved on, her face returned to sullen and Cinderella sat back down next to us. She scratched her pale ankles aggressively. They were covered in blood and scratch marks.

"Fucking mosquitoes around here. I hate this place."

"So what are you originally? An actress?" Henry asked, sneaking another hit off his pipe.

She raised her eyebrow at him. "Yeah . . ."

"Look, it's not like I thought I'd end up working in a thrift shop. But there's hope, right? We're still young."

Someone spoke back from the Dumbo-themed mini-golf course behind us.

"Not for you there ain't . . ."

A squeaky voice joined our conversation. It was Mickey Mouse. Or rather an undercover cop dressed as the Walt Disney character. He approached Henry and me with a badge and asked us to follow him. Marijuana was illegal and this was a family-oriented park.

We looked at Cinderella, hoping she would intervene, but she betrayed us.

"I'm sorry, Mickey. I didn't realize they were smoking or I would have tried to stop them myself."

"She fucking smoked too!" Henry pulled away from Mickey's grasp.

"Sure she did. Now please stop resisting or I'll have to handcuff you," said the mouse.

Henry turned to Cinderella and growled. He spat on the floor by her plastic glass slipper and told her he hoped all her boyfriends for the rest of her life would fuck her best friends for the rest of their lives.

We were guided through a series of underground corridors to Disneyland's detox rooms, also known as the Mickey jails. We were to sit in silence until the effects of the drugs wore off. The rooms were mostly populated by teenagers on hallucinogenic drugs. Henry and I both got tickets and were not allowed to drive back home. On top of that I was a minor and needed someone to sign for me. It couldn't be my parents. There was no way they would pick me up in Anaheim. I could already hear the deportation monologue on my father's lips, how I should have been more careful, how his film was on the line. When he talked about his work now he put on a serious tone and threw around big terms: the business, majors, above-the-line expenses. He had accumulated an armory of new expressions we were required to respect. When we didn't, he lost his temper or sulked, reiterating that if we wanted things to work we had to be in them together as a family. And I wanted things to work.

Henry's mother, Phoebe, pulled in to the Disneyland park-ing lot in a boxy white Buick. It made a rattling sound and bounced from left to right on its tires. I knew she was big, but I always thought Henry was exaggerating when he said she was obese. He wasn't. He helped her out of the car. She wore a pink see-through tank top and her hair, what there was of it, was up in a ruffled bun held together by a faded gold scrunchie. Below the tank top she wore a pair of silk trousers that created a floppy mount above her pubic area and Spanish-style espadrilles. Somewhere underneath the folds of her arms were the traces of a woman of style. She had been beautiful. I knew it from looking at her and from the photos I saw at the store. But her entire persona was afflicted with years of drugging, drinking, and bingeing. Her thin, meatless lips were painted with coral-orange lipstick that squished outside their contour, making her look a bit like a demented bag lady.

I expected a reproach. I waited for a snarky comment, but the moment she stepped out of the car, she smiled to invis-ible crowds, paid my fine, and shook the Mickey policeman's hand.

"Thank you for your work," she said agreeably, avoiding

any reference to the reasons we had been kicked out in the first place. It was a simple procedure, a bureaucratic trifle that need not be judged.

We left Henry's car in the Disneyland parking lot and got in the back of Phoebe's Buick.

She came inside and released a fatigued sound when her butt hit the seat. She turned to me.

"So you must be Eugenia, the girl Henry's been telling me about."

"I am. Thank you for picking us . . . *me* . . . up. I know it's a very long drive and I'm so sorry about—"

She cut me off with a wave of her hand.

"And you're from Italy. I love Italy!"

"Oh, you've been?"

I looked at Henry to see his reaction. He had never mentioned any travel in his life. He had never told of his mother doing anything except for shooting up drugs, eating, and hoarding.

"Oh yes. *Arivedershi Roma!* Do people still dance in the streets?"

I told her yes that they did, even though I had never seen anyone dance in the streets because what happened in the streets was mostly honking and cursing. On our ride back she talked about a man named Aldo who was "just so Italian" and lived in via del Moro in Trastevere. He'd given her a taste of the real dolce vita. She told us about a tavern where she drank and sang and danced on tables, about how all the men loved her because Italian women were good for cooking and raising children but not for dancing on tables. Only American women did that because they were freer.

"I was the *only* woman in Rome dancing on tables," Phoebe declared, and Henry grumbled because that was just another piece of information about his mother's youth he never knew, another corner of her life that had not included him.

"Hey Mom, where did you put the cigarettes?" he asked, trying to change the subject.

Inside the car we were worlds away from any dolce vita: trash bags filled with junk, soggy fries, half-open packets of ketchup, and empty extra-large soda cups.

"Do they still make saltimbocca? Is that what that dish is called?"

"Yes, of course . . . It's a traditional Roman dish."

"Why would you care, all you eat is burgers and fries," Henry said.

"Oh Henry, will you just shut up?" Phoebe snapped. She opened her vowels wide when she called her son's name, making it sound like a complaint. "Oh, I love those. What's in those? Is it beef?"

"Veal. With prosciutto and sage."

"That's right, sage. *La salvia.* Oh my god how I loved those saltimbocca. Do you know how to make them?"

"Every Roman does. You could"—I looked at Henry to check if I was crossing a line, but he refused to participate in the conversation—"you could come over and I could make some for you if you'd like." I offered this as a way to thank her for the ride.

"That would make me so happy." She sighed nostalgically.

Henry tapped his finger on the window nervously. "Where are my cigarettes, Mom?"

Phoebe ignored him. She started to hum an Italian song she vaguely remembered.

"Fuck, Mom. Where did you put my smokes? It's gross in here," he whined abrasively. "Pull over, won't you?"

Phoebe groaned. She slowed down and pulled over onto the shoulder like she knew what was coming. Henry darted out and around to the back door. He took out a McDonald's paper bag and started filling it with the scattered litter on the floor by my feet. The wind blowing on the freeway flipped his long hair, uncovering his missing ear as he scoured the car for garbage. He packed the bag with trash and food debris and threw everything over the emergency lane and got back in the car.

"This car is disgusting. Let's go."

Phoebe took off with no mention of the litter left behind. That's when I got it. I understood that getting Phoebe out of her den was a big deal—not only for her but for Henry as well. He wasn't proud of his mother. He wasn't happy when he spoke to her or saw her. She shot up drugs, drank, and smoked heavily throughout her pregnancy and that was the reason Henry's ear was missing, why sarcasm always coated his words. He had fought one big battle as a child and that was the one to keep his ear. The battle was lost and there was no use fighting other, less important battles after it. He had been through hospitals, surgery, infections, and years of antibiotics. Treating microtia required the coordinated efforts of a plastic surgeon and an ear surgeon. His mother's insurance would not cover all that because her addictions were considered preexisting conditions. So medical procedures were interrupted midway, doctors changed according to policies, and what should have been a normal ear disorder ended up evolving into a case severe enough to require partial amputation.

"In America it's easier to cut things off when they don't work," Henry had told me one day.

Homeless people on methamphetamines chewed their hands to the bones. When they got infected, they went to hospitals and doctors cut them off. Nurses put them in plastic bags, then tossed them out. Nothing was done to reconstruct the faces and limbs of those who could not afford it. You had to find a way to live without your missing body parts, limping through life, trying to reduce pain with chemicals and home remedies. Broken people learned not to ask for help. They lived with their digitless hands and busted knees and missing ears and certainly didn't call their parents during emergencies. They did not ask the very people who took their ears away to come and make things better.

But Henry did that day, and for that I was grateful.

We stayed quiet for the rest of the ride. When they dropped me off in front of my house, I gave Phoebe a hug through the driver's window and made a date for our saltimbocca dinner. I promised.

15

The yellow bus that drove across Topanga Canyon to the Pacific Coast Highway was almost empty. I felt a weight lift off my chest as we started climbing into the mountain. The Valley clouds cleared, pierced by oblique strands of sunlight that illuminated grasslands where sheep grazed. Deva put her feet up in front of her and looked out the window, biting her fingernails. They were painted black, but the polish had scraped off. She had a small cast around her elbow. She told me she fell in the woods. At her feet was a duffel bag filled with the clothes her father had thrown out—washed, ironed, and folded in neat stacks.

"You didn't lose them," I told her when I handed them over during lunch that day. I'd waited two weeks to see her again. She hadn't been in school. I rehearsed the line at home and imagined a series of responses, but Deva smiled as soon as she saw me. From the expression on her face I could have sworn she was also counting the days before seeing me again. She hugged me and invited me to Topanga in the afternoon. Her bones were thin like a chicken's. I was afraid they would snap. When I hugged her back I looked at the school grounds behind her— the courtyard and cafeteria, the corner with the small magnolia tree where I sunbathed, the cheerleader squad practicing for the pep rally on the football field. Everything seemed suddenly distant and shapeless. Students were dark figurines moving on the horizon. Harmless.

We stepped off the bus in front of the canyon's country store. It had rained. The weather system was different in Topanga. I filled my lungs with the cool, clean air. On the store's corkboard, local announcements and psychedelic-themed flyers promoting energy healings and crystal clearings flapped in the wind. A surfer dude bought us a six-pack of Mickey's malt liquor. We didn't have a plan, but we had a whole afternoon ahead of us. The canyon's oaks, walnut trees, and callistemons muffled the traffic noise that rose from the bottom of the mountain. They trapped it inside invisible sacs and distributed it across the hills. They were the guardians of that stillness. Things were kept safe in this remote cocoon—secrets, sounds, people. The outside world would not trickle in.

I followed Deva down a winding country road lined with crumbling cottages. We crossed an ascending dirt path through a patch of oak trees. The sun penetrated openings in the woods. It wasn't the usual Los Angeles sun, that overbearing pinnacle of light and heat that took everything in. It was different. It seemed to originate from the earth and moved up tree branches like scattered paint. We were part of a new ecosystem with its own rules.

The road dried out as we moved past the forested area. The earth beneath our feet turned golden red. Deva kept walking ahead of me and did not say a word. I followed diligently, going back and forth in my mind about whether I would seem cooler if I spoke or remained quiet. I chose silence. Deva did not appear to be thinking at all. She moved up the hill with an unfocused gaze. She probably didn't even realize we were quiet, that it might be awkward, that if we were to try and become friends, there were rules. We were supposed to talk about bands and experiences, boys, families, parties, other friends. But none of those things came to her mind and I held back from bringing in my own stories. I focused on her lips, trying to gauge if they were on the verge of emitting sound, but she used them only to taste a piece of pine pitch she'd scraped off a tree. She sucked on it, then handed me some.

"Try. It's like syrup." She smiled.

I put the chunk of dried sap in my mouth. It tasted like caramel. We walked farther on the dirt path and the landscape cleared. Trees became sparse, leaving space for desert plants— dry shrubs and wild sage bushes. Red rocks and boulders climbed to the top of a mountain. We were in a canyon within another canyon. A rocky desert rose in the middle of the hills and suddenly Los Angeles became visible from all sides: the dreamy, distant ocean; the valleys, hills, and desert plains as far as the eye could see. The rustic farmhouses in the area were unfenced and unlocked, their yards continuations of the canyon's soil. It was more like a communal garden. Open gates, open doors, open windows. Chickens running onto the dirt path. Lazy dogs on strolls without leashes. I was happy to be there.

"Should we buy some pot?" Deva asked as we ventured toward a cluster of multicolored trailer homes and cabins stacked next to one another. A purple Victorian manor towered above them. We were in a commune. A tanned gray-haired woman with bloodshot eyes and messy hair came out from the manor.

"Are you here for the *scream* therapy session?" She greeted us with a foreign accent and a sarcastic smirk.

"Hi, Heide. No. We just want to say hi to Bob," Deva replied.

"You are here for root chakra *unblocking* session?" the woman asked, sneering.

"We're here to visit Bob," Deva stated again.

Heide took a swig from an iron flask and growled, "What do you want from him?"

"We are just here to say a quick hello—"

"The last time a girl came for a 'quick hello' he got her pregnant."

"I'm sorry." Deva frowned. "But it wasn't me."

"Bob's in the yoga room," the woman finally said. "If you find him tell him he's an asshole. Tell him I didn't bring Brunhilda to school today because it was his turn."

She staggered away cussing in Dutch.

A barefoot man with a roll of toilet paper in his hand came out of an outdoor toilet and smiled at us.

"Right on, sisters," he said, and walked away.

The commune's sewers were open air and there was no escaping the smell. Deva took my hand and led me through the property. Some of the sheds had multicolored tin roofs. Hoses were linked to one another, creating an extended watering system for a few dying plants. Deva's hand was small inside mine. It was hard to imagine she could guide me through anything.

"Very peace and love, that Heide, right?"

I giggled.

"She smokes too much pot and gets paranoid."

The yoga cottage had a bamboo ceiling and a dirt floor with mats rolled out next to a gong and a broken beehive. A man in ragged patchwork overalls and long dreadlocks that were desperately hanging on to his balding skull lay on the ground in a fetal position—hands tucked under his belly.

"Fuck you, *Mom*! Fuck *you*, Mom! *Fuck* you, Mom! You're *not* my mom! *You* are not my mom! You are not my *mom*!" he screamed.

Deva glanced over and whispered in my ear, "He was adopted."

She turned to him and cleared her throat so he would notice us. "Hi Bob. Is this a bad time?"

Bob rolled out of his fetal position and looked up. His face was bright red and he was drenched in sweat. Snot poured out his nose. He seemed happy to see us.

"Deva!"

Beneath the overalls he was bare-chested except for bead

necklaces and body hair. He wiped his dirty hands on his knees.

"I'm sorry, sisters . . . I was just doing some screaming. Getting out some mother stuff, you know. Heide's been driving me nuts and it's always related: wife stuff, mother stuff. It's all the same."

"She seemed pretty upset. Said to tell you you're an asshole," Deva ventured, turning to me for support.

"Yes. Definitely upset," I added. "It was your turn to bring Brunhilda to school."

The veins on Bob's forehead began to pulsate again with rage.

"She's just jealous because I get more—" He made a raspberry sound with his lips and did a freestyle dance to shake anger off his legs. "Well I've been luckier in our open-relationship deal. It's because I'm friendlier and better-looking."

Whether he was better-looking was questionable. Certainly friendlier.

"Thing is, I don't think she knows about the open-relationship part of it," Deva said.

Bob let out a full-bodied laugh and opened his arms wide. He wrapped himself around Deva's small torso with an intense hug and hummed.

"Mmmm. Good to see you, soul sister."

Deva laughed awkwardly, muffled by his embrace.

Bob turned to me as she made her way out of his arms.

"This is Eugenia, my Italian friend from school."

"Italian? Wow, that's far-out. What brings you out here?"

"Umm . . . my parents."

"Whoa! Crazy."

His reaction puzzled me. He seemed baffled, as if I had just told him I was a wandering orphan. Or maybe that would have surprised him less.

"Yeah I know. Crazy." I went along with it.

"It's awesome to meet you." He sighed, staring into my eyes, trying to gauge the amount of past lives we had shared. Then he hugged me tight and I was enveloped by a potent aroma of sage and armpits. One of his bejeweled dreadlocks pushed into my mouth. It tasted bitter.

"Mmmm." He sighed again, stroking my back. "You're an old soul, I can tell."

I let out an awkward giggle and looked over at Deva, who rolled her eyes, signaling that I shouldn't mind him.

"I guess I am . . . from ancient Rome."

"That's right, man. The fucking Otto-Roman Empire."

Deva didn't flinch, so I didn't correct him.

Bob was the founder of the commune—one of the longest-standing co-op experiments in Topanga. His place had been around since the seventies. Originally it had been a kind of play-ground for Deva and her twin brother. Their father was always hanging out there, but when the kids grew up he had a falling-out with Bob and stopped coming around. Not that it mattered. "Everyone has their journey," Bob explained. At his commune people came and went. Everyone brought with them a learn-ing experience and left anything from musical instruments to spaceship installations to "their virginity." Bob roared laughing when he said that.

We walked back to the purple "mother house." It looked like a lurid squat with mattresses on the floor. The dining-room window opened onto a terrace that was held together by a mud-and-cement paste. A baby-elephant-size statue of Ganesh with a giant crystal in his lap overlooked the commune grounds below. Rusty bicycles, Buddha and Saint Francis statues, and generators spread out to the far end of the terrace. The back wall was decorated with Osho meditation posters and a psychedelic mural of a baby emerging from an alien's womb.

"This is the children's play area," Bob explained.

He offered us hot chai, then packed a bubbler pipe with weed.

"Are you still working with your dad?" he asked Deva, exhaling in her face.

She looked away and shrugged her shoulders. "On and off on music stuff."

Bob nodded his head like an old sage. "So much anger in his heart . . ."

Deva sipped on her tea and didn't reply.

"He should come and do some screaming. I'd rather him scream in a safe place than at home with you—"

Deva's neck burst into red patches. "We came to get weed," she cut him short, then batted her eyelashes. "Can I get some of that Vicodin too? It helps with the pain."

She pointed to the cast around her elbow.

"It's your second cast this year. You need to start watching your step, you skinny girl, or you'll crack all your bones," Bob said. He furrowed his brow and went to a cabinet on the terrace. He opened a drawer and extracted pills and weed. Deva snatched them from his hand, gave him a crumpled twenty-dollar bill, and kissed his cheek.

In that moment a little girl with dirty hair and wearing an extra-large T-shirt covered in paint peeked her head out the kitchen window.

"Da-ad!" she whined. "I'm hungry. There's nothing to eat."

"It was Mom's grocery day. She was supposed to go to the farmers' market. We have to get food for the main house!"

"She said you had funny friendships with the fruit sellers and she doesn't want to go. She said to tell you."

We left father and daughter to their arguing and took off through the sheds. The commune thinned out as we headed into the woods, the shiny tin homes disappearing behind us. We entered the forest and headed down to the opposite bank of a small stream. A string of Christmas lights hung between oak branches. They turned on and off like summer fireflies. It was suddenly warm again after the cool sunset moment. The sea breeze stopped blowing and everything ceased from its day's work. The riverbank was fringed with tangled blackberry shrubs that blocked our path, but Deva pushed them away until we reached an open meadow. In the middle of the tall grass stood an isolated stone cabin with an outdoor bathtub and firewood stacked by its side.

It was Bob's eco-cabin, Deva explained. He rented it to European tourists who wanted to live like hippies. "You get to sleep with mice in darkness and have to pay for it too." She laughed. We leaned against the door and went inside. There was a table with one leg shorter than the others; bookshelves stacked with canned food, wine, and meditation manuals; a cot and a ladder to an upper-level bed area. I pulled a bottle of cheap Merlot from the shelf. We opened a pack of Doritos and drank gulps of wine.

"Gross!" Deva laughed, spitting out the last sip. Outside we lit candles and filled up the bathtub. The air was crisp. Creatures scuttled through the woods, but we were not afraid because we were already drunk and Deva was a country girl from Topanga who knew how to battle beasts, she said. She took off her sweatshirt and the thin cotton tank top beneath it. Her breasts were small and covered in freckles like the rest of her body. Her nipples were hard and bright red like small apples. I took my clothes off too, revealing my summer tan and brown breasts. She looked at them.

"Nudist," she said. "How scandalous."

We left our underwear on and dipped our toes in the hot water, shivering and giggling at the unlikely domestic scene. A normal bathtub in the middle of a field. We lowered ourselves gingerly in the boiling water, screamed *ouch* at our burning asses.

Deva moved her cast around the tub expertly like she was

used to a permanent disability, accustomed to working around something that was broken or bruised.

"What if we get caught?" I asked.

"Bob only wishes. What would you do if you were a balding fifty-year-old dude with a crazy wife and you found two beautiful naked girls in a bathtub in the middle of a field?"

"I guess you're right."

"He's a character, Bob, huh? He's been here since forever. He gets all kinds of chic lady clients from Hollywood to do treatments with him. That's why Heide is jealous."

"What kind of treatments?"

"Scream therapy, laugh therapy, whatever therapy."

Deva cackled, took a big sip of wine, then reached for the plastic bag with the Vicodin pills in the back pocket of her jeans.

She took out three and handed me one. She chugged the pills with the wine and lowered her head into the water.

I leaned back and looked up at the sky. It was pitch-black now and filled with stars, not the fuzzy ones from the Valley— the ones I'd seen with Arash, which were trying so hard to shine through the pollution—but real, sparkling stars like the ones from cartoons, from a time when things were better in the world. I turned the faucet on with my toes. The trickling sound contained us, creating an illusion of privacy. Our legs touched under the hot water. Deva's makeup was smudged. She stared into space. I saw her leave her body a little at a time from the wine and pills until she was gone.

"We're in the middle of nature," she slurred.

"In a field," I tried to slur back, but I was too sober and she was so far away already.

I drank more wine, trying to catch up.

Deva laughed, abandoning herself to the wave that was taking her over. She seemed to want to hop on any current that took her away from the present moment—even if the present moment was perfectly fine.

My stomach growled. I needed food. I lifted my body back up in the tub and suddenly remembered it was the night I'd invited Henry and his mother for saltimbocca. They were probably waiting for me at the house already. The thought of veal chunks made me instantly queasy and when the Vicodin finally kicked in, my body started to go numb and I let the thought drown.

We stayed there, half asleep from Vicodin, feeling our bodies move in waves. Our legs entwined, toes dripping outside the tub's edge and slipping back in when they got too cold. Time passed. We added more hot water, mumbling, forgetting what we had just said. The only thing that kept us on earth was the stars above, reminding us we were beneath them and therefore, by force of gravity, on the ground. Everything inside me turned warm and fuzzy. When Deva spoke, she leaned forward and her body twisted in a beautiful spiral. The candlelight made her face soft, but when she laughed, a strange presence shadowed her features.

16

In November my father announced that I would be taking time off school. "We need help on set. In the wardrobe department. Your kind of thing," he said.

"What about classes?"

"It's okay. Max said it's extracurricular. Colleges like it when students show interest in other things."

"I think it's only extracurricular if you do it after school."

"They'll never know the difference. When did you become so uptight?"

My father was hunched over his long oak desk, trying to fix the rental camera they were using to film the auditions. He raised his eyebrows and glanced at a bulky screenplay by his elbow, then picked it up and dropped it in my hands.

"We're shooting on Monday. We're missing a bunch of outfits. Read it, cross-check the actors' sizes, find the rest."

He stuck his nose back into the camera. The doorbell rang twice. Actors paced around every room, memorizing lines. Some sat in front of the electric fireplace in the living room, staring at the modest flames. Before transforming our house into a production office, my father remembered my grandmother's last words of advice at the airport on her way back to

Rome: "There is always a fake fire burning at the Forresters' and they're the richest family in LA. Don't forget to get an electric fireplace."

Phones kept ringing, but nobody picked up. Max circled the backyard screaming in Spanish on a portable phone.

"What's wrong?" I asked.

"Absolutely nothing." My father smiled.

"Why is Max screaming?"

"His money was held up, but it's fine. We've mortgaged our house in Rome." He finally lifted his eyes to meet mine. "Everything is under control."

"What do you mean, you mortgaged our house in Rome?"

The actors all stopped mumbling and looked at me.

My father put a hand over my mouth to hush me. He sprung open the door to the backyard and dragged me outside, the broken camera dangling from his fingertips.

"Could you not talk like that in front of the *actors*? You're scaring them! Max's money is on its way. As soon as it clears he'll pay back the bank, and we'll pay off the mortgage on our house in Rome."

We stepped back inside. My mother passed in front of us with a tray of homemade biscotti and espressos for the actors. She winked at me and said there was a surprise waiting for me on my bed.

On my way there, I noticed a pile of loose mail on the floor by the front door. There was a letter for me from the University of Southern California. It was written and signed by the head of the Literature Department saying they had read and enjoyed my essay in the "Bad Sex" issue of the literary journal and invited me to consider their creative writing program. They strongly encouraged me to apply the following year, the letter said. It was the first time anyone "strongly encouraged" me to do anything. I folded the letter and hid it inside a drawer in a closet where nobody would find it.

———

In our bedroom my brother stood behind a camera filming an actress with crispy hair that looked like a wig.

"I don't understand what I'm supposed to *feel*," the woman said.

"You are supposed to feel like you feel when you want to leave a place to go back home. You worry it *might* be haunted, but you're not terrified *yet*."

"Look, honey, if I feel a place is haunted, I cry."

My brother shrugged his shoulders. "Okay, fine. Cry."

The woman repeated her lines with emphasis and burst into tears—a woman of fifty taking directions from a thirteen-year-old kid. In a corner of the room, a male figure hunched inside my wardrobe, rummaging through my clothes. I recognized the skinny legs. It was Henry.

"What are you doing here?"

"I work here," he replied in a passive-aggressive tone.

"You *work* here? Since when?"

"Since you flaked on me and never showed up at the saltimbocca dinner you organized for my mom. By the way, she was seriously hurt. She wants to start cooking classes now. It's hell at home. Thanks."

"I'm sorry I spaced on dinner. I called you. You never—"

"You called me, yes. Three days after we came to your house."

"Hey, hey! Can you guys take this somewhere else? I'm trying to get in character," the actress with the fried hair butted in.

Henry crawled out of my wardrobe, grabbed me by the elbow, and walked me out of the bedroom and into the bathroom.

He pushed me against the shower door.

"You can't do that to me," he snapped.

I had never seen him angry. I had never seen him care about anything.

"I'm sorry."

He calmed down. I removed his hand from my elbow, lit a cigarette, and closed the bathroom door behind us. It was the only place left in the house where one could have privacy.

"It would be nice to know what you were doing, going through my clothes."

"I'm working for your parents. I'm doing wardrobe for the film with you. We're using your stuff plus stuff from the store."

"My stuff? Who said you could use my stuff?"

The soporific smell of my mother's baked biscotti wafted under the bathroom door. Through the small window overlooking the backyard we could see my father and Max. They had fixed the camera and were now auditioning actors *en plein air.* The yard looked like an insane asylum, everyone walking in circles, talking to themselves.

"God, they're everywhere," I said. "In the living room, in the yard, in my bedroom! And now *you?* My parents have no boundaries. You shouldn't have accepted."

"Well, I did. So get over it. And by the way, you should get out of Topanga. Your clothes smell like cow shit."

He opened the bathroom door and stepped back out into the kitchen where my mother was getting ready to bake a second batch of sweets. They hugged.

"Biscotti?" she offered with a fifties housewife smile, identical to the one she put on for the Spam commercial in Rome.

"*Sì, grazie,* Mrs. Petri!"

"Call me Serena, please. And good job on your Italian!" She put on a maternal face and handed him a Tupperware container. "Cotoletta alla milanese for your mom!"

"Thanks, Serena. Say goodbye to Mr. Petri for me!"

Henry gave me a cold nod and stepped out through the back door.

"What?" my mother asked in an innocent tone, noticing my disbelief.

"What do you mean *what*? That's some surprise you were keeping from me."

"Oh, Henry? Yes . . . he's a sweetheart."

"Why is he working for you? You didn't even ask me if he could use my clothes."

Two actors passing through the kitchen perked up their ears. The word "working" scared them—or the idea that someone else would be working who wasn't them, did. My mother gave them a reassuring smile.

"We met him when you *flaked* on him. He told us about how you started to work at his store for fun. We all think that's great, by the way."

"Thanks."

"He seemed interested in Dad's film. So we offered him the job."

"Are you paying him?"

"Yes, of course! Seventy-five dollars a week."

"That's nothing! Why did he accept?"

"It's extracurricular."

"Henry's not even in school anymore."

"Well. We became friends. We like him. I promised to teach him and his mom Italian recipes." She blew on two biscotti and bit off their tips. "Yummy. My best ever."

Max came into the kitchen. He was on the portable phone again, arguing in Spanish.

"*¡Lo sabía! Esto no es posible! Hay que decirles a bajar el alquiler de la suite de Valentino!*"

"Get out!" I exploded at him.

"Don't scream!" my mother screamed.

"I should have stuck to writing song lyrics for rock stars. A much easier life," Max mumbled to himself and left, slamming the door behind him.

I wanted to run away but had nowhere to go, so I stepped back into the bathroom and closed the door. The truth was I'd stopped caring. I didn't want Henry's gloom lingering around me. How could he understand my Topanga days when he never even took his eyes off the screen of his arcade video game. Since I'd started hanging out with Deva, I wasn't interested in him or the store, or anything that didn't involve green pastures and communes. At home we only talked about Ettore's movie and the actors and whether Johnny Depp's agent had called. Max drifted from room to room leaving a wake of dirty plates and ashtrays. I heard him and my father laughing into the night, watching and studying horror films, but I was under a new spell. Topanga was like a force, a magnet that pulled me out of my bedroom, out of my classrooms. It was a new version of the Sicilian island, a place where I could get in touch with something primal. When I wasn't in the canyon, I was thinking about the canyon, and when I was in the canyon, I spent hours watching hawks circle the sky, feeling the rough wind blow in from the foggy beaches below. I let it strike my face. I felt the sunlight slash through the clouds and scorch my head. I allowed that savage, hungry nature to beat me and took the beating joyfully. I felt stronger. I could take in unpredictable weather changes without tuning out. I learned to not be afraid of stray coyotes, spiders, snakes, and growling frogs penetrating my sleep and dreams.

After school Deva and I took the yellow bus to Topanga and hiked to the run-down cottage where we took long outdoor baths, soaking in boiling water and drinking cheap wine. On weekends I waited for her to sneak out and meet me at the end of her driveway. We cruised the canyon at night. I returned home on an early-morning bus while my parents were still sleeping, and collapsed in bed, happy. The good nights were the ones when we walked under huge moons, immersed in nature, when the canyon was quiet and beautiful. We hid in the commune shrubs and spied on Bob and his scream sessions from the darkness. The bad nights were the ones when Deva's father overworked her or tried to lock her up. She sometimes had to take on extra shifts at the restaurant to help pay the bills. She came out of the restaurant completely drunk. She got high on Vicodin and felt like trashing things, breaking bottles in parking lots and stealing mail only to toss it out. I went along. No matter what she did, her warm laughter always sounded like a party. When I asked her exactly what she did for her father, she sighed and said something about his music and how that was a Topanga thing and I wouldn't understand. Kids weren't treated as kids there. All families were like that. There were days when working for him meant not showing up to school. I scowled, thinking how ridiculous that was, without admitting that my own father was asking me to do the same. Even though Deva occasionally complained, I understood there was some kind of canyon pact I was not grasping. That was the way things had to go there. Families were ancient clans who had each other's backs. They were a tribe and if I didn't understand their ways it was because I wasn't part of that tribe. Plus Deva's father was from Montana originally. He grew up with a big sky over his head and the sense of endless possibilities. He had raised twins alone. He knew work and grit and had dealt with bulls and ranches. He'd smelled success and failure, and throughout it all, he kept his children close to him. Sometimes there were grounding punishments and sometimes there were days when Deva just disappeared, but I rarely got her to talk about those. It made her nervous and angry when I asked too many questions. She was unpredictable. One moment violently playful, the next withdrawn and absent. She rashly diminished and increased the distance between us with nothing more than a flicker of the eye. You never knew which persona would appear, but I learned to navigate the abrupt mood swings. And it was always worth it because when I came back to Van Nuys after our adventures, I felt like a queen descending from a magic mountain. Every day I spent up there, I felt my shoulders grow wider and my chest stronger. I wandered the suburban streets with new eyes. I was not alone anymore.

17

My father thought all he needed to make a film was hire trusted family members to be part of it. And we believed him. Ours would be an Italian family affair, just like the Coppolas. The reason why family-owned restaurants had the tastiest food was because it was in everyone's best interest to run a good business.

"Same with movies," Ettore said. "When it's all in the family, stealing from the owners is like stealing from yourself."

On the first day of filming, Timoteo, Henry, and I arrived in front of the Hotel Alexandria at seven a.m. to avoid rush-hour traffic. Henry had found a way to get his car back from the Disneyland parking lot and was in charge of driving my brother and me on set. We sidestepped the limp bodies of homeless people still asleep by the entrance. My mother was already in the main hall, flustered, walking around fidgeting with a walkie-talkie, screaming at my father in Italian.

"Non ti sento! Pronto! Non ti sento! Questo coso non funziona, cazzo!"

Henry and I were in charge of costumes and set design, though I barely communicated with him. Having him there felt as if another bedroom of mine, another secret school spot, another closet had been invaded by my parents' personalities, another small thing I'd discovered that wasn't my own any longer, so I kept away. A Hispanic woman from the beauty parlor on Spring Street came to help the hair-and-makeup girls—a couple of junkies from Portland who had a tendency to fall behind. I noticed one of them pass out in front of the mirror. I told my father I thought he should fire her because she was obviously still shooting up, but he said I was being cruel, that she was just tired from waking up early.

"Plus they're both working for almost free. We're not going to get anything better."

My mother was assistant to the director and also the caterer. My brother, the line producer, ran errands and tried to make people do things on time, or just do them. Max rounded up a team of film-school students to work in the sound and light departments. Four out of seven of the film's principal actors were working actors. The rest lived on the fringes of show business. There was a thin line that divided the two categories. At first glance you couldn't tell the difference. They all seemed adequate. They were in shape, had nose jobs, permanent eyeliner tattooed on their eyelids, and breast implants—just like all first-rate professionals. But there was something askew about them. You couldn't put your finger on it until you had a conversation and discovered they were waiters, high-school drama teachers, nutritionists, and voice coaches. Still, the star, Vanessa Peters, had appeared in numerous episodes of *Baywatch* as well as *Beverly Hills 90210*. She was a runner-up to Drew Barrymore for the lead in a big romantic comedy. She was quirky and had a sexy, hoarse voice. She came on set with an assistant who had alopecia and a devotional attitude. She owned a cell phone and had dated David Lynch.

My mother took over the abandoned kitchen next to the ballroom on the ground floor. She scrubbed the old stoves clean and cooked pasta for the crew's lunch every day. Actresses initially asked for "eggs on the side" on their carbonara dishes, but when she explained that pasta was a wholesome experience, everyone let go of their diets. "You can't segregate the tastes that make the magic happen. Accept the chaos; welcome the carbs." Crew members developed secret crushes on her because of the food she cooked.

"It tastes like the home I never had, Serena," one of the runners kept saying with a dreamy expression.

The director of photography, a stoner from Big Bear Mountain with bags under his eyes, sometimes failed to press Record. The sound guys occasionally forgot to mention the roaring helicopters disturbing the live recordings, and the script supervisor usually failed to notice when actors wore different outfits within the same scene, but my father was Zen and coated each disaster with a warm balm and a smile. He never got upset. The gods were finally on his side, he said. Things would fall into place because the film had a higher purpose, a life of its own. No matter what, this was it. He just knew it and led the way like a minister preaching about predestination and unquestionable success. His Italian-style superstitions were amplified by his equally Italian-style film quirks: As long as nobody wore purple and everyone kept a red plastic *corno* in their pocket, we'd be fine.

His dogmatic approach made us feel safe and our faith paid off. *Variety* ran an article about the film. The headline read: "Ancient Downtown Hotel Glory Revived by Independent Italo-American Production." Something had clicked. We were gaining visibility. At night my father practiced his American slang in front of *90210* reruns so he could communicate better with his actors.

He talked back to Dylan McKay. "What's up, *man*? *Ma-an*? You're not *cool*. You're not *cooool*. What's up, *dude*? *Dood? Dud?*"

The importance of *dude*.

He wanted to be affable and laid-back and changed his wardrobe to project this. He paid for my mother to keep up her Meg Ryan cut and platinum blond hair, started going to the gym at five a.m. before work, and wore white sneakers and ball caps.

"That's how they do it here. Have you ever seen Spielberg? He wears sweatpants for God's sake. Sweatpants and fleece jackets and caps. I don't know a director in Rome who would even get close to a fleece jacket. I threw my church shoes out. I don't want actors thinking I'm some kind of European snob. I want to be amiable and affable, dude."

The Hollywood crowd he'd met through Max over the summer read the news in *Variety* and began to stop by the set to take a look at the film. Johnny Depp liked the premise so much, he came down for a cameo as the bellboy in an elevator scene. My father and Max took a Polaroid with him inside the elevator. They were right. Courting his agent and creating "the necessary compost," as my father called it, was paying off.

The Hotel Alexandria had been magnificent and elegant during the silent-movie era, a witness to tap-dancing, smoky smiles, cupid lips, and brushed-out ringlets. Rudolph Valentino kept a suite there. Charlie Chaplin did improvisation sessions in the art deco lobby while Tom Mix rode in on his horse. It had been a wild place with luxurious rugs, marble columns, gold-leaf ceilings, and a mezzanine ballroom with a stained-glass skylight. Now it was a run-down dump. Only sinister tenants and ghosts lived here and this suddenly attracted film directors.

The Italian horror cult director Dario Argento flew in from Rome. The Weinstein brothers at Miramax, who loved everything Italian and produced and distributed independent and foreign films, called to congratulate Ettore personally, baffled that it had taken an outsider's eye to discover and revalue one of the city's most precious lost treasures. They offered to take a look at the film once it was complete with a view toward distribution. My father and Max were thrilled. Members of the Huston family began to drop by during lunch breaks. Someone had spread the word about my mother's Italian cooking and Mario Sorrenti, the rising-star fashion photographer who had shot Kate Moss in the Obsession campaign, picked the Alexandria as the location for his next shoot. The words whispered at home were "See? *Visto?* We made it!"

I had never seen my parents so happy and confident. It made me tentatively happy. Encouraged by the general enthusiasm around her cooking, my mother started giving demonstrations in the hotel ballroom. The Tiffany stained-glass skylight had remained intact, refracting a hazy light. The room appeared even bigger thanks to the large golden mirrors that stood stoically inside the arched nooks, rotting around the edges. The hair-and-makeup junkies who normally fed on the edible balls that floated in their Orbitz soft drinks—"You, like, can drink *and* eat at the same time. It's amazing," they said—were particularly happy about Serena's culinary crash courses. My mother looked at their purple bottles, horrified.

"*That* is not food."

She set up her workstation on a steel countertop, wrapped an apron around her hips, and pulled on her reading glasses. The frames pushed her hair down next to her eyes like blinders, but she kept going.

She put a pot of water on the stove, peeled garlic cloves for the soffritto, then cleared her throat.

"Don't *fry* the garlic! Don't *burn* the garlic, just let the oil take on some of its flavor."

Crew members stood by, looking at her with folded arms and tilted heads.

They loved Serena's bluntness and even started cussing in Italian to prove their solidarity to the family. "*Che cazzo!*" or "*Madonna mia!*" they invoked every time something failed to work, which was often. As long as they were eating or cooking, they didn't complain about late payments and disorganization. Unions were never contemplated. "SAG" was not uttered once.

Henry religiously attended my mother's classes. The more he loved my parents, the less I wanted to have anything to do with him. I went on long solitary walks downtown—the only place in Los Angeles that wasn't a mall or a boardwalk, where people used their feet. It smelled like smoking manholes and street food, like what a real city was supposed to smell like. Ethnic stores and pawnshops, Indians selling jewelry, Chinese offering household appliances, Thai food joints, Latino music stores pumping salsa onto the sidewalk with massive speakers. No cops, but plenty of homeless people and cholos smoking pot. Alleyways where crack was exchanged for money in the light of day. People walked around with their flimsy shopping bags like burned-out souls—zombie faces lurching forward and inhaling smog, remembering only faintly if at all the joys of a green pasture or a blue sea. Most downtown inhabitants had never even seen the Pacific Ocean. I walked next to them, closed my eyes, and tried to imagine that ancient wave of glamour. I could feel them there—dancers, producers, and actors with their tea parties, card games, and soirees. Charlie Chaplin, Greta Garbo, Mae West, and Rudolph Valentino chitchatting next to me on the sidewalks of Spring Street. I heard their ice cubes clink inside invisible cocktail glasses and smelled their smoke as it crawled out of ivory cigarette holders.

In a building that looked similar to the Alexandria, I discovered a whole floor where Vietnamese ladies, curved over sewing machines, manufactured women's tops with blossom and bamboo patterns in fine-ribbed weaves. A tailor welcomed me and asked if I was looking for something. I told him I was working on a film—my new business card for talking to store owners. His eyes lit up. He offered a series of silk and satin curtains for free.

"Bring them on set. See if you want more. All I ask is you mention our company in the credits."

I made promises I could not keep in exchange for beautiful fabrics. A whole new chapter of vintage finds opened up for me and I began to put aside things I thought Deva would like. I collected bat-sleeved shirts from a Bombay shop, vintage haute couture, cocktail dresses, and antique-lace lingerie from a vendor in the basement of another historic building. I hauled everything back to the Alexandria and began arranging and cataloguing my finds in the back of the changing room, the same way I'd done at Henry's store. My parents had fueled their passion and I was fueling mine. At home I opened my secret drawer and looked at the letter from the University of Southern California. *We strongly encourage you to apply.* I read the words over and over.

Sometimes I got carried away and returned late on set. It happened on the day when they were shooting in the Valentino apartments. The suite had been mentioned in the *Variety* article and everyone wanted to see it, so when I arrived in the dressing room to drop off my new purchases, no one was there. Max's muffled voice spoke on the phone in a small, adjacent room. When I passed in front of him, he gave me a look I'd never seen before, a kind of goofy embarrassed grin. He switched to Spanish and I kept on walking.

18

It rained hard, soaking the earth. No more ancient glories and haunted ballrooms for me. The canyon's life force drew me as I made my way back in. Terraced apple orchards, ancient olive trees, meadows, and crooked cottages with wind chimes and prisms refracting through dirty windows. Wooden homes guarded by statues of angels and saints. Bells with rainbow tassels hanging from their clappers. The earth was claylike and the smells coming from chimneys took me back to Tuscan winters and Christmas parties. Topanga was one of the few places where seasons felt real. I walked on the fringes of the main road, high on Vicodin. Deva had been on painkillers for days. She'd said she hurt her shoulder falling off the hammock in her yard, rolling down the garden knoll. Bob was right. She needed to pay more attention. She'd guzzled all her prescription meds and wanted more from him.

We were soaking when we arrived at the commune. Heide noticed us from the windows of the main house and walked out. She pointed ten fingers in our direction as if lightning rods and pestilent rats could spout out of them. She shooed us away with a witchy face, muttering incomprehensible Dutch words.

I wanted to leave, but Deva insisted on finding Bob and gave me her last two pills so I'd shut up.

We climbed back, avoiding the front façade of the main house so Heide would not see us. The open sewers around the barracks were overflowing. Strong winds had ripped the Tibetan flags off their poles and sent them flowing down the drains. The commune dwellers abandoned the flooded cottages, running into the main house to take shelter.

When we reached Bob's studio on top of the hill my Vicodin started to kick in and I relaxed. He was in a session so we had to wait outside in the rain. We perched under the tin roof, looking through the fogged-up windows like we'd done so many times before. He breathed on a naked woman's belly, pounding against her chest with open hands. The woman sprawled on the floor, copied his moves.

"I'm a worthy mother!" she howled.

"More!" Bob encouraged her, rolling over her body with sinuous motions.

She kept screaming about how good a mother she was, while we stared at her big bush in a daze. Mud was starting to pile behind the cottages. One of the smaller ones farther up the hill began to slide down. A young man came running out barefoot with an umbrella, a bongo drum, and a knapsack. Bob didn't interrupt the session, but kept looking at the window with a ghastly expression. It was raining so hard I thought the muddy ground might wash away the commune along with its screaming naked ladies and feral children.

When the session was over Bob rushed out and we startled him with our wet hair and our indifference to rain or mud. Deva gave him a belligerent hug, still far too laid-back considering the urgency of what was happening around us.

Bob glanced at me. "Are you serious? Look at yourselves."

But we insisted on Vicodin even though the place was coming apart. Alarmed naked young women ran, sliding down the muddy hills. We didn't care. We got what we wanted and took off in the storm.

Deva's face changed once she had her pills. It opened and fleshed out. We sledded down the muck laughing, shoes and pants squelching in mud. We chain-smoked wet cigarettes that kept going out and laughed at how loose our body parts felt. The stream we usually crossed to visit the bathtub cabin on the other side of the woods was a flowing river now. When we finally reached the main road, it was crowded with firefighters and police cars flashing their lights. They looked like fuzzy luminous gems. In front of us stood a colossal, oval-shaped rock. It sat firmly on the small highway with a majestic presence, twenty-five feet tall. The boulder had fallen from the mountain, blocking traffic and tearing up a section of the highway that connected the Valley to the Pacific Coast Highway. Commuters and visitors were off-limits until further notice. We were isolated from the rest of the city.

When we got to Deva's house, we spread bay leaves over our mouths and hair to hide the cigarette smoke, but the leaves were wet and didn't smell like much. The windows and doors to the main house were open, banging into the storm.

"Deva! Is that you?" her father called from inside. "Get up here!"

She pushed me inside her cabin and closed the door behind us, sharp and sober. She quickly straightened her hair and rubbed her fingers below her eye sockets for a fresher look. She advised me to go home and hurried out. I looked at the storm, trying to gauge whether it was possible to walk down the mountain and back to the Valley, but every crevice in the canyon was now a riverbed. I waited. The room was cold. The water level beneath the cabin was beginning to rise. Soon it would flow through the floorboards and under the bed. I kept my ears pointed toward the main house. Silence and rain, then Deva's father screamed about something I could not understand. A door slammed, resolute steps came down the hill, the crepitation of mulch under someone's feet.

Deva's cabin door swung open. Her father stood there with his hair pulled back in the usual meager ponytail, beady eyes striving to open wide. His beard had grown further and was now split down the middle. The hair on the center of his chin had not grown as fast as that on either side. His face was particularly red and his jeans dirty and frayed. His crow's-feet reached the top of his cheeks, but somehow that was not the thing you took in when you saw him. It was the eyes. They were a golden brown, so penetrating and bright they made him ageless.

"So Deva says she didn't go to work because you were up in the canyon and didn't know how to get back to the Valley?"

"Yes . . . there is a boulder in the way and traffic is blocked."

He took a breath, looked around the room inquisitively, then back at me. "I've seen you before, right?"

"I came here once. With Chris."

He walked toward the bedroom window and pushed it all the way shut. "Here, otherwise it'll get so humid your bones will ache," he said.

I smiled and thanked him.

"Well don't just stand there. It's cold in here. Come up to the house and call your parents!"

I followed him up the yard toward the main house. He moved slowly like a bison, undulating from side to side. Inside was just one big room lined with dusty record covers and Deva's father's rock music awards from the eighties. The albums had earthy mystical names like *Cosmic Sands, Vesuvius,* and *Vacant Voodoo.* One of the record covers read *Sarofeen and Smoke* and featured a bunch of cool-looking musicians sitting cross-legged on a rock in what looked like the Topanga creek. Deva's father was probably one of them but I couldn't recognize him without the beard. There was a beautiful woman in the forefront.

"She had a voice," Deva's father commented, noticing my

curiosity. "Better than Janis Joplin and Ellen McIlwaine. One of those guys went on to perform with Muddy Waters, you know."

I smiled widely to show him I was impressed. Beneath the vinyl albums were boxes filled with CDs and tapes. I picked up a broken CD case. Phil Collins's face was on the cover—a sultry black-and-white profile looking down; it was *Another Day in Paradise*. I turned the cover over with anticipation, looking for Max's name in bold somewhere. I scanned the booklet, but his name didn't appear anywhere in there. I put the CD back in the box and took in the house for the first time.

It looked like a dump. Rain had blown through the open windows and soaked the floor that was now covered in mud. Wet towels and empty beer cans were scattered about, and rotten plants hung from the ceiling inside cracked pots. Only one corner of the room was dry and clean. It was furnished with a pristine office desk. Deva was sitting on a swivel chair in front of it.

Her father pointed me to the fax machine on the desk and invited me to call my parents, then disappeared into another room. Deva spun lightly in the chair and passed me the receiver. She held her pained shoulder with her hand, shielding it defensively from the space around her. Next to the fax machine was a computer monitor and a silver frame with a picture of Deva. She was a pale ten-year-old girl, squinting at the sun from a natural watering hole in the canyon. A stash of her father's glossy black-and-white portfolio pictures were set almost votively around her photo. It looked like a strange altar.

When my father picked up the phone I told him the road was blocked off and I didn't know how to get home.

"But we need you back on set! This is so *unprofessional*!" he screamed.

He liked using that word now. It was part of his new armory. He flaunted it, entitled by his Johnny Depp Polaroids and Miramax correspondences. He hung up. I acted like the line had dropped and called back.

"Don't hang up on me. It's not my fault," I said.

"I have too much to do now. Call when the road is clear." Then he hung up again.

I held the receiver in my hand and kept speaking Italian, pretending he was still on the line. I didn't want anyone to think my family would get rid of me so quickly. I glanced at the immaculate altar desk, the neatly arranged folders and portfolio pictures. It made me think of my father's oak desk at home, the only thing that was ever kept in order during those days, piled with perfect production schedules that my mother and Max printed out each week. I felt a surge of guilt. My father said he needed me, but I could not be there for him.

Chris was in the room, leaning against a wall in a corner of the kitchen, nibbling from a plastic bag of cashews. He had not said a word—just nodded at me.

A toilet flushed. Deva's father walked out of the bathroom and gave me a look.

"I guess you're staying, then?"

"I don't have anywhere else to go while the road is blocked."

He rolled his eyes at me, then turned to Deva.

"Did you fax those press releases today?" he asked her.

Deva got up immediately from her chair and started fumbling, searching through the folders on the desk. "Oh my God, I forgot!"

"I told you a hundred times! They were supposed to go in yesterday. I don't have time for this." He groaned as he walked over to us. He gave Deva a light little smack on the back of her head, then grabbed the sheets from her hands, annoyed. She giggled apologetically.

"One thing I ask! One thing."

Her father assembled the sheets demonstratively, then

handed them to his daughter so she could load them into the fax machine.

"I was doing that!" Deva complained and started over.

He stood over her, watching. When she bent forward he pulled back slightly and glanced down her back. Her shirt had ridden up and her crack was showing.

"I don't like you wearing these pants. Everyone can see your ass."

Deva didn't answer. The sound of the fax went off and she cautiously placed the papers in it. The two of them stood in front of the machine, waiting for the pages to scroll through.

"That's good," Deva's father said as the last page went through. He caressed his daughter's bare lower back absent-mindedly. "Off you go. All of you. Get out of here. I need to work. There's bread and eggs if you girls want to make dinner."

He took Deva's place on the chair, switched on the monitor, and slipped a pair of headphones on.

"Let's go," Deva whispered, rolling her eyes, implying he was a pain.

As I walked out, I turned to the desk one last time. The muffled sounds of guitars came from her father's headphones. There was a music video playing on the screen. Deva pulled me by a sleeve, trying to keep me from looking, but I lingered long enough to see her wavy long hair bounce from side to side. It was she in the video. She wore her usual bell-bottoms and a tight white T-shirt cropped above her stomach, with a silver belly chain. She walked on a dirt path through a row of aca-cias. Her lips sang a song I couldn't hear, but I could see how much effort she put in to it because she kept her fist on her belly, almost punching the music out of her body. Close-ups of her freckled face were intercut with images of her father, slightly bloated but quite elegant. Younger looking and clean shaven, not the guy with the dirty jeans and skinny ponytail who walked around the house. He leaned on a picket fence. In the video's narrative the two singers were looking for each other—desire, longing, and melancholy all showing on their faces. I turned back to Deva, but she avoided me and pushed me toward Chris, who was cracking eggs open into a pan by the stove.

"Let's have dinner in my bedroom," she said, haphazardly assembling two pieces of toast and an avocado on a plate.

Chris started scrambling.

Rain trickled through the ceiling in Deva's cabin. We put pots on the floor, lit candles, and got under the blankets making shivering sounds, still high from the Vicodin. The avocado sat on the desk, untouched. Neither of us was hungry.

"Sorry about that," Deva said. "He can be an asshole sometimes."

"How did he end up living here?" I asked, trying to keep things vague.

"He moved from Montana in the sixties. He came to the canyon because all the musicians lived here. Topanga was really special when we were kids. We used to camp out without tents at night. Our dad taught us to sleep under the stars."

"So that's where you got your wild side." I chuckled.

Deva sighed. She cracked open the window, even though it was cold, and lit a cigarette.

"We were completely free," she said, exhaling the smoke, hunching over through the crack. "Home-schooled by our mom with a few kids from the neighborhood. We were all different ages, of course. So my mom's classes were kind of strange . . . but we were happy, my brother and me. We were the canyon's mascots. They called us 'the fairy twins' because we looked like we'd come out of an Irish folk tale. You know, the red hair, the green eyes. Of course my brother looks nothing like me, so I felt even cooler, like I was the true thing. Neighbors fed us, gave us things to take home, tools to build things with, juice. It was fun."

When I asked about her mother, Deva cringed. She said that when they were kids she remembered a warm, smiling woman. She tried to think about that woman instead of the person she became later.

"Who did she become?" I asked, moving closer to her on the bed.

"My father was this bare-chested handsome guy with thick long hair, no ugly long beard yet. Super skinny, always a beer in his hand and a guitar close by, always moving someplace, or going to somebody's house to play music. His hair was so soft. I used to twist it in my fingers to fall asleep. He looked like David Gilmour, but even more beautiful. He partied a lot, but he was, you know, *present*. But my mom didn't party. She was at home, lying on a bed on the terrace. She spent her days making these really long quilts. She just quilted. All the time. She collected tons of scraps. My image of her is just pieces of fabric and sewing needles. A cigarette smoking in a glass ashtray by the bed."

I giggled, thinking about Serena. I told her my mother did the same thing. The "motionless collector." I told her about the news clippings, the stories she gathered.

"My dad was messy, but you knew what you were getting into. My mom was just completely unpredictable. She spent all her savings to open this really cool rare-parrot shop and then managed to kill off all the birds within two months. Then she went back to quilting. I think she was depressed. That's when she found Jesus. When I was eight she took off with this weird Christian hippie from Utah, Don. She met him at a county fair in Malibu. When my dad asked her why she was leaving us, she said she had done a lot of walking and talking with God and was inspired by Eve."

"Who's Eve?" I asked.

"Fucking Adam and Eve, Eve."

"Oh my God."

"Yes. Just like Eve she was ready to move on from the Garden which, it turned out, was Topanga Canyon. Now she and Don visit once a year. They have this kind of white-trash trailer attached to their car that they sleep in. Dad won't let her inside the house. I don't blame him."

Deva exhaled the last of her cigarette and put it out in a small tin box she kept tucked in a crevice between the mattress and the window. She chased the smoke out the window and curled back up on the bed.

I couldn't put the pieces together. Watering pools, camping under the stars, musical performances, hanging out with rock stars. If her father was so cool, then why did Deva have to cover herself in bay leaves and sneak out at night? Why couldn't she just wear the pants she wanted even if her butt crack showed?

Deva wrapped herself in a wool blanket and moved down to the foot of the bed. I could tell it was hard to talk about those things and I knew I should have been grateful for the little information she had given me already. She rarely liked to speak about her family. But I felt that a gap was closing between us and I wanted to go on. I curled myself in another blanket on the bed and held a candle between us. If we focused on the flame perhaps it would be easier for her to talk.

"So what happened when she left?" I asked.

"My father had to hold down the home fort while all the other canyon musicians moved on to bigger and better things. The rug had been pulled out from under his feet. He started drinking more than normal and became kind of bitter."

I gathered from what she told me that there had been an invisible moment sometime in the mid-eighties, when a group of musicians moved away from the canyon. The recording studios shut down, Deva's father, Bob, and all the guys from the commune went from being stars to becoming burned out. The men's beautiful long hair thinned out; they grew long beards to make up for it. Their taut muscles turned into beer bellies.

"By the time my dad was ready to get his feet back on the ground, the train had left the station. That's when he became conservative with us. He was afraid his wild kids might turn into wild teenagers who would abandon him like he had abandoned his parents. We were the only investment that had given him something in return."

Deva got quieter. She put her head down and rested it on my thigh.

"The problem is you can't unlearn things," she whispered. "When I was ten my father's best friend gave me a joint for my birthday, but now he expects me to work, stay at home, and help him with his music stuff. I have no life." She let out a small, incredulous snigger. "My dad took me to all-night rock concerts when we were kids and now he hates the fact that I want to go to raves. Makes no sense, right? When he found out I'd been going, he freaked out. He started crying in my lap. But it's too late for me to be a good girl, you see. I think he knows that too. And it pisses him off. He feels like he owns us because he raised us on his own. He can't handle us having lives of our own. He feels it's like a betrayal of him or something. Of everything he's done for us."

"And what do you think?"

"I mean, it's a cycle with him. One moment he's happy, the next he's enraged. You just have to be smart and find him on the right swing. Nobody is perfect."

Deva dug her fingers into the hot wax that was spilling out of the candle. She let it dry on her nails, then scraped it off. I sighed, thinking about how angry my father had sounded on the phone. I cracked a joke about his family business model and the theories about why it worked and the whole "stealing from your family is like stealing from yourself" idea.

"I mean, who says you have to be in your dad's video and I have to be part of my dad's film, right?" I proclaimed self-righteously.

Something in the air broke.

"I don't think it's the same thing," Deva said dryly. "You have a whole family. I just have my dad and brother."

She got up and placed the candle on the windowsill. She jumped off the bed and carved the pit from the avocado on her desk.

"In the video you looked a lot older—" I said.

"It's the makeup." She cut me short. She did this whenever I went on for too long about something she didn't want to talk about anymore.

"It seemed like you were playing the role of his love interest or something," I insisted.

"Not really. It's more abstract."

There was a moment of silence. Deva peeled the avocado and cut it into small pieces.

"Did your dad ever have a girlfriend after your mother left?" I asked.

"No."

She left the avocado cubes on the table, got back into bed with her clothes still on, blew the candle out, and went to sleep.

I told myself that she was just tired, that the storm and the talking and the Vicodin had drained her. I lay awake listening to the downpour. Hours into the night, through the top corner of the cabin's window, I saw Deva's father standing half naked on the windowsill of the main house, swales of rain falling against him. He was drunk. He oscillated, struggling to stay on his legs, on top of a round glass table. It was unclear what he was doing at first, but when I propped myself up for a better look, I realized

he had strapped on a guitar and was using the table as an improvised stage. I got off the bed and opened the cabin door a crack
to take a better look. He was right above me now. With a trembling jaw, he sang a wild song in the tempest. His knees shook
and his bones seemed to jump out of his body, trying to escape
his limbs. It was the first time I'd heard him sing, all upward-
curled lips and high-pitched vowels. The wind blew his beard
and the silver leaves rustled like metal chimes to the rhythm of
his music. His audience members were the spread-out branches
of the swinging eucalyptus trees. He eyed the leaves seductively
as they flushed water to the ground, addressing them like group-
ies in the first row at a concert. His performance was a lonely
cry. It welled out of a debilitating pain that was hard to look at.
He was drenched and disoriented. His intonation rose and fell
with his jerking knees. The jolts in his legs opened a space in his
voice until the whole song turned into a soaring wail. The rain
was weeping with him.

I stood there for a bit, looking at his drunk concert and feeling like I should, that *someone* should be there for him. And just
standing there, I felt good, like I was doing the right thing, supporting someone else's father since I couldn't support my own.
I swayed my body to the slurred song. I moved from foot to foot
until Deva's father was too drunk to stand or sing.

I woke up the next morning and Deva wasn't in the cabin.
The weather hadn't improved. I turned the heater on and ripped
off a piece of a stale bagel. I had slept with my clothes on. I tried
to fix myself up, pushing hair out of my eyes. I needed to wash.

The main house was empty. I opened the bathroom door
and found Chris inside, taking a shower. I closed it and waited
for my turn, leaning on the kitchen counter. There were dishes
piled in the sink. None of them contained food debris except

for bagel crumbs and jam slabs. The faucet was rimmed with a rubbery layer of mildew. I wrapped my fingers around it because that fungus was the only thing that seemed alive. Over the sink was a cardboard chore wheel indicating it was Chris's turn to wash the dishes. There were recycling bins overfilled with beer bottles and cans. Above them a Post-it read: "Deva don't forget recycling!!!" The mud from the previous day had dried on the floor. The house smelled like stale beer, but somehow I thought it was a happy smell. There were no ornaments. Nothing to give pleasure to the eyes. Yet the bareness of it all made me think there was something noble at play beneath the surface. As if that grim room was a choice, the result of some kind of idealism. This was a place where chores were divided equally and everyone took care of one another. It was crooked and imperfect and dirty, but there was a reason for it. Furniture didn't matter because art was more important than anything. It struck me how willing I was to consider Deva's father's work more artful than my father's. We'd always had paintings on the walls and books on the shelves. Our houses were cozy and tasteful. But this place made a radical statement. One that none of our houses had ever made.

In the office area beneath the framed awards, the brand-new fax machine emitted compact, electronic sounds. I walked over to the desk and looked at the framed photo of Deva, smiling from the watering hole, her father's pictures displayed around it. The clean computer monitor reflected on the desk's luminous metal surface, no beer-can marks there. I tested the drawers. They pulled out easily, making a smooth buttery sound.

Chris came out of the bathroom with a towel wrapped around his hips and another one on his shoulders. I turned away from the desk, feeling as if I'd been caught in the act of unmasking a secret.

"They went to the grocery store. The canyon is still blocked," he explained.

"I was going to take a shower. I didn't mean to walk in on you."

I gravitated back toward the bathroom and tried to pass by him. We met in front of the kitchen sink and he rubbed his wet hands on my arms. He took the small towel off his shoulders and handed it to me.

"There's no more towels. We used them for the floor. Ceiling is leaking. Don't be long in the shower. The water heater is on its last leg," he said, smiling.

He was beautiful in a similar way to Deva. I could see how they had shared space inside someone's womb. It was as if they'd assigned each other their future roles early on and established their fates. Hers would be different from his. He looked like his father did when he was young, taut stomach muscles and pale skin, except his was even paler than Deva's—translucent and dead.

"Thanks." I pulled away from him, but he held me back.

"Look. I know you really like it up here and you and my sister are having fun. I know you're sneaking out. Deva's been sneaking out since she was eleven. But do you really think you're going to change her?" he asked. "You believe in miracles, then."

"What are you talking about?" I gave him a push.

He stayed there with his wet hands planted firmly on my arms.

"This is a really complicated family."

I was about to plug in the blow-dryer after the shower, when I heard the front door open, then the rustle of paper bags on the kitchen counter. A voice was singing a tune. It didn't sound like Deva. After a moment the same song came blasting from the living-room speakers.

I opened the door a bit and peered in. The curtains on the

sliding doors in front of the desk were drawn open now. Finally some light. I could see the wide terrace outside facing the valley of oaks beneath the house. It *was* Deva singing. A big voice blasted out of her tiny stomach. She kept her hand on her belly as she spun on the swivel chair at her father's desk, singing over the recording of his song. Her father stood next to her looking at the monitor. I edged my feet back on the wet bathroom floor. It was his music video playing on the screen. The song blaring from the speakers was the same one I'd heard him sing to the wet trees last night. Deva joined in on the chorus: *"And when I say I'm looking, don't mean I wanna find what I'm looking for / When I say I'm searching, don't mean I want to search at all."*

Chris came into the kitchen, dressed now. He whistled, unloading the grocery bags by the counter as if nothing had happened. I saw Deva's father grab her up from the chair, inviting her to dance. She laughed and went with it while the video played on. I couldn't blame him for casting Deva in his video. She was so beautiful, a perfect model. When she sang from the top of her lungs, her face expanded and illuminated. She stole the show.

Chris joined in, doing a kind of goofy mashed-potato dance, swinging his arms up and down. Their father was fresh-looking and sober now. Deva was right about his mood swings. I could see the beautiful man from the early days. I could see how special he was. When he danced he kept Deva close to him, like a little doll. She was so light he could push and pull and twist her around. She followed his lead. He was overbearing, always on the verge of pushing her too hard or too close, but Deva bounced back with her own special skill. She knew how to interact with his jaggedness. Even if at times there was something strained about the way they all moved around that kitchen floor, I thought to myself that the three of them on that Saturday morning looked like a happy family.

I slunk back, closed the bathroom door, and flushed the toilet to make myself heard. I shuffled about the shower, turning the faucet on and off. When I opened the door again, I pretended to be surprised to see them. Deva casually turned off the video and put on an old vinyl record. Tim Buckley's *Goodbye and Hello* came on. His powerful, spirited voice filled the room.

"There's the Italian one! *Allora! Mamma mia! Buon giorno!*" Deva's father greeted me with unlikely avuncular affection. It was the first time I'd seen him really smile.

Rain fell through the rest of the day, soaking life with it. At night I saw it break the roof off the Alexandria and float down the hotel's marble stairs. I was late from lunch break. It was the day we shot in the Valentino suite. An important day, my father said. I ran to get there on time, but running felt like trudging in the mud from Bob's commune. I was dirty and wet and late. The red velvet from the antique suite appeared in the periphery of my eyes. I tried to walk faster toward the room. The sound of something buzzing, an incessant and repetitive hum, slowed me down. My father was there with his American cap and tennis shoes, preparing the next shot. I hauled costumes in my arms, knowing they were not the right outfits for the scene, thinking they'd just have to do because we were running out of time. When I stepped into the room I noticed there were no actors. It was completely empty except for the director. He turned around. He had long hair and beard, a plump nose, and veiny cheeks. It was the face of Deva's father that greeted me. Not Ettore's. He started to clap his hands, inciting applause, but there was nobody to clap with him. The sound of his hands echoed in the empty room. I turned my back on him and ran away, knowing I had ruined everything. The film was over. I had missed my chance.

I felt something cold holding me. I was back in Deva's cabin now, my eyes open. I was asleep but staring at the wooden ceiling. Deva's hand was shaking mine.

"Stop doing that. You are scaring me," she said.

Her long hair was on my chest. I blinked.

"I was sleeping with my eyes open," I muttered. "I was dreaming."

But the humming sound was still there.

"It stopped raining. I think they're moving the boulder from the canyon road. Should we go and see?"

I glanced up toward the main house, instinctively.

"He's passed out," Deva reassured me.

She hopped off the bed and changed into the satin fairy-princess dress she liked to wear when we went out at night. Her eyes were darting around with ideas.

We made our way toward the main road, slipping downhill through the mud. Deva climbed over a few fences and I followed. A nocturnal demolition crew had been sent out to drill the rock apart and remove it. The people from the commune had gathered around the boulder in a circle. They played drums and didgeridoos. That's where the electric hum in my dream came from. Ignoring the musicians, the demolition crew spoke on their walkie-talkies with the local police.

"What's going on?" I asked Heide. She was sitting on the wet concrete, legs and arms crossed.

"The cops are trying to tell us the boulder has 'fallen off' the mountain." She made air quotes with her fingers. "Bullshit. This is a meteor. It has landed on sacred Native American land to tell us something. These guys just want to ignore it and break it apart."

I looked at the slope from which the rock had supposedly fallen. There was a hole there.

"Maybe it *did* fall off?" I ventured.

Another woman with a long thin snake wrapped around her hissed at me.

"This meteor was *predicted*. We've been waiting for it. Earthbound spirits have been trying to tell Angelenos it's time to wake up for years now. Where do you get your information?"

"She probably doesn't!" a man in spandex pants with flame patterns screamed from inside the circle.

The musicians echoed his words, arranging them into an improvised song.

"She probably doesn't. She probably doesn't," they chanted.

The crew captain spoke into his megaphone, asking everyone to break the circle. They had to crack open the boulder. Bob stared him down.

"You'll regret it. The meteor has arrived, and we have to respect it," he said with the translucent gaze of a cult leader.

Finally the music and chanting stopped and the commune dwellers scuttled to the side of the road. From their van, the crew unloaded a power generator and a tank-looking structure with long yellow tubes attached to it. They plugged a nozzle in to the yellow tube and directed it from a distance toward the rock. They asked everyone to stay back and once the generator was turned on, a glowing white laser beam shot out toward a central spot on the boulder. It wasn't like a normal lightbulb, spreading light in all directions. It was a small but continuous shaft of focused, self-contained light emitting a warm fuzzy sound. We perched next to Bob, observing the process in awe. The hum intensified, and after a few minutes the rock began to crack open. The heat from the laser had a strange, almost palpable feeling, like it was buzzing into our own skin, an ongoing vibration that tugged at the edges of our bodies. The laser was so strong, it eliminated the debris while it drilled. Parts of the stone vaporized completely, just disappeared, and soon enough the boulder began to look like a clean-cut precious gem.

"Radical," the snake woman exclaimed.

The ray was so beautiful and precise that nobody dared speak over it. We stared, hypnotized like ancient farmers in front of fire. It felt like we were witnesses to a secret ritual. Topanga was a beautiful, mysterious place where things like this could happen in the middle of the night. Bob stood by impassively, surveying the scene. Even the demolition crew was bewildered by the power of their tool. The stone looked monumental, like a cathedral getting sawed in half. When the sacred building collapsed, the people from the commune howled. Deva and I joined in. The beam-projecting structure was disassembled and placed back into the truck. Bulldozers cleared out the rest.

"Take home a slice of heaven," Bob said, handing over broken rock bits. He gave Deva and me a deep hug. "This fell from the sky, sisters. Keep it close to you."

He was jovial and peaceful. There were no signs of the stressed-out man whose commune was sliding away in the mud. It gave me a sense of how rapidly things in the canyon could heal and move on.

I pocketed my rubble. The boulder had delivered Deva back to me and for that I was thankful. Those two days under the rain with her had been an incursion into her real world. She could hop as many fences as she wanted and duck my questions a million times, but from now on out it would be harder to keep me in the fun-only section of her life. We coexisted, our cells had spoken to each other for many consecutive hours.

I took her hand in mine. I could feel that what had been a conquest for me—being given the chance to dig a little deeper into her life—was a defeat for her. The idea that I had been part of her ordinary days, with moldy faucets and chore wheels and rain trickling through the roof onto wet towels, worried her because it meant we were just a few layers away from getting to what it was that pained her. Maybe Deva heard my thoughts because she retracted her hand from mine. She dug into her purse, took out a flask of vodka.

"Some leftovers," she said in a cheeky voice, and washed down one of Bob's pills with a sip. I took one too.

We crossed the canyon road and walked along the other side of the street to the local elementary school, leaving behind the howling hippies and the cracked boulder. The gate was ajar. Deva ran toward the playground and climbed over the jungle gym. She hung herself from the tallest bars in the semicircle. It was always like that. I tended to stay in the energy of things that had just happened—the boulder, the laser, her hand in mine—and she was always working up the impetus for something new. The road would be clear the following morning and I knew Deva didn't want me to leave the canyon with the feeling of having done it all. So she pushed us onward. We had to end those boulder days with something extraordinary, but we had nothing extraordinary in our hands: just children's rides and rubble in our pockets.

I lay back on the merry-go-round and pushed against the central wheel with my foot. I tilted my head to the ground below and looked up at the stars, spinning upside down. I felt the warm Vicodin and vodka blur into the distant anxiety that something wasn't right. Deva appeared upside down in front of me, dangling her limp body over my eyes.

"I'm so hot. It's so hot," she moaned and rolled the top of her princess dress down to her belly. She was bare-chested in front of me. I stopped the wheel to look at her. She climbed next to me on the merry-go-round and began to spin the central wheel. It made a soft, oily sound. She spun faster, laughing at nothing as we turned—anything was good as long as it could lift her from reality and plunge her into the reckless, happy confusion she loved. She tilted her head to the fast-moving ground.

"Look at the stars. They are so bright." She sighed.

But I couldn't look at the stars. I was looking at her pale body instead. She was marmoreal against the penumbra of the trees. Naked under the dark sky, her thin skin covered in goose bumps, she looked like an abandoned statue.

"Look! Look at the stars, Eugenia! They are like little sugar cubes."

She pushed her foot against the central wheel, making us turn faster. She acted like she never wanted to be still again, like she was trying to spin us into a permanent vortex, but the wheel could only spin so fast. She let go. We slowed down. She stayed folded backward, her hair brushing against the dirt, and began to cry.

When the ride stopped, I moved closer and rubbed my hand on her naked belly to warm her. When she came back up blood had flowed to her head and her face was red with cracked eyes.

"I'm sorry if this isn't fun for you," she said.

I kept my hands on her belly. "What are you talking about? It's so fun." I tried to console her.

"I'm sorry you had to be stuck here with me and . . . I'm sorry about my dad. I know he's weird."

"It's fine. I don't care what he does as long as he is not hurting you."

Deva didn't reply.

I passed my hand over her chin. She pulled back a bit, then spoke, staring at the ground. "He can be a real dick sometimes. He can be ugly and he can seem violent. He's a little crazy for sure. Sometimes he just gets drunk or uptight. By the morning it's gone."

"I don't need to have fun as long as you're okay."

Deva started to laugh, releasing tension. "Okay."

My fingers moved naturally across her belly, up to her chest.

"But I do want to keep having fun. I don't want to get sad now. I'm really fine, you know." She sniffed snot up into her nose.

"We'll keep having fun," I reassured her.

"Will we? Because we can, right? Who says we can't?"

"Nobody says we can't have fun!"

She leaned back again on the merry-go-round and pulled her dress up over her knees. The satin shimmered in the darkness. She took my hand and brought it to her inner thighs and then pressed down. I felt a kick in my legs, something opening up, and things went dark. The next moment I was on top of her. I pulled down her scrunched-up underwear, soggy and loose. She was wet. I pushed away her pubic hair to get to her exposed, unprotected parts, and pressed my lips against her. Her hands reached for my pants. I undid them quickly and in a second her fingers were inside me.

We pushed against each other, startled, not knowing what we were doing. I pulled her up and pushed her over the seat. I placed her in the same position I saw her in when her father had glanced down her back: leaning forward with elbows resting on the cold metal and her ass in the air. I wanted to own that position. I wanted Deva to know her father was wrong. She could wear any kind of clothes with me. I opened her up from behind and licked her, spreading her apart while I touched myself. I felt her taut skin become tender, then taut again. I didn't know what it was. A buttery thing, easy like the oiled merry-go-round, like her father's desk drawers. It moved and found reciprocity. Arms corresponded to arms, toes agreed with each other. A hot piece of leg merged with another. Mouths breathed the same air. Nothing needed to be explained or thought about. We were feeling the same things at the same time and the painkillers did not take that away from us. We both came.

Deva's belly rested against the cold rails of the merry-go-round, back still folded over. I could see her beauty outside the confines of vodka and painkillers, and I knew I was done with not feeling things. I was done with my rubber suit. I did not need it anymore and I hated the way it blocked my vision, how it

got in the way of the sun and the drops of rain in Deva's hair—
things I wanted to see. I kissed her shoulder and told her I had
never felt anything like that with a boy. She hung from my neck
and we let the wheel lull us through the last drops of our trailing
pleasure.

19

My parents and brother picked me up in the Cadillac at the bottom of Deva's driveway. The sun shone and Topanga felt like the Alps. I'd woken up in Switzerland to a voracious blue sky. There were no traces of the boulder except for some rubble on the side of the road and a bunch of cigarette butts and joint stubs from the drum circle.

My father was in slippers and flannel pajamas that were covered in paint. He had wild, insomniac eyes. His untamed hair was divided into three sections, a vertical funnel and two side cones ruffled into curls. A new set of hair tufts had started growing out of his ears as well. He looked mad.

"What's going on? I thought we were going out for lunch," I asked.

"Dad's been painting. We're eating at home," my mother replied.

My brother shook his head at me and tapped his forehead with his index finger, miming the Italian gesture for "crazy."

"I don't understand why you couldn't just walk down the canyon the other day. You've done it hundreds of times," Ettore scowled at me from the rearview mirror.

"It was pouring and I thought it was dangerous."

"You were much braver as a child."

Serena gave him a look, trying to stop him from speaking further. I wanted them to be quiet also, to take in the golden light over the mountain ranges, listen to the sheep bells in the pastures, and get lost in the blue distances. I wanted them to see Topanga and love that day like I did.

"We had to hire Henry to work nighttimes. He was going crazy with the costume changes. You left a mess in the changing rooms. It's full of *stuff.* Where does it come from?" Ettore protested.

"I thought I would be back the next day," I answered.

"All I'm saying is that in the *professional* world, you would have had to find a solution. You don't just call and *announce* you won't make it on set."

There was that word again, *professional.*

Serena turned to me, droopy-eyed. "Never mind. We worked it out. Two more weeks and the film is done. Dad is stressed because he had some bad news."

I could still smell Deva on my fingers. I kept them close to my nose and smiled. What happened between us felt like butterflies and sweat and a racing heart and it made me not care about being "professional" or on time or available. I felt light. Even Arash's brick was turning into a rubble of lasered powder.

"*I* had some bad news!" Ettore shrieked. "This is exactly our family's problem. When things go well, it's everyone's business, but when they turn to shit, it's *my* bad news, right? Nobody shares the pains. Only the glories!"

"Which glories, Dad?" Timoteo asked discreetly.

"The glories, the *glories*—"

"So what happened?" I interrupted as the car coasted past the canyon's last curve.

"*She* won't think it's bad news," my father mumbled to himself, pointing at me with his eyes. His eyebrows pulled up high and bushy when he was angry.

My brother and mother both turned toward me like I was the culprit.

"What?" I asked.

"She'll be happy finally. After everything I've done for her!"

"Stop talking about me like I'm not here. What's going on?" I screamed.

The temperature rose the minute we rolled into the Valley. Heat was a different concept there—a constant that one was doomed to suffer. There was no escape.

Serena gave Ettore one last glance, then looked at my brother for encouragement.

"Max left," she finally announced.

"Why wouldn't that be good news?" I answered.

"*See!*" my father screamed. "All she cares about is having her fucking bedroom back!"

My brother took my hand and squeezed it. I pulled it away, afraid he'd steal Deva's scent from me.

"Gone. Like *gone* gone," Timoteo explained.

I remembered Max on the phone at the Alexandria, his mumbled words in Spanish. I felt guilty because I could have said something then but didn't. The car screeched to a halt on the side of the road and my father turned around toward me.

"He left." He sighed. "The production money we were waiting for from his bank never came. We have no idea where he went. He didn't even leave a note. He took off with all his stuff."

"And some of ours," Serena added.

"*And* some of ours." Ettore nodded. "Including a credit card, which he has already used apparently."

"*Stronzo,*" Timoteo commented.

My knees trembled. I became instantly scared of having taken off my rubber suit because now my heart was a bigger, more vulnerable thing and my family appeared to me like a desperate, distant bunch, all of them wailing a song nobody would listen to into the rain.

"What now?" I asked.

"I'm finishing this fucking film. No matter what!" Ettore declared.

The car started moving again. I pulled toward the front seat to look at him up close. New lines had appeared under Ettore's eyes—pinkish, vulnerable skin. There was a curl to his mouth, a desperate frown. Complication dwelled on his lips.

I stayed quiet, looking at the paint marks on his flannel pajamas and wool slippers. We drove past my high school. From the street things looked like a postcard of what schools were supposed to look like in America. Something outside us, that didn't belong to our lives—as if we were taking a road trip into the idea of California. The gates and grates, the empty parking lot, I saw everything with new eyes, pretending to be a tourist.

"Is our house in Rome still ours?" I finally asked, but nobody answered.

When we got home, Max's familiar chaos was still around but none of his stuff. Ashtrays were filled with cigar butts. Empty hangers from the dry cleaner clinked against one another on the wheeled clothes racks in the living room. My bedroom smelled of men's cologne and cigar ash. A pile of receipts and empty shopping bags from the Sherman Oaks Galleria spilled across the floor. I found a Victoria's Secret body spray by my bedside table with a little note written on a small scrap of paper: *Dear Eugenia, sorry I took up so much space—in your room and in your life. I hope this spray will help you get rid of me as much as it helped me get rid of you. Gracias, Max.*

I didn't show the note to my parents and helped Serena set up for lunch on the backyard patio. The sun was strong. My father sipped whiskey on the rocks and poured her a double.

Timoteo moved in circles, shooting a basketball at a hoop over the garage, hitting the rim over and over. I noticed the patio was covered in paint drips. My father had been hate-painting. White canvases covered with abstract, angry tar blobs were propped against the house. He sat on the ground next to his new creations, sipping his drink, pouring more tar on the canvases.

"Should we call the police?" I asked.

My father shook his head without looking up from the blobs.

"We wouldn't do that to Max," Serena explained.

"But you had a contract, right? I mean he can't just leave us like this. He can't just disappear if there's a contract, right?"

"Yes . . . we . . . well . . ." Serena jiggled the ice in her glass nervously.

"Tell them," Ettore insisted without lifting his eyes.

Serena huffed and lit a cigarette. "Fine. Fine. *I!* Are you happy now? *I* didn't finalize the contract—"

"Finalize? You didn't even start!" he insisted.

"Okay, fine. I didn't do the paperwork."

"What kind of producer doesn't take care of the paperwork? That's so *unprofessional*." That word again.

"We never would have thought this of Max. He was like family to us!" my mother said, trying to justify her actions.

"Wasn't stealing from family like stealing from yourself?" I repeated my father's business motto.

"Not this time, apparently."

"You know, it's not true he wrote that Phil Collins song. I saw the album. He's not credited." I sighed.

"I mean you guys are such idiots!" my brother lashed out, throwing his basketball on the ground. He walked to Ettore and handed him a scrunched-up slip of yellow paper he had taken out of his pocket. His report card. More bad news.

"I got a D in all my classes. Too many absences. You have to sign it."

"Have you been ditching school?" Serena asked, putting on a tired, severe tone because that's what parents had to do when kids got bad grades.

My brother rolled his eyes at her. "It's the film, Mom. You took me out of school for two weeks. It's your fault. Not mine."

"It's okay. You're smarter than them anyway," Ettore sneered. He ripped the slip from my brother's hands, signed blindly, and returned it to him. "And you?" he asked me.

I had gone out of my way to make up lost tests and keep up with reading material in school. Mrs. Perks had been clear with me: If I wanted to apply for college the next year I had to stay on track. Sometimes I worked at night to catch up. I had never told anyone about my ideas about applying to a university, neither Deva nor my parents. I just kept the letter in the drawer and read it.

"I got a letter from USC," I said. "They liked an essay I wrote and encouraged me to apply to their school because they have a good writing program."

Serena took another sip of whiskey and coughed. "Well, that's good. Will you guys help me set the table so we can finally eat?"

"Yeah, let's eat," Ettore concluded.

That night the phone rang and rang. It woke me up and I thought it was Max, that he was calling to apologize and say it was all a big mistake and the money was on its way. But it was my grandmother's cleaning lady in Rome. She had found grandmother in bed in her apartment. When she opened the house she knew right away because of the smell. She'd been dead for three days.

20

Serena was the only one who was allowed to go to Rome for my grandmother's funeral. It was almost Christmas. Tickets were expensive and who knew if they'd let us back into the country a second time, now that we didn't have Max to help pull strings. Our living budget had been reduced to zero, but Ettore insisted on finishing the film no matter what. He was now editing in an underground dungeon-type studio in North Hollywood, hanging on to Miramax's interest in distributing the film once it was complete. It was a matter of finishing fast and things would pick up.

"*Vi chiedo un ultimo sforzo,*" our father pleaded, asking for a final effort on everyone's part.

In the meantime we replaced the lightbulbs in the kitchen with fluorescent lights from the 99 Cent store to consume less energy. They often flickered. We ate from the vegetable garden and watered plants with caution, always keeping in mind the miraculous effects of compost. Nothing went to waste. Every domestic action was calculated in order to save energy and money that was to go toward the realization of Ettore's dream. It was as if he had not noticed that someone had died on the other side of an ocean. Serena called every day to speak to us.

When we weren't home she left long messages on the answering machine, sometimes crying.

The day of our grandmother's funeral in Rome, my brother and I huddled on the floor listening to Serena's recorded account of the ceremony. She described a snowstorm that had paralyzed the city and told us what our uncles had cooked for the funeral party. She said she wished she'd had time to make the tortellini for the consommé herself because Alma's were *scotti*—overcooked—and the dough tasted like rubber. We heard about snow and chicken broth, but we were wearing T-shirts and drinking lemonade. Our sweaty naked thighs stuck to the living-room floor as we listened to her voice, trying to remember Rome in the winter, the way families gathered, how the pale blue afternoon light shone through the stained-glass living-room windows at our grandmother's place. I wondered what Alma and Antonio thought of us not being there. I remembered his sarcastic remarks about Ettore selling out, and imagined my mother siding with him, feeling alone and abandoned.

Instead of calling our mother back, our father asked us to send faxes to her cousin's house where she was staying.

"Letters are nicer anyway, more personal, no?"

I thought about how our grandmother would have scoffed at everything he said, every way in which he dealt with the situation. One Sunday morning Timoteo and I walked to the Iglesia Bautista Sangre de Cristo on Van Nuys Boulevard and spoke to Pastor Hernán. He agreed to do a small service for our grandmother.

"I didn't realize you were so attached to her," was Ettore's response when we told him about our plan. What was the point of wasting time and money on a funeral here, he asked. Grandma was dead. That would not change.

The service was held on the afternoon of the last Sunday before Christmas. Ettore called my brother and me from the editing studio, saying we should take the Victory bus there because he would be coming from North Hollywood and didn't have time to pick us up.

A strange thing happens when someone dies far away. The brain does not process the information. The person keeps on living in another place for you, even though the other place is not on earth anymore. It was hard enough understanding that a body was there and then not, but with a country and an ocean in between, the whole thing felt even more abstract. Deva had gone to visit her father's family in Montana for the holidays. I called her innumerable times, but as always when she was with her father, it was as if he'd sucked her away from the world. That she wouldn't want to find the time to talk to me on the phone after what had happened between us broke my heart more than anything else. I was ashamed to admit that her absence felt more tangible and important to me than my grandmother's. I felt guilty for not being able to cry, but then again none of us did. We were all disconnected.

Ettore arrived at the Sangre de Cristo church late. He hugged us and sat in the pew looking up at the rose window, distracted. During mass it was just us and the regular congregation plus the Alitalia representative from Torrance whom my grandmother had befriended during her countless telephone calls to rebook her return ticket to Rome. The woman said my grandmother had given her lifesaving advice on how to alleviate rheumatic lower-back pain and she was very sorry for our loss.

On Christmas Day we went to buy presents on Melrose Avenue. We parked at Noah's Bagels for a lunch snack and during that time someone broke in to the car and stole our gifts. We stood in shock in front of the popped-open trunk. No more presents. No more Christmas. I burst out crying. We drove back to Melrose Avenue and bought the same presents all over. My father put everything on his soon-to-expire American Express card and signed away. None of us knew how to cook a Christmas meal. The fridge was almost empty except for Hot Pockets and eggs. We cleared the table of the lingering paperwork. I lit a pine-tree-shaped candle from Pick 'n Save, a leftover from the previous Christmas, and placed it in the center. My father made carbonara. We drank wine and my father cracked a few jokes about both of our dead grandmothers and how they'd be together talking shit about him in the heavens now. After dinner he moved to his studio with a whiskey on the rocks to look at the latest film edits. I walked past him before going to bed. My throat knotted up when I saw how clean his desk was compared to the rest of the house. I thought about Deva's father's desk and stomped my foot in my father's direction to shake him up, to show him what the rest of the house looked like without our mother in it.

"Is a lawyer going to deal with the Max thing?" I asked him.

He took off his headphones. "Mom was supposed to take care of the bureaucratic side of things. I'm just an artist trying to finish a film," he replied. He slipped his headphones back on and started twirling his curls around his index finger, looking at the screen.

I felt my blood boiling. I yanked the headphones off his head. "Just how many things was Mom supposed to do? File paperwork, run errands, assist you, make food for the entire cast and crew, what else? She's one person. We're one family."

"It's very clear to me now, believe me." He took a breath and smiled. "Let's just keep going, though, okay? Finish things up and forget about Max. We don't need to call the police or lawyers or authorities. They'll make things worse. They'll shut down the film."

Authorities: invisible entities that hovered menacingly around my family's periphery since as far back as I could remember. The fascist pigs who fined you for going nude on the beach, the greedy doctors we had to lie to in order to get my brother stitched up when he fell off his bicycle in the desert, the

SS-like customs officers who treated us like criminals. That's what *authorities* did: They made your life worse.

"Nobody serves us," my father said. "We are Italians. We are less to these people than the Mexican ladies selling spicy mango salads in the Pick 'n Save parking lot."

I walked out of the house and kept going in the hopes I would get tired and finally feel sad about my grandmother. I tried to remember the last time I hugged her, the smell of her powder, her golden one-piece bathing suit and turquoise hair under the neon lights in the glass house at the Prairie Wind Casino. I told myself it wasn't strange that she used to ask me to play the tongue-to-tongue game when I was a child. I forced myself to conjure a happy memory of the smell of her saliva on my lips, her tongue licking mine, her smile. But instead I felt anger at my father and relief only at the thought of Deva's freckled face flashing in front of me.

When I came back home everyone was asleep and I called Deva in Montana, but she was rushed and distant. She spoke with a low drawl like she was high on something potent. She sounded like a different person. "I'll call you on New Year's," she said before hanging up on me. I knew she wouldn't.

I filled a cup with whiskey and ice and went to the backyard. I raised my drink to Deva and drank it fast. It was the one thing I was sure she was doing. The only way to feel what she was feeling. I drank and drank. The stars and moon were covered by smog. The sky was black. When I couldn't stand any more, I got on the ground, clutched the grass, and dug a hole. I kept digging as if my insides were jumping out of me, filling my short nails with dirt. I passed out with a clod of earth in my hand.

21

I was expecting drastic things to go down at the arrivals hall when my mother returned from Rome. I imagined her resolutions for 1994 would include anger, resentment, flung suitcases, divorce threats. I thought it would all come up like messy projectile vomit: the unanswered messages on the machine, my father blaming her for the film's financial downfall, the pain of not having her own family by her side during a death because nothing in the world was more important than finishing a horror film. I even thought Serena might call to say she would never come back. I told myself I would forgive her if that's how she chose to let her rage out.

But my mother swept across LAX with a disarming, sunfilled smile, straight into my father's arms. She kissed his lips and abandoned her head on his chest.

"How's the editing coming?" was the first question she asked.

She kissed my brother and me on the cheeks briskly.

We dropped Ettore and Timoteo at the editing studio in North Hollywood and drove straight to Food 4 Less on Sepulveda. Serena whistled, pushing the extra-large cart down the dairy aisle. I had a grocery list, but when I went to read it, I dropped an eighteen-egg carton on the floor and made a mess.

Suddenly I was screaming at my mother in the middle of the aisle. Nothing in nature was supposed to carry eighteen eggs at once, I yelled, and she should have known better than to ask me to pick up a container with so many fragile things inside. She should have known better about a lot of things and gone back to Rome. In Rome you could buy only four, maybe six eggs at a time and they were packaged in crush-resistant cartons, not flimsy Styrofoam. Six eggs! That was the natural order of things, not eighteen. Wouldn't she rather stay in a place ruled by the natural order of things?

"All we've been eating is eggs! Nobody needs so many eggs in their lives!" I insisted.

We didn't buy the carton. In the car Serena asked me what was wrong. I went off on a tangent about omelets and pancakes and American brunches, but soon I started crying and talking about her messages on the answering machine, Pastor Hernán, and the Iglesia Bautista Sangre de Cristo on Van Nuys Boulevard, our father's reaction to our grandmother's death.

"He didn't even want to have a memorial," I said, sobbing.

Serena kept driving, squinting her eyes in the sun. Her 99 Cent cat-eye sunglasses had broken in Rome.

"Well, they never really liked each other," she said. "He felt judged by her."

Deva didn't show up to school after the holidays. Nobody answered the phone in Topanga or Montana. A few days into the term, I thought I'd lost her. I dragged my feet around campus. Chris's few friends hadn't spoken to him since he left either. Nobody had news. Finally the phone rang one afternoon and Deva screamed into the receiver. She sounded happy or manic, over-vivacious. She said she and Chris had been helping their father assemble his new recording studio out in Montana, but she would return to Los Angeles on their birthday in mid-January and she was excited because we could go to the desert party she had been waiting for since September. We'd celebrate on the high Mojave plains. My job was to write down the address of where to go to get the directions to the rave, find us a ride to the desert, and get my parents to cover for us.

"I already told my dad I'm spending the night at your place for my birthday."

"What about Chris? It's his birthday too . . ."

"We each get our own special day. We've done that since we were kids. I celebrate one day and Chris takes the following. Only trick is I have to be back in Topanga by morning for our annual birthday brunch and hike," she said all in one breath. "Pick me up at eight in my driveway on my birthday."

"I miss you—"

"Remember to buy glitter. Wear bright, soft clothes. They feel amazing when you're on E."

"I miss you," I repeated.

"Oh and buy some pacifiers!" she replied before hanging up.

My mother dyed her hair roots back to blond and screened collection calls from credit card companies, while my father updated his armory of business terms with words that had to do with foreclosure and bankruptcy. He bestowed a certain kind of dignity on them, as if that too was part of the professional world of film.

Over breakfast one morning I told them the Zapatista Army of National Liberation had started a war in Chiapas against military incursions into sacred Mexican regions.

"My friends in school have organized a massive peaceful desert gathering in support of the Zapatistas. Deva and I want to go."

"That's wonderful," my father said, lifting his eyes from the *Los Angeles Times*.

"Deva's dad doesn't think we should protest the government."

"Bullshit!" My father got roiled up. "Question authority. It's the only way to ensure our brains are working."

"Exactly, so can you cover for her if her dad calls?"

"When did you become a communist?" my mother asked with a suspicious glare as she stirred sugar in her teacup.

"Actually the EZLN movement has rejected political classification," I corrected her.

My father closed the newspaper and cleared his throat. "Of course we'll cover. You know your mother and I did these things all the time when we were younger. We traveled to Peru for a whole year and camped on Machu Picchu for weeks supporting the Túpac Amaru Revolutionary Movement."

I nodded, feigning enthusiasm. I had heard the Machu Picchu story innumerable times, but pretended it was news to my ears.

I retired to my bedroom and blasted "Venceremos," the Inti-Illimani folk hit from 1970 that had been the anthem of Chile during the period leading up to the coup. Chilean flutes echoed through my thin bedroom walls. They did not smell of Victoria Secret body spray any longer. They smelled of revolution.

I showed up at Henry's store with a bagful of flea-market finds I had been storing for him, hoping they might work as currency for a trade. The electronic store bell buzzed when I opened the door. The batteries were weak and they made a distorted sound. Henry had installed it to know when to put the pot away if someone came in. I looked around. He was hunched over *Street Fighter*, the usual cigarette burning on the control panel. I hadn't been to the store in weeks. It looked like a dungeon again and I was instantly annoyed. I didn't say hello and stormed to the back room. I took out cleaning products and began to dust picture frames.

"I can't believe you let Diane Keaton get like this," I scolded him.

Henry shrugged his shoulders. "I told you I needed you around more . . . motherfucker!" he screamed at T. Hawk, *Street Fighter*'s exiled Indian warrior.

"Okay, look. I'm going to clean up, but I need your help."

"You don't have to clean up. It's fine. Oh shit!" he screamed again.

His middle and index fingers tapped violently over the control button—an obsessive clicking noise I now associated with his presence.

"I want to. And I also want your help. I need a ride on Saturday."

"So *that's* it, huh? You disappear for weeks and now you want a ride?"

"Yes, to the Mojave Desert," I mumbled. "And I'm sorry if I was mean but you'd be mean to me too if all of a sudden I turned into your mother's best friend. Plus my grandma died."

He stopped playing. "The one that used to make out with you?"

"Yes. Not exactly make out."

"Tongue to tongue counts as making out. Anyway, I'm sorry." He gave me an awkward hug. "Why do you need to go to the desert?"

"My friend Deva and I want to go to a rave for her birthday. We need a car. We have to go to Hollywood first and pick up directions."

Henry smirked. "Secret location? I hate that shit. Why can't they just give you the fucking directions right away?"

"Because raves are illegal and you have to do things last-minute or you'll get busted."

Henry shook his head.

"I totally want you to meet Deva," I said.

"Okay, first of all, I hate crowds. I hate people in general, but particularly when they are high in open spaces wearing bunny suits and tripping out on glow sticks. Second of all, you disappeared from my life and started practically living in the woods with this girl you've never even introduced me to, and now all of a sudden you *totally want me to meet her*? I'm *totally* sorry. I feel used," he said, mocking my Valley girl tone.

"Please?"

Henry let T. Hawk fall to the ground, then turned to me.

"No way in hell I'm driving two and a half hours at night into the fucking desert with a bunch of meth heads. I hate driving and I hate driving at night. Plus I have agoraphobia."

"Clearly." I scowled, glaring at the crammed store. I walked to the back of the room and started pulling my clothes from the boxes and transferring them into the new arrivals bin.

I took my shirt off and tried on the softest, most fluorescent top I could find in front of the mirror. It was bright green and cropped just above my belly button. Henry lifted his gaze.

"Dude, what are you doing? You can't get naked in the middle of the store."

"I'm not naked. I'm topless. Nobody comes in here anyway."

"That's not true. We had seven customers yesterday. They bought your *Nekromantic* knife by the way. I owe you sixty bucks."

"Just drive us to the desert and keep the money."

"I'd rather give you the sixty bucks."

I sighed and dug out more clothes from the boxes. "Deva said I have to wear soft, bright clothes."

"I hate raver fashion. Did she tell you to buy pacifiers too?"

"No. What are pacifiers for anyway?" I tried to ask with nonchalance, breezing through a pile of anime-style schoolgirl dresses.

"They satiate the need to grind your teeth when you're on MDMA . . . You'll see, the girls are all going to be sucking on them, dancing like aliens. It's just so silly."

"Better than sitting here rotting away!"

I tried on a short bright pink dress over my pants, then pulled them out from underneath. It looked perfect. Henry walked up behind me.

"You have to do the high pigtail buns. It's the style." He parted my hair, twirled it into buns, and snickered at my reflection. "You'll never be a raver, Eugenia. Italians can't survive in the desert."

I undid the buns, rolled up my jeans, stuffed them in my bag, and headed out in the pink dress.

"I'm taking it. You owe me sixty bucks."

I left the store and crossed Ventura Boulevard.

Henry ran after me and screamed from across the street. "You can't act like a spoiled brat just because I don't feel like driving you to the freaking desert in the middle of the night!"

I was already on the other side, headed for Sav-On where I would discreetly buy the pacifiers. I turned around.

"You never want to do anything! I'm so bored with you!" I screamed back.

"Does that include wrapping up the costume department on your dad's movie because you were stupid enough to get stuck in the middle of a canyon?"

"No. That's not included!"

"No shit!" Henry screamed back.

The cars driving down the boulevard between us honked at our screams. A guy stuck his head out of the window and gave us a peace sign. "Make love, not war, guys!" Henry and I both flipped him off.

It angered me that he knew I was going to buy pacifiers, that he could see through me, that he noticed when I put on an American accent to fit in. He knew how vulnerable I felt with Deva and he knew these things because I had allowed him to live in my space, breathe my air, become part of my world like a second brother.

I shut my bedroom door and took my faded tie-dyed address book out. I started leafing through it, in search of someone who might own a car, realizing, on top of everything else, that I had no friends. Some Italian names, a few classmates I had called to get homework assignments, a couple of Latino anarchists I had smoked cigarettes with in the abandoned school field where the outcasts hung out. I didn't have the guts to call them out of the blue and none of them had cars anyway. Before closing the address book, a small piece of crumpled paper fell out. When I opened it, I saw a scribble in violet pen. I could not make out the name, but I could see it was a California area code. I searched for 805 in the yellow pages: Ventura County. I began to hear drums play inside my head. Peyote, turkey beaks, loss of virginity, and trailer parks. Alo, the whiskey-drinking guy from Wounded Knee, had a car and he liked to drive it. I searched through my dresser and pulled out the leather jacket he'd given me, remembering his sweet gesture. The awkwardly romantic day-after he'd tried to conjure when we drove through the battered buttes. It had been more than a year since our Native American adventure in South Dakota. He'd written me a few letters but I had not replied. I had never called him. I never even bothered to copy his number into my phone book.

22

On the night of Deva's birthday Alo honked his car in my driveway. I ran out with a perfect plan and a pounding heart. He was supposed to have picked Deva up already and we were to head out to the desert together. I had not seen her in weeks and now she would be here, in my house. My brother was playing street hockey with Creedence and his brothers in pajamas, and though it was January, a light warm breeze blew on my bare shoulders. Even my street seemed beautiful to me, like a self-contained universe that said life brimmed with possibilities. I skimmed over Alo's truck—dusty and banged-up like I remembered— over his face and his smile and his outstretched hands, looking for Deva, but she wasn't there.

"Where is she?" I asked without saying hello.

Alo smiled at me, bursting out of a new leather jacket. This one had silver studs. He had a red silk scarf wrapped around his neck. Someone else got out of the passenger side. A guy in an oversize flannel shirt with a red bandanna covering his bald head. Both of them had goatees. I glanced at my bright pink raver dress, sparkling knee-highs, and fuzzy white fur coat. My fingers were covered with the glitter I'd smeared on my eyelids. The three of us looked like a car crash.

"Man, your girlfriend is nuts," Alo announced as he

stretched out his legs. "We drove all the way into Topanga. She came down the driveway and told us she wasn't ready. She said to tell you she'd be coming with some friends and see you in the desert."

"Yeah, that'll be easy!" His friend smirked.

I couldn't hide my disappointment. "What do you mean 'the desert'? We'll never find her there."

Alo shrugged his shoulders.

"I'm just as disappointed as you. Actually Ben here is," he said, patting his friend's shoulder with a giggle.

Alo's voice was gone. He spoke in a raspy wheeze, like a loud, strangled whisper, and he'd grown a patchy beard around his long goatee.

"Did she say *why*?"

"Nope."

"But you're better off, man. Her friends looked like freaks!" Ben cackled. "Weird alien dudes in gas masks."

They looked at each other and started laughing.

I felt a pang in my heart.

I embraced Alo briefly—a rush of stale cigarettes and the memory of his ashtray car the day of our adventure. I introduced myself to his friend. He had a sticky hand and must have been thirty. I looked back at Alo. Their presence in my driveway seemed suddenly inappropriate. I saw what I hadn't fully deciphered in South Dakota. Neither he nor Ben could ever be good enough for Deva. They were rejects. She probably saw those goatees and right there in the driveway decided to ditch them.

The back of Alo's truck was decked out with scattered blankets, dirty sleeping bags, and flannel pajamas.

"That's your spot, girl. We can't fit three people in the front."

Ben got in the passenger seat and for a brief moment I wondered if it was a good idea to ride alone in the back of a truck with two guys I barely knew. But it was Deva's birthday and she was in the desert and they were the only people who were going to take me there, so I hopped inside. Alo tucked me in. I looked at him and my eyes said *don't kill me* and he must have read my thoughts because his face softened and he caressed my cheek.

"It's really good to see you. I thought you'd never call me."

"It's good to see you too," I lied.

He leaned in closer and looked at me with a vulnerability I didn't know he had.

"I've wanted to talk to you so many times. Remember how I had cancer?" he asked.

I told him I did and asked him if he was okay.

He removed the silk scarf from his neck. There was a hole in his throat now. It was covered by a rubber cap. He tapped it.

"Took out my vocal cords. Laryngectomy."

"I'm so sorry," I said and stared at the cavity.

"My voice box is gone. Not gonna use a voice box either. Notice how I don't have a voice?"

I had, yes. When he spoke it was like he had to catch his breath, as if the air was getting sucked out of some invisible place.

"You can relax," he said. "People with holes in their throats don't hurt young girls in the back of their trucks."

Timoteo saw us. He skated over and asked me if I was going to be okay taking off with two guys. He gave Alo a suspicious scowl and leaned over the pile of flannel pajamas and blankets where I was stationed.

"Are you *sure* you want to go?"

"Of course. Just don't tell Mom and Dad you saw me in the back of a truck, okay?"

Alo gave him a pat on the shoulder. "Your sister's a big girl." He winked and got into the driver's seat.

"I don't think this is a good idea," my brother whispered.

Maybe he saw what I was trying not to see, that postcard of what things were supposed to look like, and he compared it to what was actually there. Pickup trucks in California were meant to be loaded with surfboards and girls in bikinis, not dirty blankets and flannel pajamas. But every time doubt rose to the surface, I shifted my thoughts back to the desert and waited for the anxiety to settle into visions of sand and Deva. I was on my way to see her and that was all that mattered. I hugged my brother tight and kissed his cheek.

"Thanks for caring," I said.

He kissed me, then pulled away abruptly, and skated away with his hockey stick waving from side to side. I sprawled on my makeshift mobile bed and knocked on the cab window to signal I was ready to go. Heavy metal came blasting from the inside speakers. The sleeping bag was warm enough. I looked at the stars, lulled by the movement of the car.

We rode to Hollywood to the sneaker shop where we were to pick up the secret directions. A woman in bright green body paint sat at the counter. She told me she was a leaf and that leaves were not to be confused with aliens. The rest of the store was crowded with ravers in extra-large pants, makeup, and fluorescent Super Mario suits.

"Take the 101 to the 10 East to the 605 North to the 210 East to the 58 until you are somewhere in the middle of the desert on a road called Grandview. Drive for miles until you see a boulder next to a Shell gas station. From there you will pull in to a dirt road and go straight." A mysterious recorded voice gave the vague directions on the information line we'd dialed. Trance music played in the background. Alo and his friend seemed impatient. They didn't want to go that far. They felt out of place.

We drove for hours into the night, crossing four freeways that felt like continents. Around two in the morning we reached a smaller dirt road in the middle of the dark desert. The pickup pulled over.

Alo stuck his head out the window. "Took a little detour, girl. Hope that's all right."

We were alone—just us and the desert. The two guys came out of the truck with their backpacks and proposed we get fucked up.

"I think we should go to the party. It's already so late," I said. Now I was worried and the worry took on a physical presence like one of my father's black-tar hate paintings.

The desert was cold and dry. Ben took his denim jacket off and put it on my shoulders. Alo spread blankets on the ground a little farther up from the truck and sat down. They didn't really like trance music, he explained. How about we just partied out there, the three of us? We had everything we needed, plus it seemed like Deva kind of ditched me anyway. Alo took a swig and offered me his flask of whiskey.

"To warm up," he said, smiling. And his smile was this tender thing like a child trying to convince his parents that eating candy before dinner was a good idea.

"This isn't what we agreed on," I replied, ignoring the flask.

Alo passed a loaded pipe. "No peyote this time, unfortunately," he cackled.

He wrapped his hands around my ankles and pulled me down on the blanket, hoping I'd relax. When he felt how tense I was, he giggled and raised his hands, surrendering. "We'll go, we'll go. I promise. I just wanted a chance to hang with you before we enter a sea of strangers, okay?"

"Okay."

Ben took a switchblade out of his pocket and started whittling on a piece of dry wood he'd found on the ground. It made a rough sound, like a carrot getting peeled backward.

"So why haven't we seen each other all these months?" Alo whispered in my ear.

"I was busy with school," I said, staring out into the dark.

Alo squeezed me against his chest, romantically. "I really missed you, you know? That night at the battleground was special for me."

"Yes."

He told me about the surgery. It had been bad, he said, but the good thing was he'd found a way to keep smoking. He did it directly from the hole in his throat now. It was almost the same feeling. I pulled away from him when he spoke, afraid he'd show me the new technique. I had not thought about him since he'd dropped me off in the Prairie Wind Casino parking lot in South Dakota. Now that I was close to him again—a thinner man with wrinkles around his lips, a patchy beard, and no voice box—I felt a rush of something. Guilt and pity and annoyance. He was poor, I thought. So poor he couldn't even get a full beard to grow on his face. A poor, broken man. I thought about him and how poor he was and how the hole in the throat was an entrance to his soul—a dirty, bleeding soul—and again I was thinking about the poor people of America with their missing body parts and how right Henry was about things getting cut rather than fixed. I hugged him back because if his voice box was missing, he must have been one of the worst off. But all the time I was hugging him I felt and knew I could do nothing for his missing body part.

"I'm sorry about your voice being gone," I said. "I don't think you should smoke anymore."

The chunk of sadness and worry hovering over me began to settle on us so we both got sad. It became obvious that our being in that desert together was wrong. Ben kept doing his thing, peeling his stick with the switchblade. Alo downed his whiskey in a gulp. I got up and wiped dust off my knees and leaned over to give him a kiss.

"I have to go pee. I'll be right back."

Alo's eyes lit up. I was going to stop annoying him about going to the rave and finally relax and sit with him there.

When I reached the back of the truck, I quietly picked up my bag and kept walking. I moved out of the darkness toward the sound of cars on the far-off road. I didn't look back and once I was on the road I began to run. A few cars zoomed past. I kept ironing out my dress with my fingers, hoping it didn't seem too short. The wind carried the sounds of distant electronic music. A glow-stick cactus installation and a pink laser beam shooting up from nearby plains told me I was approaching my final destination. A car pulled over and a group of kids asked me if I was going to the moon tribe party. I said I was and they let me in. They were my age. They were not dressed in leather or denim. No scarves around their necks.

The car pulled in to a new dirt road. We reached a group of men in bright orange vests who guided us toward a parking lot brimming with hundreds of dusty parked cars. When we stepped out it felt like we'd set foot on the moon or discovered a new planet populated by comets on fire and giant daisy installations.

A huge stuffed teddy bear came running toward us.

"There's a bouncing house! Let's go!" he screamed.

He searched his pockets, took out a plastic bag full of translucent pills, and gave us two each. We followed the bear and rolled down the hill until we arrived in front of a great desert sprawl. The central stage was set up with speakers as tall as buildings. Thousands of fluorescent bodies faced a wall of sound, dancing like a tribe in syncopated hopping moves—all clenched teeth and dilated pupils. Next to the stage was an *Alice in Wonderland*–themed bouncing house. The bear jumped in and reached out for us to follow. Everyone went in, but the MDMA he had given me began to kick in. I felt my jaws lock and a burst of warmth trickled inside my throat. I was afraid of the bouncing house and the girls in pigtails jumping with pacifiers in their mouths. There were too many people.

I began to wander away, but everyone appeared to me like a seamless wave of colors and electronic sounds and I couldn't tell faces from arms, human voices from electronic drones. I walked like a soul in torment and stopped in front of every swinging reddish ponytail. I chewed my tongue until my legs went out and I could not do anything that wasn't sitting down. I stumbled to the ground and knew that I looked like one of those girls who just couldn't take it. I'd gotten that far on my own and now I was stuck inside my own body. A small hill behind me was the only place that wasn't crowded. I forced myself to get up and brave the short distance. Halfway up the knoll I managed to remain standing. For a moment the music felt great. I lifted my left arm in the air and swayed gently, looking at the crowds below. Then I collapsed again. Only for a minute, I told myself, but I spent the rest of the night on that dirt patch, staring at a sea of colors, grinding my teeth. After a few hours some people running down the knoll toward the party stopped to ask me if I was okay. I tried to smile and sent them away because I could not speak. A girl with light blue hair leaned toward me and handed me a bottle of water. She pushed a pacifier pendant from her necklace into my mouth.

"That will make it better. Keep it."

And it did. I chewed and chewed until things fit back in order and bones felt like bones again, flesh became real. Angles and edges returned to my cheeks and chin.

The sun began to creep up behind the desert rocks and everyone lost their mystery at once. Smudged faces, busted eyes, swollen lips, and dilated pupils confounded by the presence of daylight. Everyone wished to shut off the light, erase the motion of the earth, kick the sun back behind the hill. The smarter ones got in their cars and drove away. I hoped Alo and Ben were among them. The vastness of the desert was too much to take in by day. The intimacy and tribalism disappeared in an instant. The cratered land had been everyone's cozy living room at night but now it was a filthy service-station bathroom with vomit and piss steaming across the dirt. I stayed to watch the lost ones under the stage who weren't ready to go home. They had sunscreen and vitamin C and Vicks VapoRub to keep their highs going, and they danced in a torment below the speakers. That's when I saw her. She was spinning in circles with her eyes closed, face smeared with glitter and gold, eyelids heavy with Egyptian eyeliner. She glowed from within, listening to a melody nobody else could hear.

I slipped off my knee-highs and put my bare feet on the ground, thinking if only I could feel the soil beneath me, I would be able to move again. A soft wind slid through my heart. I began to transpire with a warm feeling that leaked out and recirculated through my pores. Suddenly I was able to walk again and everything seemed simple. I put one foot in front of the other and kept going until I reached her cool bare arms.

"Deva," I said, moving hair away from my eyes. "Happy birthday."

She still smelled of bay leaves and patchouli, but her eyes were a darker green now, as if distance had accumulated density in her pupils. She seemed older. I held her and put my hands on her hips. The dirty desert morning transformed into California dawn. She hugged me back. I'd never seen her so thin. I kissed her hair and when I looked at her again, her strong, concrete eyes turned watery and began to dart around my periphery, unfocused, burning with their usual urge to move on. She laughed—a begging, pained expression—and introduced me to her friends, all lanky and transformed. They were too high to be friendly. We didn't shake hands.

I reached for her wrist, wanting to take her away.

"I'm sorry. I looked for you, but got carried away," she said.

I pretended it wasn't a big deal, wasn't that what everyone did at parties? Got together, swarmed in unison, split up, and found each other again at dawn like in a migratory bird dance?

"Your father," I reminded her, gripping her wrist more firmly now. "You said you had to be back in the morning for your birthday hike."

Deva looked up to a corner of the sky. The sun was out. Fun gone from her face.

"We have to go, yes! He'll kill me."

We found a ride back to Topanga with some friends of Deva's. Things seemed simpler in the daylight. We stopped at a gas station and bought Gatorade because we were all dehydrated. From the edge of the cement lot we could now see cars scattered across the land, blasting music. Impromptu parties were happening under dry plants—brief spurts of dragged-out festivities. On our way back, we popped in a cassette of the night's highlights, a kind of bootleg recording Deva's deejay friend had given her. Deva rolled down her window and stretched her arm out, her hand mimicking the movement of a boat rolling up and down on the tide. She hummed to herself, one hand waving at the Mojave moon turf, the other holding a cigarette. I kept glancing over at her, hoping she'd betray some emotion toward me, but she was in some far-off place.

The freeway that would take us back to Los Angeles was visible in the distance as we descended a sharp winding hill. Curve followed curve and I remembered I had been on that road before, driving much faster, my father at the wheel. It was the place where my brother had fallen off his bicycle and split his knee open the first week we'd moved to Los Angeles. I recognized the Mount Sinai hospital in the distant valley. I remembered my brother's little body appearing from behind a curve, walking toward us covered in blood, my mother hitting my father, crying. I saw now how sharp and blind each curve was. Why allow a kid to dash down that road without a helmet?

"Let him ride his bike down the hill while we drive. We'll wait for him at the bottom. I never used a helmet in my life," my father had said.

Ettore had put us all in danger the minute we set foot in California. He knew we needed some armor if we were to start a life here. A shell, like my rubber suit or the coarse skin that had hardened on my mother's face. She had exposed herself to so much sun that it had burned through the layers on her forehead. Her Mediterranean skin had peeled away, letting the rays charge across pores and cells. In her third eye were the flames of an imaginary star. That was her scar. We all had our own. They were indelible.

Everything ached. My limbs were stretched out as if they'd run away from my body. I was struck by a feeling of overwhelming sadness for them, as if my own body had morphed into something else while I wasn't looking, and now it was too late and I had to deal with the consequences of my recklessness. Deva closed the flimsy white curtains of her cabin to filter out the morning light and got in bed next to me. The smell of her skin came and went. I squeezed her closer to trap her inside my nostrils.

"I missed you," I told her with my eyes closed.

She rested one hand on my belly and put the other one between my thighs. "Squeeze," she said. "I'm cold."

I pushed my legs together and exhaled on her head to warm her up. The cabin was musty. Humidity seeped into our skin. I wrapped myself around her and opened my eyes, observing her face up close.

"How was Montana? I thought you'd never come back."

She avoided the question and nuzzled herself closer toward me. "You make me feel like I can lose a backpack with all my most precious things inside and you'll know exactly how to find it," she said.

I liked that, and I liked that her eyes didn't scramble around my face now. It was the first time she had looked at me that way.

But I was annoyed at the compliment. I propped myself up on the bed and told her about how I'd spent my last weeks chasing her and how difficult it had been. When she was in Montana she was always busy. She never called me back. Still, I made up a big excuse with my parents just to get her where she wanted to be for her birthday. I pretended to like a guy I wanted nothing to do with. I dragged him out to the desert and left him in the middle of nowhere. I'd been heartless and took drugs that I couldn't handle, all so I could see her again. It was hard to understand how to be with someone who didn't want to be seen, who never told you how she felt and always ran off to the next hiding place. Deva looked down and said something about how going to Montana had drained her. Her brother and father and her had built a recording studio almost from scratch. It took longer than they expected.

"But why does he need a recording studio in Montana? You guys live here," I answered.

She shrugged her shoulders.

I tried to be severe and hold my ground, but I realized as I spoke to her that I was completely enamored. She could have done anything she wanted with me. She could have abandoned me, not returned any of my calls, and I would have still been there on that bed that morning, happy just to be in her presence. I would have ditched a thousand sad Alos with holes in their throats, just to spend a night with her.

She moved across the wooden bed. Specks of light filtered through the trees outside the window and fell in streaks over her messy hair, settling on her clavicles. She hopped off and stood at the end of the bed, observing me. She removed my knee-highs. My feet were black with desert dirt. She kissed them. Her small, round head was silhouetted by light. It burst out of her margins like an electric halo.

"I was afraid you were in love with me and I didn't want to be responsible for that," she said, looking straight up at me.

I pulled her in and brushed my fingers over her chest. "I'm in love with you, yes," I replied. "So what?"

She pressed her body against the wooden footboard and kissed me. I pushed her away defensively, but she kissed me again and let out a gentle moan, something that said she was sorry. She took her clothes off and got back in bed, leading the way. She licked my lips and cheeks. I licked her back, eyes, and hair and anything in the way.

"It's okay," she said as she pulled me to her. "I want to be with you too."

My hands pressed onto her hot, bony frame. I finished undressing her. I took her in my arms and we made love. It wasn't like on the merry-go-round when we had spun around like nocturnal wind-up toys, coming fast and unexpectedly, never talking about it again. This was a declaration without words.

We were together for hours, kissing and spacing out from the drugs then reaching for each other again. Our fingers traced the outlines of each other's bodies, from inside our legs back up to our breasts and lips until every crevice was memorized. I didn't know girls could have so much liquid inside them. I had never gotten that way with a guy, but by late morning the bed was so damp, it looked like we'd spent the night peeing in it. Sand granules from the desert cluttered the inner corners of Deva's eyes, forming a bright yellow mucus like that of a kitten. Radiant dust particles deposited on her ribs and belly button. Her small breasts, illuminated by the suncatchers that hung in the window, were the last things I saw before I closed my eyes.

23

We hadn't slept long when we heard the bang on the door.

Deva poured water from a bottle and splashed it on her eyes so she wouldn't look sleepy. Her father barged in and looked at my muddled face, confused.

"Well, happy New Year to you, Italian lady. What did you girls do last night?"

"Eugenia's mom cooked an Italian dinner for me. Her parents just dropped us off so she could come on our birthday hike with us."

"What did she cook?" he asked, suspiciously.

"Veal parmesan," Deva improvised.

I'd never heard of such a dish. My mother would have rather killed herself than make something like that.

"Happy birthday, girl." He hugged her. "I remember when—"

"When I was just a little ball who rushed to come out into your arms . . . The opposite of my twin brother who wanted to stay right where he was."

His eyes relaxed when he heard her say this. She hadn't forgotten their rituals. Their inside jokes were intact. Things were okay.

"Is brunch ready?" Deva asked, faking enthusiasm.

A wider smile opened up on her father's pinkish face. He was drunk. I smelled it now. From the night before and starting again in the morning.

"I doubt my food will be as good as your mother's," he said, glancing over at me.

"I'm sure it'll be even better," I replied.

We went to the main house. The birthday brunch table was set up with banners and balloons on the terrace overlooking the oak tree expanse. There were no folders on the work desk inside, no beeping fax machines or glossy portfolio pictures. The computer monitor was turned off—the house clean. The furniture looked dead, as if it had stopped breathing when the family had left for Montana.

Chris appeared on the terrace with longer hair and a backwards cap that made him look thinner, like he was fizzling out instead of growing into a man. A gaunt, transparent creature.

"Happy New Year," he greeted me with a soft, sterile hug.

"Happy birthday," I replied.

He shrugged his shoulders.

"Deva and I don't celebrate on the same day. Dad wants to make sure he gets alone time with each of us. I'm surprised he let you come." He arched his brow at me.

Bacon and eggs fried inside.

We took our places. Deva's father poured us orange juice, then leaned into her, hugging her from behind.

"We're on TV next week. How's that for a birthday present?" he whispered.

Deva blushed and reached her arms behind to hug him back.

"A great one."

He perched in Deva's shade like a fixture to her presence, seeping into the space around her. Deva contorted her pose to seal him off, but he overspread. I'd seen him do that before.

Devour her with his presence until he made her look like a little thing.

I looked over at Chris. The banners hanging on the terrace all spelled his sister's name. I wondered whether their father would create the same atmosphere for him the following day. From the look on Chris's face I knew that wasn't going to be the case. They'd have leftover cake, melted birthday candles, cold bacon. I wondered how it made him feel to know he was not the chosen one. To be asked to step aside on the day of his birthday so his dad could have alone time with his twin sister.

Deva's father placed a wrapped gift on the table by Deva's fingers—a black Montblanc fountain pen.

She avoided eye contact.

"Thanks. It's a beautiful pen," she said, smiling wanly.

"Best in the world. Ink flows out like music. So that everything you write turns to gold." He kissed her hand. "Music contracts too."

Deva's father went inside to get the fried eggs. I reached for her knee beneath the table and gave it a squeeze. A shaft of sunlight divided us perfectly from one another at the table. I gripped her knee tighter. She, too, I thought, must have been feeling the urge to stay close to me, to keep bathing in the wide-open waters we'd dipped into that morning, our infinity pool. I saw glimpses of blue lakes and daffodils and fuming chimneys, ivy-covered cottages, and more canyon adventures on the horizon for us. I ignored her hand not looking for mine under the table.

I ate the eggs, smiled, and helped myself to more even though my stomach turned and the smell of maple syrup over the pancakes was making me sick. Deva's father drank a Budweiser and ate some strips of bacon. He glanced at his daughter then pushed his index finger over her bleary eyes, picking out crumbs of dry desert mucus.

"You both look like you came out of a washing machine. Are you sure you got enough sleep last night?"

She nodded yes, spreading food on her plate.

"You're not hungry?"

"Not much."

"Well, you better eat if you want to hike to Eagle Rock today."

"Maybe we should go in the afternoon," Deva suggested casually.

His face turned cross. He got up in a jolt, went inside, and returned with two pairs of boots. He gave her one and dropped the other one by my feet.

"We had a plan. We always celebrate your birthday like this."

He gave her a pat on the cheek, playful but stern—on the verge of a friendly slap.

"I know," Deva said cowering, too tired to come up with an excuse. "We are happy to go, okay?" she cut him short.

We set out for the great Eagle Rock. We were in no condition to go hiking, but Deva said if we didn't go, it would be worse. I'd hoped Chris would be coming with us, but he'd disappeared into his cottage after breakfast. Part of their separate birthday deal, I imagined. Deva asked me to act normal, to think about the way we hopped fences in school and how we always looked up at the sun and never turned back. I said I would, but the canyon's sunlight was dim that day, as if it had been flung off the sky. No golden rays, just faded blues and wintery metallic grays.

We hiked past the commune and red canyon rocks. Her father lifted his arm to salute Bob, who gave us a nod from the cottage he was hammering into, fixing what the rain had torn apart. I pretended not to know him. Deva waved politely as if their only connection was through her father. No traces of feral daughters or jealous wives.

The riverbanks had retired and the old mudslides from the storm had solidified into lush purple earth. We crossed the stream through the trees, guarding our heads from overgrown branches and tangled shrubs, and trailed along past the cottage with the outdoor tub where we'd bathed through the winter. A couple of Norwegian tourists hung underwear on a clothesline. Their daughter waved at us from the tub as one of the commune's stray puppies scratched its paws against the faded enamel.

"Look at that! An outdoor bathroom! Bob's a crazy cat, isn't he?"

"He sure is," Deva muttered.

Our eyes lingered on the entrance of the cabin. We'd crossed that threshold many times before, but now that we were with her father, it all seemed separate from us, as if we were walking through another version of our winter, like it wasn't us who hopped fences and broke in to cabins. We were not those kinds of girls now. We were girls who followed fathers through the woods, obedient.

We hiked back down across the main road and up into more woods through a path bordered by tall thorny bushes, down a slope, and up another hill that opened onto the entrance of the state park. The farther up we moved over rocky stretches, the colder it got.

"It's a lot of walking, but it's the best ocean view in LA," Deva's father announced. But his daughter's smile had vanished. She was meek and waxen as if she'd turned into an object during the course of the morning. Her pants were sliding off her waist and her panties bulged out of her crack in a bundled wedgie. Her breathing became fatigued. Her father noticed and walked over to her. He patted her on the shoulder.

"What's wrong?" he asked. "You look like a ghost." His tone wasn't fatherly or reassuring. He rubbed the back of her head with a noogie. Her long hair, heavy with desert dust, clumped up.

"What's this shit in your hair, Deva? Didn't you wash it yesterday?"

Deva nodded yes, pulling strands behind her ears to get them out of the way.

"It looks like you've been out camping or something. It's full of . . ." He combed through her mane with his fingers, picking out bits of sand. "Dirt . . . sand? What is this?" he asked, opening his hand for her to see.

Deva shrugged her shoulders.

He let out an impatient sigh then looked over at me.

"Veal parmesan," he said with a cackle, then turned around, and kept walking.

"Are you okay?" I whispered to Deva.

She signaled to move on with a nod of the chin, worried her father might hear us. She finally grabbed my arm, but only because she couldn't hold herself up. I made myself strong like a pole and pushed her up the hill. A little longer and we'd be on Eagle Rock. We could take a break there.

The mountains looked like distant accumulations of charcoal. Nothing was welcoming. Every leaf on the trees was like a sterile drawing. When we got to a clearing filled with oaks, they were all split in half like divaricated legs. The olive trees in a distant grove appeared remote and bare, like rickety, outstretched skeletons. Hills turned into lurching cliffs that fell off steep ridgelines into empty space. Winter.

When we reached Eagle Rock, Deva's hand was sweating in mine. The grass around the rock looked like flat patches of wire under the shadows of the clouds. Her father sat on the boulder, overlooking the precipitous bluff below, satisfied with his efforts.

"Look at that." He sighed at the view, but the ocean behind

the hills was black. His face and chest were pouring with acrid sweat, and Topanga did not seem beautiful to me anymore.

Deva took her final steps in a zigzagged line and stumbled toward a lateral bush. She leaned on her knees and threw up. I cleaned her face with dead leaves. Her father saw it and backtracked toward us.

"What's gotten into you, Deva?"

She propped herself up, resting her hands against her knees, and vomited again. I kept her hair back, but her father thrust me away with his hips.

"You want to tell me what's up?" he asked. He took her by the wrist and yanked her toward him.

"Nothing. I'm just not feeling well," she answered, collapsing into him.

He pulled her up in his arms.

"You want *me* to tell you what's going on, then? 'Cause *I* think I know quite well what's going on."

She tried to move away, but he held her still.

"You think I'm stupid or something? Italian dinner, right?" He glared at me now, then tied Deva's long hair in a knot and pulled it against his chest. She did not seem as shocked as I was by what was happening. It was as if this was a glitch or an annoyance, nothing more and nothing new.

"You went out, that's what's going on. You went to one of your all-night parties. Am I right?"

I stood on the cusp of the rock with a body that was unable to move. The chemicals from the previous night rushed back to paralyze me. There was something familiar about that feeling of impotence, a pounding heart inside an immobile body, the mind trying to bend a structure made of lumber. I was far away from Eagle Rock now, standing before Santino's wild eyes, tuned in to Angelina's sorrowful snout.

Deva untangled herself from her father's grasp.

"Yes, I'm sorry," she whimpered. "We just went out because it was my birthday."

He walked away from her, shaking his head like he was proud of himself for figuring it out. Then he stopped and caught his breath.

"It was my fault," I intervened. "I talked her into it."

He wasn't listening.

The soles of his shoes rotated against the loose gravel. He turned around and leaped back toward his daughter. Deva moved away with a jolt, causing their bodies to collide against each other on the way. The contact with her father's hips flung her across the air. She hit the rock and bounced off the quartz like a rubber ball, landing on her feet.

Suddenly I was not made of lumber anymore. I was sober and it didn't matter if Deva had fallen by mistake. My mind screamed that maybe it wasn't an accident, that this could be the prelude to something worse. I thought about the bruises I'd seen on her body, the days when she'd disappeared, the times when she'd refused to talk about things. I repositioned those memories in my head and gave them new meaning. Rage mounted inside me until it was some formless incandescent liquid. I clenched my teeth. Deva's father was coming closer to his daughter again, a look of truce and kindness on his face. That was no truce, though. It was the quiet before the storm. I screamed at him to get away from Deva. He didn't listen and kept moving toward his daughter, his head tilted sideways like he was trying to take her in. I took a step back. A quaking in my legs like an awakening, and my hands moved forward, hard and strong. I aimed for his belly. It was happening and I let it unfold like I wasn't part of the picture. I shoved myself against Deva's father with more force than I knew I had. I pushed him off the Eagle Rock into the small ditch below. I heard the sound of his arms against the shrubbery, the crackle of branches and dry leaves underneath. I didn't wait to catch my breath or listen to the final outcome. I turned toward Deva and hurried to her. She was a bundle of trembling bones. Her forehead was bleeding from the concussion.

"What the fuck did you do?" she screamed.

I replied with a slow, unhurried voice, hoping she'd made a mistake looking at me like I'd done something bad. Maybe she hadn't assessed the situation correctly.

"He was going to hurt you," I replied in a whisper.

"No he wasn't, you crazy bitch."

I peered over the rock toward the outcropping below. He was there, heaving, legs open wide on a dry bush halfway down the crag. He was far from dead, I reassured myself, and turned to Deva once again, but her face had hardened. I invited her to get up, but she was somewhere else. Her contours merged into the fading sunlight and she began to recede into the canyon. She gave me a final look of outrage and then she was gone. The sun had disappeared into the ocean, only blue hills and black shadows now. Everything caved in, and a different Deva would emerge out of that concave world. The previous one had departed.

"You're fucking nuts!" she shot at me with furious, limpid eyes, then climbed around the rock from the side and crawled into the escarpment. Her father was sprawled there. He moaned, eyes turned skyward like a martyr, bedraggled and vacant. Deva hovered over him protectively. I stayed above the rock and looked as her hair fell across his Adonis face. She was Venus, engulfing him back, conjoined. Her face was transfixed by a new light like she'd aged years in the span of a few instants. He let himself go to her embrace and abandoned his arms around her.

I felt stupid and remorseful, but also disgusted.

"Deva!" I screamed from above as she helped her father up. He limped, his arms and face scratched, but he was alive, standing.

"I'm reporting you to the police! I'm getting you kicked out of my country! You crazy Italian bitch." Even though his eyes fumed, his rage was a show. His body was squat and comfortable in his daughter's arms, his face a bright-red exploded moon.

"Deva!" I called again.

Her eyes glassed over. "You heard what he said," she said in a low drawl.

I felt myself droop. I'd heard that drawl before, on the phone from Montana. It was Deva's tone when she put up her wall. It rose above us, higher than the meteor boulder that had dropped in the canyon. It stretched over the Sicilian islands, the Mojave Desert, the Valley, and Topanga, and it was inscrutable like all the secret rules of children who'd grown up in that canyon. Topanga was a place where things were different and girls loved and feared their fathers, maybe slept in their beds, became their assistants and wives.

"You better leave or I'll kill you," her father screamed, starting to hobble his way up the trail.

I waited one more second, hoping to see Deva's translucent green eyes, if nothing else to bid me farewell, but she did not look up so I got back on my feet and ran away.

24

I galloped in a headlong descent toward the bottom of the canyon. Green patches shot across the corners of my eyes, out of focus. Suspended sycamores and rotten branches smashed against my mouth, filling it with bitter leaves. I scratched my arms with thorns, tumbling over brambles and branches, gathering momentum. I fell down and picked myself up again while the twigs sprung against my thighs. I ran through the apple orchards, the split-open oak tree trunks, past the commune's stream and the bathtub, past the red rocks. A giant hand was slapping me downhill, hitting me behind the rib cage, urging me to hurry on. I tripped and kept running down the woods toward the dark Pacific waters in the distance. I ran without looking back. I had seen my father run this way when we were kids—like a crazy spirit with flailing arms. I kept one hand on my aching spleen. On every beat, a shudder of pain shot across my back, reminding me that as fast as I could run away, it was still going to hurt in the end.

I stumbled into a gorge at the bottom of the canyon and onto a cement patch invaded by stinging needles. I crawled through a hole in a fence and suddenly I was in the lush garden of an uninhabited home in the Pacific Palisades. There was a stagnant green pond, perhaps once a private artificial lake filled

with swans. A small flight of swallows flew down to sip on the
water and dashed back up. Banana trees surrounded the pond
and tropical plants curved their thick leaves toward the ground.
On the other side of the lake, farther into the garden, I noticed
the path to an S-shaped swimming pool. I walked over. A blow-
up mattress covered in leaves drifted, half deflated, over blue
and aquamarine tiles. The water wasn't too dirty. The home had
been abandoned only recently. The pool house behind the diving board was infested with white bougainvillea trapping the
roof tiles. Climbing plants made their way toward the sky, battling for space, gripping drainpipes with furry, thirsty roots.
Two pots with overgrown flower stems drooped from the roof.

On the other side of the garden the dark ocean shimmered
through the trees, pulsating gently. I stopped. The leaves swayed
in the evening wind. The garden, overgrown and abandoned,
made me feel that time was still again. My heart settled, adrenaline dwindled. I was safe.

A faded FOR SALE sign was posted on the lawn of the
boarded up three-story mansion. Under the front porch was
a glass-topped wicker table covered in the typical last-minute
debris left behind in the final stretch of a move: open cardboard
boxes with old toys, buckets of dried-out wood paint and sol-
vent, tumbled bedsheets, dirty towels. A heap of clothes spilled
from a flung-open suitcase.

I dug my fingers into the musty fabric. I felt something soft
and pulled it out. Thanks to my time at Henry's store, my second nature now was to seek and protect any abandoned thing
coming out of a suitcase. It was a leopard coat, a real one from
the thirties at least. It was wrinkled and smelled like mold, but
the fur hadn't aged. Once I patted the dust off, it returned to life
with the slippery viscosity of an untamable animal. How could
the owners of that mansion have left something like that behind,
I wondered. The sleeves and collar had come unstitched, but
they could easily be fixed. It was cut for a size smaller than me.

I imagined it belonged to one of those silent-movie stars who vacationed in Topanga Canyon in the twenties. It had been part of the mansion for decades and now that the place was being sold, the owners, like all LA owners, had not gotten sentimental about it. I slid into the leopard fur, walked back to the pool, and stretched out on a torn deck chair.

A chilling wind began to blow. After a few minutes it was suddenly cold. The leaves still trembled, but with less electricity running through them.

I sank deeper into the coat and asked the leopard to give me paws with padding strong enough to bounce off any collision. Supreme hunter, fueled by nocturnal energies, let me be brave, I asked. I didn't know what to do or how to get home. I was afraid of something terrible happening to me if I went back into the canyon. The magnified shadow of a eucalyptus branch reflected under a dim surveillance light that was running out of batteries and a cool darkness began to cloak the rest of the garden. A fierce leopard, I thought. And with a shiver I fell asleep.

I woke up in the night to the sky crashing to pieces above my head, the roaring sound of a train tunneling through me, smashing against the pool house. My eyes flashed open and I saw Deva's father standing there, shaking me inside out, screaming. I rose in a jolt. There was nobody there. It wasn't the sky that was breaking apart but the earth. The train was being regurgitated from underground. I felt it under my feet. The soil moved in waves. Water splashed out of the pool. A part of the roof smashed to the ground bringing potted plants with it. Coyotes howled in the canyon recesses as the earth kept shaking, then everything went back to darkness and quiet. I knew what it was. We did the drills in school. They'd told us about how the land in Los Angeles rattled, but I could have never expected something like that.

I went out through the hole in the fence and walked around the periphery of the house until I emerged on a small hilltop street. There were no lights below the slope, only shimmering bits of crumpled tar. I walked down and it was like sinking into a dark gorge, guided by the sound of human screams on both sides. I couldn't understand where the drawn-out cries came from, if they were above me in the canyon or below me in the darkness, but they were reassuring. It was like having company. The earth began to shake under my feet again. This time I started to run, but couldn't steer my legs in any direction. They moved in a wobbly motion over the ribbed asphalt and I couldn't feel what I was running toward. The second rumble was shorter than the first, but when it stopped my feet kept swaying, trying to anticipate the earth's next roll. The screaming in the mountains intensified and I kept running in that awkward stumble until I realized I had landed on Sunset Boulevard. It was terra incognita, a part of the road with no houses or human signs, just trees and dirty foliage. I'd never noticed that rural pass of the boulevard from the car. We'd driven down the road countless times with the Cadillac's top down—Serena doing her best Gloria Swanson impersonation. But now it didn't look anything like that place.

Emergency vehicles and police cars lined the boulevard. Broken glass was everywhere, the smell of saltwater and cracked-open booze bottles in front of a busted-in liquor store. Sirens blared and the quiet but desperate chatter arose of people beginning to group. I walked along the highway until I found a parked police car and flailed my arms to a cop getting inside. I stuttered something about being lost and scared and needing to get back home. He frowned at my leopard fur and I suddenly realized what I looked like. It wasn't until I'd heard my own voice that I understood I was completely in shock.

"You should have stayed where you were safe," the policeman said as he let me inside his car. But nowhere was safe anymore. We pulled away from the dark ocean. In the car, alarmed voices spoke over the static on his radio. They said the Northridge Fashion Center in the Valley had collapsed and hazardous material was spilling on Winnetka, right by my high school. A building was burning in Sherman Oaks, a few blocks from our house. Ruptured gas and water mains were causing fires and flooding all over the Valley. The cop shook his head.

He said the worst of the earthquake had struck just blocks from my house. All the freeways were closed. The only way to the Valley was back through the canyon, and still he didn't know whether he'd be able to get me to the other side. The earthquake of January 17, 1994, was a 6.7 on the Richter scale.

"The big kind," the cop explained. "The kind that will have a name and a personality one day, the kind everyone will have a story about."

Police, highway patrolmen, even the National Guard were involved.

"Do you think my family will be okay?" I asked. "They live in Van Nuys."

He shrugged his shoulders.

I thought of the Sound City Studios at the edge of my neighborhood. I imagined Nirvana's platinum records falling off the wall, Kurt Cobain's bright eyes watching over the disaster from the corkboard. Another extreme event occurring in the Valley. All the more reason to love that place. What could be more grunge than a recording studio cracking open and falling into the earth?

As we got closer to the San Fernando Valley, we could see it from above shooting up in flames in the predawn light. The flat grid I'd walked far and wide and knew by heart was under siege. The city lights I used to see stretch for miles were gone. We stood over a dimmed city. I'd seen it like that before—a barren, pockmarked expanse—on the day we arrived, streets still fuming from the riots. That land had a fixed way of reacting to tragedies. Like a celebrity after a scandal, it begged for invisibility. It lay low under pressure, squat and compressed until disasters passed. Magnolia and cypress trees cowered into flaming bushes, buildings shrank, streets folded over, and lakes flung fish out of their waters. Everything waited for nature to rapidly take its course so that an ancient harmony could be restored.

I could see the Woodland Hills Mall in the distance, a beached cement whale, emanating no life pulse—a shaken slab of concrete. I thought of Arash and saluted him. For the first time he felt far away, a memory beginning to fade, replaced by new quakes.

The auroral rays intensified. The night's chill retreated behind us and we were expelled into the fiery morning below. Day broke, racing against a chorus of manic chirping birds, howling dogs, and roosters. Hungry, fast rays of sun began to climb across the crushed roofs and treetops, cracked antennas, and telephone wires that hung off wobbling poles—a far-reaching sun, responsible for the Valley's sameness, for the changeless days and odorless air. It engulfed you.

"Let's hurry home, sir," I said as we drove up Ventura Boulevard. We tried to make our way through smaller side streets, but every avenue was blocked by a collapsed building or a pile of cars. My head spun and I felt like throwing up. The cop said to stay calm. Disorientation and nausea were normal reactions to earthquakes.

From the car, I saw families huddled together. Lines formed around the few functioning pay phones, tent villages were beginning to rise while dogs roamed in packs looking for food. We met the hollow stares of those who had had a home and then thirty seconds later did not. The Valley was denuded and nakedness made no sense to a town so used to being dressed up. Without its vestments there was no Los Angeles.

The cop dropped me off on Sunny Slope Drive and I was happy to see that it hadn't fallen into the earth, that it was still there. Just more crooked.

"I hope your family is okay," he said.

I tried to hug him, but he pushed me back at arm's length.

"Just doing my duty," he said in a rush as more horrific news radioed in: the looting had begun.

"Remember what happened to this town the last time things got out of control," the cop proclaimed. "We're not going to let that happen again." He gave me a nod and took off.

Most of our neighbors were out on the street. The Mormons prayed on their front lawn. Desmond, the star, with his wife, mother, and blind dogs, wandered about in a silk bathrobe. He'd been so keen on safeguarding his privacy, but now he looked around, desperate for someone to recognize him, to talk to him and ask him how he was doing. I gave him a quick consoling nod and moved on.

Timoteo was asleep in my mother's lap. My parents sat cross-legged on the front lawn, eyes wide open. They waited silently for someone to walk over and tell them what to do. They lit up when they saw me with my unstitched leopard-fur coat and messed-up hair. Our driveway was cracked open. The living room had folded in, giving the house a crumpled Z shape. The garage door had fallen out. Boxes had toppled onto the Cadillac's windshield, breaking it, but everything else seemed fine.

"Where have you been?" my father screamed. "Your mother has already filed three missing-person reports!"

"I'm sorry. I had no way to call. I got here as soon as I could."

Timoteo awoke and walked up to me, staring at my unlikely outfit.

"You look crazy." He smiled.

"I know."

He opened my coat and nuzzled inside. "I thought you weren't going to come back."

I opened the fur as wide as I could and wrapped it around him. My parents joined us and I fit them all in. We stayed there, squeezed together in our crammed group hug.

"What about the monitors?" I asked my father. "Is the Alexandria footage damaged?"

"Don't worry about that now," he said. "I'm just glad you're okay."

Those were the words I'd waited to hear for so long, but now that he'd said them I was worried. If he had gotten to that point it meant he'd surrendered.

Someone had told them not to go back inside because there might be aftershocks. The house was not safe, my mother explained, clutching a battery-less flashlight, vaguely remembering that was something you were supposed to have handy when earthquakes struck. She set up breakfast on the front yard: dry cereal, bread, butter, and milk. She'd managed to put together a meal out of the derelict kitchen. Everything had spilled and crashed to the floor, but she was on caretaker autopilot. We were to have breakfast because it was morning and that's what people did when they woke up. So we ate, sitting on pillows on the front lawn. Neighbors trickled by to talk about loss and damage and my mother welcomed them stoically with her improvised breakfast plates. Everyone said where they were and what they heard when it happened. Some had sad stories, some had happy stories.

I curled up next to my brother on the ground.

"I didn't wake up when it happened," he said with a smirk. "I could have died."

"I'm glad you didn't."

"I didn't tell them about the guys in the pickup truck."

"Thanks." I smiled, like any of that even mattered now. I leaned against him, exhausted.

My father looked at us with ironic commiseration and started to laugh.

"What?" Timoteo and I glared at him.

"Well we can now say we've done it all. *Non ci siamo fatti mancare niente.* The whole California experience with the earthquake grand finale too. Pretty cool, right?"

Serena rolled her eyes at him. "It's not funny."

"There's dead people, Dad," I interjected.

"Okay, okay. Sorry. I was trying to be lighthearted."

Creedence and his brothers, led by their father, DeLoyal, and their pale, wide-eyed mother, Cresta-Lee, approached our house and asked us if we wanted to join their prayer circle.

My father accepted enthusiastically. He was inappropriately exhilarated, like a kid in an earthquake-themed amusement park. The adrenaline rush had stirred something in him.

"Well, it can't hurt," Serena said, trying to justify the excessive exultance. My brother and I got up and moved grudgingly toward the prayer group on the street. I heard Creedence whisper to Timoteo something about the earthquake happening in the Valley because of the porn-film industry. It was a sign from God.

Our neighbors stood in the circle. It was understood we had to be flexible with our religious affiliations in times of crisis. That day we'd have to make do with a generic, all-encompassing God, though the Mormons felt they were the protagonists of everyone's redemption since they were leading the prayers. I prayed to Mary for the first time since Arash's death. I asked her to be kind to everyone, just to be kind because we were all so tired.

The Mormons raised their hands toward the center of the circle and I saw a shadow advancing toward our street from the ruins of Victory Boulevard. A Terminator rising from the ashes. He walked hunched forward but unafraid—a duffel bag on his shoulder. I ran toward him.

Henry.

He hugged me close to his chest and kissed my head.

"How did you get here?" I asked.

"I walked."

"From your store?"

"It's not my store anymore." He grinned. "It's gone. Collapsed, exploded. A fire."

"What about your mom?"

"She's fine. She's happy. We have insurance. Only smart thing she's done in her life. She's with our neighbors right now. Her gross canned food is finally being put to good use. They're eating pinto beans on Ventura."

"I'm sorry I was a bitch," I said.

He handed me the duffel bag and made a gesture like we had all moved on. "I brought some stuff I thought you guys might need: sleeping bags, batteries, tents, Snickers bars. I'll help you through this. Italians don't know about California earthquakes."

He was right.

Henry camped with us in our backyard for a week. At night we sat around a bonfire watching the flames swell and subside under our command. It felt good to control something. We boiled water on hot coals and went to bed early. Ettore talked about practical things, like how to keep the fire going for a long time with the least amount of wood, how to recycle used water, how to make lemon and mint infusions to quench our thirst. He never once mentioned the Hotel Alexandria and the movie. During those days my brother and I felt like we were allowed to be kids again, relieved from any sense of responsibility that didn't have to do with mundane duties. We all got along like a normal family and slowly that started to feel natural.

At night sirens still blared, but things were calming down. Before falling asleep I heard the sound of Deva's body thumping against the rock—a punctual summons that reached me as soon as darkness descended. I was caught in between a feeling of paranoia and a sense of urgency and justice because of what I'd done. I tried to justify myself, but the question remained: Had I really been crazy? Had I imagined things? Once, I woke up to the sensation of my legs tumbling down a hill—the galloping rhythm from my Eagle Rock escape back in my feet. I felt my knees strike against the sleeping bag's padding. Even with my eyes open I could not stop them. My chest ached. It felt as if a wrinkled hand were keeping the surface of my heart taut, stretching the flesh out so I would know how much more painful things could get. I tried to unclench the grasp, but the hand stayed there, forcing me to feel what I did not want to feel. Slippery Deva, fleeting eyes, swaying hair. I didn't know who I was without her and without the canyon.

I stepped out of my tent in the middle of the night and stood in my nightgown in front of the fire pit, gazing at the disembodied parts of our home on display at the end of the backyard: the broken plates, the ripped couch, my father's oak desk. They all seemed so insubstantial now.

My mother came shuffling out of her tent after me, groaning.

"What are you doing up?" she asked, sleepy-eyed. She hugged me from behind in front of the dying fire.

"I can't sleep," I said, staring at the red coals.

She kept her eyes half shut as if the conversation might be brief enough to not wake her up entirely. She hated losing sleep.

"We'll be back inside the house soon."

"It's not that."

She took a breath. "I was so worried about you not coming home. I thought I would kill myself if I lost you," she said in a hoarse voice.

"You would?" I turned to her. "Really?"

"No, not kill. But I did see how ruined our lives would be without you in them."

"Thanks."

"Are you okay?" she finally asked, both eyes open now.

"Mom, I did something bad. I'm worried . . ."

She nodded reassuringly.

"I know it wasn't a peaceful sit-in in the desert, baby. I think Dad figured it out too. We were young once and you never gave a shit about the Zapatista army."

She lifted my chin to meet her eyes and I felt a surge of tenderness for her. Where had they been living all those months?

"Yes, it wasn't a peaceful gathering."

I let her fingers stroke through the front of my hair and rested my cheek on her chest. A little longer, I thought to myself. I'd rest there just a little longer.

25

I **dreaded the** moment when the phone lines would be working again, but that happened one day too. Halfway through February we were at dinner and the fax beeped and began regurgitating home-repair offers—the business of earthquakes was starting to take over the tragedy of it.

"Damaged house? Ruined interiors? We can help."

I imagined fax machines all across the San Fernando Valley overheating, spewing out papers filled with promises of those organized enough to turn tragedy into opportunity.

"Seismic businesses," my father grumbled.

We did the house cleanup ourselves, though it still smelled like mildew and rusty water.

I got up from the dinner table and pulled the curly phone cord from its base in the kitchen all the way to my bedroom. We were only one yard sale away from owning a cordless. I turned the lights off, then curled inside my bed under the blankets and made the call.

Chris picked up.

"It's Eugenia," I said in a quiver.

"My father is back from the hospital. You fractured his leg. He's in a cast."

"I'm sorry."

"That plus the earthquake. Not great timing."

"He's okay?"

There was a shuffling sound and a sigh, but no reply on the other end.

"I thought he would hit Deva." I tried to raise my voice and beat away the crackle. "He looked like he was going to do it and she was already bleeding, so I—"

"I know. Thank you." He hung up.

I called back but nobody answered.

I also called Alo to apologize, but he didn't want to speak to me. He said he never wanted to see me again and to throw away his phone number.

Deva didn't return to school after it reopened three weeks later. News spread about an outbreak of something known as Valley fever—a respiratory disease caused by airborne fungus spores carried by seismically triggered dust clouds. Valley fever: I imagined that was the reason she wasn't back—a post-earthquake refusal to return to the vapidity of our high school. Newspapers said the condition manifested itself with heavy chest pains. I felt those. Perhaps we'd both developed a San Fernando Valley allergy. Except I didn't have anywhere else to go now that she was out of my life.

Days turned into weeks. I still looked for her swinging pony-tail and kept my ears open for her laughter, but the school hall-ways echoed with her absence. I began to lose hope. It turned out Valley fever cases had been limited to Ventura County. If anyone had contracted the disease it was Alo, as if the cancer and broken throat weren't enough.

I bumped into Azar as she came out of a bathroom stall one day. Her hair had grown down to her shoulders, parted by two sparkly butterfly barrettes. It made her head look slightly less huge. She had on a short dress and white tennis shoes with wedges to make her taller. She walked to the mirror with a pur-ple compact and started powdering her nose.

"I almost didn't recognize you," I said, smiling.

She turned to me, uninterested, and narrowed her big eyes like she was trying to remember who I was.

"It's been a while," she answered. She turned back to the mirror and painted her lips with strawberry gloss. The black hair had disappeared from her arms and her mustache was also gone. She tweezed her brows now, like all the other girls in school.

"Remember when you made me believe you'd protect me after Arash died? You made me think you'd help me," she said.

"I remember our hug on the field."

"Well, you never helped. I had to figure it out on my own."

I looked at her skinny olive legs and didn't know what to say.

"I like your dress."

It had daisies printed over a burgundy background. Floral dresses were in style. She fit right in. Unlike me, she had found her place.

"Thanks," she said.

"If you ever feel like hanging out ..." I began, but she clicked her compact shut and raised an eyebrow at me. She walked out of the bathroom.

It was like the first day of school all over. On the football field I looked up at the speakers and thought that maybe Deva was gone for good and the principal would announce it with his crackling voice like he'd announced Arash's death. I swiped my hands on the fence around the school's perimeter. I waited for her by the one in front of the side doors, fingering the pieces of wire that replaced the holes that used to be there, our portals to the other side. She never came.

Mrs. Perks told me she'd take me on in her Honors English class for my senior year. She said that was an important year because it was when I had to apply for college. I thought I would feel victorious or proud of myself when that day came, but I didn't feel anything.

After school at the bus stop, a scrawny guy came up to me.

I'd seen him with Chris before, playing hacky sack in the parking lot. He went by the nickname Brain Dead. He had a green Mohawk, pants almost falling off his hips, and safety pins in his ears. His backpack was wider than his back, like a baby gorilla propped on his shoulders, suffocating his entire frame. His face was freckled and the rosy spots on his cheeks matched his mucusy-rimmed eye sockets, pinkish like those of a lab rat.

"I heard you're looking for Chris," he said as he sat next to me.

"Deva, really. Do you have news?"

"They're, like, gone or something," he replied in a faint voice.

"What?"

"They're both in continuation school. Chris's dad put them there until the move."

"What move?"

"Montana. My stepmom knows their dad through music stuff. She said he built a big recording studio out there. He's going to go with the kids. It's cheaper and stuff there."

"He didn't build the studio, his children built it," I replied defensively.

He got up. His bus was approaching. "Whatever." He shrugged his shoulders at me.

He got on and turned to me as he waited his turn to insert the coins in the slot by the driver. "See ya."

I crossed the street and started walking in the opposite direction, toward the canyon.

The bay-leaf shrubs in Deva's driveway were overgrown. I thrust my fingers against them like we always did when we came back to her place, except this time I didn't have to hide the smell of smoke from anyone. The shrubs whipped back at my arms like green armored shields protecting the crooked house—a fortress guarded by unfriendly plants. I pushed them back and kept walking up. The field of oak trees beneath the terrace hummed with the melody of Deva's laughter. It was the first thing I heard when I approached the house. My heart raced. I was back in that yard. The air smelled of woody eucalyptus, the familiar scent of all the good places I loved. For a moment it made me think maybe we could still take it all back.

Folk music played. Through the front window I saw her father sitting at his desk. His crutches leaned against the wall. Deva stood over him, hair up in a bun, a pen squeezed between her fingers. She was taking notes about something. Her father's music awards had come off the walls and the house was bare and full of scattered boxes. I couldn't tell if it was post-earthquake chaos or the looming presence of the move. Her father pulled her to him and sat her on his lap playfully as they picked out a selection of pictures that were displayed on the desk. Deva pushed him back, yanking his shirt with the deliberate gesture of a woman, yet there was something unfeminine about her or maybe it wasn't the femininity I'd known. Deva the girl was gone, leaving space for a baritone woman. And it was as if my thoughts were audible because she lifted her eyes the moment I conjured her, meeting my gaze through the window. She looked down then tapped her father's shoulder.

He let her go. Didn't look up, had nothing to fear now.

Deva came out and let her hair down as she walked to me. It flopped against her back creating the same golden veil she'd had the first time I followed her down to the river.

"What are you doing? You can't come back here anymore," she said.

"Is it true you're moving?"

"My father is filing a restraining order against you. I'm trying to convince him not to. If he sees you—"

"Are you? Are you moving to Montana? Really?" I glanced up at the main house.

"It's for his work. He got a manager there. Plus a great studio. We're going in a few weeks. LA is not good for his music anymore."

"You don't have to go. You could stay with me once you turn eighteen."

"I'm never going back to the Valley."

The bruise on her forehead was almost gone, the bluish tint had turned into a lilac patch of translucent flesh.

"I can help you," I said and meant it. "You're not seeing things the way they are."

She stood there, cold and firm. Her eyes would not blink. They looked small and beady like her father's. He must have put her on some kind of medication. She was a mask. There was something emotion-purged and unfeeling about her.

"We're finishing something up. You better leave."

She looked at my velvet bell-bottoms. They were hers. I wore them almost every day now. "You can keep them."

"You can't keep this up. You don't have to be your father's assistant."

A thick vein pumped on her forehead. She was not a kid anymore.

"Go," she replied firmly. Her eyes trembled with a slight rapid motion. She hugged me and pressed her cold face against my neck for a moment. "Don't try to stop this. It will be all right." Then she smiled.

She turned around and walked away. I felt ice-cold all of a sudden. I wanted to run after her, but instead I kept looking at her thick hair bouncing off her shoulders. I caught a final glimpse of her pale freckled cheeks before they disappeared inside the house. The door shut behind her. It was the end of halos and eucalyptus cones, of terraced apple orchards and crooked cottages. The end of the place above. I walked back down her driveway one last time and started to cry. Then I remembered how the trees of the house were like audience members. I tried to stop my tears. I didn't want them to think I looked stupid.

26

My mother stood over a marble sink holding a dead guinea fowl, ripping its feathers out a few at a time. I hadn't expected Henry to have a marble sink, but his new apartment was filled with the amenities of a new life. Everything was different after the money from the insurance came through, even his hair. He chopped it off. He didn't care about showing his missing ear anymore. The new store space on Melrose Avenue was smaller and less cluttered. This was not a neighborhood where you could sit and stare at a screen or take bong hits in the back. He lived alone in the small apartment upstairs where we now sat—Henry, Phoebe, my brother, father, and I looking at Serena's clenched teeth as she plucked the dead bird. Henry and Phoebe now took cooking lessons from her. After the quake Phoebe had moved to Agoura Hills, farther into the Valley.

"If I'm to die old and fat I'd rather do it where nobody can see me," she said. But I thought she still looked beautiful.

When I was ten years old my mother smiled and said, "Taste this," and put a sweet and gushy piece of flesh in my mouth. It was the tongue of a cow. I didn't know meat could taste that sweet. I didn't know cow tongues could be consumed and I got angry at her for feeding me a part of an animal I didn't want to eat, but that's how she was. She moved on. Dead birds, cow tongues, veal brains, she didn't care if her kids thought it was scary or wrong to eat them. The world would adjust. I looked over at her from the dinner table and wondered if I'd ever be at peace with something dead, if I'd find the courage to keep going and move forward even when everything around me said it was too much.

"It's important to massage the fowl, make it think it's loved, even if it's already dead," she explained to Henry and Phoebe, her hands reeking with bird juices. Her hair was getting longer and her darker roots were growing back in.

Henry signaled me to go to his bedroom. We slipped away. It was the middle of June. The heat wave made everything hot and muggy, but his bedroom had a new remote-controlled air conditioner. We sat on the bed next to each other, and looked out the window onto Melrose Avenue. A group of drag queens in matching outfits stampeded down the street, cackling. I felt I was in a city again, a place where people existed outside the windows.

"Looks like they're having fun," Henry said with a smirk.

I turned to look at his face. I never realized how round it was when he had long hair—like a full, pale moon.

"I wanted to ask you something," he announced uncomfortably. "I want to find and sell treasures. Real treasures. Hollywood is not like the Valley. People actually expect things here. I need help."

"I love treasures."

"Do you want to work for me? You transformed the old store and I know you could do great things with this one."

"Like a real job?" I asked.

Henry looked away, his big eyes already apologizing for having been too bold. I put my hand on his knee, not wanting him to retreat.

"Sounds amazing."

"A real job," he continued, encouraged. "After school. You

can start saving up for your creative writing at USC. You better apply, by the way, or you'll end up a loser like me."

"You're not a loser," I said. "And of course I'll apply. My English teacher said she'll help me."

I let myself fall on his bed. I nuzzled into his pillow and took a deep breath. "Your sheets don't smell like stale pot anymore."

"There's a Laundromat in the building."

He lay down next to me. I turned my back to him, pulled my knees up to my belly, and wedged my butt against the nook of his bowed legs. I passed his hands over my side, and pulled him toward me.

"Are you spooning me?" he asked.

"No, technically I'm making you spoon me."

We stayed silent, listening to my parents in the other room talking about the romantic holiday they were going to go on and how much they needed it after the Hotel Alexandria fiasco and Max disappearing into thin air. They said the same things over and over, like soldiers back from a war, tormented by recurring dreams.

"And we came home and everything was gone. Just gone. And he was nowhere to be found."

Miramax did not take *If These Walls Could Talk*. Johnny Depp and his agent didn't approve the elevator-scene cameo, saying he'd never signed a formal agreement. The Hustons kept coming over for lunch, but they were more interested in my mother's cuisine than anything else. Not even Vanessa Peters managed to pull strings. It was as if the film had been doomed the second Max left. When the final cut was finally ready, my father sold it to an Italian television channel. In America PBS came forward asking for raw footage for a documentary they were putting together on haunted buildings in America. That's what it had come down to: disembodied clips, raw footage, Italian television. It wasn't the Hollywood ideal my parents had dreamed of when they flew in.

I looked at Henry's partly missing ear and placed my index finger over the slight protuberance. The helix and upper parts were joined together in a shapeless lump of flesh and cartilage.

"What does it feel like when I touch it?" I asked.

Henry shrugged his shoulders. "Not much," he smiled. "Except it's nice to feel your hand."

"I'm happy you cut your hair."

"A missing ear is more punk rock than long hair." He giggled.

"I agree. It's probably better not to hear half the shit people say anyway."

On our way home my parents were quiet. Timoteo gazed out the window, listening to his portable CD player.

"So how about a big yard sale at the end of the month?" my mother finally said.

"What more do we have to buy?" I asked.

I gave my brother a nudge to take his headphones off.

"No, how about having one? We're thinking of moving back to Rome after this summer," my father announced, glancing quickly toward Serena before speaking.

"We didn't want to say it at dinner. We wanted to tell you alone, first."

They spoke fast like they needed to get things off their chest at once. Some part of me kept saying *no,* another said *yes* or *I understand,* but mostly I didn't understand and I looked at them like I didn't understand so they'd know they would have to speak slower.

"A couple of producers in Italy saw the film and liked it. They want to meet with Dad and talk about doing some work together. Possibly a TV series in Rome. It's good news."

"Really?" Timoteo asked, excited.

"If it works out it's a big deal. We need the money," Ettore explained. "We'll be able to deal with the house and the mortgage."

"But we need to be *there* and we can't be *here,*" Serena said.

"Can't you go and meet with these producers, and then come back?" I asked.

"It doesn't work that way." My mother sighed. "You need to live where the work is. People need to see your face." She sounded like a responsible person who now knew how things worked or didn't work. "We're tired," she admitted and just saying that made her cheeks droop and her eyes water. "We're out of money and this thing with Max took a lot out of us."

Even though there was a new prospect on the horizon, they did seem tired, both of them. A bit crooked, like they'd had enough. It was the end of a dream or the end of an idea of a dream—it was hard to tell at that point.

"It's not time for fun and games anymore," Ettore concluded. "It might be a big opportunity. And if it is, I have to take it. These Americans, they're so uptight. I'm much better off in Europe with producers who understand my artistic sensibility."

"But what about school? And the USC application and the letter they sent me and all those SAT tests I took? I have one year of high school left," I said.

"Your brother is graduating junior high, so he'll start high school fresh in Rome. You can pick whatever school you like to finish your studies. Afterward you can go to *any* university in Italy and it's free." Serena was full of solutions.

"What about your romantic vacation at the end of the month? I thought you were going because things were better. And what will you do with grandma's ashes? Smuggle them back?"

"We are still going on our romantic vacation. We've anticipated the trip. Grandma will be coming back to Rome with us. We'll find a way."

"So you won't come to my junior-high graduation?" my brother asked, disappointed.

"Your sister will come. You know, honey," my mother turned around to face him, "nobody in Italy cares when you graduate junior high. It's a ridiculous American thing. It's not like it's some big achievement."

My brother looked down. They'd been rehearsing the ceremony at school and having cap-and-gown fittings. Everyone in his class took it seriously. I squeezed his hand.

"I'll be there," I reassured him. Then I sat back and didn't say another word.

When we got home, Serena put her arms around me in the driveway. "What do you think?"

I shrugged my shoulders. I hadn't felt much of anything except sadness since the last time I saw Deva.

"What will you do?"

"I'm thinking cooking lessons. Maybe I can get some American clients. They seem to like it."

Ettore came closer to us, dragging Timoteo along with him to create a graceless group hug.

"How about it, guys? I think we've had enough of summer all year long, don't you?" He laughed, but there were tears in his eyes and I didn't understand how he could laugh if he was also crying.

My brother hugged him back. He was so terrified by the idea of going to my metal-detector school, being called "the Italian Tomato" again by everyone. He would have done anything to avoid it.

I looked away.

"You know, guys, school in Rome gets out at lunchtime. You'll finally have your afternoons back and just think about it: We can go places where it actually *snows* on Christmas."

"And we won't feel like thieves when we go through customs at the airport." My mother smiled.

"No more cops on beaches if we feel like getting naked, no more private health care!" Ettore was giving himself courage, but I walked away from their posturing and retreated inside the house to my bedroom and shut the door, fumbling for my rubber suit, hating the fact that I'd thrown it out.

I turned my TV on. Why not, I thought as I got under the sheets without removing clothes or shoes. Why not take myself out of this mess. After the earthquake, darkness had expanded until it covered everything with a feeling of indistinct gloom. Even the showerhead, as I sat under the needling water staring at the black, spiky leg hair I'd stopped shaving, looked like a grayish amoeba to me. Everything had gone downhill and I stopped sleeping. The good nights were the ones when I wallowed in the backyard crying because tears brought surprise or at least texture to my feelings. USC had accepted me as a student. Henry had invited me to work at the store. But were those reasons to stay somewhere? I was only seventeen. What would I do? Where would I live and was it worth it? Rome would be manageable, like a small town to me now—a place where cars and trees were smaller, where people cared for each other's babies and fed each other's relatives. A quaint town, the Eternal City.

I skimmed through a copy of the latest issue of *Corriere della Sera* that lay on the floor by my bed. My parents had started buying Italian newspapers at the international newsstand again. I should have known something was up. Italy was in the hands of a new leader. He came from television and was stepping into politics, promising a brighter tomorrow filled with job opportunities and modernity. He'd won the elections in March. Everyone loved him. Nineteen ninety-four had been a promising year even though some said he was a crook. He owned four national television stations, three publishing houses, innumerable magazines, newspapers, film-production companies, video-rental chains, and sports teams. At least there would be job openings, everyone said—and if he was so good with business, who knew how much better he would be with politics. He had composed a hymn for his new political party: "Forza Italia!"—"Go Italy!" Maybe he would bring good news to my family when we moved back. His face was tanned and his teeth shone. It was enough to trust him. He was five foot five and his name was Silvio Berlusconi.

As I flipped through articles about the stout smiling man, dozens of highway patrol cars and Los Angeles police vehicles appeared on the KCAL news. They rolled in perfect formation down the 405 freeway—the same freeway that roared in our ears every day—trailing behind an unhurried white SUV. It was a slow-speed chase, I gathered from the news. The man inside the white car was O. J. Simpson—a football player and actor I hadn't known much about until a few days earlier when he'd been charged with the double murder of his ex-wife Nicole and her friend Ronald Goldman. She had been stabbed in the head and neck. If he was convicted Simpson faced the death penalty. That morning his lawyers had convinced the LAPD to allow him to turn himself in. One thousand reporters waited for him at the police station, but he never showed up.

He reappeared hours later on TV inside a white Bronco. A friend drove the car leisurely while O.J. held a gun to his own head. The freeway was packed with onlookers waving from overpasses and ramps, cheering their favorite NFL star as if he were a marathon runner making his way home. Some people pulled over and got out of their cars to salute him from the roadside and I too wanted to cheer for him for some reason. It was his wax-museum face and that gun at his head and something about him that said he was done. It made you want to protect him, make sure he'd get home all right, that he wouldn't pull that trigger. I was spying on him like the rest of the nation. The only way to give him privacy was to turn the TV off.

I switched the channel and a sea of freckles hit me. I

recognized the song. I knew the face: *"And when I say I'm looking, don't mean I wanna find what I'm looking for / When I say I'm searching, don't mean I want to search at all."*

There was Deva. In the final cut of her father's music video. She leaned against a wooden fence looking up at her dad with adoring eyes. His face looked starched without the beard. His plump nose in contrast with her immaculate youth. *"Don't mean I want to search at all."*

Father and daughter clasped hands and walked down the dirt path, their voices reverberating in my ear like a drawn-out off-key note. My heart began to race. I wanted to pause the video and look at each image frame by frame, but I couldn't and I realized I should force myself to not even try. The way out of the pain, I saw, was to walk through it or drive through it perhaps, like O.J. was doing. If I could sit all the way through the video just once, putting my eardrums under siege, I could return to a time when those voices did not exist. Before being uttered, those notes had been nothing—and if I stayed there and let the music take its course, they might become irrelevant again. I remained still in bed, listening as the song stretched out infinitely, expanding backward in time. Then even the echoes dwindled. I stayed put until all sounds were dismantled and I could not hear Deva's voice in my ears anymore. Until she was a muted beauty next to a muted old man.

27

"**We're leaving in** one month, everybody! Last chance for authentic Italian food in LA County!" my mother screamed from the front yard. It was the end of July and everything we owned was out on the front lawn. My mother baked pizza pies and offered pasta alla Norma with salted ricotta to passersby. Her food stand was in the driveway and that was all she cared about, that our neighbors would remember the Italian family by the taste of the food she cooked.

My parents were proud of their choice to return now. Apart from the new job prospect, moving back had turned into a political act. America was inhumane, they said. Nobody in their right mind could live permanently in Los Angeles. It was a doomed city, destined for maniacs and workaholics. How much easier things would be once we all went back, they kept saying. The quality of life, food, even water would be better. There were people on the other side of this mess, people who actually wanted us back, who would help us. We would not return to an indifferent city.

Neighbors and visitors trickled in after my brother and I hung large signs on Sepulveda Boulevard: "Yard Sale! Moving back to Europe. Furniture, appliances, and free home-cooked Italian food by Serena." Probably the one astute marketing strat-

egy my parents had conjured since they'd moved. Ettore played
Pink Floyd from the crackling speakers that were set up on his
oak desk. It was going on sale for fifty dollars.

"If you can see it, you can buy it."

Ettore had coined the phrase to lure people in. It was
amazing how this car-salesman persona had emerged—at last.
How confident he was, pitching Jerry Garcia records and talking about Woodstock with a hippie from Santa Cruz. Now
that it was too late, now that we were leaving, he felt like he
could try on everything he'd snubbed when he first arrived.
He exuded confidence and a permanent smile. English words
slipped out of his mouth like audacious rattlesnakes: "Thank
you, ma'am." "You take care now." "How's it goin'?" "You bet."
"Dude!"

Creedence arrived at the edge of the driveway with a twenty-
dollar bill in his hands. My brother had prepared a box full of
his favorite things for him. He'd planned on giving it to him
since the day we found out we were headed back to Italy, but he
priced them first, just so his friend would see how generous he
was in giving them away—a quintessential Italian ploy. He tee-
tered at the edge of the driveway pretending to bargain. Behind
his charade I recognized a seal of love and appreciation for having been close to Creedence, for growing up on the same burning streets, bruising knees and falling on Rollerblades—the
ominous rumble of the freeway in their ears all those months.
The late afternoons coming home dirty from play, smeared with
sticky syrup from fast-food sodas, still panting with the last rays
of sun on their faces, had meant something to my brother. But
Creedence—the odd Mormon Virgil who had introduced him
to that neighborhood's microcosm—didn't get sentimental.

"I heard they are renting the house to a family with three
brothers. I'll buy the whole box from you in case we need extra
hockey gear," he said, handing over his twenty dollars.

My brother gave him the stuff and lifted his hand dismissively.

"You can just have it. I don't need dollars in Italy. Buy me a burger the next time I come to LA."

I imagined how many times he'd rehearsed that mature line, announcing that the next time they saw each other they'd have their own money to spend, but also implying that there would be a next time. Creedence gave my brother an awkward young-male hug, drawing a safe space between arms and chests. Two fourteen-year-old kids eluding the emotions of friendship.

"Hey, come to Rome sometime."

"Sure thing," Creedence said.

He rolled down the block toward his house with the box lodged between his elbow and right hip. My brother stood at the edge of the driveway, looking at him go. He squirmed at the practicality of their rite of passage: my toys, your arms. Next.

He ran back to my mother after his friend left and hugged her. She opened up to him, protectively. She had seen what I saw. My brother would be happy to go back to a place where friends were for life and moving to different continents meant breaking hearts. Here, a box of toys was enough to turn a page. People came and went, sports gear was tossed, unpaired knee pads filled boxes, cycles of friendship terminated uneventfully.

I set up my area in a corner of the front yard, beneath the oak tree, diagonally opposite my parents' sale. I dragged a mirrored cherrywood dresser from my bedroom. It looked ruined now that the sun shone on it, so I grabbed my varnishing kit to revive it. I loved painting over wood, giving it layers of life. That's how Henry and I resurrected the furniture we sold at the new store on Melrose. We picked up busted antiques from Pasadena, sanded the ugly paint off, then repainted and varnished them. We transformed bookshelves, mirrors, and dressers. I brought out two small coffee tables I had stored in the garage and the antique two-tier paper cutter. I arranged the furniture on the cusp of the street. I opened a mahogany folding library ladder and placed the Vietnamese curtains and silk tops from the downtown tailor on each step.

I draped mannequins I borrowed from Henry's store in lace and furs, then filled an antique walnut cradle with a collection of multicolored velour shorts from the seventies with matching kneesocks. I arranged a reupholstered fur ottoman and a bentwood rocking chair inside a small yurt I'd purchased at a senior-citizens arts-and-crafts sale.

Once the furniture was set up, I took out more clothes: a vintage Dior haute couture shirtdress from the fifties, ruffled cocktail dresses, Clair de Lune beaded gowns, fairy-princess slips, quilted coats, vintage Gucci silk shirts, Deva's bell-bottoms. I ironed them on a board so they'd look pristine and beautiful hanging under the oak tree against the morning light. The more my parents crammed dirty white T-shirts into boxes that read "1 dollar!," the harder I pressed my iron against each fold. I hung my earthquake leopard coat from an oak-tree branch—the ghost of a wild cat flying over our street.

"Is this part of the same sale?" a disheveled woman in pajamas with a *Los Angeles Times* under her arm and Starbucks latté in her hand asked.

"Yes."

"Oh . . ." she mumbled, glancing at my collection. "I thought you guys were neighbors and they let you use their lawn."

"No, those are my parents. I'm just selling different things."

"Obviously," she remarked, smiling and running her fingers over my Indian bat-sleeved shirts from the Bombay shop. She picked one out and tried it over her checkered pajamas. "I like these silk shirts. How much for all?"

I felt a knot form inside my throat. I hadn't thought about pricing anything yet.

"I'm still setting up. Come by in a bit and I'll have prices sorted out."

She scoffed at me and dragged her flip-flops over to my parents' area where she was greeted with more enthusiasm.

"Ricotta pie?" my mother asked.

The woman lifted her coffee cup, toasting her hospitality. She picked up my mother's earrings from a broken wicker basket and dropped them back inside. They were all unpaired or with broken clasps. More visitors arrived expressing confusion about the different areas in the front yard. I heard myself repeating the same words: "Those are my parents and that's my brother. It's the same sale. I'm just selling different stuff." I almost argued about this.

Stuff was going fast on the other side of the garden. My family was regurgitating into the city what they'd ingested when they first arrived, tossing it all back into the melting pot, the hand-me-downs' hand-me-downs. The blow-up pool was given away for free to a couple of four-year-olds along with my brother's water bed. My family stood there, sun gleaming on their wide-open faces, no hats, no sunscreen, braving the move, the changes, the influx and outflux of money.

By three o'clock the only thing I'd had the heart to sell were the Reebok Pumps I'd worn on my first day of high school. My parents had sold almost everything and were putting the rest out on the street with a sign that read FREE STUFF. On my side of the yard everything still hung untouched under the oak tree. Kids ran and jumped inside the yurt.

"What's the price on this?" one of their mothers asked, picking up a golden enamel bracelet.

I looked back at her. She had a fanny pack, a fluorescent white tracksuit, and gray hair.

"I'm not selling that," I said.

"And how much is that?" She pointed to the leopard coat.

"Definitely not selling that either."

I sneered at her and she backed off, mumbling to herself.

With each inquiry I felt my voice rush out to protect those objects. It was a waste to give them away like that. Where would they sleep at night? Would they be loved or forgotten at the back of someone's closet? For so long I thought my father was the hopeless nostalgic, the romantic seeker of glorious pasts, but really—I laughed when I saw how obvious it was—it was I who didn't want to let go of those ancient treasures, who wanted them to mean something.

My father and brother retired inside with a shoe box full of cash.

"You sure you want to stay out here?" Serena asked me.

I nodded.

"It looks beautiful, what you did," she said and walked back in, hauling trash behind her.

I was surrounded by furniture, feathers, and clothes. I held my fort down obstinately, hissing at anyone who got too close. When shoppers dwindled and yard-sale time was officially over, I began to fold and store my clothes with the same meticulousness I'd used in setting up my wing. I placed everything in big Louis Vuitton antique steamer trunks. They still had passenger labels on them. I placed the trunks, clothes, and all the furniture I could fit into the back of the Cadillac that was parked at the foot of the driveway bearing a fluorescent orange FOR SALE sign. I was allowed to drive it until it got sold.

Through the window I glanced at my parents inside the living room, counting the day's earnings. My brother hopped around them, his hand open, asking for part of the profits. I slipped into the driver's seat, scorching my thighs against the black leather, and put the key in the ignition and turned it. The white winged car rolled down Sunny Slope Drive like a tired dinosaur. I navigated the weary beast to the bottom of the street and onto the freeway without thinking. I noticed a postcard on the floor of the passenger seat. I'd sent it from Sicily last summer. They sold only two postcards at the island newsstand. One was a photo of a donkey climbing the stairs, the other was an aerial view of the island. On the card the cone-shaped island was cropped and placed over a matte blue background to symbolize the sea. That was the one I'd picked for my parents to remind them just how far away from them we were, on an island in the middle of a false blue ocean. I flipped it over and read:

Dear Mom and Dad, there are a lot of animals here. Antonio and Alma are very nice and they have a new boat. They called it Samantha Fox. We miss you. Eugenia

I knew what kind of summer they had ahead of them. I knew how happy they'd be riding *Samantha Fox* out to the Scoglio Galera, then plunging off the cliffs. My brother would be by their side with his rusty trident. As the car drove on, I felt myself slip away from the salt and the sea, from sea urchins, capers, and rock people. The island would be there for me down the line, exactly as I'd left it—immobile and prehistoric, with its ferocious birds and wild goats. I'd be greeted again. The kids, a few years older, would still make the same jokes. I'd be a film star forever for having once appeared in an outdated canned-meat commercial. Santino would have another farm with different animals—the past ones buried under porous rocks. Rosalia's crisp curls would have grown back on her head. Endless centuries' worth of volcanic stones would still be awash, unaltered under the sea.

Italy seemed to me like one of those impassive rocks now: an ageless, peninsular boulder emerging from still waters. And I knew I didn't want to be back there yet. I didn't go through the things that happened before the earthquake just so I could pretend like they hadn't existed. I couldn't follow my parents to more film sets and new beginnings, no matter what.

There were people who wanted us back in Rome, my parents said, but I didn't know who they were. I'd never spoken to them or seen their faces. Here there was a university and a teacher and a friend and a store, and I knew what those things looked like. I also knew that maybe they weren't much of anything at all, but that was okay too.

The top was down and my lace nightgowns flapped in the air. I climbed up the ascending lane toward Hollywood and Henry's store. He'd be there to help me unload the trunk. From where I was the city seemed suddenly credible. It was indeed a city, not an agglomeration of low-rise buildings. I pressed the accelerator and rode farther up, leaving behind the polluted afternoon low clouds—moving out of the Valley's last sliver of land.

Clusters of treetops on the horizon swayed in the tropical sky as a golden amber light poured in. There was silence and then the steady breath of hot air at my back—a strong, dry wind blowing from the desert, pushing me toward the city and its ocean. It streamed upon me moving in different directions at the same time, tickling the corners of my eyes. I'd felt that breeze before, I'd seen that light and knew what it was: the luminous unseen. This time I did what Max said. I didn't try to grasp it. I didn't focus on it or try to understand it. I just let it shine.

Acknowledgments

Thank you to all those who have contributed to this book with their generous reading, edits, and guidance: Claudia Ballard, Raffaella De Angelis, Gerry Howard, Sarah Porter, Sarah Engelmann, Michael Goldsmith, Emily Mahon, Bette Alexander, Karla Eoff, Yuki Hirose, Lauren Mechling, Robin Desser, Jhumpa Lahiri, Frederic Tuten, Iris Smyles, Catherine Lacey, Diane Williams, Tijana Mamula, Ines Mattalia, Derek White.

To the patient and passionate Italian team: Stefano Magagnoli, Marta Treves, Carlo Carabba, Francesca Infascelli, Francesco Pacifico.

And to those who have given me rooms, homes, and quiet time to write: Giovanna Nodari, Micah Perta, Peter Benson Miller, The American Academy in Rome, Associazione Culturale SabinARTi, Lorenzo Castore, Eugenia Lecca, Maria Clara Ghia, Emanuele de Raymondi.

A special thank you to Luca Infascelli, who walked me through the darkest passages and lost as much sleep as I did to get this story where it needed to be.

To: Francesca Marciano for sitting me down in her studio on a warm October day and giving me the talk that jump-started this novel.

And to: Kate Schatz and Taiye Selasi, who came through to save the day in crucial moments.